The Three Sisters of Victory Walk

Annie Groves is the pen name of Jenny Shaw. For many years she lived in the East End, and is fascinated by its history.

Annie Groves was originally created by the much-loved writer Penny Halsall, who died in 2011. The stories drew on her own family's history, picked up from listening to her grandmother's stories when she was a child. Jenny Shaw has been a big fan of the wonderful novels by Annie Groves for many years and feels privileged to have been asked to continue her legacy.

ANNIE GROVES

The
Three Sisters of Victory Walk

HarperCollins*Publishers*

HarperCollins*Publishers* Ltd
1 London Bridge Street,
London SE1 9GF
www.harpercollins.co.uk

HarperCollins*Publishers*
1st Floor, Watermarque Building, Ringsend Road
Dublin 4, Ireland

First published by HarperCollins*Publishers* 2022

1

Copyright © Annie Groves 2022

Annie Groves asserts the moral right to
be identified as the author of this work

A catalogue record for this book is available from the British Library

ISBN: 978-0-00-840245-7 (PB)

Set in Sabon LT Std by Palimpsest Book Production Limited,
Falkirk, Stirlingshire

Printed and bound in the UK using
100% Renewable Electricity by CPI Group (UK) Ltd

MIX
Paper | Supporting
responsible forestry
FSC™ C007454

This book is produced from independently certified FSC™ paper to ensure
responsible forest management.

For more information visit: www.harpercollins.co.uk/green

For Kate and Teresa, for all their help and trust –
there would be no Three Sisters without them.

CHAPTER ONE

August 1939

'Ugh, I hate it. My hair's filthy. It doesn't matter how I cover it up.' Daisy Harrison threw down the square of cotton that she wore as a headscarf. 'You'll have to lend me some of your shampoo, Clover. I've used mine up having to wash it so often.' She flung herself onto a ladderback chair that stood on one side of the big kitchen table.

Her sister raised her eyebrows. 'That's the third time this week. You'll just have to get used to it – and don't think I'm going to keep giving you my special shampoo every time you ask. I need it as well, you know.'

Daisy scowled. 'Can't think why. It's not as if you go anywhere.'

'Well, neither do you. And you're too young to go out anyway.'

'Girls, girls.' Their mother, Patience, always known as Patty, came in through the back door from the yard. 'Can you at least try not to argue the minute

1

you get home? I've been on my feet all day too, in case you've forgotten. Clover, be a love and put the kettle on. I'm parched.'

Clover turned to do as her mother asked, but stuck her tongue out at her younger sister as she did so. Daisy sat up straighter, ready to respond, but then caught the look on her mother's face and decided against it. She slumped back and scuffed her feet against the worn linoleum.

'I wish I'd never started work in that horrible factory,' she complained. 'There's nothing but dust everywhere. Or if it's not dust, it's little flecks of cotton which stick to you. Look!' She held up her arm. 'I'm covered in them.'

Patty smiled indulgently at her youngest daughter. 'Yes, but you'll be able to buy the clothes you're making at a bargain price. You'll like that. Besides, you know you have to work somewhere. We can't afford to have you sitting around doing nothing, young lady.'

Daisy scowled, knowing that her mother had a point. She didn't fancy sitting around being bored, and the clothing factory had seemed like the best choice, but she hadn't reckoned on all the discomforts of actually doing the job. 'That dust makes me itch,' she said crossly, rubbing her wrists beneath the cuffs of her summer jacket.

'It could be worse,' said her mother, gratefully accepting the cup of tea from her middle daughter. 'You aren't out in all weathers, now are you?'

'And you don't even have to deal with customers,' Clover pointed out. 'We had some real old sourpusses in today. One wanted to know why we didn't have any swedes. I said to her, you do know it's August, don't you? But she just stared at me, like it was my fault. There's no pleasing some people.'

'True,' said Patty, but she didn't rush to add any examples of her own. She valued her job at the greengrocer's around the corner and never liked to cause trouble. Many a time she had quietly wondered if she'd done the right thing, getting Clover to work there alongside her. She knew the girl wanted more excitement, but a job was a job and the pay wasn't too bad. They were lucky that the owner, old Mr Morton, trusted them to get on with running the place and didn't interfere. However, she knew Clover didn't share her own love of the produce. What Patty would have asked for, if granted just one wish, would be for a good-sized garden where she could grow her own fruit and vegetables. How she would have enjoyed that, and the sight of her family's faces as she fed them food grown by her own hand. She gave a short sigh. Fat chance of that ever happening.

Nobody she knew had a garden, not a proper one. Everybody had back yards, some bigger than others. That was a fact of life in Dalston. The terraces of houses weren't built for gardening. There was room for a washing line and maybe some pots if you were lucky. Anything more was just a dream. This was the East End of London, after all.

Besides, Patty counted herself as lucky in many other ways. She loved their house. Even though it was near the main road that ran from Stamford Hill and beyond, all the way down to Liverpool Street and the city, the actual terrace of houses was called Victory Walk, with no traffic passing by to bother them with noise. While their home was no palace, it was as spick and span as she could make it, and with just about space enough for everybody. She and her husband, Bert, had the big bedroom facing the front, and their oldest son, Peter, had had the smaller room behind that. She drew in a breath at the thought of him; her beloved boy had recently joined the army, going off to train at the start of the summer. She was proud of his choice but it didn't mean she wasn't worried. The bedroom facing over the back yard was shared by Clover and Daisy, which no doubt partly explained why they argued so much. Robbie, the youngest of the family, was tucked into the smallest room, not much more than a box room really, next to the main bedroom.

The Harrisons' firstborn child no longer lived at home. To their immense pride, Rose had qualified as a nurse and now lived at the nurses' home attached to the hospital over at Homerton. It was only a bike ride away and she still came back whenever she could, but Patty acknowledged that she missed her clever, steady eldest far more than she would ever admit out loud. Not least because Rose had a lifetime's experience of settling disputes between her two rowdier sisters.

As if reading her mother's mind, Clover set down her teacup and asked, 'Isn't Rose here? It's her afternoon off, isn't it?'

Patty nodded. 'She was going to meet Robbie after school as she'd promised to take him for a teacake when she was here on Sunday.' She smiled to hide yet another worry; Robbie was a constant headache. Sometimes she was astonished that he'd made it to the grand old age of ten, he'd been so sickly as a baby. If there had been an illness going round, he'd caught it, and always worse than any of the others. All winter long he would struggle with bronchitis, the sound of his laboured breathing from his cramped room haunting her as she tried to sleep. She couldn't help fussing over him, even when he wasn't ill; protecting your children was the first duty of any mother. It could have made him spoilt and timid but if anything it was the reverse. If there was trouble, Robbie would be right there in the middle of it.

Still, he couldn't get into mischief if Rose was looking after him. And it was August, warm and sunny and dry, all good for Robbie's poorly lungs. Patty took a last sip of her tea and stretched out her legs under the wooden table. She should make the most of such moments. Soon she would have to get to her feet and begin preparing the evening meal. But for now, her children were safe and well, and fed; who knew how long that would last?

'Shoes, Robbie. Wipe them straight away. Doesn't matter if they aren't muddy, they'll still bring in stuff from the pavement.' Rose stood over her little brother, knowing that she shouldn't have to check that he knew what to do, but also knowing that if he brought dirt into the hall, it wouldn't be him who had to clear it up.

Robbie shrugged, and dutifully scraped his feet across

the doormat. His thin summer plimsolls were wearing out but they'd only be needed for a few more weeks. Rose nodded and he ran up the stairs, away from the grown-ups and their increasingly worried discussions.

She made her way to the kitchen, where her mother and two sisters were sitting at the table, empty teacups in front of them. Patty noticed the direction of her gaze and made to stand up. 'Would you like a cuppa?'

Rose smiled and shook her head, taking a seat beside Clover. 'I had plenty while Robbie had his teacake.' She sighed. 'Have you thought any more about what to do about him?'

Her mother didn't need to ask what Rose was referring to. It was all anyone spoke about these days. The threat of war with Nazi Germany hung over them, heavy and almost inevitable. Robbie's school had written to them over the holidays, setting out arrangements to evacuate all pupils in the event of war being declared. Trains would be laid on to take the children to a safer place, somewhere in the country. Everyone expected London to be hit hard, and because Dalston was known for its factories and wasn't far from the docks down on the Thames, there was every likelihood that it would be right in the firing line.

Patty briefly shut her eyes. 'I've thought about nothing else, love. I know they say they'll be looked after properly, but how can we be certain? Shipping them off to strangers like that – it doesn't seem right. What if he has one of his bad days? Or goes down with pneumonia? They won't know what to do for him. He's too delicate, I can't let him go.'

Rose clasped her hands in front of her on the table. 'Even if all his friends go?'

Her mother nodded. 'They don't get bronchitis like he does. They'll manage all right, but he needs special care, you know he does.'

Rose squeezed her hands even tighter. She knew what an attack of bronchitis was like, from looking after Robbie since he was a baby. It was partly that experience which had prompted her to become a nurse. Moreover, she'd seen plenty of cases of adults with pneumonia and wouldn't wish it on anybody. Yet they had to balance the risks, surely. 'The school wouldn't put him in danger,' she reminded her mother.

Patty shook her head. 'I'll talk about it with your father when he gets back from his shift, but I can't see how anyone can look after him like we do.' Her voice showed the strain she was under at having to make such a decision, and Rose decided to leave it. Her mother was feeling bad enough as it was.

Daisy pulled her chair in closer to the table. 'Perhaps it won't come to that. Perhaps we won't have to go to war at all.' She reached down to pick up the cotton headscarf that lay where she had thrown it.

'Oh, come on, Daisy. Get your head out of the clouds.' Clover had no patience with her sister's optimism. 'Don't you ever see the newspaper headlines? Or listen to the wireless? It's heading our way whether we like it or not. Better get used to the idea.'

Daisy was instantly nettled. 'You're the expert now, are you? You left school at the same age as I did. You don't know anything more than I do.'

7

'I know enough to recognise what's staring me in the face,' Clover replied at once. 'The only question is when, not if.'

Rose turned to face her middle sister. 'Horrible to think of it but I reckon you're right, Clover. We're trying to make preparations over at the hospital, although it's hard when we don't really know what we'll be up against.' She did her best to ignore the look of anguish that flashed across their mother's face.

Clover grinned, pleased to have won Rose's approval. She tossed back her tight curls, in the same shade of chestnut that all three sisters shared. 'Well, that might be your ticket out of the clothing factory, Daisy. You know that booklet what the government sent out a few months ago. We'll all have to do our bit, if it comes to it.'

'Do our bit?' Daisy looked dubious.

'Don't you remember? It'll be around here some-where. Unmarried women with no dependents will have to join a service or do essential war work.'

Daisy shifted in her seat. 'Well, I won't have to. I'm not eighteen yet.'

Clover smiled mischievously. 'There's always the Land Army. They take you earlier. How about that? Going to work on a farm, up nice and early every morning, mucking out cows?'

Daisy shuddered. 'Ugh. Not likely.' She looked down at her nails, which she prided herself on, and made great efforts to keep beautiful despite the rigours of factory work.

'Yes, you might meet a nice young farmer,' Clover went on, getting into her stride now. 'A fine strapping lad, not like those whey-faced boys in the factory. Big muscles from heaving around all those heavy hay bales. He'll probably smell of cows but you won't mind by then, cos you'll be used to it. Probably won't be able to live without it, in fact.'

'Stop it!' Daisy shoved her chair back again. 'You're being horrid. Join the Land Army yourself if you're so keen.'

'Yes, stop it, Clover,' their mother said, which made Daisy laugh in triumph and Clover scowl. 'We'll all have to make decisions we don't like soon enough, if what your father says is right. And in the meantime we'll make the most of whatever peace is left to us. And that means inside this house as well as outside.' With that she pushed herself to her feet, leaving her daughters staring at the tabletop.

CHAPTER TWO

'What are you up to at the weekend, then, Daisy?
Planning on breaking any hearts, are yer?'

Daisy stopped in her tracks as she came through the
clothing factory gates to glare at the young man who
had called out to her. He was pretending to clutch at
his heart and made a woeful face. She knew it was for
the benefit of his friends who were clustered around
him, not because he particularly cared about her.

She shoved her hands firmly into the patch pockets
of her summer jacket. 'Never you mind, Terry Foster.
Whatever I'm doing won't concern you.' She gave him
what she hoped was a firm look and made to walk on.

'See, you're breaking my heart already,' he protested.
'What about a smile for us brave boys, then? Don't
you care that we're putting our lives on the line to
defend the likes of you?'

Daisy was caught despite herself. 'Brave, what? On
the football field? What are you on about?'

Terry laughed in triumph at having piqued her
interest. 'Not sure how much football there's going to

be where we're going. We'll be training all right, but not for playing games any more. This is serious stuff, life or death, you know.'

'What is?' Daisy was annoyed at having been delayed but hated the way the group of lads always teased her, and Terry was the worst. It was as if he could sense she was a bit younger than the rest of the girls on her section, and homed in on her as an easy target. Still, she was used to being the youngest and always considered the baby. She had plenty of practice at hitting back.

'We've only gone and joined up.' Terry was grinning broadly now, evidently pleased with himself.

'For what?'

'Fighting for king and country, of course. Defending the likes of you, so you can carry on dressing up and having fun, breaking all our hearts along the way.'

'Don't be so daft,' Daisy snapped. 'You don't even know that there'll be any fighting.'

Terry raised his eyebrows. 'Stands to reason there will be. Didn't you hear the news they broadcast before the shift ended? Germany just invaded Poland. That's it, no question about it. Give it a day or two and we're in. So we aren't waiting to be called up, we all went to put our names down at lunchtime. No point in hanging around. At least this way we choose what we're in for. I'm off to the army. The uniform will suit me.' He laughed again and his blue eyes danced with excitement.

Daisy couldn't deny that plenty of her colleagues admired Terry, with his strong physique and thick sandy hair, and no doubt he would be the ideal poster boy

11

for the army. Something about him grated on her, though. He was always so pleased with himself, and she couldn't see that he had anything to be especially pleased about. 'Are you all going into the army then?' she asked.

A couple of the others nodded, Terry's regular hangers-on who loved to follow him, in the hope that his popularity and reported success with girls would rub off on them. 'Course we are,' one of them said, and Daisy struggled to remember his name.

Only the tallest member of the group shook his head. 'Not me,' he said. 'I'm going into the navy.'

Terry laughed again, not quite kindly. 'Taken with that Fred Astaire film, were you? Think you're going to see the world, but all you'll see is the sea?'

The other one joined in. 'Or will you look better in the uniform? Think you'll fit in better with the other trainee accountants rather than us what work on the factory floor?'

'Yep, that's it, you're right.' The tall, dark-haired young man nodded easily, clearly not bothered by his colleagues' teasing. 'Dark blue sets off my colouring, although I didn't have you down for a follower of fashion, Chalky.'

Daisy nodded, remembering the film they were talking about. Rose had taken her to see *Follow the Fleet*, a couple of years ago. They'd emerged out onto Kingsland Road and sung at the tops of their voices: 'We joined the navy to see the world, but what did we see? We saw the sea.' There was something stirring about it. She wouldn't mind seeing the sea herself.

'Are you really doing that?' she asked the tall one. She couldn't remember his name either. He hadn't been at the factory for very long. There was something about him that set him apart, not just that he hadn't gone along with the rest of the gang's choice or that he did something in the main office.

He nodded and held back to face her properly. 'I am. My uncle was in the navy and always talked about it. Made me wonder what it would be like to try it myself.'

'And do you think you'll be needed?' Daisy briefly looked at her feet, in their sensible flat shoes, the inevitable flecks of cotton caught in their brown laces. 'I mean, is it certain that it's going to be war?'

Terry would have laughed at her question, she was sure, using it in some way to emphasise that he was a man of the world and she was too daft to know anything. But this young man didn't.

'Sorry, but yes, it's certain,' he said, and though his dark eyes were kind they were steady, with no sense of triumph or teasing. He wasn't talking down to her. 'We can't back away now Germany has done this. It'll be any day now. Do you have anyone joining up?'

Daisy gulped. 'My brother. He left for his army base a couple of months ago.' She didn't want to think about what that might mean now. It had seemed such an adventure, Peter hefting his khaki kitbag and joking that he'd be able to lift ten of them once he'd completed his training.

'Good for him.' The young man smiled a little. 'I'm Freddy. Frederick Lawrence, at your service.' He smiled more widely.

'Daisy. Daisy Harrison.' She knew she was blushing, which was annoying, but she couldn't stop it. What was wrong with her? He was just one of Terry's mates, Terry who would do anything to get a rise out of anyone. But before she could say more, the leader of the gang himself interrupted.

'Oy, Fred, you coming down the pub or not? Don't want to waste a minute of what might be our last weekend of freedom, do we?'

Freddy shrugged. 'Nice to meet you, Daisy. I take it you aren't coming down the pub?'

'Me? Oh . . . no.' Daisy didn't want to admit that she wasn't old enough, not in front of this young man. Besides, it would mean having to endure still more teasing from the gang. 'I – I 've got to help my mother make our tea, you know.'

'Another time, maybe.' One more grin, and he was off with the rest of them.

Daisy nodded and watched as the group of young men sauntered down the pavement to the main road, their voices loud, full of high spirits at the great adventure they were about to embark on. Slowly she followed them, a huge feeling of uncertainty swirling through her, and then she hurried up, suddenly filled with the urge to get home, to the safety of her family.

Rose lay on her bed, staring at the ceiling, her hands behind her head. She'd heard the news on the wireless and now there was only one way in which events could unfold. All the hopes and fears of the past few weeks and months, even years, were about to come together in the fact of war. She couldn't quite work out how she felt.

She shifted and turned onto her side on the single mattress, grateful at least that she had this cosy room in the new nurses' home of the Hackney Hospital. Compared to the old home, it was luxurious: built only a couple of years ago, it had modern metal windows, proper bathrooms, and plenty of room downstairs for socialising and eating. Guiltily she acknowledged that it was far more comfortable than the room she'd had to share with her sisters back on Victory Walk. It was far quieter, too: no squabbling Clover and Daisy, no Peter running up and down the creaking stairs shouting about his mislaid football boots, no agonised coughing from little Robbie.

That was only fair, she reasoned. When she was on shift it was often pandemonium – organised, but pandemonium nonetheless, exhausting physically and mentally, having to cope with whatever came her way and no option but to get on and do the job. She wouldn't have had it any other way. It was what she had wanted to do for ages and had saved for, what she'd trained for over three gruelling years, and now what she loved, having qualified and settled permanently at this hospital. Tonight, though, she couldn't deny that her feet ached. She'd been running around for, what? Twelve hours solid? Something like that. No wonder they were sore.

Rose suspected that she'd look back on today's shift as the calm before the storm. What were they in for? She couldn't begin to guess and didn't know who to ask. Even if plenty of her parents' generation had been caught up in the Great War, things would be different now. This was 1939, the modern world. Weapons had changed, but so had defences. She desperately wanted to know what to expect, but that was impossible. You couldn't foretell the future at the best of times.

She pressed her face into the freshly laundered pillowcase, her thoughts turning to what had happened last week. She'd been making the most of a half day off, wandering down to the shops on Mare Street, when she'd bumped into her cousin Faith. Faith was only a little older, but always treated Rose and her sisters as if they were somehow beneath her. Rose blamed her Aunt Vera, her mother's big sister. Aunt Vera lived only a few streets away from Victory Walk and never missed an opportunity to interfere with what she regarded as her younger sister's inadequate way of raising a family. She had three girls as well: Faith, Hope and Joy. Faith was by far the most annoying.

That afternoon, Faith had simpered, a sure sign of trouble.

Rose had nodded warily. 'Having a look around the shops?' she'd said, politely enough.

'Well, I thought I might as well, although I tend to buy everything from the West End these days,' Faith had replied, with a toss of her long blonde hair. 'Still, as I was passing through, I thought, why not.'

Rose sighed inwardly but had kept a smile on her face with some effort. 'Oh, yes. Your mother said you'd got a new job and wouldn't be living at home any more.'

Faith nodded with ill-concealed delight. 'That's right. I'm a secretary now, a very important and responsible position. So I've moved into lodgings closer to the office. It's very convenient for all the best shops as well.'

'Gosh, well, that must be nice.' Rose couldn't remember her cousin undertaking any training that might have led her to such a job but perhaps she had hidden talents.

Faith smiled smugly. 'It's very different to Dalston,' she said. 'But I have a good reason to come back now and again.' Her smile grew wider and over-bright as footsteps sounded behind them on the pavement. Rose caught a glimpse of the familiar figure reflected in the tailor's shop window before she heard his voice.

'There you are – I was waiting outside the baker's . . .' He stopped when he realised who Faith had been talking to. 'Ah, hello, Rose.'

'Hello, Martin.' Rose kept her voice even, despite being taken aback for a moment. If he was willing to go shopping with her cousin, then Martin Fletcher clearly knew Faith a whole lot better than he'd ever let on.

Tall, brown-eyed Martin Fletcher had been part of Rose's life for longer than she could remember and they'd been in the same class at primary school. They had always been spoken of as children who would do well for themselves, given the right chance. He'd been hard-working, always top of the class at arithmetic, and the teachers all loved him.

As they'd grown up, there had been a widespread assumption that they would end up together romantically

17

as a couple, because everyone agreed they were so well suited. Martin had lived up to his promise and been the sole child from the class to sit and pass his eleven plus, something that had never been on the cards for Rose. None of her family had even considered trying for grammar school – the uniform cost too much for a start.

Still, they lived just a few streets from each other and they'd stayed close. The trouble was, Rose had realised as she grew older that she was truly fond of him but more as a friend. He was almost like another brother. But she didn't need another brother; she had two already. She didn't like to cause a fuss, though, and so everybody carried on assuming there was romance in the air.

Martin had, if anything, grown keener, and often asked her to go to the pictures or out for a walk but Rose came up with excuse after excuse, and finally had to explain that she didn't want to string him along, to encourage him to believe her feelings would match his. She hated to let him down but she couldn't pretend there was something there when there was not. If she listened to her heart, she knew the truth.

Martin had nodded but his eyes still held hope that she was mistaken. Meanwhile friends and family loved the story of the childhood sweethearts and were reluctant to let it go. If Rose protested, they said it was typical of her modesty. There was no convincing them.

Now it seemed he'd turned his attention elsewhere. Or had it turned for him.

Faith had laughed lightly and allowed Martin to take the bags she'd been carrying, while touching him briefly but deliberately on his arm. 'We'd better go, we don't want to be late,' she'd purred.

'Er, no. Um, well, nice to see you, Rose.' Martin had made off with Faith, with a look of what Rose could have sworn was guilt on his face.

What was she to make of that? For ages she had told herself that this would be the best possible outcome: Martin would meet somebody else and realise that what he felt for Rose was just the tail end of a long friendship. But Faith of all people! That hadn't been in her mind at all.

Maybe Faith would appreciate what Martin had to offer. He was good-looking, he was amusing, and what Clover called a 'good catch': nowadays he worked in the local high-street bank, so that meant he had a decent income and prospects. Although, knowing her cousin, that might not be enough. Faith wanted the world served to her on a platter. But they were all adults now and Martin was free to make his own decisions.

Her sisters and mother would be more disappointed than she was, Rose decided. Auntie Vera would be unbearable once she found out, if she hadn't already. Rose groaned into her pillow. She'd better take the bull by the horns and warn everyone herself, before Vera could turn it into a point-scoring exercise.

Rose rolled over onto her back again, wriggling her toes and flexing her ankles in an attempt to ease her poor feet. She'd go round to Victory Walk on Sunday, that's what she'd do. She was on late duty tomorrow and so would have the next day off until evening. She

19

shut her eyes. This room might be the last word in up-to-date comfort, but it couldn't compete with her mother's kitchen when it came down to what really mattered.

Besides, she wanted to check that all was well with her family now that most of the schoolchildren had been evacuated. Robbie had not gone with them in the end, so had been spared the tearful farewells on the platform of Hackney Downs station, but it was another sort of risk to keep him at home when the future was so uncertain. Some of the nurses who had younger brothers or sisters had arrived on shift red-eyed. There were few who had not been affected by it in some way. Rose would rest easier once she had gone round to Victory Walk once more.

CHAPTER THREE

Patty made sure that the wireless was tuned in properly, wary that Daisy or even Robbie had tried to spin the dial to find something more entertaining than the BBC Home Service. The prime minister was due to make an announcement later this morning and she didn't want to miss it.

When it came to the moment, though, she very nearly did. Chaos had erupted once Rose had arrived and told them her news. Patty was of course sorry to hear that Martin wasn't as interested in her eldest daughter as they'd all assumed, but Clover and Daisy were beside themselves with indignation.

'He's nothing but a two-timer!' Clover exclaimed, folding her arms across her chest, gripping onto the cuffs of her old blouse. Her knuckles were white, as though she would have punched the young man if he'd dared to show his face. 'How could he!'

Rose sat down at the table and shrugged. 'Really, it doesn't matter. I never thought we were more than good friends. I only told you so that Auntie Vera couldn't make a song and dance about it.'

Patty raised her head from where she'd been darning her husband's socks. 'Don't speak like that about your auntie,' she reproached her eldest, although she spoke mildly.

Daisy huffed and turned around on her heeled sandals. 'Well, good luck to him if he's walking out with Faith now. She's stuck-up and he's welcome to her.'

Patty turned around in her fireside chair. 'Don't speak like that about your cousin.'

'Ma, you know what I mean. She thinks she's a cut above and she's got no cause to,' Daisy said hotly. 'I bet she only agreed to walk out with him because she knew it would annoy Rose.'

'Really, I'm not annoyed,' Rose protested, but her sister ignored her.

'Yes, she's just showing off that she can get Martin to follow her round like a puppy.' Daisy nodded emphatically.

'I said he offered to carry her shopping, not that he was following her round like a puppy.'

'Same thing.' Daisy was adamant.

'Yes, and then she'll have her sights set on someone grander than Martin Fletcher,' Clover predicted. 'New job in the West End, what's all that about? She's on the hunt for someone with plenty of cash to keep her in the style she'd like to become accustomed to. Poor mug, whoever that is.'

'Look, I really don't mind either way, but can we just leave it alone now? I was never going to walk out with him anyway.' Rose could see this was all taking on a life of its own.

'No, you're being very brave and I'm sure I wouldn't be half so kind.' Clover was enraged on her sister's behalf and enjoying every righteous minute of it.

Patty set down her mending basket by the side of the gleaming range and got to her feet. 'Girls, girls, a moment of quiet, please. Daisy, turn up the wireless and don't change the station. Clover, call for your father, he's in the back yard. We've all got to listen. Oh no, we've missed the beginning.'

Bert Harrison came through from the back door, as the voice of Neville Chamberlain spoke from the wireless which held pride of place on the wooden sideboard. 'This country is at war with Germany.'

Silence fell, all quarrelling forgotten, as the Harrisons stared at one another, the steady words of the prime minister slowly sinking in. No matter that they had known this was coming – hearing it out loud was something different. Now there really was no escape. The ground had shifted beneath their feet and the world was changed.

Daisy gave a small cry and her hands flew to her face as she tried to stifle her fear. Bert moved to put his arm around her slim shoulders as they shook. Patty gasped and her grey darning wool fell to the floor. Clover looked as if she was about to say something but no words came out. No words would be enough to describe this feeling of the future being destroyed in ways they could not begin to guess.

It was left to Rose to restore a sense of normality. 'Tea?' she said, rising to her feet again. 'I'll put the kettle on.'

'I'll help,' Patty said, standing to join her eldest in the back kitchen where the tap was to be found. She reached for the old kettle that had been a wedding present so many years ago. 'Clover, Daisy, you set out the cups. And put some plates out too – I made a ginger cake yesterday and it'll put some heart into us.'

'Just what we need.' Bert looked affectionately at his wife, his eyes twinkling; to him she was still the most beautiful woman in the world, the passage of time and the arrival of all their children notwithstanding. 'Where's Robbie? He'll have to be told what just happened.'

'He went out in the street to play football with the Glanville lads. They didn't get evacuated either,' Patty called over the noise of water hitting the metal base of the kettle.

Rose glanced at her mother in concern. 'The Glanvilles? They're a bit older than him, aren't they?'

Patty turned off the brass tap. 'Yes, but the children of his age have all gone, so they're the next nearest. I know they're a bit wild but they aren't bad boys. He has to play with someone.'

Rose nodded but bit her lip. A bit wild was somewhat of an understatement but her mother was right. Robbie couldn't be shut away in his room wrapped in cotton wool.

'Let him play a bit longer,' Bert said. 'Let him make the most of the end of summer.'

Patty nodded, knowing that at least she had all her children safe for the time being – or at least, the ones near to hand. Peter was a worry she could do nothing

24

about. Casting her eyes across her girls she had to smile. They might squabble among themselves but, as they'd shown this morning, if one of them was in trouble from outside then they closed ranks. They were a strong team, and she would bet on them against anybody. Now she just had to hope that they stayed that way in the face of what was to come.

Clover sat on her bed in the room she shared with Daisy, shivering despite it being a warm September day. She was frightened, as she could sense they all were, but a part of her was excited too. This dreadful declaration of war might just be her way out of the greengrocer's. She knew that her mother had got her the job and it wasn't that she was ungrateful; she simply didn't want to spend the rest of her working life there.

She stared out of the window – her bed was nearest to it, on account of her being older. The rooftops of East London stretched for miles, terrace after terrace, broken up by some tall trees in the park beyond the main road. Later on there would be the big beams of the new anti-aircraft searchlights over towards the West End but at this time of day their yard was bathed in sunshine, as was the yard behind it which belonged to the house on the next street over. Both had a collection of pots – or whatever big containers could be used as pots – and Clover's father had set up a rough work bench for sawing wood and light repairs. He'd be out there again soon, she thought with a pang of affection, knowing how much the entire family relied on him.

She didn't want her mother to think she was disloyal. Rose had worked at the shop as well after she'd left school, while she was saving up to begin her training as a nurse. It was almost like a tradition for the Harrison women. Even Auntie Vera had turned up now and again when they were short of staff, although Clover was quite glad that this hadn't happened often. Vera was prone to lecture everyone and managed to put some customers' backs up. She sighed loudly, gazing out as Bert emerged from the back kitchen, his shirt-sleeves rolled to his elbows, saw in hand. He was mending a shelf, she could see.

No, Clover thought, this was her chance to try something different. She reached into the pocket of her skirt, her favourite green striped fresh cotton one. Her mother had helped her make it and had added two big patch pockets at the front. Clover drew out the leaflet that had arrived months ago. The government had listed ways in which women could do their bit, should war break out. Well, now it had.

Clover knew that she could do more than weigh vegetables and make polite conversation with people she'd known since she could walk. She'd been good at school; not brainy like a handful of classmates, but no dunce either. She'd liked arithmetic, although she'd kept quiet about that, and learning to read had been a doddle. Her teachers' most common complaint had been that she'd have done much better had she only not talked so much.

She screwed up her eyes. This was her opportunity, to find out what else she could do. All the young men were joining up – Daisy had said that many of her factory colleagues had done so already. Peter had decided the army was for him months ago, but now his friends who were still at home would be enlisting. There would be vacancies for young women, she was sure.

She remembered the conversation about the Land Army. *Mmm, perhaps that won't be my first choice*, she thought. She'd seen enough of vegetables for a start, lifting the big sacks when they arrived at the shop's side entrance, heaving them around in the storage section, piling boxes of potatoes out front. She could conjure up that earthy smell of them right now. The only good thing was arranging all the produce in ways most likely to tempt the customers. No, she wanted something else.

Slowly she turned the pages of the little booklet, allowing her mind to wander. Where would she like to end up? Would they send women abroad? Clover had never been further away from home than a day trip to Kent. She wasn't at all sure she'd like foreign food, and nobody she knew had ever tried to learn a language. Then again, whispered a little voice in her ear, you won't know until you try, will you?

What about the women's branch of the navy, she wondered. Would they expect her to work aboard a ship? At the moment it seemed as if the women worked on land, but that might change. She couldn't swim. So maybe not that, then.

There was also the Women's Auxiliary Air Force. What might that involve, she asked herself. Would they want her to fly a plane? Even if she was after an adventure, that felt like a step too far.

So then there was the Auxiliary Territorial Service, the women's branch of the army. That sounded safely land-based, no high seas or skies. Clover pondered it for less than a minute and then made her decision.

On her next half day she'd go to the recruitment office and sign up. She'd join the ATS and make her family proud of her.

Then her mind was snapped back to the immediate present as Daisy came in. Clover instantly recognised the baby-blue cardigan she had on. It was hers. 'I never said you could borrow that!' she cried indignantly, and Daisy folded her arms.

'You never wear it.'

'I do.'

'You said it would only get dirty down at the shop.'

'But I keep it for when I go to the cinema!' Clover protested, and then she relented a little. If she went ahead and joined the ATS, then arguments like this might be a thing of the past. For a fleeting moment she felt a pang of regret. She'd miss them.

CHAPTER FOUR

'Daisy, Daisy, give me your answer, do.' The group of young men burst into laughter and their leader smirked as if he'd invented a completely original joke.

Daisy groaned. If she had a penny for every time she'd heard this, then she'd have been rich enough to buy her entire family a beautiful house – possibly one each. Not for the first time she cursed her name. Her mother's love of all things that grew had lumbered all the girls with flowery names but her sisters didn't get teased the way she did. Rose and Clover: nice sensible names. But Daisy – there was always that horrible song. Terry Foster was breaking into the chorus again as he swayed in time to the beat, while his followers leant against the factory wall.

'Or if you won't share my bicycle built for two then at least come down the pub,' he suggested, throwing his hands wide as if he was about to take a bow.

'I'll do nothing of the sort,' Daisy said sharply. 'I've got better things to do than hang around with the likes of you.'

At this, all the young men groaned, and Terry put his hand to his forehead as if in despair. 'You're so cruel!' he protested.

Daisy scowled and tightened the scarf around her neck. Summer had turned to autumn and the air was growing chilly, the evenings beginning to draw in. She noticed it after coming off the factory floor and stepping outside after a day's work. Inside they were kept moving and usually felt warm, but now she could tell the difference.

'Why are you all still here anyway?' she demanded. 'I thought you were off to join the army. What's kept you?' As she said this, she registered that the tall one, the one who had said he was choosing the navy instead, wasn't with them. Freddy, his name was. No sign of him.

Terry shrugged as his gang looked to him for an answer.

'We're waiting, that's all,' he told her. 'We got to stay home until we hear where they want us to go.'

'They're not in a hurry to turn you into heroes then,' Daisy replied.

Terry held out his hands again. 'It's not as if there's anything really happening, is there,' he said, and the others nodded. 'The odd false alarm when they set off the sirens and that's about it.'

Daisy tried to hide her shiver at those words; she had been terrified the first time and wondered how they could dismiss the warnings so readily. She didn't want the group to spot her anxiety though.

'That's all there's been,' chipped in the young man nearest Terry, who had hair that stuck up in all directions. 'My ma and pa ran under the stairs the first couple of times but they don't bother now. Pa says it's all a load of baloney anyway. We got nothing to worry about.'

His friends seemed to agree but Daisy wasn't anywhere near as sure. Her own father had said only last week that this was a temporary lull and they should keep their wits about them. He had begun to build an Anderson shelter in the back yard, and had blamed himself for not starting it sooner. If he'd done it a few months back then Peter could have helped.

'Chalky's right,' Terry declared. 'They said we'd be gassed by now, but look at us! Fit as fiddles. We got Jerry on the run. I reckon they're scared of us, that's why those gas attacks haven't happened.'

Daisy wasn't convinced. 'I see you're carrying your gas masks, all the same.' She pointed to the chunky little cardboard boxes slung by straps over their shoulders. She wore one exactly like them, although she'd tried to make it prettier by changing the strap to look more like one from a proper handbag.

'No flies on you, are there, Daisy?' Terry flashed his teeth. 'Doesn't hurt to take precautions, does it now?'

'And the ARP will be on at you if they find you out and about without one,' Daisy reminded him.

Chalky sniggered and Terry looked put out. 'There is that, I s'pose. Anyhow, much as we'd love to pass our precious leisure time with you, we've got an urgent appointment with several pints of beer down the pub. We got to say goodbye to Chalky's brother and cousin, 'cos they're off to training camp tomorrow.'

Daisy thought that was rich – it was them who'd accosted her, not the other way around. 'What have they been doing up to now, then?' she asked. 'Were they at the factory as well?'

Chalky shook his head. 'No, they was down Old Street, working in the office for the Underground. Hardly saw the light of day so they can't wait to get out in the open doing all that hard exercise. Like what we'll be doing soon. You won't recognise us next time you see us, what with all our new muscle and everything.'

Daisy huffed. 'We'll see about that.'

'It's true. Our mate Freddy what's joined the navy left a few weeks ago and already he says he's miles fitter. If a great lank like him can do it, imagine how we'll turn out.' Chalky visibly swelled with anticipation.

Daisy's ears pricked with interest but she knew better than to admit this to the group of young men. She'd never hear the end of it if she let slip that Freddy had stuck in her mind. But before she could think of a suitably damning reply, Terry cut in.

'Come on, we don't want to keep them waiting. They've got to have a decent send-off 'cos they'll be keeping the likes of you safe as you work in your nice warm factory.' He gave her a jaunty wave and led his loyal troops off down the pavement, whistling as if he didn't have a care in the world.

Daisy pulled a face at their departing backs, and then began to walk down the other side of the street, along the white-painted kerb stones. Now that a blackout had been imposed during the hours of darkness, cars and bicycles couldn't use headlamps and there were no street lights, so the white paint was meant to help prevent accidents. Rumour was that several people had been injured because the scheme wasn't working, but the very thought of it made Daisy hasten her pace. She didn't want to get caught out as dusk fell; she didn't have a torch, and even if she did she would have to be very careful how she used it.

For a moment she cursed the lads for delaying her, but then the last thing Chalky had said came back to her. His brother and cousin had been working down at Old Street. That wasn't too far – a bus ride away, or a longish walk if it came to it. If they were leaving that kind of job, it made sense that others would be doing so too. There would be vacancies.

She recalled that Auntie Vera used to tell them about some of her friends who'd worked for what was now the London Passenger Transport Board during the Great War. Back then, women had been bus and tram conductors, and performed all manner of roles that you only saw men in nowadays. But if all the men had to go to war . . .

Daisy stopped in her tracks. There would be opportunities right there for the taking. How much more fun it would be to join an organisation like that. She could do all sorts of new things. Maybe Auntie Vera would know.

Or maybe not, Daisy hastily realised, resuming her walk home. If she didn't succeed, then Auntie Vera would have something to tease her with for ever after. No, she'd do better to keep this quiet. She'd make stealthy enquiries of her own and not tell a soul until she'd got a new job. Something where she could meet new people, help them out. It wasn't as if she had any particular friends at the factory, as nearly everyone was older than her.

Lifting her chin to the chilly breeze in resolution, Daisy strode ever more quickly down the busy main road through Dalston, eager now to find out what her mother would have ready for tea. Lunchtime in the factory canteen felt like an age ago, even though there had been steamed pudding with custard, one of her favourites.

Idly she found herself wondering what sort of food they served at the training camps. Would the army meals be better or worse than those of the navy? What would Freddy be eating, and what was he like now he was so much fitter? Then she gave her head a shake. She wasn't interested in him, it had just been the quickest of conversations. He'd have forgotten her already. The best thing she could do was put him to the back of her mind.

'Now, you're sure you want to help?' Bert Harrison regarded his middle daughter as she stood at the back door. She was shrugging off her jacket, having just arrived back from somewhere – he couldn't remember if she'd said what she'd been doing.

'Of course I do.' Clover was indignant that her father would even ask. 'Look, I've changed into my old shoes and everything.'

Bert nodded slowly, wondering if the girl knew what she was letting herself in for. He'd never thought of her as very practical. Rose, yes, and Peter had always been his right-hand man when it came to making or mending things around the house. Well, it wasn't Clover's fault if she hadn't had much chance to practise. It had always been easier to ask her brother or eldest sister to help with whatever needed doing – but they weren't around right now. The main thing was to complete the construction of the Anderson shelter. While there had still been no actual raids, he couldn't rely on that state of affairs continuing. Besides, he wanted his family to feel as if they had somewhere safe to go. It was nerve-wracking when the sirens went, even if they were false alarms.

'All right, then see if you can lift that corrugated sheeting. Then you come over here on this side and hold the roof in place,' he said, moving so that she could slip past him. 'That's it, just there. Then I'll nail down that corner. Make sure you keep your fingers out of the way when I do.'

Clover gave him a straight look. 'I know that. I'm not daft.' All the same she shuffled a little further away.

They had been lucky that the yard was not paved over, and so they could dig beneath the surface. The shelter had just about fitted into the rear portion of the yard, and Patty had been far from happy to begin with although she knew it was for the best. But she'd had to move her pots and containers full of plants, and they were now all crowded together close to the back door.

There was always the option to join plenty of their neighbours in the communal shelters that had sprung up in the church halls, but Patty had to admit she was happier at the thought of their family having their very own refuge. It would be far quicker to get everyone inside, and if they forgot anything then it would be mere seconds from the house. Plus – and she knew it wasn't a very nice thing to think – they wouldn't have to put up with the noises and smells of a big group of people all squashed into one place. It was bad enough when Bert snored and the combined ranks of the residents of their part of Dalston all snoring merrily away would rid her of any chance of sleep.

Now Bert held the nail exactly where he wanted it, raised the hammer with his other hand and brought it down with force. 'Ow!' Clover shouted.

Bert looked up aghast. 'Did I hit you? But you're well away.'

Clover was embarrassed. 'No, no you didn't. It was just louder that I thought it would be.'

Bert raised his eyebrows. 'It's corrugated iron, it's bound to make a bit of a clatter. Now mind yourself. There's a lot more where that came from.'

Clover pursed her lips and stood in readiness, holding the metal sheet tightly as her father swiftly finished nailing the corner. Bert watched her out of the corner of his eye, noting how she got the hang of what was needed. 'Very good, now help me lift the next one. Move along a bit more – careful, watch that mud on the ground. I'll do the opposite corner next.' He was glad he had finished digging out the actual shelter; no matter how keen she was, he just couldn't see Clover wielding a spade. But perhaps he had underestimated her. 'That's it, you keep this bit steady. Don't jump when I bang the first nail in.' He grinned at her to show he was joking.

'I'm used to it now,' Clover assured him with a bright grin in return.

She did seem to have got the hang of it, Bert told himself as they progressed around the edge of the shelter, even when she had to support the weight of the next metal sheet on a tricky bit at the back. There hadn't been room to form a tidy right-angle, and he'd had to make do with a cut-off shape which meant that the roof was harder to fit. Still, she didn't blanch as he tapped away, gently bending the corrugated iron so that it covered the odd gap and overhung enough to keep out any rain.

'I don't believe it!' They were interrupted by a hoot of laughter from the back door. Daisy stood there, arms folded, shaking her head. 'Is that really you, Clover, or am I seeing things? Are you sure you know what you're doing?'

Bert turned to face his youngest daughter. 'Now don't be mean to your sister. She's doing a grand job helping me out here.'

'If you're so clever then why don't you try helping as well?' Clover suggested, glaring at her sister.

Daisy pursed her lips. 'All right, I will. Just let me change – it looks muddy out there.'

'You'd better not have taken any of my clothes again,' Clover warned.

But Daisy had vanished into the back kitchen and then re-emerged a few moments later, this time wearing

Wellington boots and an old jumper which they all knew was a hand-me-down from Rose. 'So, where do you want me?'

Bert nodded approvingly. 'Now there's two of you we can tackle the most difficult bit. We've got to bend the iron sheet into a curve to go over the far side, without damaging it, or else the rain will come straight through rather than rolling off. So you two catch hold of it here and then push down, steadily and both at the same time.' He paused, hoping the importance of that last instruction had sunk in. He didn't want the pair of them to start arguing or competing to see who was strongest.

Clover winced as she caught her hand against the sharp edge of the sheet but otherwise there was no complaint and the two girls did as they were asked, which allowed Bert to weave between them and make adjustments, tapping more nails into place as he did so, squatting down on his heels to check everything was as even as possible, and finally pronouncing himself satisfied. 'Good, you did well there, girls,' he said, wiping his hands on his faded brown overcoat. 'I'd be here until next week if I'd had to do that alone. Now all I have to do is sort out the door, and then it'll be ready for you and your mother to fit out the inside. I know she's got some ideas about how to make it warm and comfortable.'

Clover made a quizzical face. 'Not sure it'll ever be what you could call comfortable, Pa,' she pointed out.

'We'll make it as comfy as we can,' Daisy declared, pulling her woollen sleeves back down, as it was cold once you stopped working. 'Shall I put the kettle on when we've cleaned ourselves up?'

Bert nodded in approval. He certainly had underestimated the pair of them. They hadn't minded a bit when it came to getting their hands dirty, so he wouldn't hesitate to ask for their help next time it was needed.

Patty had heard them coming in and was already filling the teapot with hot water, and so it was not long before all four of them were sitting around the big kitchen table, welcoming warm cups of tea in their hands.

Clover cleared her throat. 'I have some news.'

Daisy looked sceptical but Patty leant forward eagerly. 'Oh, do tell us, Clover. I hope it's something good.'

Now that it came to it, Clover hesitated for a fraction. She spread her fingers wide on the table's surface, her chilly hands pale against the patterned tablecloth. She took a deep breath. 'I've joined the ATS.'

There was a clatter as Patty shakily set her cup down in its saucer. 'What did you say, Clover?' She stared at her daughter as if she'd spoken in a different language.

Clover pressed her hands into the table more firmly. 'I've joined the ATS. The Auxiliary Territorial Service, you know, the women's branch of the army. That's where I was earlier today.'

'Yes, yes, I know what it is,' Patty said hurriedly. 'But what do you mean, you've joined it? What about your job in the shop?'

Clover winced at the mention of the shop, but kept her voice steady. 'I wanted to do more, you know, like Peter's doing, and Rose too. They need young volunteers, more than the shop needs me. I don't mean that I don't like working there,' she added hurriedly, noticing Patty's stricken face. 'But I'll be more use wherever the ATS send me.'

Bert coughed briefly. 'And where might that be?' he asked, his eyes gazing intently at his daughter's face. 'Did they say? And when would you have to go?'

Clover shook her head slowly. 'Well, I don't really know,' she confessed. 'They just took my details and said that they'd let me know. It might take a little while – there were lots of people there, all with the same thing in mind, so I suppose they'll have to sort everyone out bit by bit.' She took a sip of tea. 'I'm sorry I didn't tell you beforehand, but . . . well, I thought I might lose my nerve if I didn't just jump right in and do it. You aren't cross, are you?'

Daisy was simply staring silently, caught out by the surprise. Patty was biting her lip, her hands holding the teacup tight enough to snap the handle off. For a wild moment she wondered why it had to be her beloved girl who'd done this: none of her nieces had taken such a step. Faith, Hope and Joy were staying out of the conflict, she was sure.

It was left to Bert to reply. He took a moment to gather his thoughts but when he spoke he was completely sincere. 'I think that's wonderful, Clover.' His eyes shone and his voice was full of pride. 'It can't have been an easy decision. I bet you worried about letting your mother down in the shop, but you've done the right thing. Somebody else can fill in for you there. You're young, and fit, and even this afternoon you surprised me by how quickly you picked up how to help fix the shelter roof. We're proud of you, my girl.' He gazed lovingly at his daughter, whose eyes welled up with tears at the unexpected praise. 'And may I say, they're lucky to have you. No doubt about that.'

CHAPTER FIVE

Daisy cursed silently to herself as she strode along Old Street, dodging the sandbags that some business owners had piled up in readiness for any aerial attacks. Windows were criss-crossed with strips of brown tape in case the glass broke in one of the raids they were all waiting for. If her mind had been on such details she would have recognised that the area had been transformed since the last time she had been there, which was before the war began. However her thoughts were replaying the conversation that she had just had at the Underground station office.

She could see now that she had gone wrong, right from the start. She had blithely assumed that they would be delighted that somebody wanted to work there now that their staff numbers had been reduced by the young men joining the army. She hadn't actually said that she knew at least two had left recently, the ones that Chalky had gone on about. But secretly she'd thought they might be impressed at her initiative. She'd gone there after work, as she'd had an early factory shift and had finished in the middle of the afternoon.

At first they hadn't taken her seriously. The man who seemed to be in charge, her father's age if not even older, had looked down his nose at her – not difficult, as he was tall and Daisy was only five foot three. His face was almost grey, due to not being out in the daylight very often, she suspected. He had frowned, and then asked, 'Is this part of a school project?'

Daisy had bristled. 'No, not at all. I left school years ago. Like I said, I'm here about the vacancies I heard of.'

He had taken off his wire-rimmed glasses and polished the lenses on his handkerchief as he spoke. 'Well, you don't look old enough to have left school.'

Daisy could have stamped her foot in frustration but managed not to. 'I can assure you that I am. I'm working full time but want to do more to help the war effort.' Somewhere that would offer more exciting opportunities, she might have added – although she was beginning to get the distinct impression that this man was not keen on excitement.

'Well, young lady, you have come to the wrong place.' He sighed with impatience. 'To work here you would have to be at least twenty-one. Don't even try to persuade me that you are anywhere close to that age.'

'I'm older than I look,' Daisy declared.

'No matter. You aren't old enough and therefore won't be mature enough to cope with the responsibilities these jobs entail. Now if you wouldn't mind, I have important work to return to. I wish you good day.' With that he had turned his back on her and gone back inside his office with the solid wood door.

Daisy had clenched her fists but had been powerless to do anything to change the man's opinion. He had obviously made up his mind and that was that. Besides, she thought ruefully, she wasn't anywhere close to twenty-one. She wasn't even eighteen yet.

Now she kicked her way along Old Street, scuffing her shoes, little pieces of gravel flying in front of her. Buses trundled past, full of people who no doubt worked in places far more interesting than the clothing factory. Daisy was furious with herself. She should have thought this through.

Of course there was going to be an age barrier. Office jobs were different to factory ones, where they'd take you on at fourteen as long as you could reach the equipment. Even if she had tried to lie about how old she was, there was a chance that someone here would recognise her; lots of people knew her family, as her father was a well-respected foreman at Sutherland and Company, the big paint factory, and people came to the greengrocer's from all around. The only reason she'd come here was because of that connection with Chalky's brother and cousin. Any lies she got away with at the start would soon have been found out.

Berating herself for her own stupidity, she turned left after the grand façade of Shoreditch Town Hall and headed north to a bus stop for Dalston. There weren't many people waiting, which probably meant she had just missed one. It was turning out to be that sort of day.

As she leant against a lamppost, tucking her wayward hair behind her ears to keep it out of her eyes, she began to calm down. She couldn't give up at the first hurdle. Look at Clover, all ready to go and do her bit by joining the ATS. Hearing that news had bolstered Daisy's intentions still further.

Perhaps she had gone about it all wrong this afternoon, but there were other tube stations. It didn't have to be Old Street. In fact, it would be better if it wasn't. The fewer people who might recognise her, the better. It would only have to be for a few weeks, she reasoned, as she was bound to do so well that even if they learnt the truth about her age, they would forgive her, as by then she would have become all but indispensable.

She would have to make herself appear older – and not simply turn up in her factory clothes. If she wore higher heels to make her just a little taller . . . and perhaps a touch of make-up? She could borrow some that Rose had left behind – she wasn't about to risk Clover's wrath by taking hers. Perhaps do her hair differently? Anything had to be better than how it looked after a shift tied back in that horrid scarf, which made it all dull and flat. And finally, dress up to appear professional. That was it. She had to seem more sophisticated, not some scrappy girl who didn't know what was what.

The bus finally wound its way up from Bishopsgate and Daisy took a seat on the top deck so that she could look into the windows of the buildings close by. Even though she was seventeen she never tired of that. Now she felt better. She had a plan. She'd practise her look and then, once she was confident that she could carry it off, she'd go to the next-nearest tube station. Manor House was in her sights . . .

Clover shoved the brown envelope into her coat pocket after she'd swiftly read the message it contained which was far from what she'd hoped for. Before she could think straight about what it might mean, there was a loud crash from the other side of the front door, and then a shriek, followed by laughter.

She opened the door to the broad pavement and stared at the sight that met her eyes. Robbie was practically at her feet, groaning and laughing at the same time, his knees grazed and dripping with bright red blood. 'Robbie! What have you done!' she exclaimed crossly, although she could see well enough for herself.

A little further down Victory Walk lay the wreck of what must have recently been a go-cart, smashed panels of wood strewn about, wheels still spinning. The younger Glanville boy was crouched beside it, examining it. 'Don't think those brakes work, Robbie,' he said, his face creased with merriment.

Robbie groaned again and rolled onto his back. 'I was sure I did them right this time,' he protested, then his gaze met that of his big sister. 'Don't worry, Clover, it's not as bad as it looks. They're only scratched a bit,' he added, pointing at his bloody knees.

'You get inside right now so that we can clean you up,' she spluttered, knowing that this was her responsibility. Her mother was still at the shop, her father at his factory, Daisy at hers. And no Rose around, who would have been the most capable person to sort this out.

'He was only trying out our cart,' Ricky Glanville told her, prodding the splintered side of the wreck. 'We're going to have to patch this up good and proper, or it'll never hold your weight again.' He was about a year older than Robbie, his light brown hair falling into his eyes, his shoelaces undone. 'Pity, I thought we'd sorted it out this time.'

Clover glared at her brother. 'Don't even think about it. You're never going near that contraption again. You could have been killed.'

Robbie shook his head as he tried to get to his feet, attempting not to show he was in pain but failing to hide the wince as his knees straightened. 'Oh, don't take on, Clover. I wasn't going that fast. No harm done, not really.'

'Only to our cart,' Ricky said ruefully.

Several people at the other end of Victory Walk had noticed the commotion and one of the neighbours began to make her way along towards the crash. 'Oh no, that's all we need,' Clover breathed. 'They'll complain that they're not accustomed to anything going that fast along here, even though those district nurses in the end house race along day and night. Ricky, you gather up this mess and get rid of it. I know you were behind it to begin with, it's got your name written all over it. Robbie, get inside sharpish. We'll put some Dettol on those scratches and meanwhile try not to bleed all over the hall mat.'

Robbie stuck out his tongue at her back as she turned to open the door more widely but did as he was bidden, straightening up fully.

'Not to worry, I'll keep it safe,' Ricky promised, carefully balancing the least damaged pieces of wood in his arms and collecting the wheels. 'We can try again. Just don't let on.' He nodded towards where Clover had disappeared into the hallway.

'Quick, you'd better scarper,' Robbie advised, shutting the door as his friend moved away down the pavement.

Clover sighed as she ushered her little brother through to the back kitchen, where she made him sit on a low stool while she fetched the bottle of pine-scented amber liquid and some cotton wool. Remembering how Rose had done this on countless occasions, she filled a shallow bowl with hot water from the kettle. 'This will sting a bit,' she warned.

'I know,' said Robbie glumly.

Carefully Clover cleaned and then disinfected her brother's knees, noticing how he bore the discomfort with no complaint, just catching his breath a little as the cotton wool sometimes stuck to the skin. A shaft of late autumn sunlight came through the window, warm and golden, and suddenly she couldn't feel cross with him any more. He was only doing what children had always done, playing outside with a friend. After all, most of his other friends had departed a couple of months ago, everyone in floods of tears and afraid they wouldn't see one another again. It was only him and the Glanville boys left on Victory Walk, and he must miss the others even if he never said so. A small part of her recognised that building the cart must have taken some ingenuity. Pity that they hadn't worked out how to make brakes for it.

'Up you get,' she said, more gently now, tipping away the bloodstained water and disposing of the last of the cotton wool. 'Let them dry a bit and then we can find you some lint dressings.'

Robbie huffed. 'I shan't need those. I'll be all right. I don't want to look like a baby.'

Clover ruffled his hair, thinking he was still their baby, no matter what he might believe, as he batted her hand away. 'I'm going upstairs to read my comics,' he said, and he set off, limping slightly.

Well, he was probably right, no real harm had been done, Clover sighed to herself as she sat down on the little stool to make the most of the unexpected sunshine. Even Rose couldn't have fixed him up any better, she was sure – although their parents would undoubtedly have something to say about it.

She'd slung her coat over the hook on the backyard door, and now she retrieved the envelope from its pocket. Slowly she straightened out the creases from where she'd crumpled it up in frustration. It contained just one page, official-looking, all typed up with her name in full: Clover Elizabeth Harrison. It informed her that for her initial period in the ATS, she would be able to live at home, contrary to the usual conventions, as she was being allocated a role near the War Office in Whitehall, which she could commute to by bus. That wasn't the part that had annoyed her. But the role – she might as well not have bothered signing up. After all that anxiety and waiting for news, she was to be a storekeeper. A bloody storekeeper! From weighing vegetables for the families of

Dalston to counting . . . she didn't know what, but maybe woolly socks, for the army. That wasn't the adventure she'd hoped for. She'd been prepared to put her life on the line – and here she was, again, stuck with being a storekeeper.

CHAPTER SIX

Rose hurried to disinfect her hands before she saw to the final patient on the ward. Now that autumn was on its way out and winter was arriving in a shower of hail and chilling rain, the flu season had also begun. While the remaining younger members of Hackney's residents could usually shrug it off after a few days in bed, older folk struggled and the worst cases ended up in hospital – if they had the means to see a doctor in the first place.

Her job was to get them assessed, treated, and then back into their own homes where they could be looked after by the local team of district nurses. Rose had great faith in them and had got to know a few since she'd taken up her profession. The last and largest house in the terrace of Victory Walk was the closest district nurses' home, and she'd grown up impressed by their uniform and their energy as they cycled to and from their cases.

The remaining patient was an elderly woman. 'It's cos I live on my own, you see,' she said shakily, as

Rose took her temperature, pulse and respiration – the elements known as TPR which began any examination. 'Now my boys have gone off to fight, I don't bank the fire up like I should. Then that cold air gets in me lungs.'

Rose nodded. 'Well, you've got to look after yourself, Mrs Parfitt. Plenty of hot meals, even if it's only soup, and don't sit still for too long if you can help it.'

The woman sighed. 'Easy for you young ones to say. You don't have arthritis like what I do.'

Rose regarded her steadily. 'Even so, a bit of regular movement will help. Keeps your circulation going which means you'll stay warmer and helps to oil those painful joints.'

The woman shook her head. 'Ain't you going to give me medicine to take home, then?'

Rose smiled. Patients often asked her that. 'The best medicine you can take is a bit of regular exercise,' she assured her. 'Doctor might well give you something while you recuperate but long-term, you just see if I'm right.' She tucked in the blankets at the end of the bed and made to move away. 'I'll make sure the district nurses check up on you and they'll tell you the same thing.'

'Thank you, Nurse. I suppose you know what you're on about.' The old woman still sounded a little put out, but her expression showed she was grateful for the attention.

Rose smiled once more and then went across to the nurses' station in the centre of the brightly lit ward, to finish her notes. Then her shift would be over.

She was going to an early showing at the new Odeon on Hackney Road with her cousin Hope. Just that morning, as she'd taken a quick walk for fresh air before starting work, she'd been greeted by a cry. 'Fancy seeing you here!'

Hope was as unlike her sister Faith as chalk and cheese. She'd inherited Vera's stockier build, and her hair, although fair, was cut to her shoulders in a wavy bob. She put far less effort into her appearance and that morning was wearing a tweed coat with slightly frayed cuffs which she must have hidden from her exacting mother.

'I'm just helping out at the church hall, sorting kiddies' clothes,' Hope went on. 'Don't suppose you're free later on? I'll be dying for a sit-down come the afternoon. Have you seen *Wuthering Heights* yet?'

Rose chuckled. 'I have. In fact, it was the last film I went to with Martin. It was all right but I don't fancy watching it a second time.'

Hope hooted with laughter. 'He's seen it twice though! He took Faith to it last week. Or so she said, when she bothered to show up at our house, and that was only because she wanted to borrow something from Ma.'

Rose made a face. 'He didn't seem to enjoy it much the first time. So good luck to them. What about *The Adventures of Sherlock Holmes*? Clover loved that one. I reckon she's got a thing about that Basil Rathbone.'

Hope gave a mock-shiver. 'She can join the queue. He was so handsome in *The Hound of the Baskervilles*! You can tell her she'll have to fight me for him.' Then she fished in her large shopping bag slung across her body like a satchel and drew out the local newspaper. 'Here, look, it's on at the Odeon. I've hardly been there since it opened. Shall I see you outside ten minutes before curtain-up?'

Rose had agreed with enthusiasm and now she hastened to her room to get changed out of her uniform. It never ceased to amaze her that Hope had turned out so friendly and sensible compared to her glamorous but shallow sister. She wondered if Martin knew what he was letting himself in for . . . Stop it, she told herself, as she fastened her neat green gloves, and picked up her gas mask. He's moved on, and rightly so. She took a deep breath. In her heart, she wished he'd moved on to someone more suitable, someone kinder. But it wasn't her concern any more.

Clover wiped the small windowpanes with a cloth, breathing on the glass in an attempt to let in more light. At least this storeroom had a window. Earlier this morning she'd had to put up with the senior officer in charge of training, an older woman known as a section leader, droning on about the best way to lift and stack boxes while peering at her in the gloom of one of the basement rooms in the huge old office building. As if she didn't know how to bend her knees when moving heavy weights – she'd been hoisting sacks of potatoes far bigger than these puny cardboard boxes.

'Clover, snap out of it! You've got your head in the clouds again!'

Clover turned around to find her fellow storeroom attendant standing right behind her. Sylvia was about her own age, wiry of build and with long, almost black, hair that she always wore in two plaits. She was a Londoner too, only she came from Tottenham. Clover perked up at the sound of her voice.

'What've you got there?' she asked, looking at the large paper bag that Sylvia was carrying.

Sylvia set it down on a bench and brushed pine needles from her khaki uniform. 'Bits and pieces that they didn't need in the War Office,' she said. 'My sister works over there and I popped in to see her on the way here as we're so close to Whitehall. They've got a tree and everything, but they had some spare pine branches and leftover tinsel so I thought we could brighten this place up.'

Clover stepped away from the little window and rummaged in the bag. 'That's a good idea.' She delved into the depths of the bag to see how much it contained. 'Oh, I know. We could make a hoop. You know, you make a circle with a coat hanger or something like that, wind branches around it and then add tinsel or any baubles if you've got them.'

Sylvia's face brightened. 'We did that once and my gran put candles on it. Then she lit them and forgot all about it. Nearly burned the house down.'

'Well, we won't do that,' Clover replied hastily. She looked around the small room, not much more than a square box itself. There were some crates of light wood in one corner, the topmost of which was falling apart from overuse. 'Look, we can use that. Take the slats and tie them at the corners with thick string, to make a diamond. Doesn't have to be round, any shape will do.'

Sylvia did as Clover suggested and before long the two of them had assembled the frame and covered it with the bright green branches. 'You wouldn't know what was underneath,' she chuckled. 'Let's make stripes of tinsel across the middle.'

'We could alternate the colours,' said Clover, unfurling a ruby-red length. 'I'll put this at the top and bottom and you put another sort across the centre.'

Sylvia drew out a bundle of gold and began to untwist it. 'This will go perfectly. You've got a real eye for this, Clover.'

'Thanks.' Clover beamed and was filled with a warm glow. It felt like ages since anyone had praised her. The stores section leader was dull and impossible to please, no doubt from having to take on so many new recruits in a short time. When she'd worked with her mother they'd known each other so well that there had been little need to say anything. So this unprompted comment delighted her.

Perhaps she did have a talent for this kind of thing. For a moment her imagination ran away from her, conjuring pictures of designing decorations for bigger rooms, grander spaces, on all sorts of occasions. Then the sound of approaching footsteps broke the spell.

'Quick, sweep up those needles,' Sylvia muttered, swiftly returning all the unused bits and pieces to the bag. 'This might brighten the place up but it's not what we're being paid to do. Let's look busy!'

Clover nodded in agreement and between them they managed to tidy the floor and still give the impression that they'd spent the last few minutes studying lists of equipment, as their sour-faced section leader swept in. 'All in order?' she demanded. 'Have you checked the last batch of supplies?'

Sylvia nodded and pointed to the sheet of paper in front of her. 'It's all here,' she said seriously, all traces of enjoyment gone from her voice.

'Very good, very good.' The officer ran her eyes along the columns to ensure that all was as it should be. Then her interest was caught by what she noticed propped against a pile of packing cases. 'Oh, I say.'

Sylvia and Clover's eyes met. Now they were in trouble.

The officer put down the list and went over to the decoration, lifting it up in the daylight from the little window. 'Did you make this? Well, clearly you did.' Her usually solemn face broke into a smile. 'How ingenious. I can see that you have repurposed waste material and made something pretty from it. Well, that is to be commended. I shall make a note of it.' She smiled once more. 'Right, carry on.' She swept from the room, leaving the pair astonished.

Finally Clover breathed out. 'I thought we were for it then.'

Sylvia shivered. 'I did too. Perhaps she's not such a bad old stick after all.'

The two of them started laughing, in a release of tension, and Clover glowed again. She'd really missed this feeling. At the shop she'd had no companions her own age; sometimes Hope or Joy would drop in, but otherwise she'd lost contact with girls from school. As she carefully looped a final piece of string around the apex of the Christmas diamond so that she could hang it where it would catch the light, she made a decision. 'What do you like to do after your shift ends, Sylvia?' she asked. 'Shall we go out together some time?'

Patty prided herself on her Christmas preparations. Usually she would begin months in advance, making the cake and the pudding, checking that she knew where the decorations were, buying in crepe paper to make new ones if necessary. This year she had been more cautious, although heaven knew that they could all do with a big celebration to cheer everyone up. However, not knowing who might be home or what might happen in the immediate future, she had put off making a start.

Now she'd had the longed-for news that her eldest son Peter would be home on leave, there was no stopping her. 'What's the rush?' Bert said, as he finished his breakfast of toast and marmalade. 'He only left a few months ago. He won't have forgotten what we're like. It's still the same old house, you don't have to change it completely.'

Patty paused in the middle of the back kitchen and dried her hands on a tea towel. Sometimes men could be so pig-headed. 'I'm not changing it completely, I'm making sure he has a Christmas to remember,' she replied. She didn't add that already there were forecasts of food shortages and restrictions. It might be the last time they could celebrate in style. 'It's got to be even better than the last one. I'll get the girls to help, and Robbie too if he can put those blessed comics down for two minutes. He's a dab hand at paper chains when he puts his mind to it.'

Bert nodded, with only a scant idea of what his wife was up against. 'Would you like me to bring back anything from the factory?' he asked.

'Brown paper, if there are any offcuts from the packaging,' Patty said promptly. 'I can use that to protect anything breakable before wrapping it in the Christmas paper proper – and also Robbie can paint it and then cut it up, to glue together for his paper chains.'

Bert put his plate of crumbs on the draining board. 'I'll be sure to check,' he promised. 'Right, I'd better be off.' He lifted first his jacket and then his overcoat from the back door hook, shrugged them on and then stepped across the scrubbed tiles to give Patty a peck on the cheek. 'See you later.'

'Bye.' She smiled at him as he went out, but sighed with a little relief now that she was on her own. She loved him dearly but at a moment like this he didn't appreciate the urgency of what she was up against. The clock was ticking. She'd have to make lists and then swing into action.

Two hours later, the kitchen was filled with the smells of cinnamon and nutmeg, as Patty stirred the cake mixture while a tray of biscuits was already baking in the oven. She sang to herself under her breath, an old carol she'd learnt in Sunday school when she was younger. She felt a lump forming in her throat; it reminded her of her own parents, who had died just a couple of years ago. First her mother had got sick, and then her father had followed a few months later. Everyone said he hadn't wanted to carry on without the woman to whom he'd been married for the best part of fifty years.

Patty blinked as tears came unbidden to her eyes. This wouldn't do. She missed them, of course she did, but she had her own family now and, against all the odds, they were to be together for Christmas; therefore it was up to her to make sure they had the loveliest time ever. None of them could predict what next year might bring, and so they had to seize the day. Touch wood that the predicted raids still held off, at least until the festivities were over. There were rumours of incursions along the French border but nothing serious close to home – yet.

'Are you all right, Ma?' Rose arrived through the back door, her cheeks rosy from the cold, which set off the reddish flecks in her chestnut hair. For once it wasn't scraped back in its neat bun, but hung in waves around her flushed face. She wore a cornflower blue coat, collar turned up against the chill wind, which set off her blue eyes.

'Yes, it's just this nutmeg making me sneeze.' Hastily Patty pulled herself together. She didn't want her sensible eldest daughter to catch her coming over all emotional. 'Here, take these oven mitts and check the bottom shelf, would you? I don't want anything to burn.'

Rose set her coat over the back of one of the dining chairs and reached for the old mitts, their padding coming through the tired stitching. Right, she thought, that's one Christmas present sorted out. She'd get a new pair from the market at the nearest opportunity. 'Mmmm, Christmas biscuits!' she exclaimed in appreciation. 'Let's see – they could do with another couple of minutes.' She checked her nurses' watch, which she wore even when not on duty as it was so useful. 'I'll keep track.'

Patty nodded, knowing that Rose would do exactly that. If it had been Daisy she might have been distracted, and Clover was liable to forget such details, but not Rose.

'Did you hear that Peter has got the dates for his leave?' Patty asked now. 'He'll be here the day before Christmas Eve and he can stay for four nights. Won't that be wonderful?'

Rose smiled; she had missed her brother and longed to hear all his news. 'I don't have my rota yet but I'm sure I'll be able to come over at some point and I want to hear all his news. I bet Clover will too – I know she's been pining for some real adventure.'

Patty's face clouded with worry. 'Don't go giving her ideas. I know she's disappointed to be stuck indoors checking boxes, doing what she's always done, just in a different setting, but I can tell you, I'm glad. It means at least she's not in the way of danger.'

Rose shrugged as she reached for the mitts once more. 'Well, you've hit the nail on the head.' She bent to the door of the well-polished range and opened its heavy door. 'Oh, these are just right now.' She lifted out the tray of sweet-smelling biscuits and set them on the range top, beside the wire rack her mother had laid out in readiness. 'Clover's itching to get out of the storeroom, isn't she? We might want to keep her safe, but she's in the army now.'

Patty leaned across the counter for the cake tin that she had lined with greaseproof paper. 'I know, and she's almost an adult. But she's my little girl when all's said and done. Just don't let your brother fill her head with tales of bravery and risk-taking. I want you all to stay safe.'

CHAPTER SEVEN

Patty had been cleaning the kitchen floor when the knock came at the front door, and then she heard it swing open. She leapt to her feet and nearly knocked over the bucket of warm water, catching the handle just in time.

'Where is everybody?' came the deep, familiar voice, and she thought she would die of pride, relief and delight. He was home. Peter was home after all those months of training and here she was, hands reddened and with her oldest apron tied around her waist, totally unprepared. She'd known he was almost bound to be delayed and so had not got her hopes up that he'd be back before late evening. Now here he was, doing the impossible: arriving early.

'In here!' she called out, throwing the dirty water into the back yard and drying her sore hands as he came through into the warmth of the kitchen. For a moment she simply stared at him. He'd always been fit, thanks to his love of football, but now he'd filled out across the shoulders and lost any roundness in his face. What a fine, handsome boy he was. He took after his father in his facial features, and had the family thick chestnut hair, only his was now cut very short.

Then he was striding across the worn rag rug and sweeping her into a hug, and it was all she could do not to sob into his scratchy greatcoat, she was so glad to see him.

'It's good to be home, Ma.' Those few short words made her heart sing. Then her practical nature took over.

'You must be gasping for a cuppa,' she said, as he released her and took off the heavy uniform coat and slung it over the back of a chair. 'I'll get the kettle on and then we'll see what we've got to eat. There's a lovely ham that I was going to keep for Christmas Day, but we need to celebrate.'

His newly mature face broke into a broad smile. 'I won't say no to that. They feed us well, and I had a pie from a van outside the station, but it's just not the same. And it's a long way from East Anglia, even if the train didn't arrive late.'

Patty nodded with satisfaction. 'Of course,' she said happily.

One by one the other members of the family arrived back from their jobs or, in Robbie's case, from playing at the Glanvilles', all but Clover who was on a late shift. Bert promptly brought out the whisky that was kept in the parlour for special occasions, while Daisy rushed to help lay the table and peel potatoes to accompany the glistening ham. Peter was shouted down every time he offered to help, and subsided onto a chair at the table, enjoying all the activity and lapping up the attention.

Daisy pinched her cheeks to make them redder, wondering as she did so if that added to the effect she was after, or made her look younger. If she couldn't use rouge, then this was the next best thing, but she had a horrible feeling it made her seem childish with a big red face.

'What are you doing?' Peter asked. After they'd finally finished the impromptu celebration meal, Daisy had managed to catch him for a quiet word.

'Let me show you how I helped put on the roof of the shelter,' she'd said, glad that Clover was not there to point out that she'd helped as well.

Peter raised his eyebrows at that, but obligingly shrugged his uniform coat back on and stepped outside into the yard – even smaller now that the shelter was completed and taking up the rear of the space.

'Shut the door,' Daisy hissed.

'What? Why?' Peter's good-tempered face took on a teasing air.

'Keep the heat in for the others,' Daisy said loudly. Then, once he'd done what she asked, she drew him down to the shelter. 'Cos I need to ask you something.' She huddled into her baggiest woolly jumper, a cheerful crimson colour, rubbing her upper arms for warmth.

'Well, out with it, then. You're obviously freezing.' Peter tapped the corrugated metal. 'Nice roof, couldn't have done better myself.'

'Never mind that! Look, I need you to do me a favour.'

Now she had her brother's full attention. 'In trouble, are you?'

Daisy shook her head crossly. 'No, nothing like that.' She took a deep breath and then quickly explained her plan: to work for the London Passenger Transport Board, and what she'd have to do to fool them. 'I've been planning it for ages but didn't know if I could get away with it,' she continued. 'So when I heard you were coming home I had an idea. You take me down the pub, I try to have a proper drink, see if they believe I'm eighteen. Which I will be next birthday anyway.'

Peter took a step back. 'Hang on, Daze. You could get in trouble.'

Daisy made a face. 'Not really. I'm allowed in at my age and I can have a soft drink. I'd be allowed something stronger with a meal, so if they ask I can say we got confused.'

Peter laughed. 'So we have to go to a pub that serves meals, do we? Not just the local?'

'Better not the local,' Daisy said hurriedly. 'I don't want anyone I know to see me. Specially not any of Ma and Pa's friends. Or one of our cousins – that'd be just my luck if Joy or Hope came strolling in. You know what it's like round here, can't do anything without half the place knowing.'

Peter nodded. 'True enough. But I'm not lying for you. If anyone asks me direct, I can't swear you're over eighteen.'

Daisy tossed back her deep brown curls. 'They won't. I'm going to show you just how grown-up I can look. Thanks, Peter, I owe you.'

'You do. Well, you better show me the rest of this precious shelter, to make your story convincing.'

Daisy swung back the door, which had come from an old shed that Bert's friend was getting rid of. 'Look, we got a bench along each side and one at the back. Ma put in cushions so we'll be comfy, and there's even a little methylated spirit stove so we can make tea if it comes to it.' She pointed to a dented kettle and row of mismatched cups propped on an upturned wooden box.

'Which it hasn't yet. And hopefully won't.' Peter bent over and tapped the box. 'Touch wood.'

Daisy crouched down and copied him.

Now they walked along the pavement, down a side street off the main road which ran south to Liverpool Street, Daisy concentrating on balancing in the heeled boots she'd taken from the cupboard of things Rose had left behind. Fortunately they had the same small feet and Daisy reasoned that Rose hardly ever wore the boots as she was on her feet all day in flat shoes and so now these hurt her ankles.

She'd carefully studied the pictures in Clover's magazines and tried to copy the popular hairstyles, sweeping her hair up from the sides and fastening it with grips. She'd had a serious go at making a stylish wave at the front but her hair was having none of it, and so she'd given up. A dab of mascara and lipstick added to the effect, she'd decided as she posed in front of the bedroom mirror, hurrying in case Clover came in. The lipstick matched the dark pink of her blouse. Then she overheard her mother say that Clover was going out with one of her new friends from the ATS and wouldn't be home until much later so Daisy had added more of her sister's mascara for good luck.

The December evening was cold and she wished she'd been able to wear her thick knitted scarf, but the square of patterned silk she'd tied at an angle across her throat was much more stylish. Peter had laughed when she'd come down the stairs adjusting it. 'You'll freeze,' he'd said. 'I won't,' she'd automatically replied, but now she knew he'd been right.

'This wind's coming straight in from Siberia,' she said, trying to stop her teeth from chattering.

'Told you,' said Peter cheerfully. 'Anyway, if you think this is bad, you should see what we have to put up with. The huts we sleep in on our base are leakier than that Anderson shelter, and the wind is sharp as nails. It's so flat up there, there's nothing to stop it coming direct from the Steppes. Course, we're all hardened army fighters now and we don't take a blind bit of notice.'

'Course you are.' Daisy flashed her brother a look.

Finally Peter took pity on her. 'Nearly there,' he said. 'Normally you'd have seen the lights of the saloon by now but what with the blackout, you can't tell it's only at the next corner. Here we are. The Dog and Fiddle.' He made a show of gesturing to the big wooden door, its brass handle gleaming in the moonlight and sporadic beams from the searchlights. 'Don't show me up, there might be some others from my battalion there, lots of us Hackney boys got leave together.'

'As if.' Daisy gave a sniff and then sailed through the door as he held it for her.

So far so good, she thought, as she edged her way towards the bar, avoiding any big groups of friends standing around. The air was warm and the walls were decorated with paper chains. In the furthest corner stood a Christmas tree, shiny bells and stars hanging from its branches, a doll dressed as an angel perched lopsidedly on top. She couldn't stop to gawp as it might single her out as someone who'd not been in a pub before. Her parents had very occasionally taken them to a beer garden in the summer, but the girls had never been allowed inside.

Peter was directly behind her. 'Better let me order,' he said in her ear.

'Why? How will I know if I look the part?' She turned to argue but he put his hand on her shoulder.

'Don't make a fuss, people will wonder what you're on about. The gent buys for the lady, that's the way it's done. Right,' he took up the one vacant space at the gleaming brass-fronted bar, 'what'll you have?' A middle-aged barman stepped across to take their order.

'I'll have half a shandy,' Daisy said boldly. She'd heard Rose say that this is what she had, very rarely and when she wasn't on shift the next day.

'Half a shandy and a pint of bitter for me,' Peter said to the barman, who set down the tea towel with which he'd been polishing glasses and went to the pumps at once. 'You tried this before, have you? Do you even like shandy? Don't make me look like an idiot, mind.'

'Of course. And I won't,' Daisy said, crossing her fingers inside her coat pocket. She'd have to drink it, no matter what. Anyhow, the barman hadn't questioned her age when Peter ordered, so she must be doing all right.

Now she allowed herself to gaze around the room. It was Saturday night and the saloon was crowded, some older couples sitting on padded banquettes near the fire, a few solitary old men nursing pints in the corners, and plenty of young people, a fair few in uniform. There was a piano on the far side, sheet music flapping in a draught as drinkers pushed past. She must be the youngest person here, but who would know that? There were two WAAFs, by their uniform, and as they wore no make-up she was sure they looked younger than her at this particular moment.

Then her gaze froze. The drinkers had moved away from the piano to reveal a big wooden table, covered in empty glasses although it was still early evening, and all the seats around it occupied by young men, most of them in khaki uniforms similar to Peter's. Half of them had their backs to her, but even so that hair was unmistakable. Chalky, who'd recently left the clothes factory. Sure enough, beside him, his profile visible, sat Terry, holding forth with a loud tale, to gales of laughter.

Daisy hastily turned around before they could see her. At once she came face to face with an even more familiar figure.

'Daisy! What on God's earth are you doing here?'

Daisy almost dropped her shandy. 'Clover!' was all she managed to say. A cold feeling of dread crept over her. Her sister was bound to reveal her secret, blow her cover.

But then Clover caught sight of Peter. The two hadn't seen one another since he'd left home and their reunion was full of joy. Peter gave his middle sister a big hug and Clover hugged him in return, clearly glad and relieved that he'd made it back for Christmas.

'You should have got word to me where you were going to be, what your plans were,' he said, grinning to show he wasn't annoyed.

'Well, I just assumed you'd be delayed getting back just like everyone else seems to be these days. Besides, we hadn't really decided where we'd go,' Clover told him. 'I'm here with my new colleague, Sylvia. Look, here she is, come to say hello.' She turned to a wiry young woman with long dark hair that shone as it spread across her shoulders. She was wearing a neat pea-green knitted jumper tightly belted at the waist. 'Sylvia, this is my big brother Peter, who's just got back on leave. And this,' she indicated Daisy, who was hanging back, 'is my sister Daisy.'

'Very pleased to meet you,' Sylvia said, smiling up at Peter, who was at least half a foot taller than her. 'I'm Sylvia Ellis. And Daisy – I've heard so much about you.' Their eyes met, almost on a level, and Daisy had to smile back.

'I bet,' she said. Then she raised her glass. 'Cheers and Happy Christmas,' she added, taking a brave sip of the deep brown drink. With everyone's gaze on her she had to swallow it, although it had a sharp taste she wasn't at all sure she liked. Never mind. That wasn't the point.

Their activity had drawn the attention of the young men at the big table across the room, and now Terry stood up and called out.

'Hey, Daisy! Thought that was you! Didn't you say you never went to the pub?' His friends hooted as if he'd come up with the funniest comment in the world.

'No, I just said I never went to the pub with the likes of you,' Daisy shot back smartly.

There was a chorus of ooohs and Chalky nudged Terry in the ribs. 'She got you there, mate,' he said cheerfully.

'Here, don't do that, you nearly made me spill my pint.' Terry didn't like to be upstaged. 'Get yourself over here, Daisy, and bring your friends. There's plenty of room.'

Daisy looked dubious, but Clover shrugged and Sylvia looked pleased at the invitation. 'Why not?' she asked. 'There's nowhere else to sit down. I wouldn't mind taking the weight off my feet. We've been running around doing last-minute stocktaking all day.'

Clover cocked her head at her sister. 'What are they like, Daisy? They don't seem a bad lot, but you know them and we don't.'

Daisy sighed. They wouldn't be her ideal companions for the evening, but if she could hold her own and not get teased about her age with them, then that would serve her purpose well. 'Oh, that one with the sandy hair is a bit of a big mouth,' she said. 'The one next to him is all right even if he follows Terry around like a puppy. I recognise a couple of the others from the factory – that's how I know them, Sylvia – but the rest I've never set eyes on before.'

Peter made the decision for her. 'I won't turn down an offer from a fellow soldier, that'd be rude,' he declared. 'And you heard Sylvia, she'd like to sit down, so we'd better accept.'

Daisy took another gulp of shandy for courage. 'All right,' she agreed. As she let Peter lead the way through the other groups of drinkers standing around, she couldn't help but check the circle of Terry's friends. There was no sign of Freddy. Still at his naval base, she thought, gripping her glass tightly. Not that she cared, one way or the other.

Terry had made the others shuffle closer together around a curved banquette, and Chalky had somehow found a spare couple of padded stools so that there was just about room for the four of them to sit down. Clover and Sylvia got the stools, since they'd been standing for longest. Peter cheerfully shoved up next to Chalky, and Daisy perched next to him, glad that she hadn't had to cram shoulder to shoulder with her former colleagues. That would have been far too intimate. To deflect their teasing, she took the initiative with the conversation.

'So, how did the first weeks of training go?' she asked. 'Bet it seems like ages since you left.'

'Oh, we've taken to it like ducks to water, just like we knew we would,' Terry assured her and Daisy wrinkled her forehead. Exactly what she might have expected him to say. 'Me and Chalky are in the same barracks; they let us bunk together in fact.'

'Yep, they didn't have the sense to split us up like the teachers used to have to do when we was in school,' Chalky chipped in, his upper lip covered in foam from his beer. 'I spect they'll learn soon enough.'

One of the others across the table cut in. 'Chalky, you haven't introduced us properly. How come you're so rude, didn't I teach you anything?' He flashed his teeth in a smile but there was a slight edge to his comment. Daisy registered that he looked a lot like Chalky but was perhaps a couple of years older.

Chalky swept the back of his hand across his forehead in a dramatic gesture. 'Whatever am I thinking of. Daisy, this fellow here is my cousin Victor. And next to him is my big brother Bernard.'

Daisy nodded, noting that the second man also looked a lot like Chalky. Both of them were looking at her expectantly. 'Ah, right, so this is my brother Peter, my sister Clover and her friend Sylvia.'

The three of them smiled in acknowledgement, and Sylvia flicked her hair back a little.

Peter and Terry immediately fell to talking about the army, and Daisy realised that the two soldiers across the table were the very people who until recently had worked at Old Street tube. While she had no intention of recounting her embarrassing afternoon there, it wouldn't hurt to pick their brains. 'Chalky said you'd been with London Transport before joining up,' she said brightly.

Bernard's eyes lit up. 'So he's been talking about us, has he?' He glanced at Victor, but his cousin's attention was fixed on Sylvia. Smiling as he saw he had Daisy all to himself, he leant forward and folded his hands on the table. 'Well, it's no walk in the park, let me tell you . . .'

Daisy nodded and listened as he related anecdotes of tricky customers and emergency situations in which he'd been the saviour of the day. She slowed her sips of shandy, knowing that if she finished he would offer to buy her another and then she'd never remember any useful nuggets that he let slip. 'And did you have to know all about the other transport, the buses and trams and everything?' she asked innocently.

'Oh, of course.' Bernard gave her a look that suggested he was worldly-wise beyond imagining. 'Say there was a problem on the tube, you'd have to know what other ways the passengers could complete their journeys. That's a lot of detail to remember.'

'It must be.' Daisy smiled sweetly. Now there was something she could work on. She'd be the expert in buses from Manor House, if she had to stay up all night swotting. She sat back a little, pleased that she'd achieved more than she'd set out to, even if she'd had to pretend to like shandy.

Meanwhile Clover watched the others, her glass of lemonade nearly untouched in front of her. What was Daisy up to? She could tell her little sister was behind this – Peter would never have volunteered to bring her here. And who were these lads they'd somehow got stuck with for the evening? Sylvia seemed very taken with them, the one in uniform opposite them in particular, who hadn't taken his eyes off her since being introduced. All the same, he was a bit too smooth for Clover's liking. She couldn't put her finger on it but his chatter was just a little too practised. Also, she remembered now that at the start of the evening she'd seen him chatting up another group of girls. Clearly he was trying his luck tonight. Still, he was on leave and it was nearly Christmas. She mustn't be mean. All the same when he offered to buy her another drink she shook her head, while Sylvia said she'd love another port and lemon.

'Well, after that we really must be going,' Clover found herself saying. 'It's Christmas Eve tomorrow and we'll have to be up in time for church. Our parents will expect it.' She ignored the puzzled looks from Daisy and Peter. Nobody at home would demand that they went to the service, what with Peter only just home and Clover working all Saturday. Their mother would like it, of course, but it wasn't compulsory.

Clover wondered if she was turning into her sister Rose, always keeping an eye on everyone and looking after them whether they needed it or not. Sylvia was, after all, an adult, who could most likely take care of herself. Still, Clover thought, this was the first new friend she had made for ages. She didn't want her to end up in the clutches of that Victor bloke. That would be no way of celebrating Christmas.

CHAPTER EIGHT

Patty ran a critical eye over the last-minute preparations. The turkey had been roasting for most of the morning, after she'd risen before sunrise to make sure the oven was hot enough. The root vegetables had gone in, either tucked around the bird in the same tray or in separate ones on the other shelf. The sprouts were all prepared, thanks to Clover, and would be put on to boil at the last minute.

She sighed with satisfaction. That was one advantage of working in the greengrocery; she had ample opportunity to buy the fresh produce, and didn't have to try several shops or stalls to find what she wanted. Her sister had complained non-stop the last time they'd met, telling of empty shelves and shortages. 'People should get everything in without waiting till the last minute,' she had declared, and Patty had resisted the urge to point out that this was exactly what Vera herself had been guilty of.

Vera and family were due any minute, for a pre-dinner glass of sherry. They always did this. Hope and Joy would be bound to tease their mother for drinking when she always complained it gave her a red face, and this was now almost a family tradition. No doubt Faith would grace them with an appearance too.

Her only sorrow was that Rose wouldn't be with them until at least tea time. 'It's only fair, Ma,' she'd said when she'd popped over the day before. 'I had last year off, and so it's my turn to work and right now it's really Christmassy because we try to make it as cheerful as possible for the patients by decorating the wards and everything.'

'Yes, of course, and they'll be glad of that. And you sing them carols, don't you?' Patty had done her best not to let her disappointment show. Rose was needed at the hospital and that was that. She'd save her some turkey and trimmings, though, just in case the canteen couldn't provide enough for everybody.

Providing food was going to get ever more tricky, she realised. There was talk of rationing coming in, for essentials at any rate. Petrol was already rationed of course – not that it affected her immediately, although deliveries to the greengrocer's were often late. But when it came to things like sugar, well, Patty was grateful that she'd had the foresight to buy it when she'd seen it available. It wasn't what you could call hoarding, she told herself; just being prepared for the future. She kept it in old biscuit tins, so that it wouldn't become damp and solid, and had put it on the highest shelf so none would get used up by accident.

Clover came into the kitchen wearing her best frock, a warm cherry colour with a velvet ribbon at the collar.

Patty beamed. 'Don't you look smart!' she exclaimed. 'Come and look at the table with me. Do you think it's all right?' The two of them went over to the big wooden table, now covered with the cloth that came out only for special occasions, and laid with the cutlery that Patty had been given as a wedding present so many years ago. She had polished it lovingly and now it sparkled in the golden light of the fire burning in the grate.

'Of course it is. It couldn't be better,' Clover said, knowing how much work had gone into this. 'Why don't you pop upstairs and get changed now, and I'll get the glasses ready for when Aunt Vera comes. She is coming, isn't she?' Her voice was the very opposite of enthusiastic.

'Thanks, Clover.' Patty kept her tone neutral, not inclined to criticise her sister. 'You're such a help, I don't know what I'd do without you.' She headed off before another small emergency could occur, and Clover set to, fetching the small sherry glasses that hardly ever left the cupboard, polishing them with a tea cloth.

Daisy came into the room and immediately made a beeline for the fire, stretching her hands out towards it. 'Oooh, this is lovely!' she said. 'Our room is freezing. I don't need this cardie after all.' She undid a button on her delicate cream cardigan, chosen to complement her bottle-green frock with fine fancy stitching at the neck.

'Yes, thank you for your offer, you can help,' Clover said dryly. 'See if you can find the bottle of sherry in the parlour.'

Daisy shrugged. 'No need to be like that. Where's it going to be?'

'No idea. It won't have been seen since this time last year.' Clover then relented. 'Try the cupboard next to the fireplace, under the photograph of Peter in his uniform.'

Daisy reluctantly left the fire and passed her brother as she left and he came in. 'Someone say my name?' He was in civvies today, his hair carefully Brylcreemed into place, a shiny pair of cufflinks flashing at his wrists. He'd gone to the trouble of looking his best in order to make their mother happy, Clover realised.

'Could you get in a bit more fuel? There, take the coal scuttle,' she suggested, knowing that nobody would feel like fetching more once they'd started eating.

'Smells lovely in here.' Peter sniffed the air with appreciation. 'I mean, the grub's all right where we are on the base but it's nothing like Ma's cooking.'

'I should think not,' said Clover.

'Well, it's been lovely to see you but I don't want to keep you from your dinner.' Vera made a show of knotting her elegant scarf as she prepared to set off once more, now fortified by two glasses of sherry, which had indeed made her face go red. She was taller than Patty, and a little stouter too, especially as her coat was of bulky heavy wool, in a deep shade of mustard. 'Arthur is so sorry not to see you today but he's had to go to a most vital drinks meeting for the Chamber of Commerce, otherwise he'd have loved to be here, you know he would. They take it amiss if anyone doesn't attend, even on a day like this.'

'Yes, so you said.' Patty smiled brightly to hide her annoyance. Not that she missed Arthur's presence – she could happily do without her self-satisfied brother-in-law – but Vera was making such a hoo-hah about this blessed businessmen's meeting. She could imagine only too well what it would be like. Good luck to him, she thought, but it wouldn't do for her own family to pick up on her irritation. They were rude enough about Vera and family without giving them any more ammunition.

Still, every cloud had a silver lining and she'd never seen Clover and Daisy all but fight over who would finish off peeling the sprouts, the perfect excuse to lurk in the back kitchen and not come under the critical scrutiny of their aunt. In the end they had both gone, and she could pick up the sounds of them now, water running from a tap and then the clank of the enamel colander as it hit the draining board. Hope had pitched in to help as well – she was turning out to be a lovely young woman, Patty thought. Joy had joined them, though when she'd glanced in, the third of Vera's girls had been leaning against the back door, checking her fingernails.

'Have a lovely day,' Patty said. 'You too, Faith. Such a smart brooch you're wearing.' She nodded at the twist of golden metal her niece wore on the lapel of her pale grey coat, with a few green and red stones nested in its loops.

Faith gave her tinkle of a laugh. 'Oh, yes, isn't it? That was from Martin. He's good like that. Gave it to me before he left for training.'

'Oh, has he enlisted?' Patty said, feeling that she ought to find out in case Rose asked, even though she didn't want to encourage Faith.

'Yes, bless him, he's just joined the air force,' Faith said, 'even though he didn't need to; being in the bank he could have argued it was a reserved profession. But he wanted to do his bit.'

Patty couldn't work out if Faith was proud of his bravery or annoyed that he wasn't around to buy her presents any more. 'Of course,' she said steadily.

Vera fussed with the buttons of her coat. 'Come along, Faith. We don't want to keep your father waiting. He'll be wanting his dinner after his meeting. I put the turkey in the oven before we came out.'

Patty had to bite the side of her mouth hard not to laugh, as she could hear Daisy in the background mocking her aunt. '. . . very important meeting,' she was saying, except her voice was obscured by the noise of plates and cutlery being assembled, and was only intelligible if you knew her voice extremely well. This wouldn't do. 'I'll go and call your other two,' she offered. There they were, Hope laughing at Daisy's mischievous impersonation, and Joy still looking bored. 'Your mother needs to go soon,' she told them, staring meaningfully at Daisy to ensure she didn't say any more. Coats were fetched, and the inevitable gas masks retrieved from the newel post.

'Off you go then, don't let me keep you.' Patty waved her sister and nieces goodbye as they set off down Victory Walk, and then hurriedly closed the front door to keep in the heat. Right, that was the end of today's obligations. Now she could enjoy herself with her own beloved children, and Bert, who had managed to down his sherry in two gulps and then claim he had an emergency repair to make to the shelter door. She could hear Clover calling to him in the yard.

'You're safe to come in now, they've gone.'

The meal was everything Patty had hoped it would be, all the elements ready on time and more than enough to go round. She'd made sure to heap extra helpings onto Peter's plate to feed him up, and would have done the same for the girls except they'd said no. It was a comfort to her to know that she'd provided for them all, and something to concentrate on rather than join in with the discussion around the laden table.

With Peter home, Bert was more inclined to speak his mind about the way in which he thought the war might go. He was a keen reader of the *Daily Express* and the *Hackney Gazette*, as well as tuning in to as many bulletins on the wireless as time would allow. 'There's no doubt that tensions are rising,' he said, and Patty felt her stomach turn a somersault. She didn't want to think about the atmosphere of foreboding that hung over them from day to day. She poured the last of the gravy for her husband instead.

'You're right, of course,' Peter replied, and Patty had a desperate urge to put her fingers in her ears. Not today, let's have one day away from all the doom and gloom, she thought. But Peter was making the most of his chance to talk to his father, and Clover was joining in; she must hear all sorts, walking around the pavements near Whitehall.

'Come and help me clear the cutlery,' she said to Daisy, and used the excuse to run the tap noisily in the back kitchen, dulling the discussion of possible raids. At least we've got the shelter now, she told herself. Then she pasted on a bright smile. 'You bring the clean spoons, I'll fetch the side plates, and we can start the pudding,' she instructed her youngest daughter and it was only when everyone had finished the final course and settled in the front parlour for once, that Peter made his announcement. He'd deliberately waited until Rose was there too so that he could tell all of them together.

'Better make the most of me over the next couple of days as we're shipping out to France,' he said. Anything else he might have said was interrupted by the sharp gasp from Patty.

'France?' she said faintly. 'All the way over there?' She put her hand to her throat.

Bert glanced anxiously at his wife, hoping she wasn't going to become upset. 'Well, yes, of course, you've got to be sent to where the action is,' he said. 'France and Belgium is where it's all going on right now, isn't that right?'

Peter sat up a little straighter. He'd been slouching back comfortably in one of the old easy chairs, their brick colour matching that of the sofa where his parents sat in front of the roaring fire. Now he pushed himself more upright, his broad hands on the starched armrests with their pretty tatting edges. It somehow felt fitting that he should tell them of the biggest event of his life so far in the formal room. It was as if it marked the seriousness of the occasion.

'That's it. That's where we'll be of most use,' he said, trying to be matter-of-fact about it. Underneath, he was a roiling mix of apprehension and excitement. Yes, he knew there would be danger, but this was what he had trained for. He'd dreamed of being sent into action ever since he'd decided to join up. Finally his new skills would be tested.

He hoped he looked confident and ready for whatever fate threw at him, even if he couldn't meet his mother's eyes. Of course she was bound to be anxious. He mustn't let that affect him, he was an adult now and had a job to do.

'Ooh, you'll soon be speaking French and everything,' Clover teased, pleased for her brother. She knew he was itching to do more than march around a parade ground. 'And you'll have to eat that foreign food. How do you like the thought of that?'

'I know some of the lingo already. Inky pinky parlay voo. That's right, isn't it, Robbie?' Peter made a lunge for his little brother and tickled him.

'Let me go, let me go,' he protested. 'That's just a silly song, don't tickle me.'

Peter set him back on his feet. 'You'll miss me when I'm not here.'

Robbie shook his head. 'No I shan't.' But then he looked at his big brother and everyone could tell he didn't mean it.

Patty dashed her hand across her eyes and then pulled herself together. 'Well, I dare say you won't get a dinner like the one you just had over there,' she said stoutly.

'Of course he won't.' Bert backed her up at once.

'Good old boiled beef and carrots if we're lucky,' Peter said. 'Anyway, nobody can cook like you can, Ma. You outdid yourself today, even by your high standards.'

Patty smiled even though the tears were still threatening to break through. 'I should hope so too. That's what I wanted. I knew you might be called away at any time. None of us can say for certain where we'll be this time next year, so I wanted it to be extra special. Not that your father and I plan to be anywhere other than here,' she added hastily, registering Robbie's look of alarm. 'But you girls, who knows what the new year will bring?'

Clover shivered, partly in trepidation but also in excitement. If Peter was able to put a brave face on what lay before him, then it was up to her to do so too. 'Who knows . . . ?' she echoed.

CHAPTER NINE

'I've only agreed because tomorrow I won't be here to take the blame if Ma and Pa find out,' Peter reminded Daisy as they strode once more along the chilly pavement towards the Dog and Fiddle. 'One quick drink and we're leaving. Don't go trying to persuade me otherwise.'

Daisy ran a hand through her hair and fluffed it up. 'I wouldn't dream of it. You can trust me.' She was delighted Peter had reluctantly said he'd accompany her one more time so she could be fully confident she could pass for over eighteen.

Peter was keen to enjoy his last night at home before France beckoned and had arranged to see some of his old schoolfriends and work colleagues later on, but couldn't turn down his little sister's cry for help. Although he knew they'd be in trouble if caught out, he had to admire her determination to do whatever it took to get that job.

'Right, you wait there by the door. This time I've got to see if I can order the drinks,' Daisy insisted, as they stepped into the warm fug of the saloon bar. It was not as crowded as last time, being a weekday and earlier in the evening, and she could make her way without pushing and shoving. She'd see if she could get served in her own right, ordering a pint of beer for her brother – even if this time she'd stick to lemonade, as she'd really struggled to get through that sour-tasting shandy.

Unknotting her new turquoise scarf, a Christmas present from Rose, she squared up to the bar and smiled brightly at the barman, letting him know she was waiting, while he poured a dark, plummy liquid into a small glass and passed it to a young man in army uniform. Daisy could see only his back as he fished in his pocket for his wallet. Then she saw his face in profile as he passed some coins across the gleaming countertop.

It was one of those lads from the previous time. Chalky's cousin, what was his name? Victor, that was it. She watched as he took the little glass and a pint of what looked like Guinness over to a table in the corner, and there was his companion – surely Clover's new friend from the storeroom. Daisy's interest was piqued, but before she could angle for a better view, the barman came across to her.

'Yes, miss? What'll it be?' She was so intrigued by what she'd just seen that she forgot to be nervous. He didn't bat an eyelid when she asked for a pint and set about pouring it as Peter, fed up waiting, came across the room to stand by her side.

'What's up with you?' he asked, not fooled by Daisy's carefully casual expression.

'Look over there,' she hissed.

'Over where?' Peter gazed around.

'Keep your voice down!' Honestly, men were useless at this sort of thing. Now people were looking at them, alerted by her brother's obvious staring at all the other customers. 'I'll tell you in a minute. You're attracting attention. Just for that you can buy the drinks then at least you'll have to face the other way when you pay.'

Peter shrugged. 'All right, keep your hair on. I was going to buy them anyway. Can't have my little sister spending all her money, now can I? Not when I'm earning a decent wage with the army. You can return the favour when you get that new job.'

Even though she was cross with him, Daisy had to smile, buoyed by his certainty that she would succeed. Picking up her lemonade, she made her way over to a vacant table by the window from where she could see Victor and Sylvia but remain hidden from their line of sight.

'Out with it,' Peter said, flipping a coaster as he took his seat.

'That couple there. Recognise them?'

Peter peered across to where Daisy had indicated, and nodded. 'Yes, of course, they were in here last time. So what? Must be their local. That's hardly a surprise.'

Daisy threw her gaze up to the smoke-yellowed ceiling. 'Don't be daft. Don't you remember? Sylvia lives in Tottenham. She only met that fellow the same time as we did. So what are they doing here together?'

Peter gave her the same sort of look he'd used when they were growing up and that Daisy hated – reminding her that she was a baby who knew nothing worth speaking of and he was a grown-up, well versed in worldly matters. 'I should have thought that much was obvious,' he replied. As if to back him up, Sylvia's giggling reached them over the background hum of conversation, and they could see Victor leaning closer to her.

'I bet Clover doesn't know,' Daisy muttered. 'I'll have to tell her.'

Peter set down his pint, from which he'd taken a sip. 'You girls,' he said lightly. 'Tell her, don't tell her, what's the difference?'

Daisy treated him to a look very similar to the one he'd given her. 'She'll want to know. That's her friend, and she's out drinking with someone she scarcely knows. I got the impression that Clover didn't like that fellow very much and so might have something to say about her friend having a drink with him.'

Peter glanced across again. 'Seems as if she's getting to know him better by the minute,' he observed, and sure enough the two were now closely huddled together, Victor with his arm around Sylvia's shoulder. 'All the same, it's their business, isn't it?'

Daisy scowled and had some of her lemonade. Something didn't feel right, and it wasn't just the unfamiliarity of being in a bar, with her nerves still a little on edge. It was the way Sylvia was sitting – or, as became apparent, more like slumping. The young woman was still laughing loudly, so loudly in fact that a few heads turned, but nobody said anything. Victor's uniform acted like a shield; nobody was going to spoil the fun of a soldier on leave.

Peter took a final gulp of his pint. 'Come on, let's get going. I've kept my half of the bargain, now you do the same. I've got my old gang waiting at the Cock Robin.'

Daisy picked up her drink once more and then put it back down. 'Hang on, they're going. Let them leave first and then we won't have to talk to them. That would be awkward.'

Peter sighed dramatically but went along with her request, realising that there was some kind of undercurrent to do with female logic that he didn't understand, nor care to.

Victor was now holding Sylvia tight around the shoulders, as much to keep her upright as out of affection. He seemed to be trying to shush her as they wove their way back towards the big door with its shiny brass handle. 'No, of course not, I'm a gent, I am,' he was saying as they passed by.

Sylvia laughed uproariously.

Daisy drained the last of her lemonade as the door swung shut behind them.

Peter rose to his feet and reached for his coat. 'Tell you what, Daze,' he said as his sister refastened the gorgeous scarf around her neck, 'now you've got a taste for shandy, don't you go getting in a state like that. Seriously, I mean it. You don't want to let yourself get into a pickle. It don't look good. You could come to harm that way – and if you don't know what I'm on about, then ask your sisters.'

Daisy bit her lip. She knew what he was on about. 'It's all right, I'm not that wet behind the ears,' she snapped and then she relented. He wasn't saying it to make her feel small; he was trying to protect her. She swallowed the lump that had just appeared in her throat. He felt he had to say something because he knew he wasn't going to be here in person to look after her, and he was concerned.

'Look, I know you're not daft,' he went on, speaking quickly now. 'Just say if, only if, you was to get in a sticky situation with someone like that, I'll tell you what you got to do. You got to bring your knee up into his crotch. Do it fast, don't give him no warning. That'll get him to stop. But best you don't get into anything like that, so lay off the shandy.'

'I promise,' she said, a little shaken by his intensity. 'You don't have to worry. I didn't like that shandy much anyway.'

He grinned broadly as he held open the door for her. 'I could tell,' he said, smug and relieved at the same time.

Daisy tutted in mock-indignation, but she couldn't shake the image from her mind: Sylvia apparently enjoying herself but hardly able to walk, and in the clutches of a man that she hardly knew. She wondered if she should say something when she got home, but nobody liked a snitch. Perhaps she was showing her inexperience after all.

CHAPTER TEN

A new year, a new decade, thought Patty, as the wind slammed shut the back door. She heaved the basket of heavy washing through the narrow gap between their wall and their neighbour's, balancing it on her hip. She refused to admit this caused her an annoying twinge of pain in her lower back. The washing had to be hung out to remove the worst of the water, no matter what, and so she'd just have to tell herself that the pain wasn't there.

Good job it was a decent breeze, she thought, as it would dry everything off that much quicker. Even if the washing line was blowing around like a crazy beast and it was all she could do to wrestle the slippery wet clothes into position and peg them firmly into place. It was all so much more difficult now that the space in the yard was so cramped. Standing back, checking that nothing was going to brush against the roof of the shelter, she paused for thought. What would 1940 bring?

She rubbed her cold hands together to bring the circulation back into her fingertips. Her biggest worry was for Peter, of course, now on his way to France as part of the British Expeditionary Force. It sounded very grand, and despite her fears she was deeply proud of him. She'd done everything she possibly could to make his stay a good one; now his future was in the hands of fate.

Rose was her anchor, the voice of common sense and always to be relied upon. Sometimes she wondered if her eldest wasn't just a little too sensible and serious. When did she ever let her hair down? Did she have a secret life of adventure over at the nurses' home? No, Patty didn't think so.

Clover was settling into her new position, even though she'd clearly hoped for something more exciting. Patty pursed her lips. Be careful what you wish for, she thought. She was no expert, but every instinct told her that excitement of one kind or another was coming their way, and Clover would soon be doing more than unpacking boxes of army uniforms.

As for Daisy, she was clearly up to something. Patty's maternal sense was on red alert with her youngest daughter, knowing without being told that a kind of change was in the air. It was the little signals that gave it away – Daisy practising a different sort of hairstyle when she thought nobody was looking, Clover mentioning in passing that one of her magazines had been moved or mislaid. It all added up, but quite to what Patty couldn't say – or at least not just yet.

She winced as she rubbed her chapped fingers a little more briskly. What she could really do with was some of that lovely soft hand cream that her sister used. Hmph, thought Patty, fat chance of that.

A shriek from inside the house brought her back to the present. Robbie was evidently running down the stairs, late for school. Her beloved youngest, and she wanted nothing more than to shield him from all the world's problems with the force of her love. But he'd have none of it and probably quite right too. More of his friends were beginning to trickle back from the villages they'd been evacuated to, because everyone was saying the danger had been overstated and therefore it was as well to have the youngsters back where they belonged so their worried parents could keep a close eye on them.

Again, Patty was by no means convinced. Surely the government wouldn't have gone to the trouble of arranging the evacuation in the first place if it was all for nothing? Robbie was different, he was delicate – although you wouldn't believe it from the whooping and hollering going on in the kitchen.

Time to go and sort him out, my girl, she told herself. Get him off to school and keep things as normal as possible, for as long as possible. Then they'd see what 1940 had in store for them.

She picked up her empty laundry basket before the wind could whip it away and headed back for the kitchen. 'What's all this noise!' she called, trying to sound strict.

'It wasn't me, it was on the wireless!' Robbie did his best to convince his mother, but the solemn voice of the newsreader in the background made that very unlikely.

'Robert Harrison, you deserve to have your mouth washed out with soap and water,' Patty admonished him. 'Now pull up those socks. I don't know how you manage it, you've only had them on for a matter of minutes.' All the same, as she drank in the sight of her youngest with his socks around his ankles, she was relieved beyond measure that he was so lively and healthy. Pray God he stayed that way.

William Rathbone stood up stiffly from his desk and straightened his collar. Not much daylight filtered down into his office, just a little, from the many sets of steps leading up to ground level from the ticket hall, but not enough to read by. He adjusted the small lamp a fraction, as he did scores of times a day. Its beam fell upon the application form, its ink not yet dry.

Mr Rathbone hadn't been fooled for a minute. The applicant hadn't lied outright when he'd asked her age, but he could tell she'd gone to some lengths to exaggerate how long ago she'd left school and her experience in her current factory job. He would bet that she didn't usually dress as soberly either. He had to hand it to her: it was a very good act.

The fact was, she ought to be twenty-one to even think of being considered for a position with the London Passenger Transport Board. Management had been quite clear. If women had to be admitted into their organisation, and it was with some reluctance in some quarters, then mature ladies were preferred, as they would be steady and reliable. Mr Rathbone thought some of the bosses would have forty fits if they could see the young woman in front of him.

She was neatly turned out in a calf-length maroon skirt and cream blouse with a small bow at the collar, and she had hung a dull grey jacket on the coat stand before taking the seat opposite his desk. She held a plain brown handbag on her lap and was fiddling with its strap – the only visible indication of her nerves. Mr Rathbone had interviewed many hopefuls over his years in this job and he knew all the signs.

He should send her away right now, of course. Yet he'd rarely had an applicant so well prepared. He'd tested her general knowledge of the area – excellent, but no real surprise, as she'd grown up not that far away. What about other forms of public transport, should the Piccadilly Line fail? She knew them all. She named all the bus routes, and when he'd asked her what the fastest route to the West End would be, she'd instantly recommended the correct bus. She'd known about the nearest overground train line north on Green Lanes as well, and that there were no trams running from this junction any more.

'And so why do you wish to work for the London Transport Board, rather than any other organisation?' he asked.

The young woman had straightened up and lifted her chin a little. 'Because I know how many people rely on it,' she said emphatically. 'Whether it's for work, or seeing family and friends, it's all down to transport. I love meeting people and helping them if I can. Nobody likes being late or getting lost.'

'Very true,' he replied, even if he himself was rarely late and never lost.

'I believe I can get along with most kinds of passengers and give them a helping hand if they need it,' she assured him. 'Also, I know this station and can remember it being built. It's so modern and I'd love to feel I was doing my bit for the war effort in such a place.'

Despite himself, Mr Rathbone had been impressed. He loved his job and he loved the sense of being at a vital spot in the map of the capital city. This was the major intersection of the Seven Sisters Road and Green Lanes. His wife Poll sometimes teased him about it. 'You're like a spider at the centre of your web,' she'd say. He didn't mind. He was tall and thin, with receding hair, and not remotely like a spider, but he did enjoy the sense of the roads stretching up to Hertfordshire and out to Essex as well as into the West End and the City.

This young woman knew her stuff. She spoke clearly, not posh or anything like that, but with confidence. She gave the sense of being able to deal with tricky customers and boy, did they get a lot of those. He'd known plenty of colleagues who'd looked good on paper flounder when under pressure. Age often had nothing to do with it.

Besides, the fact was that the junior members of staff were leaving, either called up or volunteering before they got their papers. Young men were needed else-where. Samuel was still here, and was likely to stay, as he had flat feet and was therefore unsuitable for the services. But even he, with his five years of experience, couldn't do the work of three clerks.

Mr Rathbone drew in a deep, wheezy breath. Who was he to condemn this young woman for trying? He knew what it was like, to want to do your bit. He'd lied about his age twenty-five years ago when he'd gone to the army recruitment office, claiming he was eighteen, when he'd been only fifteen. Some days he wished he hadn't; his lungs had never recovered, though he hadn't been gassed as badly as many of his comrades. He'd never been able to play football properly again though, he simply couldn't run for long.

Poll hadn't minded about that when she met him. He gave thanks to whoever was watching over them that she'd taken a shine to him, and couldn't believe his luck when she'd accepted when he'd proposed. Nearly twenty years ago, that had been. They'd been happy together ever since, except for one thing: they hadn't been blessed with children.

Was it the gas? No, others worse than him had come back and had families. Still, he couldn't help wondering. He'd have loved to have had kiddies, little versions of Poll. The world needed more like her.

He knew he was being sentimental and allowing this to cloud his judgement, but he couldn't help thinking that if they'd had a daughter she might have looked a little like this young woman sitting in front of him, playing with her handbag strap. Her hair colour was similar: that rich chestnut, although Poll's was beginning to fade now. Those bright eyes, full of curiosity and energy. That sense of wanting to play her part in the world.

He sat down again, and looked across the neat office to his colleague Sam in the corner. 'Mr Collins! I seem to have left my cup of tea on the filing cabinet near you. Would you be so good as to bring it over?'

If Sam was surprised, he didn't show it, simply looked up and nodded. He put down his pen and quickly straightened a stack of papers on his desk and then moved to the cabinet, his swift action belying those treacherous flat feet. If fate had dealt him a different hand, this smart young man with his open face and dark blond hair would have loved nothing better than to join up. Smiling politely now, he acknowledged the newcomer's presence and then set down the plain white cup, minus its saucer.

Raising an eyebrow, Mr Rathbone reached for it and then tutted. 'Oh dear, I seem to have smeared the edge of your application form.' He smiled inwardly. Yes, he'd judged it just right. It didn't look like deliberate damage – more like the form had been handled before the ink was properly dry. These things happened. Nobody was likely to have the time to examine it and file a complaint.

The section headed 'Date of Birth' now showed the day and date of the month but not the full year.

'Well, now.' Mr Rathbone set the cup aside and folded his hands in front of him. 'You have shown thorough knowledge of the local area and wider transport system. Your handwriting is adequate and your appearance is suitable.' He paused and then smiled more broadly. 'Miss Harrison, I am pleased to tell you that you have passed your interview. You have got the job.'

Daisy froze for just a second and then smiled even wider, as if she couldn't quite believe it.

CHAPTER ELEVEN

'Haven't seen you for ages! I thought you must be avoiding me.' Clover swung around in the storeroom as Sylvia hurried in, late for her shift. 'Sightings of you have been rarer than hen's teeth since New Year.'

Sylvia hung up her overcoat, almost missing the hook on the back of the big oak door. 'Didn't they tell you? I got seconded over to my sister's office, cos heaps of them went down with the flu. It's going round, you know.'

Clover pursed her lips. She did know – it was the talk of Dalston, and her mother had been worried sick that Robbie would get it and then he'd be stuck in bed for weeks. But Robbie had breezed along as normal and hadn't had so much as a sniffle, to everyone's relief. 'Nobody told me,' she said, feeling cross that their section leader Miss Linton hadn't thought to mention the temporary transfer, but she couldn't be angry for long. Not when she was so pleased to see her friend back.

'You haven't missed much,' she said, putting down the box of stationery she'd been carrying. 'It's been the same old routine, here, only I had to do more of it myself. Not like at home, where it's going to be tricky to get hold of ham and butter and sugar, thanks to this new rationing.'

Sylvia straightened her uniform jacket and then tugged back her sleeves, ready to get stuck in. 'Oh, I know. Our mum is at her wit's end already. I said to her, it's no use complaining, it's not going to change any time soon and we're just going to have to get used to it. Easy for me to say, though, cos I don't take sugar in my tea and she likes two heaped teaspoons every time she has a cup. And she has a lot.'

Clover nodded. 'It's going to be tough on anyone with a sweet tooth. My little brother loves his cakes and biscuits and we spoil him, cos he was so sick when he was small. He's going to find it harder than the rest of us.'

'I'm more worried about the bacon,' said Sylvia. 'I love a fried breakfast when I've got the time. There's nothing like the smell of sizzling bacon – just the thought of it makes my mouth water.'

'Well, we'll just have to make do with a cup of tea,' said Clover, moving to the little shelf where they kept the cups. 'I'll get cracking and you can have a look at the lists for what's to be done this morning. And you can tell me all about what you got up to over the holidays, even if we didn't really get a proper break.' She stopped as she could see a trace of a blush creeping up her friend's face. 'Oh, go on, spill the beans. You look as though you've got something to tell me.' She reached for the teapot as she teased the other girl.

'Well . . .' Sylvia hesitated, and then started to giggle. 'Now you come to mention it, I did have a bit of fun over Christmas. I don't suppose anything will come of it but it was all right while it lasted. Nothing wrong with going out and enjoying yourself, is there?'

'Well, no,' Clover replied. 'I'd be a fine one to talk, wouldn't I? After all we went to the pub together before Christmas.'

'We did.' Sylvia giggled again. 'In fact, you're to blame for what happened, you could say.'

Clover took a step back in surprise. 'Me? What did I do?' She racked her brains for anything likely.

Sylvia twisted her hands together and cleared her throat. 'It was those blokes. You know, we went and shared a table with them. You remember the ones in army uniform, the ones your sister knew?'

Clover cast her mind back to that evening. 'Ah, so it's Daisy's fault,' she said. 'I'll be sure to blame her, whatever it is you're going to tell me.'

'I got talking to a couple of them, as you saw,' Sylvia went on, 'then when we all came to leave, you and your sister set off one way, with your brother – it was all right for you two, you had that big strapping fellow to look after you. Well, I was going up to Tottenham and had to get the bus, and one of the others offered to see me to my bus stop.' She paused and Clover gave her a straight look.

'Very kind of him,' she said. 'Quite the gent.'

Sylvia nodded. 'Exactly what I thought. Don't get that often, do you? So I said yes, and we set off and . . .

well, we did get to the bus stop eventually but we might have taken our time about it, if you get my drift.'

'Sort of,' Clover said dubiously. She wasn't sure she liked the sound of this.

'So, anyway, Victor, that's his name, he asked if he could see me again as he had a few days before he had to go back to his base and of course I said yes.'

'Of course.' Clover liked it even less now.

'He was ever so generous, took me back to that same pub and bought me drinks all evening.'

'I bet he did.' Clover had a sinking feeling. It was one thing to go out and have a bit of fun, but you had to know when to stop. She wasn't inclined to let blokes have fun at her expense, that was for sure. But then again, she shouldn't judge Sylvia. Perhaps that was the extent of it – a few drinks in the Dog and Fiddle. She could hardly get on her high horse about that, having been the one to introduce her friend to that pub in the first place.

'Well . . .' Sylvia cast her a glance, now a little more nervous. 'Don't think badly of me, Clover, I only wanted to enjoy myself and so did he. It didn't seem right, him heading off to fight, putting his life at risk over in France, without a bit of something to remember . . .'

'Oh.' Clover knew soldiers used this line to get what they wanted, and what better opportunity than everyone setting off to fight in France? Only she wouldn't have stood for it.

'Yes, it could have been his last evening down here for a while, so I thought, why not? He knew this place, sort of like a pub but it called itself a hotel, that stayed open a bit later, and his mate behind the bar lets him go up to the staffroom for a bit of privacy . . . Well, I'm not rightly sure I remember where it was, but he did get me on the last bus home, I know that, so he's still a gent.'

'A real gent,' said Clover, trying to keep the sarcasm from her voice.

'So, we both enjoyed ourselves and no harm done.' Sylvia straightened her sleeves again but struggled to meet her friend's eyes. 'Don't look like that, Clover, I wasn't sure as I should tell you, and you're not to blame him. He didn't take advantage or nothing. I knew what I was about, so don't get on your high horse.'

Clover shook her head and wondered if she was putting two and two together and making five, but one more glance at her friend's face and she knew she wasn't. Whatever had gone on at this place that stayed open late had obviously been a whole lot more than a few drinks and a quick fumble by the bus stop. She was no prude, she knew such things happened, but she wouldn't want to go so far herself. Certainly not with somebody she hardly knew. It was far too risky.

'Well, I hope you were careful,' she said seriously. Her mother had drummed into all three of her daughters the possible consequences of such behaviour and stressed that it was just plain wrong. Clover wasn't sure it was quite that simple, and one of her old school friends had confessed they'd gone all the way when her fiancé had been posted abroad, not long after the war had begun – but that was different. They were engaged. If anything went wrong, she wouldn't be left high and dry. Quite how much of a gent this Victor would prove to be was anyone's guess.

Sylvia tossed her head and her plaits swung around her shoulders. 'I know about all that,' she insisted. 'You don't grow up around where I'm from and not hear about how to look after yourself. I got him to promise to take care of things and he did. So there's nothing to worry about. You don't think the worse of me, do you?' she added, biting her lip, her confidence slipping a little.

Clover sighed. 'I'm only anxious that you don't get caught out,' she said quietly. 'None of us wants that to happen. Anyhow, what's done is done and that's that. Like you say, he's off to fight in France and you're back here working with me, and it's a new year and who knows what it'll bring. Just as long as you were careful.'

Sylvia was about to respond when the heavy door swung open and their section leader came in, bearing an armful of files. 'Here you both are, good. We must have these checked through before the end of your shift today.' She gave them both a close look. 'Careful about what?'

Sylvia's mouth dropped open, but Clover stepped in as easy as could be.

'Careful not to have forgotten how the supply forms work, as Sylvia's been in the other department for a couple of weeks,' she said smoothly, and if the section leader was suspicious then she didn't show it.

'Quite so. Not that I'd expect you to slip up after such a short period away,' she said generously. 'Still, Harrison is wise to check. It never hurts to be careful.'

She deposited the files on the biggest table and swept out again, leaving Clover and Sylvia looking at one another, the woman's final sentence left hanging in the air.

If Daisy had imagined that she would be advising passengers all day long, as the public face of Manor House Station's ticket hall, she was soon proved wrong. Much of the work of a clerk was behind the scenes, at a desk like the ones she had seen Mr Rathbone and Sam Collins using on the day of her interview. It was cleaner than the factory, of course, and less tiring, but she could tell she was on a sort of probation.

It was sometimes almost as noisy as the factory, especially when tube trains thundered in and out of the platforms far below, and crowds of rush-hour commuters swarmed in and out of the many entrances. There were the other members of staff too, many of whom worked on the lower level, making sure train doors opened and closed properly, checking signals, making announcements. Some came and went, like those who changed the posters or brought supplies. They were mostly older men, some of whom had come out of retirement to replace the younger men who were joining up.

Several were openly curious about their new recruit and not above making sly assumptions and impertinent comments: she was young, she was female, and so her primary purpose must be to make them tea. Mr Rathbone would have none of it. 'You take no notice of them,' he insisted, and Daisy did just that. She'd had plenty of practice ignoring Peter and his friends when it suited her, and she was used to sticking up for herself.

It was different in the office. There, she was the newest member of staff and so that meant her duties *did* include making the tea.

From the very first day, Sam had emphasised that he liked his good and sweet. However, her first day almost coincided with the start of the very unpopular sugar rationing. So it wasn't exactly the best way to make a good impression on her colleague, having to inform him that he'd have to cut down, or bring in his own from home.

'But I can't do that!' he'd protested in horror, with his usual barely contained energy. His blue eyes gleamed with mischief. 'My old dear would have forty fits if I started taking things from her kitchen. That's her kingdom, that is.' He ran his hand through his sandy-blond hair, which would have had to be cut much shorter if he'd been in the forces.

'Can't be helped,' Daisy had to tell him. 'We got this one tin to last us all, and that's for the entire week. If you want it very sweet on Monday, there'll be none left by Friday.'

Sam had sulked for the rest of the morning, but had come to his senses by lunchtime. 'You're right, Daisy,' he'd said. They'd soon agreed he didn't have to call her Miss Harrison, although their boss Mr Rathbone still did so. She liked being able to call him Sam; it felt like they were part of the same team. He seemed like a friendly sort and she was glad that he didn't have the swagger of Terry from the factory.

'I got some friends that work down the docks,' he said, 'and they sometimes get hold of molasses, when they have a shipment. Do you know what that is? It's like treacle, it's lovely and sweet, it is. Not sure what it would be like in tea though.'

Daisy shuddered and grimaced. 'Ugh, no, that doesn't sound very good at all. I bet your teaspoon would stick up straight if you tried it!'

Sam shrugged and picked up his empty teacup. 'Well, we're not likely to find out,' he replied. 'I dare say it'll be in high demand now we can't get hold of proper sugar. Anyway they been talking about trying for the merchant navy, although dock workers are exempt from the call-up. If my feet weren't so blooming flat I'd maybe give that a go.' He sighed deeply and then rallied. 'Go on, then, Daisy, I'll try one with just half a spoonful. Just don't expect me to enjoy it.'

'Daisy, come and give me a hand with this.' Patty was struggling to move a large basket from the front step and looked up in delight as her youngest appeared from the far end of Victory Walk.

Daisy was proudly kitted out in her new workwear, with its smart little insignia and Patty had a certain sense of self-satisfaction that she'd guessed correctly that change was in the air. Her maternal instinct hadn't been disrupted by the war after all. But what was clear was that the girl loved her new job. Look at her now, walking with a spring in her step and a wide smile on her face.

'What have you got there?' Daisy asked.

Patty gave a little puff of breath as she stood up properly from where she'd been bending over the basket. 'That nice Mr Banham, the ARP warden, helped me bring this back from the shop. He put it on his bike, which was kind of him. The trouble is, it's so heavy I'm having trouble lifting it again.'

'Blimey,' said Daisy, 'What have you got in it? Rocks or something?'

Patty raised her eyebrows. 'Not quite. But something that we might be able to use for rock cakes. On account of the sugar being rationed.'

'I've had it up here with rationing,' Daisy groaned, remembering Sam's face at the tea with reduced sugar. Coming closer she peered with curiosity into the basket. 'Root vegetables,' she said, poking the ones at the top to get a clearer idea. It was dusk and of course there were no streetlights so in the shadow by the front door, it was hard to see for sure.

'Parsnips,' Patty said.

Even in the fading light there was no mistaking the look her youngest gave her. 'Parsnips?' Daisy echoed. 'For cakes? Don't you mean for soup, or Sunday dinner?'

Patty shook her head firmly. 'No, there's all these new recipes coming out. We got to save our sugar, but you all like your cakes, specially Robbie, and he needs building up, you know he does. So I thought I'd try something a bit different.' She unlocked the front door, indicated the basket, and between her and Daisy they got it inside and into the kitchen. Patty lit the gas lamp and the big collection of parsnips was revealed.

Daisy pulled another face. 'Really, Ma? Must we?'

Patty took off her coat, hung it up on its hook and reached for her apron. 'Yes, my girl, we must. I do have a bit of sugar put aside from last year, but it's for special occasions, so don't you go saying nothing. Especially to your Aunt Vera,' she said meaningfully.

Daisy tapped her nose. 'Mum's the word. But all the same—'

'I wouldn't even mention it to you a minute ago out on the doorstep, that's how secret it is,' Patty went on. 'So for everyday stuff we're going to try some substitutes. Makes sense – I get first chance to buy the vegetables after all. It'll be good for you. Better for your teeth, for a start.'

'There's nothing wrong with my teeth,' Daisy said at once, running her tongue over her top row, checking they were all right.

'Then let's keep it that way. We got no call for visiting the likes of the dentist,' Patty said firmly. 'You wait and see. It's going to be delicious. Don't say anything to Robbie, let's see if he notices.' With that she set to, emptying the basket handful by handful, stowing the parsnips away in the cupboard furthest from the fire, where they would be dark and cool.

Daisy watched dubiously. She had no great desire to eat parsnips in a cake. Still, if this was the worst privation that the war had to throw at her, she supposed she should be grateful.

CHAPTER TWELVE

Rose had always loved strolling round a market, especially when she didn't have anything in particular to buy. The busier, the better. There was something about the hustle and bustle of the crowds, the colourful stalls, the hawkers' cries and the constant hum of chatter that she found comforting, restful even.

This morning, the air was crisp and clear, with just a hint that winter was coming to an end. Her cheeks and the tips of her ears were tingling with the cold, but it was a good feeling. She'd put on her warmest coat, and teamed it with a bright green woolly hat, a Christmas present from her mother. She'd managed to persuade Daisy to join her, as her little sister was on a late shift. Daisy had protested that she could do with a lie-in, but Patty had shooed her out of the house. 'Do you good,' she'd said. 'And see if there are any bargains while you're there.'

Daisy told her sister all this as they approached the entrance to Ridley Road, making it all sound much more dramatic than it had actually been, as Rose realised at once. Her little sister loved to tell a good story, and she'd enjoyed the entertainment. 'I don't know what there might be in the way of bargains, not at this time of year,' she observed. 'Doesn't mean we can't look, but don't get your hopes up.'

Daisy rolled her eyes. 'And after all, there is a war on,' she chanted. 'Which is all anyone ever says when I ask for something they don't have. Which is just about every time I go shopping.'

Rose tucked her hand through Daisy's arm and patted her sister's sleeve. 'I know. Happens to me as well.' She steered her past the main aisle of stalls and on to one of the side rows, where it was easier to see what was on sale.

She'd been pleased just before Christmas to have found their mother a replacement pair of oven mitts, in a bright pattern of white polka dots on an orange background. They were stoutly padded too, more than enough to cope with the hottest dishes that would come from the oven shelves. Patty had been delighted with them, recognising the thought that had gone into the gift.

Now Rose caught sight of a similar pattern a few stalls away and hurried across to find out what it was. The stallholder, an elderly man with a nose made red by years of standing outside in all weathers, perked up when he saw her. 'Can I tempt you to a bargain, miss?' He rubbed his hands together. 'All of the finest quality, this is – as you can no doubt tell for yourself.'

Rose grinned back at him, enjoying the game. 'Well, let me take a look.' She pretended to be interested in a tablecloth and matching napkins before turning to what had caught her eye in the first place: a pile of tea towels. The topmost ones were patterned with polka dots, this time orange on a white background. She smiled to herself. How her mother would appreciate these, and again they'd be useful too. They'd bring a welcome bit of colour into the kitchen.

'Those are fresh in this week,' the stall holder assured her, nodding seriously. 'You can take them home safe in the knowledge that you'll be the first round here to have such a thing.'

Rose held one up to check its texture. Neither she nor Patty would think twice about being the first or only people to have them, but it was all part of the patter. 'What do you think of these?' she asked Daisy, who had been momentarily distracted by another stall.

'Oh, that's pretty,' Daisy said, and the elderly man beamed.

'You got a good eye for quality, miss,' he said. 'If you're interested, I got some more in a box here somewhere . . .'

As he bent down to check under the stall there was a commotion from further down the aisle, as a woman called out, 'Oy, you cut that out right now!'

A blur of a young boy barrelled around the corner and came hurtling towards them at speed. His head down, he could hardly see where he was going and collided with Daisy, who would have fallen if it hadn't been for the side of the stall. The accident broke his momentum, but he was going to carry on, when Rose exclaimed, 'Ricky Glanville, you stop right where you are! Don't even think about running off. You say sorry to Daisy and to that woman over there. I don't know what you've done but she's not very happy.'

Ricky came to a stop and his shoulders slumped. 'Hello, Rose,' he said sheepishly. He stared at his feet, his grey socks gathered in folds where they'd fallen around his ankles.

Rose drew herself up to her full height of five foot five. 'Ricky. You nearly knocked Daisy over. What do you have to say for yourself?' She gazed at him with an expression she usually reserved for difficult patients. It was too much for Ricky and he caved in.

'Um, sorry, Daisy,' he said glumly. 'I didn't mean to hurt you or nothing.'

Daisy straightened up and tugged at her coat. 'No harm done,' she said, a little shakily.

The woman who ran the stall further along came up and folded her arms, looking down at the boy. 'Now what do you think you're up to?' she demanded. 'You could have damaged my stock back there.'

Ricky sighed. 'I just wanted to see what was over that wall. I didn't know them boxes were yours. I thought I'd be able to see better if I stood on them. I didn't know they'd fall over.'

The woman cleared her throat, and Rose stepped in before she could accuse Ricky of anything worse. 'Ricky, apologise to this lady and we'll say no more about it,' she instructed him firmly. She raised her eyebrows and he got the message good and clear.

'Sorry,' he said. 'I won't do it again.' He looked up to see if he was going to be in even more trouble.

The woman seemed slightly mollified. 'Well, see to it that you don't,' she replied. Rose cut in before she could complain about anything else.

'There, that's settled,' she said brightly. 'Off you go, Ricky. I'm sure you should be in school. And we'll let this lady get back to work.' She nodded expectantly and the woman could do little other than follow her suggestion and go back to her stall.

Ricky dawdled for a moment, watching her go. 'We ain't got school all the time this week. They got to change all the classes around cos of some teachers going off to fight in France and whatnot.' The hem of his woollen jumper was unravelling, and Rose couldn't help but think it wouldn't be much use against cold weather.

'Well, then, I expect they've set you homework to be getting along with,' Rose remarked, and the look in the boy's eyes showed that she was right. 'You'd best catch up with that, don't you think? You won't want all those children who were evacuated to be ahead of you, will you?'

'No.' That point had hit home. 'Bye, then, Rose – and thank you.' He gave a final nod and turned for the exit to the main road, his small frame soon disappearing among the other shoppers.

The old man behind the stall had been watching this exchange, having abandoned his hunt for the rest of the tea towels. He pursed his mouth, seeming impressed. 'You done well there, miss,' he said, wiping his palms on his brown overall.

Rose shook her head. 'The boy didn't mean anything by it, he's just a livewire.'

'Know him, do yer?' The man refolded the polka-dot towels.

'He lives nearby,' Rose explained.

'Nippers, eh?' The man looked skyward for a moment and chuckled. 'Had two of me own like that, and they got to let off steam somehow. They don't know no better half the time.'

'Yes, well, with luck he won't do it around here for a while.' Rose sighed, still eyeing the pretty pattern.

'I could do you a good price for those, by way of thanks for keeping the peace.' The man smiled and Rose perked up.

'Well, now . . .'

Daisy tuned out as her sister began bartering, knowing how she loved to haggle for a bargain, and scanned the crowds of shoppers milling around them. She bit her lip a little as she rubbed her arm, which was now beginning to throb where it had met the side of the stall.

She wondered idly if there would be any lipstick that she could buy. She couldn't go on sneakily borrowing Clover's or hoping Rose had left behind one that would suit her. Now she had a job that involved meeting the public, she ought to have something smart. It would make her feel more presentable, more grown-up. Nothing too flash, though, because Mr Rathbone wouldn't approve, but just a little touch of pink to brighten her up.

She was so caught up in the idea of finding the perfect shade that at first she didn't hear the question.

'I said, are you all right? I saw what happened.'

Daisy swung around and gasped.

'I'm sorry, I didn't mean to startle you.' The man's voice was full of consternation.

Daisy could feel a blush rising up her face. How embarrassing. He'd think she was a silly girl. 'No, no, you didn't. I mean, I'm perfectly all right.' She took a breath. 'I didn't know you were back.'

Freddy smiled, and she knew for sure that her face must be glowing like a tomato. 'Well, it won't be for long. It's embarkation leave; just a short time to see my parents and family and a few friends.' His naval uniform certainly suited him – Terry and his gang had been right when they'd teased him about it, all those months ago. It fitted him perfectly. Daisy couldn't help notice how he'd put on muscle in all the right places, just as his friends had said. Then she pulled herself together.

'My brother had some leave just before he was posted to France,' she told him. 'We don't know where he is exactly, but lots of them went together.'

Freddy nodded. 'Yes, there are a lot of them being sent over there.' He narrowed his eyes. 'Are you quite sure you're not hurt? I was too far away to help but you went into the side of that stall with some force. You want to get that seen to,' he went on, noticing how she was holding her arm.

Daisy gave a quick smile. 'Oh, I shall. That's to say, Rose – that's my sister there – is a nurse. She'll make sure everything is all right.'

'I'm pleased to hear it,' he replied, and though his tone was light he wasn't joking. 'That puts my mind at rest.'

'That's Rose for you,' Daisy laughed. 'She's a very useful person to know.'

People continued to mill around them but somehow their noise and chatter seemed far away. Freddy looked at her intently. 'Good, because I'd hate to think you'd come to harm.' It was almost as if he was leaning closer to her. Daisy leant forward a little too, in order to catch exactly what he was saying. For the briefest of moments, she caught a scent of spice and citrus, and a tingling sensation crept up her spine as their eyes locked. Then he cleared his throat, and the spell was broken. 'Are you still working at the factory?'

'Er, no. I'm in the ticket hall at Manor House now,' Daisy told him proudly.

'So you don't see any of the others—' Freddy was starting to say, when a woman's voice broke in.

'There you are! I've been searching all over the place. Come on, we should go.' The woman had one of those voices that carried effortlessly, bright and shiny like a bell, full of confidence. She put her hand on Freddy's arm, and Daisy noticed how pale and elegant her hand was against the dark material of his uniform. She was wearing the very shade of pink lipstick that Daisy had been thinking about earlier and for a wild moment she wondered if she could ask where it had come from. But no, it occurred to her that this question would not be at all welcome.

'This is Miss Harrison, Daisy, whom I met at the clothes factory,' Freddy said, easily bringing her into the conversation, but the woman was impatient.

'Pleased to meet you. The factory, how nice,' she said, suddenly icy. 'Freddy, you know we can't hang around, we promised we'd be back in good time.' She tucked her hand around his arm more firmly and started to pull away. 'Excuse us, Miss Harrison, we're dreadfully late. Good day to you.'

And they were gone, the woman, who was perhaps a little older than Rose, moving smartly away and Freddy having not much choice other than to be dragged along with her. For a second he looked back over his shoulder and threw Daisy a brief apologetic smile.

Daisy stood rooted to the spot. What had just happened? Freddy hadn't even had time to introduce the woman to him, but they certainly seemed very close. Just look at how tightly she'd held on to him. That was claiming possession, if ever she'd seen it. Not that it mattered. Not that she had any hopes of anything more from Freddy. He was just a former colleague, that was all. He'd asked after her arm in politeness, that was the extent of it. But if that was the case then why was she feeling so peculiar?

'Daisy, what's wrong?' Suddenly Rose was back at her side, her expression one of concern. 'Is it your arm? Let's get you home. I shouldn't have spent so long chatting to the stallholder, I didn't realise it was causing you pain – and don't bother denying it, I know you too well. I'll give you a proper examination once we're back. But see, the kind man gave me four for the price of three. Won't Ma be pleased?'

Daisy smiled wanly. Now she came to think about it, her arm was pretty sore. The hunt for the perfect lipstick could wait until another day. 'She will,' she forced herself to say, to think about something other than the strange scene she'd just been part of. 'She'll be delighted.' She bit her lip, trying to ignore how fast her heart was beating.

CHAPTER THIRTEEN

'Most irregular, most irregular.' The section leader, Miss Linton, was muttering to herself as she read a memo that had arrived first thing. 'I'm not at all sure we can assist with this. Oh, Harrison, I didn't realise you were there.'

Clover stepped through the doorway into the storeroom, as the mid-morning sunlight streamed through the little window, now minus its cheery tinsel wreath. All was back to the usual stark boards and shelves, the greys and the browns and the khakis. She tried not to feel too miserable looking around the place but sometimes it was enough to get you down. She moved across so that she could stand in the beam of sunshine, for warmth and to lift her spirits.

'I was fetching some more string,' she explained, holding up a ball of twine.

'Yes, yes.' Miss Linton was distracted, rereading whatever instructions she'd received. 'We always need string. Now, where's your colleague? I haven't seen her this morning yet.'

Clover didn't want to admit that she wasn't sure. Sylvia had arrived late, which had been the pattern for the last week or two, looking rather pale. Her near-black hair framed her almost white face in stark contrast and her cheeks were hollow, her cheekbones sharper than usual.

They'd hardly begun their work when Sylvia had made an excuse to sit down on one of the metal chairs, scraping the legs along the floor with an ear-splitting screech. 'Ow. Sorry about that. Ouf, I'm out of breath already.'

Clover had pulled a face. 'Blimey, you are unfit these days. What's the matter? Are you going down with something?'

Sylvia looked glum. 'I'm not sure but I think I might be. I'm right off my food and that's not like me. And I don't seem to have the energy for anything.'

Clover grew concerned. 'That's not like you either,' she said. 'Would you like me to get you anything? A cup of tea, maybe?'

Sylvia gulped and shook her head. 'No, even tea is no good at the moment. I don't know why but it somehow doesn't taste right.'

'That's terrible!' Clover loved her regular cups of tea. 'Maybe it's the tail end of that flu that was going around. We were all afraid our little brother would get it. So don't you come near me if you think that's what it might be!' She mock-shuddered but her friend would not be consoled.

'You could be right,' she'd said morosely. The old fun-loving Sylvia was nowhere to be seen this morning.

'Look, cover for me if Miss Misery-drawers comes along, would you? I'm going to pop out for a bit of fresh air, it might do the trick.' She'd got up with another screech of chair legs and swiftly made for the door. That had been half an hour ago.

Now Clover felt that her friend had put her in a bit of a tight spot and wasn't very happy about it. Still, on the plus side, their superior was obviously distracted by whatever lay in the contents of her memo, and for once was not on the warpath.

Clover put the twine away in its correct box and began to check the shelves for any other missing equipment, as Miss Linton hummed and tutted, at one point bringing out a pen from her skirt pocket and tapping her teeth with it.

Clover couldn't very well say that this was all very irritating and was putting her off her job. Three times she had to start counting the tins on the farthest shelf, as she'd get so far and then Miss Linton would appear to be about to speak, and she'd lost concentration – but all for nothing.

Finally the section leader made a decision and spoke about what was troubling her.

'There's a possibility of a transfer,' she said. 'It has to come either from this department or the one down in Holborn. I don't mind telling you, I am in two minds.'

Clover raised her eyebrows in surprise. The formidable Miss Linton was not in the habit of showing any form of self-doubt, or of confiding anything. Now she tucked a rare loose strand of short greying hair behind her ear and frowned.

Clover wasn't completely sure if she was waiting for an answer or simply airing her thoughts, but she ventured a question anyway. 'What sort of transfer?'

Miss Linton tutted again. 'Experienced volunteers are needed, for army logistics.'

Well, that sounded equally as boring as counting tins in a dim storeroom. Clover waited to see if there was more.

'Attention to detail is paramount, and demonstrable examples of teamwork.'

That didn't shed much light on the subject.

'Travel will be involved and the posting will be of no limited duration.'

Clover carefully set down a tin she'd been wiping and stood up straighter. 'Do they say what sort of travel?' she asked.

Miss Linton gave her a sharp look. 'They have not specified but you seem like a bright sort of girl, Harrison. You're enlisted in the auxiliary branch of the army. You may well be aware of where a great number of army troops have recently been posted.'

Clover's eyes widened. 'What, you mean to France? Like my brother?'

'I couldn't possibly say,' Miss Linton replied dryly.

Clover gazed at the dust motes tumbling in the beam of sunshine. 'But isn't it only men who go? I don't know of any women sent abroad, not for this war, anyway.'

Miss Linton wandered over to the window and ran her hand along the shallow sill. Clover pitied any cleaner who might have left a layer of dust, but apparently there was none today. Her supervisor met her gaze.

'For the most part you are right,' she conceded. 'Of course, the greater portion of our troops abroad are male. However, there is a small number of women in the contingent: nurses, of course, some ambulance drivers, and some dedicated ATS girls, many of whom are telephonists or the like. Obviously, they are all highly trained. Then there are also some clerks, organising the stores and logistics, matters of that nature.'

Clover nodded, speechless. Was this her chance? Or was her supervisor talking in general terms?

'I . . . I would be interested to know more about such posts,' she said cautiously, not wanting to overstep the mark, to volunteer for something that was not in fact on offer.

Miss Linton nodded sagely. 'Indeed. I dare say you would, Harrison. You strike me as somebody who's capable, hard-working, and not afraid to show initiative. Not to mention ingenious, as your fir wreath demonstrated. However . . .' She folded and refolded the piece of paper in her hand. 'The stress here is on teamwork and it strikes me that the positions would best be filled by at least two women who worked well together, and not one or more talented individuals.'

Clover blinked slowly, trying to judge what the woman meant. Could it be that her dreaded supervisor actually appreciated her work, didn't think she was totally hopeless, as seemed to be the case most days? And if so, might she recommend her for a new position? But then, it couldn't be just one person. To be considered seriously, it would have to be her plus at least one other.

And where was that one other? What had happened to Sylvia?

A swift glance at her watch showed her that her friend had been gone for the best part of an hour. That was an awful lot of fresh air. Perhaps there had been an accident, she'd been knocked over by a bus or tram—

The door swung open and there she was, her plaits lank and flat but with a little more colour in her face. Her face registered surprise at the sight of Miss Linton but she said nothing.

'Oh good, you're back,' said Clover smoothly, as if she'd stepped out only a few minutes ago. 'Did you, er, find what you were looking for?'

Sylvia stared at her for a second and then shook her head. 'Not quite, they were, um, right out of the size I wanted.' She cleared her throat. 'Do you need a hand with that?' She nodded towards the shelves.

Miss Linton turned towards her, her face giving nothing away, but Clover had the feeling she was not fooled for a moment. 'Good morning,' she said brightly, directing her piercing gaze at Sylvia. 'Well, I shall leave you two to get on with your tasks. I trust you are in good health, Ellis?'

Sylvia looked nonplussed. 'Well, er, yes, why wouldn't I be?'

Miss Linton maintained her steady gaze. 'No reason, of course, merely a polite enquiry.' Her glacial smile was worse than her habitual stern expression. 'Just remember, Ellis, walls have ears. We need you to be in tip-top form in this department.' She opened the door to the corridor, but had one last comment before she left. 'As you well know, it pays to be careful.'

'Blimey, what did she mean by that?' Sylvia sounded aggrieved, once their supervisor was safely out of earshot.

Clover gritted her teeth. She wasn't sure – but the woman had clearly intended something. All Clover knew was that she'd been given a glimpse of life beyond the storeroom, a position of adventure and undoubted danger. The question was, did Sylvia want to find out more? And was she up to the job?

Patty usually loved the early days of spring, with the breezes growing warmer and the buds appearing on the trees along Hackney Downs, the big green space near Victory Walk. It meant it was time for her to think about sowing her first seeds into the back-yard pots, and soon there would be the new vegetables in the greengrocer's. The sight of all that greenery always cheered her up, no matter what the other news might be from further afield.

So she tried her best to feel happy at a delivery of spring onions and smiled dutifully at the delivery man, who wheeled his cart around to the side entrance of the shop so that he could help her stow them away. 'You'll be missing your daughter lending a helping hand,' he'd said, heaving a heavy sack of potatoes out of the way, as the small room was filled with their earthy smell. 'She always brightened up my day and that's a fact.'

Patty nodded and gave a genuine smile at that. 'Of course I do,' she admitted. 'But she's got an important job to do now, with the ATS.'

The man had looked impressed. 'Well, good for her,' he replied. 'Do give her my best – we all appreciate these young'uns what step forward in our time of need.'

'I shall, and thank you,' Patty said, waving him off and then wiping her hands on her apron.

It wasn't worry about Clover that preoccupied her thoughts. She was far more concerned about Peter, away in France. He wrote regularly, even though his letters were never very long – he'd never been one for reading, always preferring to be out and about doing something, working or playing football down on Hackney Marshes. Even so, it was wonderful to hear his snippets of news, although they didn't add up to much. The food was all right but he was sick of boiled beef. He didn't want to try the French stuff. He'd been on patrol. He'd been trained in making observations in the field. He was wearing the thick socks she'd given him for Christmas. Could she send some more?

With no customers around, Patty whipped out her knitting needles and wool from beneath the counter and began to cast on stitches, knowing she could do this without concentrating too hard. When it came to turning the heel, she'd need to pay attention, but for now she could clack away and not fret about being interrupted. She'd chosen a nice deep brown colour, rich and warm, thinking it would go well with his khaki uniform, if he was in a position to care about such details. It made her feel better to think of him wearing them anyway.

The shop doorbell rang and she looked up to see who it was. Her sister Vera came in, huffing and puffing as she hoisted her shopping basket through the gap between the doorpost and the first set of shelves. 'You need to sort out the entrance to your shop,' she announced. 'There's hardly room for your customers to get in. They're not likely to buy a lot if they can't fit their bags through the space, now are they?' She plonked down her basket at her feet and stood up with a small groan, waiting for Patty's reply.

What Patty wanted to say was that most customers could manage quite easily; the problem stemmed from Vera being too stout to begin with. But she didn't. Instead she said, 'That's a lovely coat, Vera. Is it new?'

Vera beamed and the distraction worked. 'It is, isn't it?' she said happily. The coat was in a vivid shade of pinkish purple; Patty knew that Daisy would have called it Dark Windolene. In truth it made her sister look a bit on the sallow side, but a little white lie couldn't hurt.

'I found it in the sales at John Lewis,' Vera went on. 'That was a couple of months ago now. Faith insisted I went with her. She has to buy all manner of smart clothes for her position as a secretary, you know. It's vital that she looks the part, to fit in with her boss's office.'

'Of course,' said Patty and she couldn't help but sigh. It had been a very long time since she'd last been to John Lewis.

'You want to try it some time,' Vera went on. 'Get Rose to go with you on her next day off. I suppose she does have time off now and again?'

Patty pursed her lips at the veiled criticism that Rose spent too much time at the hospital and not enough with her family. If Faith had been a nurse then nobody would ever have heard the end of it. 'She sees us whenever she can,' she replied neutrally.

Vera looked around to see if there was anything she needed. 'Have you got any spring greens?' she asked, peering at the wooden shelves which lined either side of the shop. 'I can't see any.'

'They're still out the back. I haven't put them out yet,' Patty explained. 'I can fetch them for you if you like.'

Vera nodded gratefully. 'Yes, please. Arthur does love his bit of greens. Joy never would eat them, of course, though heaven knows I tried. Hope will eat anything, that's for certain.' She leant against the counter. 'And have you had any word from Peter? We do think of him, all the way over there, far from his nearest and dearest.'

For a moment Patty couldn't speak, transfixed by the worry that was never far away. Then she mastered her emotions. 'Yes, got a letter from him at the beginning of the week in fact,' she could answer quite truthfully. 'He's well, sends his love.' That was stretching it a bit but wasn't quite a lie, and it immediately lightened Vera's face. Bless her, thought Patty, she drives me round the bend but she does care about my children. She's all right underneath, I must remember that.

'Does he say what's happening wherever he is?' Vera went on, her brow furrowed with concern. 'France, isn't it? Or is it Belgium now?'

Patty shook her head. 'He can't really say, you know that. Bert's been piecing it together from the news and

131

reckons Peter's near Lille. That's in the bit of France near Belgium,' she added hastily, spotting Vera's swiftly covered confusion. 'It's all very strange. From what Bert reads in the papers or hears on the wireless, there's no real fighting yet, just skirmishes. Makes you wonder if it's ever going to really happen. You know, proper battles and all that.'

Vera shuddered. 'Don't even say it. It was bad enough all those years ago, all those boys we were at school with who never came home.' Her hands automatically went to her gas mask in its cardboard case, which was slung over one shoulder. 'Perhaps this is all it will turn out to be. Let's hope so.'

Patty's eyes met those of her sister, and each read the desperate hope in the other: that this time all the boys would make it back, that there would be nothing more serious than a few standoffs on the Belgian border. Patty broke away first, unable to bear the hope when her heart told her that she shouldn't assume any such thing. That, having massed the troops, the great powers would not back down and something worse was bound to happen soon. 'I'll fetch you those greens,' she gulped.

By the time she returned with a generous bundle of leaves, wrapped in newspaper, Vera was ready to return to her new favourite topic of how hard it was to buy goods now. 'Having to register with just one grocer, it's ridiculous,' she grumbled, packing away her vegetables. 'Now we've all got those blessed ration books I suppose we'll be in deep trouble if we lose them. All that fuss about keeping count of everything. And the queues! You'd think I had nothing better to do all day than stand in a line in the cold!'

Patty again bit her lip, so that she didn't snap that it was ten times worse if you worked all day and still had to queue, before or after, or in your precious dinner hour. Saying it wouldn't help. Vera was only voicing what everyone was feeling. The restrictions were beginning to bite. At least fruit and veg weren't subject to restrictions, and so she didn't have to deal with customers confused by the new systems or trying to get around them.

'Give my love to Robbie and the girls,' Vera said as she rebuttoned her vivid coat.

'I will. And send mine to your girls.' Patty folded her arms and sighed as her sister struggled to manoeuvre her heavily laden basket out through the door once more. The truth was, they didn't know what was in store for any of them. Shaking her head, she tried hard to hold on to the old adage that there was no point in worrying about things you couldn't change. She'd never been very good at that. It was what came as part and parcel of being a mother.

CHAPTER FOURTEEN

'What are you doing after work?' Clover asked Sylvia as they started to pack everything away at the end of the day. Now that spring was here the storeroom stayed light until the end of their shift and they didn't have to coax the reluctant light bulbs any longer.

Sylvia was still subdued after what they'd decided was a bout of flu. 'I said I'd meet my sister and that we'd get the bus back home together,' she said flatly, reaching for her overcoat.

Clover reached for her own. 'Oof, it's getting a bit warm for these,' she observed. 'Mind you, I could do with a walk to stretch my legs. Shall I come along with you? I can get a different bus back myself.'

Sylvia shrugged and her plaits swung around her shoulders a little. 'All right.'

Clover thought that this was not exactly an enthusiastic response but better than an outright rejection. She'd asked Sylvia a few times over the last couple of weeks if she fancied going out for the evening but Sylvia had always come up with some excuse. Clover tried not to be offended, as the girl might have her reasons; she was still obviously under the weather, and maybe she was trying to save money. All the same, Clover couldn't help but feel slightly miffed. She still held out hopes that the old Sylvia would return, and then they could see if that chance to be posted to France was still open.

The pair picked up their handbags and gas masks before stepping outside into the late afternoon. For all that it was a busy London street, birds were singing and the trees bore new leaves. Clover felt her heart lift as it did each time she noticed these details, and she breathed in with pleasure. How could she be cross when the season was so full of new life?

'Don't you love this time of year?' she asked, spinning around on her low heel, gazing up at the blue sky visible above the tall buildings to either side.

Sylvia was having trouble with the top buttons on her coat. 'Damn thing's too tight,' she muttered.

Clover remembered what her mother had said recently, and sympathised. 'Oh, they get like that after a while – perhaps it shrank when you got caught in the rain. My Aunty Vera only went out and bought a new one at John Lewis a few weeks ago. Lewis's, I ask you! All right, it was in the sale, but still, she spent more than any of my family have *ever* spent on an item of clothing. Not even Pa's wedding suit, and Ma said he wore that for every special occasion for the next twenty years. And Ma said Aunty Vera's was bright pinkish purple – how will she get anything to go with th—'

'Clover!' Sylvia came to a halt on the pavement. 'I didn't get caught in the rain.' Her lip trembled. For a moment she couldn't speak, then it came rushing out. 'I did get caught, though . . . just not in that way.'

She hung her head and turned away and for a moment Clover didn't understand what her friend meant but then she took one look at Sylvia's face and the pieces fell into place. The supposed late flu. The reluctance to go out. Now the coat being too tight. 'Oh, Sylvia,' she breathed.

Sylvia's back was to her, and the girl had wrapped her arms around herself. Clover could see that her knuckles were white. 'I suppose you won't want to be seen with me now,' Sylvia said in a low voice. 'I've got myself into trouble good and proper, haven't I? Just like you warned me about after Christmas. It all seemed like a great lark, then.' Her voice wavered and she would not face her friend.

'Oh, Sylvia.' Clover couldn't think of anything else to say for a minute. Every detail of that conversation came back to her, Sylvia's assurances that she'd been careful, that it had all been a bit of fun but there was nothing to worry about. In some ways this was her fault; she'd asked Sylvia to come to the Dog and Fiddle in the first place. It was through her that they'd met Daisy's former colleagues and their gang. Then reason reasserted itself; *she* hadn't told Sylvia to go out walking with one of them, hadn't known that they'd met up again afterwards. Sylvia had done that of her own free will.

All the same, she couldn't turn her back on her friend in her hour of need. That would be no sort of friendship at all. She'd put aside her annoyance that she was unlikely to be chosen for the posting to France. That might come up again. The most urgent matter was what Sylvia was facing, right here and now.

'Of course I won't want to stop being friends,' she assured her. 'I want to help. You know I do.'

Slowly Sylvia turned around, her face drawn, tears trickling down her cheeks. 'Really? Are you sure?'

Clover nodded immediately. 'I'm sure. We can work out what's best to do. Have you told anybody else?'

Sylvia groaned softly. 'No. Ma and Pa will kill me. They've always said that we should watch out for ourselves, that this is what could happen, but I always thought it would be someone else who got into trouble. That it couldn't be me. Well, now it is.' She gave the ghost of a grim smile.

Clover shivered, despite the warmth of the afternoon. It seemed so wrong that Sylvia could be in such a pickle when she'd never intended any harm to anybody. 'What about your sister? Does she know?'

Sylvia gave a stifled sob. 'I haven't said anything but she might have guessed, and if not yet, then she will soon. We share a room, so she knows I've been dashing out in the mornings. If it was flu then she'll wonder why she hasn't caught it too. In fact, she asked me that yesterday, wondered if I thought it was funny.' She dragged her leather lace-up shoe against the paving stones. 'I suppose it was her roundabout way of finding out if I was hiding anything. Well, I won't be able to hide it for much longer.' She glanced down to where the buttons were straining across her chest. 'I'm all sore up top which is really uncomfortable, that and being sick all the time. Then the rest of me has lost weight so I look like a bleedin' skeleton when I go to the mirror.' She met Clover's gaze. 'So what for having fun, eh? This is no fun at all. It's deadly serious. They'll throw me out when they learn what's happened. Then Misery-drawers will hear about it and I'll be chucked out of the ATS as well.'

Clover didn't know if that last thing was true but she suspected it was. Even so, Sylvia couldn't have been the first one to come unstuck this way. Perhaps they had a way of dealing with it. 'You don't know that for certain,' she pointed out, but Sylvia was having none of it.

'I bet you it's true. I can't see why they'd keep me on, or let me come back after – after it's over. I can't even think about what's in store. Clover, I'm scared, it's all becoming real now. I didn't believe it myself at first, I really did imagine I had flu, and that . . . Well, you know my monthlies had stopped cos I lost weight when sugar got rationed. I didn't lie to you, honest, I didn't.'

Clover could tell that Sylvia was totally convinced and she had to nod. After all, what would she have done? It was such an outside chance – but that didn't change what lay ahead.

'We've got to make a plan,' she decided. 'We can't stay here, standing about. People are beginning to notice.' She fished a clean handkerchief from her pocket – one her mother had embroidered with a cheerful letter C in crimson chain stitch in one corner. 'Here, take this, and wipe your face.'

Sylvia gulped again. 'Are you sure? It's such a nice one.' She rubbed the white cotton between her shaking fingers.

'Doesn't matter.' Clover hoped her mother wouldn't notice it was missing. 'Make yourself presentable and then we'd better go and find your sister. She'll be waiting, won't she?'

Sylvia nodded as she dabbed at her cheeks. 'I'll tell her we had to work late. She won't know no different.'

Clover tucked her hand beneath the other girl's elbow and gently encouraged her to walk on, aware that crowds of Londoners were finishing their days at the office at the same time, and not wanting to draw any more attention. The fewer of them who saw, the better.

Sylvia leant heavily on Clover, as if she could hardly walk, exhausted by the effort of finally confessing what was at the root of her troubles. She dragged her feet and breathed heavily. As they rounded the corner onto the street where her sister worked, she slowed down and said, 'I'm so sorry.'

Clover turned to face her friend and grasped her arms firmly. 'You don't need to say that. You've got to be strong, stay in control, when you're around other people. Save your tears for when you're with me.' She flashed a smile. 'Do you have Victor's address? Why not write to him, share the burden? It takes two, you know.'

Sylvia grimaced. 'I do have it. He gave it to me almost like he didn't care either way, but he did give it to me nonetheless. That must mean something, mustn't it?' She brightened at the thought. 'He wouldn't have done it otherwise.'

Clover was by no means as sure, but knew it wouldn't help to voice her doubts. 'So you'll write to him?' she pressed.

Sylvia took a deep breath and steadied herself. 'I'll think about it,' she said.

Daisy ran down the steps to the tube station ticket hall, not wanting to be even a minute late after her lunch break. She'd taken advantage of the warmer weather to stroll around Finsbury Park while eating the fish paste sandwiches that Patty had made that morning before leaving for the greengrocer's.

She'd watched two robins competing for the same worm and almost lost track of time, so she'd ended up sprinting through the park gates on the corner of Green Lanes and Seven Sisters Road, past the end of the bus stop where a number 29 was setting off for Wood Green, and down the wide stone steps to the level beneath. This tube station was sleek and modern, having been built less than ten years before, but she had no time to appreciate its design today.

She paused on the bottom step to straighten her collar. She didn't always have the responsibility of answering queries from members of the public, although that was far and away the best part of working here. Sometimes she was allowed to sell the tickets, now that they trusted her to get the sums right and count the change.

There was a passenger coming towards her now, and she could see that he was about to ask her a question. Sure enough, he stopped just in front of her and smiled.

For a moment this threw her. It was such a tiny thing but somehow his smile reminded her of Freddy's. His mouth went up very slightly more on one side than the other, and his lips were similar too. How silly she was being. She hadn't even realised that she remembered what Freddy's mouth looked like. Besides, this man was even taller than Freddy, although a bit older, maybe closer to thirty. Hastily she pulled herself together.

'. . . was wondering if you could help me,' he was saying.

Had she missed what he wanted to know? 'Certainly,' she replied brightly, hoping he would expand and she would not look like a fool.

'You see, I'm not familiar with this part of London, I'm from south of the river,' he went on. 'I know all you North Londoners think we're a foreign tribe but really we aren't so bad.' His eyes were alive with merriment and Daisy gave him a grin in return.

'Well, you're a long way from home now,' she said.

'I am indeed. And that's why I need help finding my way to Camden.'

Daisy nodded and breathed out a soft sigh of relief. That was an easy one. 'You can get the tube south from here and change to the Northern Line at King's Cross,' she suggested, 'or, seeing as it's such a nice day, you might prefer to take a bus. The 29 goes straight there. You'll pass alongside the park for the first part of the journey.'

The man smiled again but then asked, 'Will it take much longer, though? I'm expected there for a meeting and can't spend all afternoon looking at trees. Much as I'd prefer to.'

Daisy shrugged. 'Why don't you come with me to our big map of the tube network over there and I'll show you how many stops there are and where to change, and then you can decide.'

'Fair enough.' He followed her across the ticket hall, and she could see through the office window that Sam and Mr Rathbone had noticed what she was doing. Good, or they might have thought she was late.

Sam was watching her and his usually cheerful face had a slight scowl on it. She'd have to ask him why later on, but now she was busy. The man was right behind her as he took in what she had to say about his choice of route. She could almost feel his breath on her neck as she pointed out the interchange. He had a smell of fresh soap, quite unlike the young men at the factory, who had virtually all smelled of cigarettes. She decided she much preferred the soap.

'Thank you,' he said now. 'I won't take up any more of your time, but you've been most helpful. I'll take the tube and save the bus trip for next time.'

She grinned again. 'Glad to be of service.'

'I expect there will be a next time,' he said, and once again his eyes were alight. Then he headed off down to the lower level from where the trains departed, and she turned for the office.

That short encounter had made a good day even better. He had seemed such a pleasant man, and if he reminded her of Freddy – well, somebody was bound to. Not that she cared one whit. She almost broke into a whistle, but remembered in time that it was frowned upon. A pity – she loved a good whistle. But now she was going to make Sam tell her why he was in a bad mood.

CHAPTER FIFTEEN

'I've got to give him time. It stands to reason.' Sylvia twisted her hands anxiously as she and Clover sat in the little park around the corner from their workplace, which had a row of benches well placed to catch the spring sunshine. Plenty of the civil servants and forces staff from around Whitehall would gather there to enjoy it. 'Letters must go missing all the time between here and France. It's not like sending someone a postcard from Southend before the war started.'

Clover could tell her friend was trying to make excuses. While of course she couldn't say for certain that Victor had received the letter Sylvia had finally managed to write, setting out her predicament, she knew damn well that Peter was getting all the ones their family sent and was replying regularly. Only yesterday he'd let them know he'd got the new socks from their mother and was planning to wear them the next chance he got for an evening out. 'It'll impress the mam'zelles,' he'd written.

'Are you sure you won't have one of these?' Clover held out the packet of sandwiches wrapped in waxed paper that she'd hastily cobbled together this morning. 'I love Marmite. Go on, take a couple.'

Sylvia shook her head and pulled a face. 'No, you have them. Marmite tastes really funny now. I've lost my appetite and that's a fact.' She swung her legs out in front of her and then back under the bench. 'Shame, as otherwise I'd be eligible for extra rations – well, that's if I told them that I'm expecting.'

Clover took a bite of her sandwich, with its delicious crust. 'Hmmm.' She put the packet down in her lap. 'So you haven't said anything to your parents or your sister?' She surreptitiously glanced at the other girl's figure, but there was no noticeable bump. Early days yet, she thought.

Sylvia's plaits swung as she shook her head. 'No, I'm going to wait until I hear from Victor,' she said firmly. 'The more I think about it, the more I know he will write back. I just feel he won't let me down.'

'If you say so.' Clover was increasingly certain that Sylvia was clutching at straws, but she didn't have anything better to suggest. And who knew, Victor might yet surprise them and come good, offering to support Sylvia and take responsibility for them once he got back from France. She gazed up at the white clouds scudding across the sky. Huh, far more likely that she'd see a row of pink pigs floating along in front of them flapping their wings than Victor doing the right thing.

* * *

Mr Rathbone made a note in the margin of the report he was reading about last trains on Sundays, his mind not fully on the numbers in front of him. He was anxious about another report that had reached his ears, this one not as official. Or at least, not yet. He did not know how seriously he should take it.

Despite all the warnings, nothing had come of the fears that London would be under attack. He continued to carry his gas mask everywhere, as did everybody; his was slung over a hook on the back of the office door at this very moment. It was never far from his reach, and that was well and good, but there had been none of the dreaded gas attacks. He of all people would not wish those on anyone, not even his worst enemy. Not after what he'd seen in the Great War. Gasphyxiation, they used to call it. Please God, never again.

His wife had asked him to build a shelter for them in their back garden but he had realised it was impossible. There was no space. The little yard was paved over and even if he'd been twenty years younger he would have struggled to dig it up and then go down deep enough into the packed earth beneath. If the worst happened, they would go to their local church hall and take their chances with their neighbours.

He was not at all keen on the other alternative that was in the air: that people should come to the tube stations and take shelter underground, along the platforms. Admittedly, he could see the logic. Those tunnels were already far under the surface and had ready-made access for many passengers at a time. That side of things made sense.

But the very idea of his precious platforms being clogged up with sleeping bodies, not neatly moving onto trains and thus making space for those who came along next or who descended from the trains – no, it was unbearable. The disruption, the inevitable mess. How would the Piccadilly Line keep to schedule? What would it do to the carefully calibrated movements across the entire network? If he allowed himself to dwell on the details it made him break into a sweat.

Still, he reminded himself, it might not come to that. The lull that had typified the war since September might continue and the whole thing fizzle out. That would be best for everyone.

He looked up from his desk and caught sight of his newest employee. Well, perhaps not best for quite everybody. If the war ended then all the rules that had been changed or bent would come back into force and the women who had stepped up to men's roles would find themselves back where they started. He couldn't see Miss Harrison relishing that. He congratulated himself that his faith in her had been justified; she worked hard and learnt fast, clearly loving every minute of it. It shone out of her as she busied herself around the place, and it fair lifted his spirits to see her in action. The clothing factory's loss was most definitely his gain.

He was pleased to see that Sam always went out of his way to show her how everything worked, the location of whatever she might need, the nuts and bolts of the job. He had wondered whether his junior colleague would take umbrage, feeling slighted at no longer being the youngest, but far from it. He also seemed to come alive when Miss Harrison was around and he couldn't do enough for her. That certainly made life in the office much more pleasant. Now and again he had his off moments but who didn't?

Mr Rathbone tidied away his report and sighed again. Like it or not, he had better prepare for the unthinkable eventuality of the general public sleeping downstairs, on his well-regulated platforms.

'What's got into him?' Sam mused aloud, as he passed Daisy at the back of the office. 'Did you see? He's got a face like a wet weekend. Something's going on and he's got a memo about it, I shouldn't wonder. He hates a difficult memo, does Mr Rathbone. *"I must confess that I do not see why they have to make these changes."*'

Daisy giggled as Sam did a fair imitation of their boss, but she didn't want to be disloyal. Mr Rathbone had put his neck on the line by employing her and she knew it. 'Maybe he's got to work extra-long hours for the same salary,' she speculated.

As if aware that he was being talked about, Mr Rathbone looked up at them and then came over. 'Everything all right, Mr R?' Sam asked cheerfully.

Mr Rathbone paused. Then he decided that if the plans came to pass, everyone would have to be prepared. 'There is an idea, and at this stage it is no more than an idea . . .' he began.

'An idea?' Sam repeated.

'Yes. Well. It has been suggested that the general public might use our platforms to shelter from any future raids.' It all came out in a rush. 'It would involve some disruption, of course. Say nothing for now. But just to warn you, your duties would have to adapt somewhat.'

'Blimey,' said Daisy, not sure what to make of it. People needed to be safe. But there had been no raids, so why was he getting so het up?

'Yes, well. As I say, keep it to yourselves for now.' Mr Rathbone retreated to his desk once more.

'Blimey just about sums it up,' Sam groaned. 'He won't like that. That's too much change in one go. In view of that, Daisy Harrison, we need cheering up. What say I take you down that nice pub near Finsbury Park on Friday for a quick drink before the weekend begins?'

Daisy wondered what would be the best way to bat this back. It wasn't the first time he'd asked her. 'That's all very well for those of us who have the weekend off,' she retorted smartly, 'but I'm on shift Saturday morning, thank you very much. What's worse, it'll be alongside that daft ha'peth who's been brought in from Wood Green who doesn't know the routes. You'd think that being only two stations up the line he'd have all that information at his fingertips, but no. I'm surprised he makes it this far without getting lost.'

'True. He don't know his left from his right, let alone his north from his south. I pity you, Daisy, I swear.' Sam struck a melodramatic pose, but his face was eager. 'Another time, then. Just name your evening. You could have a drop of port and lemon if you've a mind to.'

Daisy shuddered and she wasn't putting it on. It was bad enough having had to drink shandy. She hadn't repeated the experience since Christmas. If she recalled rightly, port and lemon was Sylvia's tipple and look what a state she'd got into. In any case, she was far from keen to try that stuff.

Besides she couldn't give her real reason: that she was still seventeen. Sam didn't know her exact age. He teased her about being under twenty-one but he didn't know how far short of that landmark she actually was. She mustn't blurt it out now.

She didn't think there was anything much behind his invitation other than them getting along well in the office and perhaps him being lonely after all his friends and former colleagues had joined up. That must be horrible. He never talked about it but sometimes she caught sight of his face if Mr Rathbone mentioned a headline from the newspaper or an article he'd heard on the Home Service that morning. All those brave boys off fighting, and Sam being stuck at home because of his flat feet. What a strange reason for being left behind.

She ought to be kind to him. 'Perhaps not this week but later,' she said. 'Only don't try to get me drinking port and lemon. It looks like medicine. Where's the fun in that?'

Sam's face glowed with pleasure. 'I'll take you up on that, then,' he said happily.

CHAPTER SIXTEEN

Rose sank onto the chair in the dining area in the nurses' home and pulled it under the table. She knew she should eat now that her shift had ended but the conversation that had just happened had put her right off her food. Damn that doctor and his superior air.

Although that could be said of many of the doctors. Not all of them; some were perfectly nice, and appreciated the skills of the experienced nurses, of whom she was now considered to be one. However Mr Prendergast – not Doctor, he insisted, he was a surgeon and must therefore be addressed as Mister – was a nightmare.

He had been for as long as she'd known him, and she wasn't the only nurse to think so. He made little secret of his opinion that nurses were there not only to assist him in theatre but outside as well, in a personal capacity. He wasn't as crude as to do anything obvious such as back them into corners or physically intimidate them. That would have been easier in many ways – lots of the nurses had dealt with bad behaviour from patients. No, he was more subtle, but the pressure was there nonetheless.

Her meal steamed before her, corned beef and hot vegetables, and the smell was enticing, but still she hesitated to eat. Ugh, that man was a menace. Downright creepy in fact. He would stand just a little too close and speak softly so that you had to lean in even closer to hear. He might be saying something vital to an operation; you didn't have a choice.

This time he had come up to her as she was leaving the ward. 'Nurse Harrison! What an unexpected delight.' He had blocked her way, not so that any patients would notice if they happened to be looking that way, but so that she could not get past without touching him. Typical.

'I do look back on our days in theatre with pleasure,' he had purred. 'How is it you are never on rotation with me any longer? We must do something about that.' He had smiled and that was even worse. His lips were wet and slimy.

Rose wanted to tell him to get lost but that was impossible.

'Well, don't let me detain you,' he had continued, oily and just very slightly menacing. Then he'd paused. 'You'll be hoping to move up the ranks at some point in the near future, won't you? I dare say all your superiors are pleased with your performance.' He had leered as he'd said it. 'I'd be very happy to give you a hearty recommendation – that is, if you'd consider giving me a helping hand.'

152

Was he suggesting what she thought he was? Truly this man was disgusting, and within earshot of vulnerable patients too. 'I really must be getting along,' she had replied tightly and ducked around him, feeling his unwelcome gaze on her back as she'd walked quickly down the corridor, resisting the urge to run as fast as she could.

Her gravy was congealing by now. She stirred it with her fork to make it look more palatable. How could this horrible man have such influence? She wasn't sure who she could talk to. Several of her close colleagues had been transferred and more than one had volunteered for the services. The more junior ones might not understand; the more senior ones were the very people who would have a say in her progression, or not.

That left her family. They might not understand exactly how the hospital system worked, but they wouldn't say she was being stupid or imagining it. Whatever else happened, they would be there, backing her up.

'Come on, Sylvia. I can't hold this big box much longer, I need help.' Clover's arms ached as she tried to move the stationery from one end of the shelving to the other. Dust went up her nose and her eyes itched. The damn thing hadn't been shifted for ages, that much was clear.

Sylvia slumped. 'Sorry.' But she gave no sign of coming to Clover's rescue.

Clover huffed and balanced the big box against the middle shelf, supporting it by leaning against it. 'What's up? I thought you'd stopped being sick in the mornings but you look pale and wan today.' She grinned, trying to chivvy her colleague into action, but it didn't work.

Sylvia shrugged. 'I got a terrible backache and I don't know why. It's not as if I done any heavy lifting. I must have slept funny, though I don't remember it.' She twirled the end of one plait around her fingers, and her forehead gleamed with sweat.

'Don't tell me you're coming down with something,' Clover groaned. 'We're past the flu season, thank God, so it can't be that. Well, perhaps you shouldn't lift anything big today. We can leave this where it is or I'll ask Miss Linton to give me a hand later.'

'All right.' Sylvia didn't sound grateful at all, only tired.

'Still no news?' Clover felt she had to ask, although she was sure that if there had been a letter from France then Sylvia would have told her in a flash. Her friend didn't even dignify that with a reply, simply gave her a look which said it all. Victor hadn't written, and she was beginning to lose hope that he ever would.

'Well, I reckon we should cheer ourselves up with a trip to the cinema,' Clover suggested, grabbing a duster and setting to work on the corner that had caused her to sneeze so much. 'Tell you what, they're showing *Goodbye, Mr Chips* again near us. Do you fancy that at all? You've probably seen it already but I'd go again. I love Greer Garson, she's so beautiful. I wish my hair would curl like hers.' She ran a hand through her chestnut mop and transferred a speckling of dust as she did so.

Sylvia could not summon up any enthusiasm for the idea. 'I might,' she said dully. 'I did see it when it came out last year. It was all right. I don't really mind.'

Clover pursed her lips. If it was only all right and Sylvia didn't mind, then there wasn't really much point. 'Would you rather see something else?' she asked, determined to get some sort of positive response. 'How about *Jamaica Inn*? Or *Dark Victory*? I love Bette Davis.'

Sylvia groaned and rubbed her back. 'Not really. I can't think about it right now.'

Clover all but threw down her duster. 'Well, you just let me know when you can, and we'll plan a night out. I love going to the pictures.'

Sylvia gave her a glance that was almost a thank-you but then she groaned again. 'Blast, this isn't getting any better and now I think I need the bathroom,' she confessed. 'Will you cover for me if Linton comes over? Sorry, got to dash!' She almost ran from the room, the current from the door opening and closing making all the dust fly up into the air again.

Clover had a fit of sneezing and then rubbed her itching eyes. She knew she should be sympathetic but really, she was doing the work of two people and it felt as if that had been the case for ages. She would have enjoyed seeing that film again but there was no point going with someone who didn't really like it. Rose would be working, and it wasn't Daisy's cup of tea. Joy was always a misery at the cinema and Hope would have gone umpteen times already. Perhaps she'd go on her own and the hell with the lot of them.

If Sylvia hadn't messed around with Victor they could both have been in France by now, doing something far more exciting than stacking boxes all day, every day. It wasn't fair.

Clover had never taken much notice of the young recruits who ran messages for the stores operation, as they tended to get moved around a lot and no sooner did you learn one's name than she was gone and somebody else turned up in her place, only to be transferred a short while later. So when a slight girl with short blonde hair and freckles knocked on the door and stuck her head around it, she couldn't remember her name or how long she'd been around.

'Are you Miss Harrison?' the girl asked, slightly out of breath.

'Yes, that's right.'

The girl gulped. 'It's your friend, she says you're to come.'

Clover felt her stomach lurch. But it could be anything, she mustn't jump to conclusions.

'What's happened?' she asked, sounding calm on the surface.

'I'm not sure. It's just . . .' The girl had come into the storeroom proper and was shuffling her feet in anxiety. 'I had to go to the bathroom and she was in there and she don't sound well, miss, and I asked her was she all right and she said no and to come here and fetch you so that's what I done.' She stopped, and sneezed.

Clover forced herself to take a breath. 'Right, well, sounds as if I'd better do as she asked. Thanks for telling me, ah . . . ?'

'Bella, miss. Bella Farley.' The girl brightened at being thanked.

'. . . Miss Farley. I'll just set this pile down on the counter and then I'll follow you out.' Clover shoved the mound of papers she'd been reading back where they came from, hastily wiped her hands on her skirt and headed out to the corridor, trying to prepare for what might come next.

As soon as they approached the cloakroom door, Bella made her excuses. 'I got to get back to the dispatch desk upstairs,' she said, and disappeared around the corner as fast as she'd come.

Clover hesitated for a moment, her hand on the doorknob. Then she summoned her courage and went in. A low groaning came from one of the cubicles.

'Sylvia? Is that you?' Clover went over to the end cubicle, embarrassed at the thought that she might have got it wrong and someone else was in there.

'Clover . . .' It was Sylvia all right.

'What's going on? Is it your backache?' It was cold in the cloakroom with its white-tiled walls and row of shining porcelain sinks. The spring warmth didn't penetrate this far and a smell of carbolic hung in the air.

Silence for a moment, and then, 'No – Clover, can you get me a towel or something? I can't move.'

'What? How do you mean?'

There was a sob from the other side of the cubicle door. 'There's blood all over,' Sylvia cried. 'Loads of blood and it won't stop!'

Clover gasped. 'What, how . . . ?'

Sylvia sobbed again. 'From me, it's coming out of me. And the backache is worse, much worse. Clover, I'm frightened. I'm all shaky, and cold.'

Clover wished that Rose was here. She always knew what to do. But her big sister was miles away, coping with many sick patients all at once, balancing their needs and priorities, not flinching at the thought of blood. There was just Clover here and now.

She'd managed to clean up Robbie, hadn't she? Admittedly, that was on a different scale but she'd done it all the same. She mustn't panic.

'Don't worry, I'm here,' she said firmly, to convince herself as well as Sylvia. 'I'll find you something, never fear.' She turned around in a circle, surveying the sinks, the gleaming taps, the pipes. In the far corner was a cupboard. Of course, they had to restock it now and again, managing the supplies of soap and toilet paper – and towels.

Sometimes it was locked but luckily today it had been left open. Clover wrenched back the wooden-panelled door and rapidly scanned the shelves. Disinfectant – that might be useful, so she grabbed a bottle. Cotton wool, what was that doing there? And then, behind the supplies of soap, some towels. White from many rounds of bleaching, rather rough in texture, but towels and they would have to do.

She grabbed an armful and rushed back to the other

end of the chilly cloakroom. 'I've got them. Look, I'll throw them over the top of the door. I don't want to pass them underneath, because we don't want them picking up whatever might be on the floor.'

Sylvia made a wordless noise that Clover hoped was a yes. Well, she'd been fairly good at games at school, and she could throw accurately, so she bundled up several towels one by one and threw them over, willing Sylvia to catch them.

'Come out as soon as you can and then I can help you much better,' she called in encouragement.

After what felt like hours but in reality could only have been five minutes, Sylvia emerged, her face even whiter, her hands stained with blood.

'Lean on me,' said Clover at once, trying not to dwell on what she was seeing, 'and come across to the sinks where we can get you cleaned up.' She'd already run the tap so that there was instant hot water, a luxury indeed.

Sylvia was a dead weight but somehow she manoeuvred her across the serviceable floor tiles to the sinks, running the warm water on her poor hands. Clover could see that there were splatters of blood on her clothes, which would take some explaining if anyone were to come in so she positioned herself to shield the sight of her friend from anyone at the door.

'Here, use this nailbrush. And there's plenty of soap.' She kept her voice steady, as Sylvia's sobs continued but quieter now.

Clover thought hard. She had a spare set of clothes hanging on the back of one of the storeroom cupboard doors; she'd got caught in the rain one time and had vowed never again to spend the day in sopping wet clothes. If she could get Sylvia to wait in here, and then nip back—

'Ah, so there you are.' The stern voice cut across the room and through her thoughts.

Just when they didn't need her, Miss Linton had arrived.

'Yes, we were just – we were just . . .' Clover couldn't think of a credible way of explaining what was happening, certainly not enough to convince the hawk-eyed supervisor.

Miss Linton nodded. 'I see. Don't bother trying to cover it up, Harrison, I understand completely what is happening.'

Sylvia groaned more loudly now.

'Come away to the staffroom, and we'll get you tidied up and decide whether you should see a doctor,' Miss Linton said, her usual sharpness replaced by concern. 'We'll save the explanations for later. Come quickly, now, there's hardly anybody about and you won't face unwanted questions and scrutiny.'

Clover didn't have time to be surprised but helped support her friend along to the more comfortable quarters of the staffroom, where the more senior members could take their tea breaks. As Sylvia sank onto a well-worn sofa and curled up into a ball, her eyes met her superior's.

The older woman raised an eyebrow. 'Perhaps it's for the best. We'll get her through this immediate crisis and then see how the land lies.'

Clover gasped again. 'But . . . you knew? How could you have known? We never spoke about it unless we were outside, Sylvia was so careful . . .'

Miss Linton sighed and spoke quietly so as not to disturb the worn-out young woman. 'I see the pair of you day in, day out,' she replied. 'Of course I knew, you meet a lot of young women in the ATS. I tried to convey that I was aware of what had occurred.' She gave a tight smile. 'And, believe it or not, Harrison, I too was young once.'

CHAPTER SEVENTEEN

Daisy sat on her bed, staring out of the window as the sunset drew streaks of pink and red across the golden sky. The late evenings of spring made her remember being a little girl, refusing to go to sleep because it wasn't dark. Her sisters had despaired of ever getting her to drop off before they themselves reached their later bedtimes. Now she knew it was almost at the point where she should pin up the blackout blinds, but the sky was so pretty that she didn't want to, not quite yet.

Her thoughts turned to the last hour at work. Sam had reminded her of her promise to go for a drink with him one Friday and she'd laughed it off, but could see he was a little hurt. Damn, she'd meant no harm, but now it looked as if she'd have to go through with it one day. He wasn't going to forget it and let her off the hook.

So she'd been feeling more than a little unsettled when the passenger who'd reminded her of Freddy arrived once more in the ticket hall, this time up the escalator from the lower level where the platforms were. She'd smiled at him before she could even think about it, and out of the corner of her eye caught Sam's dark look as he noticed. But the passenger had smiled back in recognition, which was a relief. She didn't want to presume that he'd remember her and be made to feel a fool, grinning like an idiot at some random man.

'Well, hello,' he'd said, as she came out of the office on the pretence of polishing the shiny fittings around the big network map. 'You're on duty again, I see.'

'I am,' she'd said, stating the obvious but not really minding. He really did have the most intriguing eyes – sparking with life, and giving the impression that you held his full attention.

He cleared his throat as if he was just a little nervous, although that couldn't be right, not really.

'The last time I was here, you mentioned a bus route that would take me directly to Camden,' he said. 'I don't know if you recall?'

Daisy went through a brief show of searching her memory, so that she didn't seem too obviously keen. 'Oh, now, yes, that's right. You mean the number 29.'

He nodded happily. 'If you say so. I don't want to presume upon your time, but would you be good enough to point me in the right direction of the bus stop? I seem to remember that there are lots of them once you get above ground here.'

Sam was really glaring now. She could see his pale face through the office window.

Emboldened, she had laughed and smiled even more broadly. 'Come with me, I'll show you,' she offered.

The man's eyebrows rose. 'Really? Would you be able to do that?'

Well, strictly speaking, she really shouldn't, but she wasn't going to take back her offer now – and she certainly wasn't going to return to the office with Sam shooting daggers like that.

'Of course, it won't take a moment, and like you say, there are so many that you could easily end up at the wrong one.' She'd led him up the correct staircase to the outside world and indicated where the buses to Camden went from. The streets were busy and she didn't hang around, but knew that the man was extremely grateful and, if he hadn't remembered her properly before, he'd certainly do so again now.

'You've certainly gone above and beyond the regular call of duty, Miss . . . ?'

'Harrison. Daisy Harrison,' she'd said without missing a beat. Not that she gave out her name to just anybody, but he was an exception, standing there in his well-cut suit, smart collar and tie, every inch the gentleman.

'Well, thank you again, Miss Harrison. I'm Edgar, but my friends call me Ted. Ted Burnett, at your service.'

'Pleased to be able to help you, Mr Burnett. Now I really must be getting back.' She soaked in his appreciative gaze for one blissful moment, before turning away and descending the steps once more, to face the resentful Sam.

She was still gazing out of the window at the fading light when Clover came in.

'What are you sitting here in the dark for? Get that blind up or we'll be for it from the ARP,' she snapped, flinging down her cardigan on her bed.

'All right, keep your hair on. What's getting your goat?' Daisy turned around and then caught the expression on her sister's face. 'Blimey, Clover, what happened? You missed tea and everything. What's going on?'

Clover gave a huge sigh and collapsed onto her bed, skewing the candlewick bedspread as she did so. 'Oh, you wouldn't understand.' She bunched up the cardigan and threw it at her pillow.

Daisy sniffed. 'Don't be like that. I might.'

Clover rolled her eyes. 'Look, Daisy, I know you're working in a proper job now and you've had a taste of shandy but that don't mean you understand some things. I'm just a bit upset, that's all.'

Daisy hated it when her sisters reminded her that she was younger than them and less experienced in the ways of the world. Besides, she'd grown up a lot over the past few months. Trust Clover not to notice. All the same, something was evidently seriously wrong.

'Well, try me,' she said seriously. Now was not the time to pick a fight, she could tell. If the positions had been reversed and she'd come back after a bad day at work, she'd have wanted sympathy, not a quarrel.

Clover stared at the ceiling. For a long moment she hesitated but then appeared to come to a decision. 'All right, but this isn't pleasant, I can't pretend that it is. And you mustn't tell Ma.'

Daisy felt a flash of panic, but said, 'Doesn't matter. And I won't say anything.'

'Right.' Clover passed a hand across her face. 'You know what a miscarriage is, right?'

'Of course.' Daisy had heard of such things, but that was about as far as it went.

'Well, Sylvia had one today. At work. It was awful. She was in such a state, and we didn't want anyone to see, and we were stuck in the cloakroom . . .' Clover cleared her throat and took a deep breath. 'I mean, I knew she'd got in trouble and was expecting a baby, but I didn't want it to end like this.'

Daisy stared at her sister. 'Is she all right? Sh-she's not dead, is she?'

Clover gave a sad smile. 'No, no, I didn't mean that. She's all right really, just very wrung out and sad. Our supervisor turned out to have known all along and came and took charge, almost as though she knew exactly what it was like. She had the name of a doctor who she said would check Sylvia out without blaming her. That's why you can't say anything, not even to Ma, cos people love to point the finger and the fewer folk who know the better. I had to run off to Woolworths to buy a cheap golden ring so Sylvia could wear it to the doctor's, just in case.'

'Poor Sylvia.' Unbidden, the image arose of Sylvia in the pub just after Christmas, drunk and hooting with laughter, being all but carried by that soldier home on leave. And then Peter's comment, about not turning out like that, for her own safety.

'Was it . . . who was the father?'

Clover glared. 'Isn't that her business?'

Daisy shrugged sadly. She hadn't breathed a word of what she'd seen that night but perhaps now was the time. 'Was it – was it what's his name, Chalky's cousin?'

Clover stared.

'Victor, isn't that his name?' Daisy persisted. Now she had to know.

'Why do you ask?'

Then it all came flooding out, how Daisy had watched them in the pub, and wondered then if Sylvia had known what she was doing.

Clover sounded as if she didn't know whether to be glad or angry at what her sister was telling her. 'You've known this since December? And you never said?'

Daisy hunched her shoulders. 'Peter said not to be a snitch, I didn't know if she'd told you or not. Anyway it might have come to nothing.'

'But it didn't,' Clover said flatly. 'It came to something good and proper. And Sylvia wrote to tell Victor but he hasn't written back, the sneaky bastard. He's over there having the adventure of his life, and she's back here dealing with the consequences.'

All at once it felt like too much for Daisy. The undercurrents of adult life were sweeping her away, all the hope and betrayal and secrecy. No wonder Peter had wanted to shield her. She was very close to being out of her depth but that would be of no use to Clover at all. Her sister had borne the brunt of events all day and needed comfort.

'You did your best,' she said, moving across to sit by her sister. 'You stuck by her and didn't run away, or report her. She'll appreciate that when she comes to think about it.'

Clover pulled a crumpled hanky from her skirt pocket. 'Well, maybe. I bet she's got a whole lot else to think about right now. Besides, she'll be off sick for a few days, I should imagine. Anyway,' she sat up straighter, 'we got through it, somehow. I don't know how Rose stands it, dealing with blood and all that. I wished she was there to help but . . .'

'You did it, Clover. You saved her from something really horrible happening.' Daisy's voice was full of admiration. Even if Clover annoyed her, she recognised that she would be a good person to turn to in a crisis. Before she could tell herself not to, she gave her sister a quick hug. 'You're a good friend, Clover.'

Her sister gulped and then nodded. 'Thanks, Daisy. I'm sorry to blurt all that out at you. But then, seems as if you weren't too surprised anyhow. I suppose you must be growing up after all.'

'Suppose so.' Daisy grinned in the last of the light. 'Come on, there'll be some food left over downstairs. Ma put some potato pie aside for you, it's in the enamel dish in the kitchen.'

Clover stood and smoothed out the creases in her skirt. 'Thank God for that. I'm famished. But first we'd better put up that bloody blackout blind.'

CHAPTER EIGHTEEN

Patty arrived slightly later than usual but she was humming to herself as she opened up the shop. It was the little things that mattered. Daisy had insisted that she didn't want a fuss for her eighteenth birthday, now that she was in a responsible grown-up job, but her mother hadn't been fooled. She had secretly made a cake – not a big one, but something to mark the occasion nonetheless. Clover had been sworn to secrecy, but had managed to bring back a pretty decoration from her workplace.

'It's only a paper ruff to put around the outside of the cake but Miss Linton said I could have it,' she'd explained, and Patty had smiled broadly. Clover might argue with Daisy until the cows came home but when it came to the essentials, she could be relied upon. She had saved some dried fruit and used it for the top of the cake, making a big letter D.

Clover had suggested asking Hope and Joy over to join them but neither had been able to make it midweek; Hope was helping with the Women's

Voluntary Service tea van at Liverpool Street and didn't want to let them down. Joy hadn't wanted to come without her sister. Clover pointed out that meant more cake for everyone else. The small tea party had been a big success and afterwards they'd sat up talking; now this morning Patty was running behind. She was determined to hang on to the good mood brought about by her two younger girls getting along without a squabble for an entire evening.

By the late afternoon Patty was glad to see the back of the old woman who'd come in to buy cabbage and whatever else she could use in her stew. She knew her well by sight although they'd never really had much to do with one another; she vaguely recalled that the woman's grandchildren had been at school with Clover, or perhaps it had been Rose. No reason for the old bat to be so personal, when it was rubbing salt into the open wounds of Patty's deepening worries. The happiness from yesterday had dissolved in the face of the woman's anxiety.

'Well, I don't trust him,' the woman had said, her voice a little querulous, as she prodded the cabbage with a suspicious forefinger. Patty glared. Was she going to buy it or not? She herself wouldn't want to eat a vegetable that had been poked about by somebody else. She cleared her throat.

'That's fresh in this morning, Mrs Ramsbottom.'

'I should hope so too, prices you charge these days.' The old woman's expression showed that she thought Patty was having her on. 'Why they have to go changing things beats me. That Mr Chamberlain knows what he's doing, you take it from me. He's got all the right ideas. This Churchill fellow, what does he know?'

Patty pursed her lips but simply put the cabbage into Mrs Ramsbottom's basket. Quite why she should trust her customer's opinions over those of her own husband, she didn't know. Bert always listened to the news on the wireless and these days read the papers even more thoroughly from front page to back, and if he said the new prime minister was the right man for the job then she believed him.

'Got any carrots?'

'I'll check under the counter.' Patty was glad to duck behind the till, where the old bat couldn't see her. She pulled a face when she was safely out of sight, which made her feel better. 'Here we are, just look at their bright colour, enough to put a spring in your step.'

The carrots were a lovely vivid orange, just as they should be.

Mrs Ramsbottom looked dubious. 'I suppose they'll do. Fat lot of comfort they'll be when the Germans invade. Look what they're doing now, overrunning Belgium and Holland. And bits of France. We're next, just you wait and see.'

Patty could feel herself growing hot under the collar. 'Well, that's why they had to get a new prime minister,' she said stoutly. 'Now things are finally starting to happen, we need someone who'll take them on, beat them at their own game.'

Mrs Ramsbottom tutted. 'That's as may be. But I can tell you, I don't like the shape of his face. Nothing good will come of it.'

Patty let out an exasperated breath. She couldn't stand anyone who predicted defeat with such obvious relish. 'Will that be all?' she made herself say politely.

Mrs Ramsbottom had harrumphed, resentfully paid up, and stomped out, or as well as her arthritic hips would let her.

Patty tried not to let the wave of worries swamp her. How could she go about her business when all the news was of the German blitzkrieg over the Channel, tanks rolling into the Netherlands and Belgium, right where Peter might be? It had happened less than a fortnight ago but already his regular letters had stopped.

Bert had reasoned that the army probably had more pressing matters to attend to than sorting out the mail for home, but that must mean her letters to her son weren't getting through either. It didn't stop her writing or sending them but she had less and less faith that they could reach him, her beloved boy, out there in the face of danger. If she thought about it too much she thought she would go mad, but how could she not think about it? On top of that she had the daily concern of wondering if the regular supplies to the shop would continue, not wanting to let down Mr Morton, her ageing boss. How she longed for a letter from Peter.

The shop door swung open once more and she briefly hoped it would be someone who might lift her spirits, or at least distract her, but it was her sister Vera. Patty braced herself.

For once, though, Vera did not launch into an immediate onslaught about what Patty was doing wrong or how mistakenly she was bringing up her children. She seemed unusually subdued. Patty wondered if the grim news from the Continent was at the root of it.

'You all right?' she asked, when Vera remained strangely quiet.

'Of course,' Vera replied automatically. 'Daisy's birthday go well, did it?'

'Very nice, thank you,' said Patty, wishing she could turn back the clock and have those few happy hours again.

'Good, I mean, I'm glad. Not every day you turn eighteen.' Vera pursed her lips. 'It's nearly closing time, isn't it? Do you fancy a cup of tea at that place down the road? I bet you could do with a change of scenery.'

Well, that was a first. Patty almost said that she couldn't, that there were still five minutes to go, but then she remembered what an early start she'd made every day this week. 'Give me a mo and I'll be ready,' she said, swiftly bagging the day's takings.

With everything securely stowed away, Patty picked up her coat and gas mask. She ushered her sister out and locked up after her, wondering what this was all in aid of. Vera did not make such offers without reason.

The café was quiet, just a few women at the tables near the sparkling clean windows, and they made their way to the furthest corner from the counter. Vera began to describe a concert she'd heard on the Home Service a few nights ago, but then she'd added that it had been an ENSA one for the forces abroad. 'They couldn't say where of course, just somewhere in France.' Then her hand flew to her mouth. 'Oh, silly me. I've put my foot in it, haven't I. You'll be worried about Peter.'

'Yes, yes I am,' said Patty at once, in a rush of relief that she could say the words, and only afterwards registering that Vera had had the tact to recognise her faux pas.

'Well, Winston Churchill is the man for the job,' Vera declared, in complete contradiction of the previous customer. 'My Arthur says so and he should know.'

Patty conceded that as Vera's husband mixed with councillors and local business leaders these days he might well be in a position to have an informed opinion. 'Bert says so too,' she said. 'We heard Churchill's broadcast on Sunday night and he sounded like he knew what he was doing. Calling for the country to be men of valour.' She brushed back a loose lock of hair that had escaped from her scarf, which she was wearing more as a hairband. 'He means us women too, we got to be ready, he says. So that's what we're trying to be.' She looked askance at her sister. 'You got something on your mind,' she said.

Vera turned away to gaze at the pictures on the opposite wall, advertising Bovril. 'Well, I might have. There's such a lot to consider these days, isn't there?' She was playing for time but finally came out with it. Glancing around to make sure there was nobody else within earshot she leant closer. 'It's Faith I'm worried about.'

Patty raised her eyebrows in surprise. Faith was in a cushy job in the West End, not stuck out in France somewhere, or even on the frontline at the local hospital like Rose.

'What's wrong?'

Vera swallowed hard. 'I think it started when Martin went off to do his training.'

'Oh, yes.' Patty did her best not to show any resentment towards the young man, who she had had great hopes of for her eldest girl. Not that Rose seemed to care, quite the opposite.

'And as you know, Faith has always been held in very high regard by her boss. Very high regard indeed. She was hand-picked for the position, I may not have mentioned it, but she was.'

Patty nodded, and remembered Rose saying something at the time along the lines of she didn't know that her cousin had any experience or qualifications that would have won her the job.

'And then . . .' Vera sighed. 'Well, his wife took the sensible option to join her parents in the country, back when the children were evacuated, you remember. Faith gave me to understand that it was, er, welcomed by both sides. So he has to turn to someone for support, doesn't he, businessmen like him have such a lot on their plate, such heavy responsibilities.'

Patty's instant reaction to that was to object, what, more than Bert had? Foreman in a factory that kept losing staff to the forces, under pressure to produce more but with less? But she didn't. 'Go on,' she said instead.

'It's just that – well, I'm not really sure, Patty, but I think it's gone further than a . . . strictly professional relationship. She hasn't told me as much directly, it's more that as a mother, you know, you guess, don't you, when something's not right. You'll have had similar moments with your girls.'

Patty counted herself as lucky that actually she hadn't had to deal with such a situation. None of her girls had given her much to worry about in that way. Not yet, anyway – they were still young. Robbie was always highest on the list – or at least, before the recent bad news from France. There, she was worrying about that again, when she'd had two whole minutes thinking about something else. 'You know when they're hiding something from you,' she suggested, remembering how secretive Daisy had been before her interview.

'Exactly.' Vera looked relieved to have shared her concern. 'She is most certainly not telling me something and that's so unlike her. You know we talk about everything, we're almost like best friends rather than mother and daughter.'

Patty frowned. She didn't care for such ideas. She loved to be on good terms with her children, of course she did, but there were very clear boundaries. She was not their friend. She was their mother. It was different.

'So I don't know exactly what has happened but she's not the same as she was. She's got this funny look in her eye, sort of distant, and she keeps saying his name, can't talk about anything else.'

Oh dear, thought Patty. That all pointed to one thing. Vera surely knew it as well as she did. And the man was married – it did not bode well.

'I don't suppose she would consider changing jobs?'

'Oh, no. That wouldn't do at all. Where she is now is so prestigious. She won't want to come back to working in Hackney in some office or anything.'

Or doing something useful, like nursing, or working for the transport board, or joining the forces, thought Patty, offended on her daughters' behalf. 'How about a different office? One of the civil service HQs? She'd meet all sorts of officers there, I bet.' Patty paused. 'Would she have said anything to Hope or Joy?'

Vera shook her head. 'I shouldn't think so. After all, they've not left home, they don't have Faith's experience of the wider world. Don't get me wrong, they're lovely girls, but just not as sophisticated.'

Patty thought that Hope was far too sensible to be hoodwinked by a married man, if that was really what was going on, but then, young people did all sorts of silly things when it came to love. 'In that case, you'd better wait to see what happens, and make sure she knows you have a shoulder for her to cry on. If it comes to that.'

Vera's shoulders sank. 'Maybe.' She made to pick up her wicker basket. 'Thank you for listening, Patty. I'm probably imagining things and it's all this tension about what's going to happen next. I'd best be getting along. I'll have to queue at the chemist, I expect. I need some linctus for Arthur, just in case he gets one of his bad throats.'

'Of course,' said Patty, cutting off any long speech about Arthur and his many conditions which were all a result of his hard work. 'Give her our love anyway.'

Vera nodded. 'I will. And I'll be thinking of Peter. Goodbye now.'

Patty gave her a half-hearted wave, wondering what would come of this. She briefly wondered if their own parents, dead for some years now, had ever had to worry about Vera and her – but no, they'd surely never caused anything like as much trouble. Vera clearly valued the prestige of Faith's job even though it appeared to put her in the face of a very different sort of danger. Well, something would have to give. Patty couldn't help but be glad that her girls weren't tempted by such enticements. There was a limit to how much she could worry, wasn't there?

'Where's Sam?' Daisy hung up her jacket and put her handbag down by the desk. 'He's usually here by now.'

The underground office was as bright as it would ever get from the filtered sunlight above. Now that it was the end of May, the days were almost as long as they could be, dawn breaking early and sunset later and later.

Mr Rathbone looked up from yet another report. 'Good morning, Miss Harrison.'

Daisy smoothed her flared skirt before sitting down. 'I hope he's not sick,' she went on. 'Would we have to have that fellow from Wood Green in as a replacement if he is? Have you heard?'

Mr Rathbone took a moment to reply. 'If you mean Mr Fraser, then yes, I do believe he will be with us this afternoon.'

Daisy's face fell. Mr Fraser was no fun at all, and still didn't know how to navigate the travel system. He was slowly improving on direct routes, but ask him anything that involved a change of lines or, heaven forbid, two changes, and he didn't have a clue.

At moments such as this she realised how much she relied on Sam to add some enjoyment to her work day. He was usually so lively, and knew the job so well that it was easy to overlook just how much he got done in a short time. It was only when someone like Mr Fraser came along that the contrast was so stark. She made a mental note to appreciate Sam more, and to tell him so once he showed up again.

'So, have you heard from him?' she pressed, seeing as her boss hadn't answered her directly.

Mr Rathbone steepled his fingers over his reports.

'You'll have heard the news last night,' he said.

Daisy had; they had all listened to the wireless, desperate for any word that would shed some light on where Peter might be. Since Mr Churchill's stirring speech a week ago Sunday, things had gone from bad to worse. Not only had the Germans invaded the Netherlands and Belgium, they had now swept through even more of France. It sounded as if the British Expeditionary Force, the army that Peter was a part of, had been forced back towards the coast. What had started with such optimism was now at risk of turning into a rout.

All the same, Sam couldn't be affected by that, or to no greater extent than they all were. Any setbacks on the Continent brought the threat of a Nazi invasion a step closer. Everyone was muttering about it and the atmosphere of fear hung over them all.

'Yes, yes I did,' she replied. Dragging her words, now not sure that she wanted to hear what her boss was about to say.

'Our troops are being forced out of France and are cut off from a retreat back to Britain by the waters of the Channel.' Sometimes he could be so careful and literal. Daisy nodded, dreading what was to come and yet now impatient too.

'I know, it's awful.'

'You might not have heard the rest. The Royal Navy, of course, is coming to the rescue, to pick up as many of the soldiers as it can. The air force will be there too, to defend the ships.' He fiddled with his fountain pen, a sleek maroon one that he took home with him at the end of every shift.

'Reading between the lines, it'll be tricky for the larger vessels to come in close enough to the beaches. It's a stretch of coastline at Dunkirk, not a set of harbours.' He took another slow breath. 'So any smaller craft have been asked to come to their assistance.'

'Smaller craft?' Daisy had never had much to do with boats, and was never quite sure what any of the words meant.

'Yes, the little vessels. Pleasure craft, fishing boats, that kind of thing. They can safely navigate much shallower waters, you see. Every single one within reasonable distance of the French coast has been called upon to help.'

Daisy frowned, unable to imagine such an enormous endeavour. 'What, boats like what you see down at Limehouse?' she asked. 'Or on the canal?'

'The small to medium ones, yes. Well, not the rowing boats, they would never manage the distance. But it's not far from Kent to northern France. A whole fleet of small boats is setting off.'

Daisy frowned again. 'But why does that mean that Sam's not here at work with us?'

180

Noise filtered through from the platforms below, of trains arriving or leaving, passengers calling out or just the thrum of dozens of conversations. The staff based on the lower levels appeared and disappeared at the big office window. Buses halted at or departed from the crossroads above. Silence fell between the two colleagues.

Finally Mr Rathbone said, 'Because he's gone with them.'

'What?' Daisy exclaimed at once. 'Sam? But – but he can't even swim!'

Mr Rathbone nodded in acknowledgement. 'No, as I understand it, you are right. However, you may or not be aware that plenty of fishermen can't swim. That doesn't stop them from going to sea day after day. The call went out for volunteers, and Sam has chosen to go.'

Daisy felt an icy chill sweep over her.

'As you are aware, he's often mentioned his friends who work down at the dockyards,' he went on. 'Several of them have decided to go together. They apparently have a medium-sized boat that's sometimes used for smaller cargo, transporting it up and down the Thames. So it must be seaworthy. We shouldn't doubt it. He won't be in any danger from that, at any rate.'

No, thought Daisy. Just from a hundred other things. Like bad weather, high waves, being shot at. Getting hit by a bullet. Drowning. The image flashed into her mind before she could stop it.

Mr Rathbone looked at her sharply. 'Miss Harrison, I realise this has come as a shock, but you must not

181

allow it to distress you. He will be just as capable as anyone else in his position – that is to say, he's a very able young man and we must have faith that he will do his duty and then return unscathed.' He kept his gaze on her anxious face. 'Take heart, Miss Harrison. He won't be alone, he'll be with his friends, and they can handle a boat. It will do none of us any good if we fail to keep things running here. To keep things on track, you might say.' He smiled at his weak pun but Daisy could not bring herself to respond.

She had known Sam resented being unable to join up, thanks to his hated flat feet. It made sense that he'd rushed off to join the rescue mission. She gripped the edge of her desk, forcing away the mental pictures of the cold water, the men floundering. Mr Rathbone was right. It was up to them to carry on in Sam's absence. She'd not realised until now how fond she was of him, how she relied on that friendly, open face.

'I suppose so,' she agreed quietly.

'Very good. Now, we'd better apply ourselves and get as much done as we can, before the arrival of Mr Fraser.' Mr Rathbone gave a sudden grin and Daisy recognised he had about as much faith in their temporary replacement as she did. Still, set alongside what Sam was about to endure, it was small cause for complaint.

CHAPTER NINETEEN

Daisy persuaded Clover to go to the cinema with her while they waited for more news. *Band Waggon* was on and as they were both fans of Arthur Askey, it was the obvious choice. 'It'll take our minds off everything,' Daisy suggested hopefully.

It was still light as they left the Picture Palace, the early summer evening still warm, and people were out enjoying the last of the rays. It was a far cry from the woes of winter, trying not to twist your ankle on the white-painted kerb, avoiding sandbags, wishing you could at least use the full beam on your torch.

What had felt like the disaster of Dunkirk was now being spoken of as a great act of heroism, an example of British bravery and pluck. Newspapers and the wireless carried stories of men who had made it home and the intrepid sailors who'd brought them back, from the experienced fishermen to the total novices who'd wanted to have a go. Some of their tales were hair-raising, but all had contributed to saving many thousands of lives. It was a moment when you felt history being made all around you. It was all very well, but not knowing what had happened to Peter, or Sam, or, as Daisy tried not to think, even Freddy made it hard to celebrate.

Clover stepped neatly to the side to get out of the way of a man shouting that he had the *Evening Standard* for sale. She could guess what the front page would be. 'Did you hear if Sam got home all right yet?' she asked her sister, as a family in front of them stopped so that the mother could buy a paper.

Daisy shook her head. 'No, not yet. Mr Rathbone says we're not to put any store by that, because lots of boats are still to return. So we're going to assume he's fine until we're told otherwise.' She said this staunchly, but Clover wondered if it was quite that simple.

'That's probably very sensible,' she said, because it was true; there was no point in worrying about something that you couldn't change. If she repeated it enough to herself, she might believe it in the end. 'Tell you what, shall we stop off for a drink before heading home? It's such a lovely evening, and who knows when we'll get the chance again. I don't even have to go to work tomorrow, and you don't have an early start.'

Daisy gave a little laugh. 'It would be very daring, wouldn't it. Ma wouldn't approve.'

'Ma needn't know,' said Clover. 'Besides, I used to go out with Sylvia and nobody turned a hair. Things are different now. We don't have to be escorted by a man any more. People respect that we work hard all week for the war effort and deserve a bit of time off at the end, same as anyone else.'

'I should hope so,' said Daisy, straightening the strap of her gas mask.

'Besides, you're eighteen now. You don't have to sneak in.' Clover smiled. 'My treat, for my little sister who seems to be growing up before our very eyes.' She turned off the main street, pointing out the building at the far end of the side road. 'That's not a bad place, and it's got a little beer garden at the back. I bet that catches the last of the sun. We should try there.'

Daisy squinted up at the painted sign as they drew closer. 'The Golden Lion,' she read. 'It rings a bell. Perhaps some of the old gang from the factory talked about it but of course I was too young to go with them then.'

'Course you were.' Clover raised an eyebrow, and then pushed open the door, which had coloured glass panels inset in the top half, although they were criss-crossed with brown tape in case of bomb blasts, just like every other window around.

She led the way to the bar and ordered two lemonades, correctly guessing that her sister was in no hurry to taste shandy again. The glasses were pleasantly cool to the touch and the bubbles rose up in the clear liquid.

'Oooh, that went straight up my nose,' giggled Daisy as she took a sip, keen not to spill any as they wove around the other customers to reach the far door to the garden.

Blinking as she stepped from the dimness of the bar into the brightness of the beer garden, it took her a moment to register the figure sitting on his own in one corner, at a small wooden table. 'Clover, wait a mo,'

she said, as her sister was about to head in the opposite direction. 'I've seen someone I know. If I'm not
much mistaken, that's Chalky – you remember, one of
my old colleagues from the clothing factory.'

Clover stopped and faced her sister. 'I remember all
right. He was there that night when Sylvia met Victor,
wasn't he? I'm not likely to forget that.'

Daisy nodded. 'That's right, but we can't blame him
for what happened. He can't be held responsible for
his cousin. Let's go over and say hello. It'll look odd
if we don't.'

Clover pulled a face. 'All right, but don't go spending
the rest of the evening chatting to him. I know he can't
help it if he's got a cousin like that but I'm not thrilled
at the thought of any of that lot, to tell you the truth.'

Daisy flashed her a look of sympathy. 'I know, I
know. All the same.' She glanced back at the young
man, who was staring at the pint in front of him, and
showing no sign of having seen them. He was in civvies,
not his army uniform, his shirt sleeves rolled up. It
looked as if his hands were shaking, the closer they
got to the table.

She smoothed her skirt as she came to a halt in front
of him. 'Chalky,' she said brightly. 'Thought it was you.
You remember my sister Clover, don't you?'

His hands were definitely shaking, though he was
trying to hide it. The old Chalky would have made a
joke of some kind or at least have responded equally
brightly, but there was none of that now. His eyes were
sunken as he raised his face to look at the sisters, his
lips bitten.

'Daisy,' he said dully, as if it cost him a huge effort. 'Daisy Harrison, as I live and breathe. And Clover, yes, of course, Clover too. Well, it's good to see you both again.'

His voice was croaky and rasping, and he didn't sound pleased at all. It wasn't that he sounded displeased either; it was more as if he didn't care either way. His beer sat in front of him untouched. His shoelaces weren't tied properly and his socks didn't match. Daisy took in all these details without realising that she was doing so. Her eyes grew wide and then she asked the question she almost did not want the answer to.

'Chalky,' she said, the brightness all gone from her tone, 'what on earth has happened?'

'You better sit down,' he said after a long pause. With a trembling hand he reached for his pint and lifted it, managing to take a long draw from it while spilling some from the side of his mouth. Clover found a couple of wobbly wooden stools and pulled them across to the small table. The sisters sat and waited, while Chalky set down his glass once more.

'I just got back,' he said. 'Look at me, not a mark on me, is there? So I must be all right, but I tell you, I don't feel all right. I can't sleep, can hardly sit still, and that's a fact.' He shook his head. 'Our captain said as I should take a few days' leave, come home and get myself right again. We came ashore in Kent, it weren't no distance really. But before that . . .'

Daisy leant forward. 'Go on, Chalky. Do you good to let it out.'

'Don't know as it will.' He thought about picking up his glass again, changed his mind. He cleared his throat and then raised his gaze so that he was looking over the back wall, not meeting their eyes. 'I seen things I never thought to see, things nobody should have to see. So so many . . . they was all in the water, Daisy. All trying to get home, to get on the boats, but there weren't no room.'

Daisy and Clover waited, a chilly knowledge of what was to come creeping over them.

'Start from the beginning, Chalky,' Daisy suggested, as the silence stretched out.

He shook his head again, and then began. 'We was all over in France, like you knew. Nothing happened for ages. We was going on patrols and marches and it was all quiet. We was all together, me and my brother Bernard and Terry and Victor, we was having a great laugh to be honest. We tried the local wine and it was gut rot but we kept trying anyway. Victor even got himself a girl. Well, we all wanted to but Victor was the one who managed it, like he always done.'

I bet he did, thought Daisy. And I bet Terry kept on trying as well.

'Then all that came to an end when Jerry decided to come through France. It was all so fast. Then we was leaving our camp and moving west and we had to leave all our equipment behind. For weeks and months it was nothing but look after your equipment, polish it, everything in order, and then it was leave it behind, don't go back for anything, just keep what you can carry and move like the clappers. I don't reckon anyone saw it coming; it was chaos, that's what it was.

'For ages it was all little lanes and fields and then we got to the beaches and there weren't nowhere else to go. We all set up as best we could, on the sand or just behind. We were still together, us four, we shared a tent and ate together, had our cups of tea on the beach. If you just looked straight ahead at the sea you could tell yourself you were on holiday with your mates, but of course it weren't like that really. And Victor was in a terrible temper because he hadn't wanted to leave his new girlfriend.

'So the captain says we're going to get rescued and the navy is sending ships.'

Daisy held her breath in case by some good fortune there would be news of Freddy, but she was disappointed.

'Then the big ships can't get close and all these little boats turn up and we have to walk into the water to reach them. All of us all crammed together in the cold water, in our uniforms, and they got all wet and heavy and dragged us down. We couldn't swim, not one of us ever bothered to learn, you know, Daisy. I mean, why would we, we never went to the beach except one week down Margate when we was nippers, Bernard and me that is. Anyway. So the boats get close and some of the others start climbing in or getting pulled out of the water. We think we're going to be all right, a bit wet maybe but all right.'

He stopped for a moment, took a swig of beer.

'Turns out we wasn't all right at all. Jerry's planes arrive and start shooting at us in the water. Like sitting targets, we was. Nowhere to go, you couldn't even duck under the water, they still shot at you. There was blood everywhere; one moment we're standing up to our armpits in sea water, the next it's all red and we're surrounded by blood.' He shut his eyes. 'It was everywhere and I can't stop seeing it. Like a big red river, and all over our clothes, our bags if we still had them, all red with it.

'But it didn't stop the little boats, they kept on coming in as well. I don't know how long it was, it felt like days but it wasn't, and one gets close to us and they somehow pull Bernard up over the side. I start shouting, that's my brother, that's my brother, and then hands reach out to me, and one old man with a beard catches hold of my arm and he says, you come up here with me and you can be with your brother. And he pulls me up as well and I fall on top of Bernard but neither of us care, we're in the boat.

'Then Bernard says, that's our cousin down there and our mate. We got to rescue them too. The boat's already full with other solders we don't know but the old man says, all right, let's have a go. And he turns to look over the side and I sort of sit up so I can point out who we mean.'

He halted again, and passed his hand across his face, as if steeling himself to go on.

'And then . . . then that's when Jerry comes back. The plane went right over our heads – and the noise of it, Daisy, I'll never forget it. The engines, and then the gunfire. They didn't stand a chance. I saw it right in front of my eyes.'

'You don't have to tell us if you don't want to,' Clover said, anxious now, as Chalky took a deep breath. He continued as if he hadn't heard her.

'They shot Victor and Terry like they was fish in a barrel. Them and scores of others. Almost as close to us as you are now. Not a thing we could do to help them, we were only yards away but I couldn't . . . I couldn't . . .' He took another deep, heaving breath. 'They were goners. Only good thing about it is, at least we know for certain. Saw it with my own eyes so there won't be no doubt, no waiting around for news. Then the old man says, right, boys, we can't do no more, we're heading for home. Somehow he points that boat at Blighty and brings us home. I don't remember much about it, to be honest, I don't know if I slept or collapsed after what we saw or what. After a bit they shake me by the shoulder and say, wake up, son, that's Kent over there, that is. And we got home.'

Daisy didn't know what to say. She realised she had been gripping the side of the wooden stool, her knuckles white. She opened her mouth to try to respond but nothing came out.

Clover blinked slowly, as if trying to take in the horror of it. 'You got back. You did it somehow,' she managed to choke out, finally.

Chalky shrugged. 'They say in the papers we were all brave but we weren't. We just did what we were told. It wasn't like we thought it would be – we didn't even get to fire our guns. Just mown down in the water, they was.'

'I'm so sorry,' Daisy said, very quietly.

'Bernard, he didn't say much, but he got hurt in the middle of it all. Turns out he caught a bullet in his arm, so they took him off to hospital soon as we landed.

191

There were all these ambulances ready and waiting. So he tells us he's been shot once he knows he'll be taken care of, and they send him off in the back of one of them. They check me over and say I'm all right but my captain was there somehow, he must have been picked up by a different boat, and he comes over to talk to me. I tell him what happened and he says I got to come back here for a few days, like what I said to you before.'

Chalky slumped as if he had no more energy left in him, now that his tale had come full circle. Then he straightened a little as one last thought came to him.

'Tell you what, though, I know who was brave. That old man. He must have been my granddad's age, and there he is, out on the sea, no guns or nothing to defend us or his crew or hisself. He should have a medal.' The sisters nodded in agreement. 'He saved us, me and Bernard and all the rest packed into that boat. We owe our lives to him. That's what bravery is.'

Daisy and Clover began their walk home in stunned silence, each replaying what Chalky had said. Eventually Daisy asked, 'Do you mind if we stop here for a moment?'

They were near the solid wall outside St Mark's Church, and its grand shadow gave them a little privacy. Daisy leant against the wall and covered her face with her hands, her shoulders shaking as she sobbed. 'Oh, Clover. It's too much. What must it have been like? All that blood and your friends dying right in front of you. It could have been Peter, it could have been Peter!'

Clover rubbed her back through her thin cotton top. 'But he wasn't serving alongside them, we don't even know if he was there,' she said. 'Now at least we know some made it back.'

Daisy turned her tear-stained face to her sister. 'Yes, but it was luck, wasn't it? Like Chalky said, it's not whether you were brave or not. It's chance. He got back, Victor and Terry didn't.' She shuddered. 'I know I didn't like Terry that much but he was always the life and soul of the party, and I can't believe he's dead. He wasn't that much older than us.'

'I know.' Clover sighed. She'd hardly known the young men but remembered how excited they had been at Christmas, in their uniforms, the big adventure lying ahead of them. Now that adventure had come to a sudden end, nothing like they'd imagined. 'And I don't want to speak ill of the dead, but Victor – well, he treated Sylvia badly but he didn't deserve to die for it. Nobody deserves that. And like you say, not that much older than us either. Poor Chalky, losing his friend and his cousin like that.'

Daisy groaned as the sharp surface of the wall began to dig into her back. 'I bet he feels it should have been him. He looked up to Terry, all that gang did. He won't forgive himself for living when Terry died. Like he said, he doesn't have a mark on him but he's hurt all the same, it's just a different sort of hurt.'

Clover looked sadly at her sister. She couldn't call her a baby any longer, not when she came out with ideas like that. This war was making them all grow up fast. She was meant to be the adult here, if only by a couple of years, but her heart was heavy. It was too huge a feeling to put into words but she did her best.

'Look, everything's chance when you think about it,' she said slowly. 'We were born here and not in France, or anywhere else. We haven't got the Nazis overrunning our country, or at least not yet. That's nothing to do with us, just an accident of birth. The thing is, we got to make the best of what we've got, and that's what we're doing.'

'Suppose so.' Daisy gave a sniff. 'I'm going to try really hard, like Terry won't have a chance to do. It's as if, we got to do that bit extra to make up for those who can't do it no more. If you see what I mean.'

Clover nodded. 'Yes, I do. I sort of feel the same. It's up to those that are left to carry on, cos we don't want the Nazis to win. I bet Peter will be back fighting the moment he can, cos that's what he's like. We got to assume he's all right because we haven't heard anything different. And we got to hope that Chalky gets some rest and then feels better, so he can do whatever he's needed to do.'

Daisy raised her eyebrows. 'It might take more than a few days by the looks of him.'

'Maybe. We don't know, do we? Perhaps Rose deals with that sort of thing. We could ask her. She's coming over on Sunday for tea.'

Daisy stood up and brushed dust from the wall from her sleeves. 'Let's do that. Poor Chalky. At least he's still got Brendan. That must help. Oh, I do hope Sam's all right. Mr Rathbone might have heard more by tomorrow.'

Clover gave a small smile. 'That's the spirit. We can't do nothing about it so don't lose hope. Tomorrow might bring better news. Come on, we should be getting home. Ma will worry, and she's got enough on her plate.'

'She has,' Daisy agreed, and Clover thought again that her baby sister had changed over the past six months. She might not have seen things so easily from their mother's perspective before.

Daisy hesitated. 'Clover, will you tell Sylvia about this? She ought to know, oughtn't she?'

Clover's smile faded. 'That's the first thing I thought of, as soon as Chalky told us what had happened. I couldn't say anything then as he probably didn't know anything about it. We don't even know if Victor knew about the baby, or what he planned to do if he did get that letter.'

'He got himself a French girlfriend though, didn't he. So I bet we can guess,' Daisy said darkly.

Clover exhaled loudly. 'Well, I shan't tell Sylvia about the girlfriend. She's got no need to know that and I can't see how it would help. But yes.' She scuffed her feet along the pavement, not wanting to imagine how the conversation was likely to go. 'Yes, I'll have to tell her, won't I? I don't want her to hear it from anyone else, that's for certain. So it had better come from me. I don't want to, Daisy, but I will. I'll tell her.' Having made her resolve, she tucked her arm through the crook of her sister's elbow and the two young women sadly made their way home in the last rays of the bright June sunshine.

CHAPTER TWENTY

Patty didn't know what was worse, being rushed off her feet with a batch of new deliveries and having nobody to help unload – the usual man had gone off to Dunkirk to join the rescue effort and pulled his back – or getting home to find there was still no news. Whichever way she turned, there was the huge wall of anxiety. It was up there with the worst of Robbie's days of sickness, when they'd wondered if he would pull through.

At least then she'd been able to do something to make things better: putting Vicks on his chest to help the breathing, rubbing his poor little back when it ached from coughing, making his favourite comfort food, like mashed potato and bringing him cups of Bovril to make him strong again.

What she wouldn't give to be able to do the same for Peter now. She tried not to think of him lying dead in a French ditch. Maybe he was cold on board a ship, shivering on deck, his heavy uniform sodden, or lost on a beach somewhere. How he'd love a mug of her pea and ham soup.

Snap out of it, my girl, she told herself as she tidied the kitchen for the umpteenth time to give her hands something to do. You can make him pea and ham soup when he's back. In fact, she'd start a list of what he'd like. She could save her rations to come up with something special. Perhaps she'd even ask Vera if she could put a little aside from hers, just because it was Peter.

Stepping through the door from her kitchen to the back yard, she felt the rush of welcome warmth from the sun. At this time of day, early evening, its rays had moved around from her collection of pots by the door to fall directly on the far end of the shelter. Patty bent down to inspect her plants, which she'd been tending diligently come what may.

Her tomatoes were coming on nicely, even though she'd feared they would hate their new position, that it would be too crowded for them. They were some way off fruiting yet, but they showed no sign of mildew or straggly growth. Carefully she pinched out some side shoots, and reached into her apron pocket for a piece of twine. Handling the stems gently, she tied a loop around a bright green branch and fastened it to the length of wonky wooden offcut that she was using as a cane.

Then she checked her rosemary, the scent of which always calmed her no matter what. When they'd run out of Vicks, she'd sometimes poured hot water over a few cut sprigs to make a strong-smelling steam, which she would encourage Robbie to inhale. It had seemed to help him. She hadn't thought of that for a while; she must remember to ask Rose if it actually did any

197

good. These days, thank heaven, she mostly used it to flavour her roast vegetables on a Sunday.

The next couple of pots held her mint plants. She pressed some of the leaves together so that their aroma would rise through the warm air. She loved to breathe in that distinctive scent, and she wondered if she could use that in pea soup if they couldn't get enough ham. That would be an idea. She was sure she'd manage something.

Inspecting the plant more carefully, she decided that it needed watering. That was the trouble with everything being crowded together in this part of the yard. It all got the full heat of the midday sun, and you had to remember to water the pots morning and evening. Now that they were in the shade she could go ahead and do it without the water going to waste, evaporating into the air. She scanned the yard for her watering can.

There it was, by the drainpipe. She was glad that Bert had had the foresight to buy a new one for her last summer, correctly predicting that such things could be hard to come by in the event of war. It clanked as she carried it through the doorway to the kitchen sink, where she could just about fit it under the tap.

It was touch and go, however. She hadn't liked to tell Bert that it was really too big and she had to jam it in sideways. She'd just about got the angle right when there was a knock at the front door and she looked up in annoyance. Typical. If she left it now, it would tip over and all the water would spill over her lino.

The knock came again, and she hurriedly dried her

hands on her apron and ran through the hallway. For once she was the only person in the house: Robbie had gone round to the Glanvilles, apparently to do homework together although she wasn't sure she believed it; Bert was working late, as was Daisy; Clover could never say what time she would be home as she was at the mercy of the buses.

So it was just Patty who was there when the telegram boy drew out his envelope and asked if she was Mrs Harrison. Patty automatically said yes, held out her hand for the telegram, and thanked the lad, but it was as if she was watching herself do all of this from out of her body. There she was, a woman of middle age, with faded chestnut hair partly held back by a scarf, a well-worn striped apron tied over an old pleated skirt and off-white blouse full of creases after all day in the shop. Her shoes were in need of a polish, her fingernails could do with a scrub after tending the plants.

The smell of those plants brought her back: the rosemary, mint and lingering green scent of tomatoes. She swallowed hard and stared at the paper in her hand. Suddenly she couldn't bear the sun, and shut the door on it and the outside world. She sank onto the lowest step of the staircase and folded forward on herself, gasping for breath. If this was the news she had been dreading, she didn't want to see it.

But she had to know. With shaking fingers she fumbled the dreaded paper open and tried to focus as the words swam about before her eyes.

The telegram had only one line.

Ma, Pa. Back safe. More to follow. Love Peter. Stop

For a moment she feared that she'd got it wrong, that she'd seen what she wanted to see rather than what was there – that in truth it was to tell her he had perished in his attempt to escape the sands of Dunkirk. But no. She read it again. The words were the same. Back safe.

Then all the worry she had carried with her ever since the news of the invasion broke, and the weeks and months of anxiety before that, hit her in a wave. The tears came, the ones she'd never dared release in case any of her family saw them. She was the one who had to dry their tears; they must never know the dread she carried inside. Yet now Peter was safe, she could let them flow at last, knowing her boy had made it home.

CHAPTER TWENTY-ONE

It was as bad as Clover had thought it would be. Part of her wanted to postpone the dreaded conversation, to hold on to her own delight that her brother had survived. But she knew she couldn't. She waited until she and Sylvia were taking their sandwiches to the bench under the trees in the park nearby and there was no risk anyone from their department would see them or overhear.

Sylvia had known that something was up. 'Out with it,' she'd said, pausing the unwrapping of her food. A pigeon hopped around on the gravel at the end of the bench, its eyes bright with hope of finding some crumbs.

Clover had shut her eyes briefly, praying for inspiration, but then had jumped right in and repeated what Chalky had said. She left out the reference to the girl-friend, the blood and the terror. She kept it as short as she could. Even so, the bare basics were horrific enough.

At first Sylvia was totally silent, taking in what her friend had said. Then she had started to cry, softly to begin with, but then great heaving sobs. Her sandwich lay forgotten beside her. Clover watched sadly, knowing her friend had to let the tears flow. When the worst of the sobs had abated, she edged closer along the bench and took Sylvia's hand.

'It's horrible, I know. I wish I hadn't had to tell you, but you needed to know.'

Sylvia nodded, and rubbed her eyes. 'It's the shock of it. I mean, of course you know that not everyone made it back and that people died, but you don't ever think it'll be anyone you know yourself. Those poor boys, that's all they were really, just boys.' She stopped and blew out a long breath. 'As for Victor, well, I don't know what to say. I thought I'd got it all straight in my mind, and knew what I'd tell him if I ever saw him again, but that isn't going to happen now.'

She paused once more, shaking her head slightly. 'I'll never know if he got my letter or not. And if he did, what he was going to do about it. He'll never know that there wasn't a baby after all. After everything that I went through, he'll never know, and to tell you the truth I hated him for it. I had all that happen to me and he was off living it up in France, or that's how I saw it. And then he goes and dies. Oh, I'm horrible, to say such a thing. Clover, do you hate me?' She turned to her friend.

'No, of course not,' Clover said at once. 'You're bound to feel that way. None of this changes what happened before, it just puts it in a bit of a different light. You're in shock, it's only natural. You let it all out, it doesn't matter. I won't hate you for any of it, I promise.'

Sylvia sniffed and rubbed her eyes some more. 'Thank you, Clover. You're a good friend.' Then she laughed bitterly. 'Bet you didn't reckon on all of this when you first met me, did you? Just as well we didn't know what was around the corner.'

'Don't be silly,' Clover said.

Sylvia reached for her sandwich and idly broke off a small piece of crust. She threw it to the pigeon, who immediately pecked at it in delight. 'It might as well have it, I've lost my appetite,' she said in a small voice. 'It's so strange – here we are sitting on a bench under some nice trees and the sun's out, and it'll never shine on Victor and Terry again. Or on all the rest of them. It doesn't seem real.' She crumbled some more crust and scattered it on the ground.

'I'm glad you told me,' she went on. 'What if I'd heard it down the pub or something like that, and it all got changed in the telling like Chinese whispers? That would have been awful. At least here I can make a fool of myself and nobody's any the wiser. I'll go back and tidy myself up and carry on like nothing's happened.'

Clover nodded. 'I wanted to tell you, so you'd know exactly how it was. It's only fair. Well, if anything can be fair in all of this. Look, I'll eat my sandwich and we can have a bit of a breather. We don't have to go back for another fifteen minutes.'

Sylvia took out her handkerchief and blotted the rest of her tears, and after a while began to nibble on what was left of her own sandwich. Then she glanced at her watch and saw that Clover was doing the same.

'Better be getting back now,' she said, her voice steadier. The tears had dried. Her eyes were still red but it was only apparent up close. She stood up and brushed the last of the crumbs from her skirt. 'Do you know what, Clover, it's a terrible thing to say but maybe the miscarriage was meant to happen. I thought I wanted to die myself for a little while, but now I can see it was for the best, in the long run. I'll make a new start somehow. No baby, no Victor; none of that's going to happen now.'

Clover stood as well, folding her greaseproof paper back into her bag so that it could be re-used. 'We don't know what's in store,' she said gently. 'Maybe you'll meet someone who treats you right and then it'll be the time to think about babies.'

Sylvia shrugged. 'Maybe. I shan't go rushing into anything, that's for sure.'

Clover nodded. 'Exactly. Come on, time to go.'

They made their way towards the park entrance, and the pigeon hopped happily across to the fallen crumbs.

Even Mr Fraser was pleased to see Sam back safe and sound, although they scarcely knew one another. Daisy was doubly pleased; she'd just about kept her lip buttoned working with their temporary colleague but she couldn't wait to see the back of him. Now he would be returning to Wood Green for his next shift and truly they were welcome to him.

Then, of course, she was both delighted and relieved that Sam had returned. The short delay in his reappearance had preyed on her mind, even if she realised rationally that it did not help to assume the worst. After all that she now knew about the horrors of Dunkirk, it was hard not to conjure up an image of Sam perishing in a similar fashion.

However, this morning Mr Rathbone had arrived with a spring in his step and a smile on his usually solemn face. He told her the news at once: that he'd received a telegram from Sam's mother, saying they were to expect him before midday. Sure enough, at half past eleven the sound of the young man's footsteps heralded his arrival in the ticket hall and then through to the office.

Mr Rathbone and Daisy instantly stood up, unplanned, and Daisy couldn't help clapping. 'Sam! You're back!'

'As you can see.' Sam held out his arms and turned full circle, although his movements were slightly clumsy. 'I'd have been here earlier only my old dear insisted on calling in the doctor to check me over. Weren't no need but it put her mind at rest, so I went along with it.'

Daisy rushed over to him. 'Are you hurt? What happened? Did you get shot at in the boat? Why did it take you so long?'

Mr Rathbone cleared his throat. 'One thing at a time, Miss Harrison. Give the fellow a chance.'

Sam laughed off the barrage of questions. 'Any chance of a cuppa? You know I never expect you to wait on me hand and foot, Daisy, but just this once?'

Daisy collected herself and nodded, rushing to do as he asked. They could be in for a long bout of story-telling and explanations and the least he deserved was some refreshment to help him along.

Once settled at his desk, Sam recounted how he'd joined his dockworker friends in their boat, heading across the Channel in the flotilla of small craft. 'I never been so cold in all me life, not even that time it snowed and we ran out of coal. Good job it was summer, I'd have hated to try it in the depths of winter.' He shivered to emphasise his point. Then they'd followed the rest of the vessels to the French coast, 'and we could get in closer than most, on account of the size of our keel.' Daisy had been mystified but hadn't wanted to interrupt to check what he meant.

Sam had made the rescue sound very matter-of-fact, and again Daisy hadn't wanted to chime in to see if he'd witnessed the bloodbath that Chalky had described. Sam played down the difficulty of filling their boat with soldiers. 'Some of them was injured and they was all soaking wet, our poor little boat was heavy as could be. My mate what knows about these things was a bit worried, said we were low in the water, but we turned around and got back to Blighty. We were a bit slower than we wanted, what with all of that. Main thing is, though, we all made it and we unloaded all those injured lads in Kent.'

Daisy looked at him askance. 'So if it all went so well, how come you had to see the doctor?' Doctors were expensive; they weren't called in for any old complaint.

Sam tried to shrug off her concern but Mr Rathbone cleared his throat. 'Samuel, do tell us, or we won't be able to make allowances if it becomes necessary.'

Sam pulled a face. 'You don't need to go making allowances or nothing. The truth is, I ricked my ankle, like a bloody idiot, pardon my language. All that way over to France and back and not a spot of bother, but when we was unloading the casualties – well, the quayside was all slick and wet, you can imagine, and I fell over like a fool. Turned my ankle, that's all it was. My mates what are used to the slippery jetties down the docks had a good laugh at my expense. Still, it's not broken, and I can get about on it now.'

'Well, we're very glad to have you back,' Mr Rathbone had said warmly, and Sam had glowed at the praise.

'Are you pleased then, Daisy?' he grinned.

'Of course,' she said, and he beamed even more widely.

But later that afternoon, he was less pleased.

Daisy couldn't help it; she was all but hugging herself with anticipation. She couldn't quite believe her daring. While it was hardly on a par with sailing to France on a pitifully small boat and rescuing injured soldiers, she felt she had done something rather brave, in a totally different way.

Ted Burnett had appeared once more in the ticket hall and of course she'd gone out to see if she could be of help. She didn't want his journey ruined by one of the last acts of Mr Fraser, who was departing for his usual post in a couple of hours' time. Perhaps buoyed by Sam's reappearance, she'd been even more cheerful than usual and couldn't help but notice that Ted had picked up on this. In fact she was not even surprised when he had, at the end of their conversation, asked if she might be free on Friday evening. 'There's a lovely little pub I know not too far from here, very respectable,' he'd said. Daisy had tried to appear doubtful and to pretend to consider the matter, but her heart wasn't in it. She'd accepted almost at once.

Fancy her, Daisy Harrison, being asked out by such a good-looking and sophisticated man as Ted Burnett! Despite herself she could not help but be flattered. She knew it was silly to start to imagine where this might lead, but she gave in to temptation anyway. She could see herself being taken to lovely restaurants, where they would serve food the likes of which she'd never tasted, perhaps never even heard of. Trips to the theatre. Something more adventurous than the usual cinemas with her sisters. Suddenly they seemed like very boring choices indeed, in comparison to what Ted could offer.

She had done her best to keep her cool as they'd said farewell, with him smiling in that special way that he had, promising to meet on Friday. Once he'd disappeared down to the platforms, she'd practically done a little dance of happiness.

Then she caught sight of Sam's face. All his pleasure from the morning's praise was wiped clean away.

Once she was back at her desk he would hardly meet her eyes, let alone speak to her. He deliberately turned his back, apparently finding something overwhelmingly urgent in the filing cabinets behind him. Daisy waited until Mr Fraser had finally departed and Mr Rathbone had stepped outside for a moment to tackle him.

'Sam! Whatever's wrong?'

'Nothing.' He had not turned round.

Daisy got up from her desk and went over to him. 'Is it your ankle? Is it hurting more that you let on?'

'No,' he grunted impatiently. 'My ankle's fine.'

'Then what is it?' She folded her arms, determined to get to the bottom of whatever was troubling him.

Finally he swivelled round to face her. 'Oh, come on, Daisy. How long has it been – weeks, months even? – since you said you'd come out for a drink with me on a Friday evening after work? You agreed, and then you never actually do it. It's always something – you got to help your mother, or you've arranged something with your sisters, or got an early start the next day. But when that bloke turns up who, let's face it, you don't know from Adam, you're all over him. I heard you clear as a bell. You're off with him on Friday night without so much as a second thought. Well, I hope you know what you're doing, that's all I can say.'

Daisy gasped. 'What do you mean? I do know him! I've spoken to him lots of times.'

Sam raised his eyebrows. 'You know exactly what I mean. You don't know him well at all, don't pretend. He's flashy as can be, anyone can see that. Ask yourself why he's not off fighting. Paid someone to look the other way, has he?'

Daisy was incensed. 'How can you even think such a thing. He's a real gentleman. He's smart and funny and good company. Why shouldn't I go for a drink with him? It's only a visit to the pub, I'm not running off with him.'

'Why shouldn't you go for a drink with him? Why do you think? You don't know him from Adam.'

Daisy felt herself blushing. Why was Sam being so mean? It wasn't as if there was anything between them. They were colleagues and she had thought they were friends. Perhaps she had been wrong.

'I think that trip to France has addled your brain,' she said sharply. 'You were never like this before.' As if she didn't have enough people at home telling her what she could and couldn't do, that she was too young to make her own decisions. Well, she'd decided now. She was going for a drink with Ted and nobody would stop her.

Sam leant back a little and closed his eyes. 'Have it your own way, no doubt you know best, Daisy,' he said quietly. Then he tried to lighten the atmosphere. 'Seriously, what's a man to do to get you to keep your promise, eh? I go all that way and rescue a boatload of our brave boys, bring them home to Blighty and this is the thanks I get.' He gave a wry grin.

Daisy smiled, relieved he was joking again. 'Don't be daft, we were worried stupid while you were gone. We even had to put up with Mr Fraser. So we were thankful to see you again.'

Sam looked at her sadly. 'Were you really, Daisy? Maybe. But not worried enough to come for a drink with me. You'll go out with that smarmy stranger, but you won't raise a glass with your old mate.'

Now she was sure there was nothing more to it, he was just being friendly, even if he was a bit put out. 'Of course we were worried. Just as Mr Rathbone said.

Anyway, it's not the same. Like you say, we're mates. We can go out at any time. We do go out, like at dinner time. It's completely different.'

Sam lifted his hands in surrender. 'All right, Daisy. If you say so.'

'I do say so.' The sight of Mr Rathbone returning brought an end to their conversation, and she tried to push it from her mind as she got back to her work.

At the end of her shift she picked up her handbag and gas mask, departing without looking back, and so she missed the expression on Sam's face.

CHAPTER TWENTY-TWO

'I'm sorry, Clover. You do understand, don't you?'

Sylvia wrung her hands and looked so woebegone that Clover hastened to reassure her, even though she was still absorbing what her friend had just said. It was a morning like so many others, transferring boxes to and from the storeroom, keeping careful notes of what went where and what needed reordering. Now Sylvia had decided she didn't want to do it any longer.

'It's all the memories. Knowing what happened to me in here, all those weeks beforehand of trying to keep it a secret and then being so sick. Every time I pass the cloakroom door it reminds me. I can't even bear to go in there – if I need the bathroom I have to go to a different floor.'

Clover had nodded, realising that this was all too likely. She could recall the scene all too vividly herself. It made sense, and now Sylvia had applied to work alongside her sister in her department.

All the same, Clover felt slightly offended. She knew it was unreasonable to react in that way, and yet she couldn't help it. She'd done everything she could to help her friend, talking through all her options, supporting her and covering for her, and now she was being left alone in the boring old storeroom. She might have to train up a newcomer, and there was no saying if she'd get on well with her. When it was just the two of you for protracted periods of time, you had to rub along together or it would be a disaster.

And then, of course, there was always that lingering resentment: she had given up her chance of going to France when Sylvia confessed she was pregnant. Never mind that the BEF's days on the Continent had ended so terribly. Logically, she recognised how dreadful it would have been – but she had longed for that chance, and still a part of her regretted not trying for the posting.

However, there was no point in spilling all this to Sylvia. Clover had chosen to stay and help her friend; it wasn't Sylvia's fault. 'No, no, of course I understand,' she said now. 'It will do you a world of good to get away from here, and to work with your sister.'

Sylvia gave a small smile of relief. 'I'm glad you see it like that. I'd hate to be the one left in the lurch and I wouldn't have done it if everything hadn't happened the way it did. I've told my sister the full story,' she went on. 'She wasn't very surprised and she'll look after me, just like you've done.'

Clover kept her expression kind and understanding, but that made her want to scream. So she was being chucked aside for Sylvia's sister, now the painful crisis was over. 'Yes, I expect she will,' she managed to say. 'Have you spoken to Miss Linton yet?'

213

'I'm going to see her later this morning,' Sylvia said. 'I don't suppose she'll be very surprised either. Funny the way it's turned out. She used to drive me mad but now we've seen a different side to her. Maybe it's just because she's over thirty. We might be just like her when we're that old.'

Clover pulled a face. 'Maybe you're right.'

Even so, she hadn't been expecting a summons to the staffroom that afternoon, where Miss Linton sat straight-backed in an armchair, a notebook open on a small table at her side. 'Harrison. Clover. Thank you for coming.'

Clover nodded politely, thinking that it wasn't as if she had much choice in the matter. She racked her brains for any misdemeanour that might merit a telling-off, but came up with nothing. She'd been a model of good behaviour and discipline lately.

'I dare say you are wondering what this is about.' Miss Linton waved her to a chair and smiled. 'Don't worry, you aren't in any kind of trouble.'

'Oh, good,' said Clover, sitting as indicated. She cast a curious glance at the notebook but there was little to see, and nothing that gave any more clues.

'Well.' Miss Linton clasped her hands together and rested them on her lap. 'As you are aware, your colleague has requested a transfer to head office and I shall be recommending her. It would be unkind not to, given her history in this building.'

Clover nodded again and waited.

'The question therefore is, will you wish to remain?' Miss Linton arched an eyebrow. 'I recall how keen you were to apply for the posting to France, but that is now no longer possible.' She paused, to gauge Clover's reaction. 'It strikes me that you would be well suited to something a little more challenging, shall we say. We none of us know what is coming but you will, like all of us, have heard the rumours of a possible invasion. I am in no position to predict whether that is likely or not but I am certain our defences must be further strengthened.'

Clover frowned. What was her superior officer suggesting?

'Of course our government is very concerned that women should not bear arms as such, no firing of guns or anything like that. Still, there are opportunities to be closer to the front line. We need women who are not afraid of action, who are disciplined and committed to the cause and who can show initiative under fire.' Miss Linton looked Clover directly in the eye. 'I've already told you that I feel you are ready for more, Harrison, and permit me to add that the recent unfortunate events only confirmed that impression. You are obviously not squeamish and can cope with sudden and unpleasant emergencies.'

Clover blushed. 'I don't know about that. I only did what anybody else would have done.'

'Pfft.' Miss Linton was having none of it. 'Take it from me, Harrison, that there are plenty of young women, men too, who simply fall apart when faced with such situations. You, as I have seen for myself, do not.' She leant forward. 'Now, don't think I'm saying this to get rid of you. I should be sorry to lose someone so competent. But I can train up new recruits to do your job. It might take them longer and they may not be as reliable but I do not feel I should stand in your way should you wish to progress.'

'I see.' Clover was not actually sure that she did, but was beginning to form an idea.

'Nearly every other position would involve moving to a training camp. It's highly unusual that you have not had the regular basic training, and then you would need to specialise. Will that be a problem? Are you especially needed by your family?'

Clover thought quickly. Rose was working nearby and always available to help if, to imagine the worst, something befell Robbie. Daisy was maturing at a far faster rate since the war began. Peter was safe, for now at least. Her parents would encourage her to try something new, and would be proud of her, while her mother would hide her anxiety.

'Not especially,' she said firmly. 'I'm very happy to relocate.'

'Good. I thought as much.' Miss Linton picked up her notebook and flipped a page. 'South Coast, Harrison. Many airfields, primed to take the fight to the Nazis in the air. Many big towns, even cities. A prime target in so many ways, and in need of stout defence. May I put your name forward?'

Clover swallowed hard; this was all very sudden. Then she remembered how she'd felt when Sylvia admitted she was leaving.

'Yes please,' she said, before she could reconsider. 'Thank you, Miss Linton. Yes, I'd love to try.'

CHAPTER TWENTY-THREE

Daisy checked her appearance in the mirror on the staff cloakroom wall. She had bought herself a lipstick, rather than borrowing her sisters', and now carefully painted a bow shape on her upper lip. She blotted it and repeated the action, frowning as she did so, wanting to make sure it was absolutely accurate. It was a cheerful shade of dark pink: not too showy, but not too subtle either.

She had changed from her sober work blouse into a brighter one with a vivid pattern of green leaves winding around blue flowers, which livened up her dark skirt. She couldn't fit an entire change of wardrobe into her bag, but she reckoned this would do the trick. She was only going to a local pub, not an expensive restaurant in the West End – yet.

She had debated whether to tell Clover what she was doing and using that as an excuse to borrow her perfume but had decided not to. Clover would be bound to tease her and, after all the trouble with Sam earlier in the week, Daisy had had enough of that. Still, he'd seemed happier the next day and they'd kept the peace in the office, and if Mr Rathbone had noticed that the atmosphere was strained at times, he hadn't said anything.

She hummed to herself as she checked her collar, tugging it so that the last few creases fell out. She looked smart and she knew it. She would not let Ted down by looking shabby. She might be young and new to this adult life, but she had standards and was determined to show them.

She'd spent so long on her preparations that she was almost late, so that she had to dash through the ticket hall and up the steps, with no time to say goodbye to Sam, still at his desk in the office. The angled rays of sunlight caught her well-brushed hair as she emerged at ground level, and several workers waiting for the number 29 at the bus stop turned to catch a second glance.

Daisy was scarcely aware of it as she hurried to the street where Ted had said he would meet her. Then she wouldn't have to walk into the pub on her own. She thought this was kind of him, recognising that some women would be embarrassed to do such a thing. She hadn't liked to say that she didn't actually know if that was how she would feel, as she'd never done it.

She slowed her step as she approached the street, the noise of the Seven Sisters Road fading as she walked away from it. The houses here were taller than her home, mostly three storeys, and some had women and children sitting on the broad stone steps leading up to the front doors, enjoying the early evening sun. The houses were arranged in terraces, with alleys every now and then, which she might not have noticed but a cat ran out of one of them. You didn't see domestic pets around much any more; people didn't know if they would be able to feed them as the war restrictions tightened and so tended not to get them.

'Good puss,' Daisy called quietly, for a moment missing the cat they had had when she was little, who had long since gone to meet its mouse-catching maker. Then she stopped herself. She wasn't a child now. Besides, the tabby was not in the slightest bit interested, as it sleekly vanished behind a dustbin.

There was the street name she'd been looking for, and there was Ted himself. He was reading a newspaper and so she had a minute to take in the sight of him: a light summer suit, a shirt that was open at the collar, thanks to the heat. His shoes were shiny, his hair groomed, and he looked every inch the gentleman. Her heart skipped a beat when he glanced up and saw her.

'You came after all!' he said genially, stepping towards her. 'I thought I might have got the time wrong.'

Oh no, she'd made herself late by looking in the mirror for too long. 'No, no, it was my fault,' she assured him, now wrong-footed. 'I – I couldn't get away from work any earlier.'

He smiled widely. 'I know how hard you work at that place. Well, you'll have to make it up to me by allowing me to choose you a drink. What do you say?'

He steered her by the elbow to the pub entrance, which was altogether more impressive than that of the Dog and Fiddle or Golden Lion. It had solid pillars to either side of the double doors and an archway over the top, with plaster decorations of geometrical shapes. From inside came a hum of conversations and laughter, and when Ted opened one of the doors for her she could see it was already busy.

'Well, all right,' she said, impressed by the scale of the place, even though she'd been intending to ask for a lemonade. But that would be babyish. She wasn't out with Clover now, or trying to convince her big brother that she liked shandy. Ted would choose something suitable. He seemed at home here – he was most likely one of those people who were at home anywhere.

'I'll find us somewhere nice to sit,' he said, somehow clearing a path for her through the throng. 'How about over there? It will be quieter if we are a bit out of the way, around that corner.' There was a table and velour-cushioned bench seat in a far corner, almost in an alcove, away from the cut and thrust of the Friday-evening crowd celebrating the end of the working week, or at least those of them who didn't do extra shifts over the weekend. A Friday was a Friday, after all.

Daisy sat and watched as Ted made his way to the bar, reaching it apparently without effort. He wasn't one of those men who had to push and shove to get where he wanted, Daisy marvelled. Space seemed to open up for him. She decided she liked that in a man. There he was now, talking to the barman, a middle-aged fellow with a red face. The man looked across at her and observed her for a moment before turning back to Ted, saying something which made them both laugh.

She wondered what drink he thought she might like and hoped it wasn't shandy. No, this looked darker and it was in a smaller glass. It looked horribly like that stuff Sylvia had been drinking when she'd seen her in the pub – but now Ted had bought this for her, so it must be all right after all. She would make herself like it, no matter how it tasted. He set it down before her and it sparkled in the light from the window behind her, the panes of which were of patterned glass with the usual tape across them.

Ted raised his own drink, a pint of bitter. 'Your very good health, Miss Harrison.'

She blushed. 'It's Daisy, please. And, er, your health.' She picked up the glass by its delicate twisted stem and took a sip. 'Oh, that's very sweet.' And strong, she didn't add. More like medicine than anything else. It reminded her of the linctus that Robbie had to take when his chest was bad, but she couldn't very well tell Ted that.

'It is.' His eyes were bright with humour. 'As sweet as your face, may I say.'

'No! That's silly.' She laughed but she was flattered all the same. It was like one of those lines in the films. You weren't meant to believe it but it showed he appreciated you.

'So, tell me about yourself, Daisy,' Ted said now, all his attention on her, which made her feel as if she was the most important person in this crowded room.

'Oh, there's not much to tell.'

'Tell me anyway.' He leant back against the velour padding, his face open and interested, his arm draped along the top.

And so she did, recounting what her family was like, how she'd worked in the factory and hated it, and so had decided to find a better job. She skirted over the issue of faking her age. She didn't want to come across as deceptive, even though lots of people had done the same thing. 'And what about you?' she finished.

'Oh, you don't want to know about me.'

'I do, I really do,' she protested, her head swimming a little from the unaccustomed strong drink.

'Well, if you insist. But first let me get you another one of those.'

Daisy looked down and somehow the little glass was empty. She didn't remember finishing it. She supposed it was because it was so small, when she was used to having half pints of lemonade. 'I'm not sure . . .' she began, but he was out of his seat and heading back to the bar before she could form the rest of her sentence.

Daisy could feel a warm glow spreading through her and it was very pleasant. She leant back against the cool window, letting her attention drift. Some of the drinkers nearby were eating snacks from the bar; pickled eggs looked as if they were popular. She wrinkled her nose, not tempted in the slightest. She wasn't hungry at all, but perhaps she would like another glass of that sweet, strong drink.

Here was Ted now, with a fresh glass of it for her. He settled himself once more on the velour window seat, a little closer than he'd been before. She didn't mind. She could catch notes of his aftershave, a combination of woody and smoky. She didn't know anyone else who smelt like that. Her father and big brother smelt of coal tar soap, if anything.

He began to tell her about himself, just as she'd asked, and yet she couldn't quite concentrate on the words. She let the lovely warm flood of his speech wash over her, enjoying the rhythms of it, the bass tone. Such a lovely deep voice he had.

'. . . ended up crossing the Thames even though I'm from south of the river,' he said, then stopped. Clearly he was expecting her to comment.

'Oh, south of the river!' she echoed, as if he'd just told a great joke, and he basked in her reply.

'I know, I know, but you mustn't hold it against me.' His eyes grew even brighter.

'I won't, I won't hold anything against you.' She struggled to make sense.

'Oh, now you needn't say that.' Now his expression held something else in it, some kind of meaning. Perhaps she'd said the wrong thing. What was it she'd just said? The heat of the bar was clouding her mind. 'Do drink up,' he urged.

She tried some more of the deep purple liquid, more bearable now that she was used to it.

'Do you like it?' he pressed.

She smiled and nodded. 'It's a bit like when we make jam – the juicy bit.'

He smiled even more widely. 'Yes, you're right. My mother used to make blackberry jam. We used to ask for the juicy bit, as you call it, to put on our rice pudding.'

That was a nice picture, she thought. 'My ma makes rice pudding sometimes. Tapioca as well.'

'I expect it's delicious.' There was that look again.

'Yes.' She shifted, suddenly not quite comfortable.

'Ted, I think I need some air. It's hot in here, that's what it is.'

He glanced at her sharply and then grinned. 'You're right, it can get a little stuffy sometimes. Why don't we step out the back. You'll be cooler out there.'

'Oh, has this place got a beer garden?' Daisy asked, standing, and automatically slinging her bag and gas-mask container across her shoulder. He raised his eyes at that but didn't comment.

Ted seemed to know his way around, taking her to a much less grand door towards the rear of the bar, his hand resting on the back of her waist. She wasn't sure how she felt about that. She'd seen it in the films, and it seemed like something a gentleman would do, but it was a surprise all the same. She told herself not to react like a girl, to take the compliment that she was sure it was.

The cooler air from outside brought her out of her stupor. The dusk had fallen, which must mean it was later than she'd intended to stay out. There was enough light to see by, but she had to peer into the gloom along the brick-wall-lined passageway that they had entered.

She gazed around. 'Which way is the garden?' she asked, puzzled.

He gave a brief laugh. 'Don't you worry about that. We don't need a garden.'

'Oh.' That was a strange thing to say. The bar had been nice, what Aunt Vera would call classy, but this area wasn't nice, wasn't really anything at all. Perhaps it was a passageway to the garden. But Ted wasn't making any attempt to go anywhere else.

Vague memories began to tease her brain. 'What sort of drink was that?' she asked.

His laugh was louder this time. 'Oh, do you want another?' he teased. 'You must have seen it before, it's very popular with the ladies. Port and lemon, that's what you've been drinking.'

Port and lemon? That was exactly what Sylvia had had that night, wasn't it . . .?

As she was trying to remember, he came even closer and now his hand was fully around her back, pulling her against him. His other hand came up to her neck and caught in her hair. 'You see, we don't need a garden, this will be just fine,' he breathed, and his voice sounded peculiar, more like a growl, and his words kept catching.

'No, no, it isn't.' She tried to wriggle free but he held her in a tight grip.

What was happening? She didn't like this at all. Where was the gentlemanly Ted of a few minutes ago – or was it hours? The memory of Sylvia in the Dog and Fiddle came sharply into focus in her mind, Victor laughing, all over her, then how they'd lurched out of the pub.

Look at what happened next.

The sickly taste of the syrupy drink rose in her throat but she couldn't even cough it away. He had her too tight and now his hands were moving all over her, tugging at her blouse. He'd stopped asking her anything, but was pushing her backwards against one of the brick walls.

'You're so sweet,' he crooned. 'You're just like I imagined . . . just get this bloody gas mask out of the way . . .'

Another memory came to her from that night – of Peter and what he'd said. What to do if a man got a bit too much, how to make him stop. Dare she try it?

She had to. He was gasping and then came the sound of the material of her blouse being torn, her lovely new blouse that she'd chosen with such care.

Without warning, she brought her knee up sharply into his groin as hard as she could, and then when he backed off with a sharp grunt she ran, down between the brick walls of the horrid alley. She caught sight of his face in the dull light as she turned – surprise, most of all, and then pain. Good.

Would he try to follow her? She reached the end of the passage, sped past the tall, terraced houses, their steps now empty, and ducked into the mouth of the next alley. She crouched down, wrinkling her nose at the smell of rubbish and something even nastier, but she didn't have the luxury of caring what it might be. She had to see if he'd followed her, if he was going to pounce and overpower her. She didn't know how long the effects of her action would last. Peter hadn't said.

Gradually the last of the dusk left the sky and a pale moon cast its feeble light on the street. Sounds of households came from open windows. The Home Service was broadcasting a concert, and several houses were listening to it. Just a normal domestic Friday evening.

Daisy groaned out loud. How had she been so stupid? She'd fallen straight into the trap, and it was of her own making. She didn't know this man at all. She'd spun herself a fantasy, of glamorous living and expensive meals and outings. He'd seen her as nothing more than a casual amusement, assuming she'd be grateful for the attention and willing to give him what he wanted – and not bothering if she agreed or not.

Well, she'd shown him. A good job she'd acted when she did – the element of surprise had helped her there. A few moments longer and she'd have been unable to get away.

She shuddered, the effects of the alcohol wearing off and the shock beginning to hit her. That was a narrow escape and no mistake. How ridiculous to think that a man so much older would be genuinely interested in somebody like her. He was just an old lech. He'd probably gone back inside to hunt down some other poor mug. She shivered, slowly standing up, trying to keep her bag from whatever rotten detritus was on the ground.

Then she realised it wasn't just the shock that was making her so cold. Her blouse was ripped in several places, half of its buttons missing, its collar hanging off. If she thought about this too much she would start to cry. How dare he! Did he think she could afford new blouses at the drop of a hat? At least she still had her old serviceable work blouse rolled up in her bag.

Shuffling around, but quietly just in case anyone was nearby, she opened her bag and got out the now extremely creased old blouse, and shrugged out of the remains of her new one. Trembling with cold and nerves, she wriggled into the safety of her drab top, managing not to drop anything onto the mucky ground beneath her feet. Thank goodness for the blackout. Nobody was likely to see what she was doing.

Inhaling a deep breath, she tucked the scraps of blue flowery material into a nearby dustbin and set about retracing her steps, the route she had taken with such naïve hope only a couple of hours before. She'd cut through to Green Lanes and catch a bus down to Stamford Hill and beyond, south to Dalston. Even now the work side of her mind recited the routes she could use. She'd be safe then, well away from that monster of a man.

Grimly she mounted the first suitable bus and settled onto a seat by herself, leaning against the window. She couldn't wait to get home to have a thorough wash in the hottest water she could bear. Sam had been right all along, she thought. She'd allowed herself to be swept away on the basis of nothing.

Then she dipped her head in sadness as the reason why she'd fallen for Ted in the first place came back to haunt her. He'd reminded her of Freddy, in his bearing and smile. Well, she would bet that Freddy didn't treat women like that. Not that she was in a position to find out. Freddy had that stuck-up girlfriend and that was all there was to it.

Daisy sadly realised that she'd just have to carry on, setting aside any thoughts of romance. All that was really at stake was the imaginary future she'd allowed herself to dream up. It wasn't like those who'd lost loved ones at Dunkirk. In all honesty she had nothing to complain about. There was nothing else for it, but to wake up tomorrow and keep on putting one foot in front of the other.

She was still shaking, but decided that when she felt more in control then she would tell Clover. Now that they had shared the sorry story of Sylvia and the miscarriage, she felt that her sister wouldn't dismiss her, or blame her, or anything horrible. She would understand and sympathise. That was all Daisy wanted. She couldn't undo what had just happened, and nobody could blame her more than she was already blaming herself. A day to calm down, she thought, and then she'd be in need of a shoulder to cry on.

CHAPTER TWENTY-FOUR

'So, what does this mean? When will you be leaving?' Patty stared at her middle daughter and wondered why her children often saved such important moments until after the family had all eaten together.

Clover put down her fork on her empty plate. The roast dinner had been delicious and all the more so because she alone had known that it might be her last for a while.

'On Wednesday,' she answered with a very slight shake in her voice. 'This week.'

'Oh.' Patty sat back down again. She'd been about to clear away the plates and cutlery but for a moment the wind was knocked from her body. Another of her children leaving her. It cut her deeply.

Then she rallied, knowing that this was bound to happen at some point and that she had been lucky that Clover's first posting had been so close to home. 'Well, it's sooner than I imagined but I dare say they'll want to get you trained up for whatever you'll be needed for.' She smiled gamely although her heart ached.

'Let me take those plates.' Rose stepped in to help

as usual. She could tell how her mother really felt. Reaching for the pile of crockery, she smiled at her sister. 'You could be right in the thick of it, Clover.'

Clover almost blurted out that she hoped so, but realised in time that this would not reassure her mother. 'We don't know,' she said, 'but Miss Linton did say that the south coast will need strong defence. I don't know much more than that – not even where I'll be stationed, exactly.'

Daisy was unusually subdued. She simply added her cutlery to the pile and nodded absently. Rose observed this but did not think too much about it. Her little sister was lost in a world of her own but she'd snap out of it soon enough.

Bert sat up straighter in his chair. 'Well, we're pleased you're going to step up when you've been given the chance,' he said warmly. 'You'll be an asset to them, Clover. It's not to say we won't miss you, of course we will, but we know you've got to go.'

'Like that old song from the Great War, you mean. "We don't want to lose you but we think you ought to go".' Clover grinned, relieved now that both her parents had taken the news so well. She wished she'd had more time to prepare them but once she'd said Yes to Miss Linton's proposal, events had moved speedily. Already a young new volunteer had turned up in the storeroom, and Clover would train her for the remaining two days in Central London before packing her bags and heading south.

'That's the one.' Her father nodded sagely. 'Just be sure to write to us often.'

231

'And longer letters than Peter sends,' Patty added.

Clover sniffed. 'Well, that won't be difficult. I'll tell you all about it.'

Daisy stared at the tabletop, registering the conversation but with no desire to take part for once. Her plans to tell Clover about her terrible evening were suddenly in ruins. What was the point in confessing all that, only for Clover to leave? Her sister's mind was on her forthcoming adventure, that was for sure. But there was nobody else Daisy could tell.

Rose was too sensible, she wouldn't understand. Her parents would be aghast that she'd put herself in such a position to begin with. Hope, maybe? But she was so caught up in her WVS work that she'd barely have the time to listen. Joy was out of the question; she'd use it as an excuse to make herself even more miserable. No, she'd just have to keep the whole incident to herself.

She realised that Clover was looking at her. 'What do you think, Daisy?' she asked. 'Will you miss me?' It was said lightly but Daisy could tell her sister was surprised by her silence.

'Oh . . . oh yes. B-but good for you,' Daisy stuttered. 'I mean, you hated being shut up in that storeroom. Now you'll get a chance to, I don't know, see the world.'

Clover frowned. 'I wouldn't go that far. See Southampton, maybe.' She gazed quizzically at her younger sister but didn't press the point.

Daisy smiled but said nothing further. She felt like screaming all of a sudden. A year ago she might have given in, or picked a quarrel to release her anger, but she resisted. Clover was heading off for her big adventure and it would be mean to spoil it. Gritting her teeth behind the pasted-on smile, she knew she must suffer in silence.

Rose had strolled over to Victory Walk from the nurses' home rather than ride her bike, determined to make the most of the warm weather. It was so refreshing to breathe in the air, feel the sun on her skin. When she was on duty she rarely got a moment to step outside and if she was on late shifts she might not even see much daylight. Everyone knew natural light was good for Vitamin D, and that in turn was good for your bones.

Now she set off for the return journey after the roast dinner, feeling pleasantly full, and heartily grateful that her mother was such a good cook. The nurses' home provided all their meals but it just wasn't the same. She was glad she'd been there for Clover's announcement. Patty had appreciated her presence, she was sure.

Her mind was caught up in what might happen to her middle sister when a voice said, 'Hello, Rose.'

Rose turned from the view of the big trees along Hackney Downs to see who had spoken. It was her cousin, looking even more elegant and expensively dressed than the last time she'd seen her. 'Hello, Faith. What brings you out this way?'

Faith was honouring Dalston with her presence in a deep pink summer suit, jacket lapels edged in cream piping, her high sandals in a similar cream with delicate crimson bows. Rose wondered how she managed to walk along the uneven paths around the edge of the Downs in such creations.

Faith tucked back a lock of her expensively styled hair. 'I came to see my parents obviously. Then I decided I'd have a bit of a walk before getting the bus back to my flat. You know how it is. They ask so many questions, it makes my head spin.'

'Oh, I see,' said Rose, although she never found that to be the case at her parents' house. She tried not to feel dowdy in comparison to her cousin. Her own summer dress in pale blue was perfectly good, she knew, and yet, when set beside Faith's outfit, it felt second-best.

'Yes, they just don't understand the sort of life I have now,' Faith continued with a small sigh. 'It's no wonder, though, they've never lived or worked anywhere other than around here. Whereas I know what it's like to be at the very heart of things, right in the centre of London. It's so different, I can't tell you.'

Rose tried to look sympathetic. 'I'm sure you're right.'

Faith beamed. 'It's the pressure, you see. I always have to look exactly right and not a hair out of place. It's what's expected. My boss is extremely particular.'

Rose inclined her head and said nothing. What was it her mother had told her after a recent conversation with Aunt Vera? Something about Faith seeming to be very close to her boss.

'That must be tricky,' she said, thinking that her superiors were pretty particular as well. They had every reason to be. If any of them made a mistake it could be a question of life or death, which was unlikely to be the case for Faith.

'He's very insistent that I get everything exactly as he wants it.' Faith stroked her lapel as she spoke. 'I'm learning such a lot. I never would have had a chance to do half the things I do now if I'd stayed in Dalston. I don't regret it for a moment.'

'I expect Aunt Vera misses you though,' Rose suggested, knowing how proud Vera was of her daughter's success.

Faith sighed again. 'Oh, she does. And I do miss her, but I'm being given opportunities now that I could never have dreamt of before.' Her expression grew distant and Rose had no desire to enquire exactly what those opportunities might be.

She wondered what she could say that wouldn't bring forth more gushing comments about the mysterious boss or the demanding job. 'Have you heard from Martin recently?' she asked neutrally.

Faith laughed, a tinkling little laugh. 'Oh, Martin. He's such a sweetheart. Isn't he? Didn't you think so? I do write to him now and again and he always sends me back such long letters. He's very busy but never so much as he can't spare time to tell me everything he's doing. Not that he can tell me all the details, of course, the censors won't let him.'

'Well, of course.' Rose couldn't argue with that.

Faith nodded, now playing with her jacket cuffs. They too were edged in neat piping, obviously not the result of dressmaking at home. Rose felt a stab of jealousy. Fancy being able to afford such quality clothes. Then she wondered exactly who was paying.

'In fact, I'm sure he'd love to hear from you,' Faith said. 'You were very close for a while, weren't you?'

'Well, we were friends, but no more than that,' said Rose, wondering what Faith was up to.

'He'd appreciate it, I know. He's so far from home, he'll be thinking of you, I'll be bound.' Faith's tone grew more insistent.

'I'm sure he isn't,' Rose protested. What was her cousin insinuating? A few months ago she'd all but flaunted her relationship with Martin, as if to rub it into Rose's face who had the upper hand, who he cared for most. She'd been wasting her time. Rose hadn't been worried in the slightest. If anything, she'd been concerned for Martin, that he was being taken in by her cousin. So why would anything change now?

'No, he surely will be. A few lines from you would do him the world of good, you know. He's so fond of you.'

Rose was more confused than ever. There was no way on this earth that she was going to start up a correspondence with Martin after all this time. She didn't want to encourage him – and now he had Faith to come home to.

Whatever games her cousin thought she was playing, Rose wasn't going to go along with them.

'Lovely to see you, Faith, but I have to be getting along now,' she said. 'Do give my love to your sisters and Aunt Vera.'

Faith gave a polite smile. 'Oh, of course. You'll be on duty again soon, won't you. Martin always said how dedicated you were to your work.'

That was a barb if ever there was one. Well, she wasn't going to rise to the provocation.

'Yes, got to be ready to go on shift this evening,' she said cheerfully. 'I'd best be off.'

Faith looked as if she was going to say something more, but changed her mind. 'Good to bump into you, Rose.' She waved prettily as Rose set off down the eastward path.

Honestly, thought Rose, some people had no idea. All right, she herself wouldn't have objected to the chance to fill her wardrobe with lovely clothes. But they were nothing in comparison to the satisfaction she gained from doing her job, and doing it well. And whatever other activities Faith's position required, she was not remotely interested in them.

CHAPTER TWENTY-FIVE

Clover was shaking, and not only with the cold. It was a clear night and the stars were twinkling against the darkness of the midnight sky. The old truck, however, was not built for the number of young women crammed onto its flatbed base, and it laboured horribly as it struggled uphill, threatening to loosen their teeth in their jaws.

'Blimey,' said one of the other girls opposite her, with a Midlands accent. 'If I'd wanted to be chucked about like this I'd have gone to a fairground.'

The next woman along smiled stiffly. 'It's not so bad. We could have it worse.'

The first one pulled a face and swiped back her dark ponytail. 'This is bad enough. Oh, what I wouldn't give for a warm bed. To think I left my lovely snug barracks for this. I wonder how much further we have to go? Or where we are?' She scanned around her but all was shrouded in the gloom of blackout.

'At a guess, we're heading north-west from Southampton,' said the one with the stiff smile.

Clover perked up. 'How do you know that? I haven't seen any kind of sign since we pulled out of Clapham Junction.'

The woman turned to face her directly. 'For a start we could see which way the moon came up as we left London and that showed we were heading south – although I bet you were told like me that this is where we'd be going. Then when we got off it was clearly at Southampton – not all the signs had been fully painted over. Now we are heading north-west – you can tell by the stars.'

'Can you?' Clover couldn't.

'Yes, it's easy. See that shape up there, the one that looks a bit like a saucepan? Well, follow two of its stars – where I'm pointing, look – and you get to one lone star on its own. That's the north star, Polaris. As long as you can find that, then you can work out in which direction you are headed.'

'Blimey,' said the other young woman again.

Clover was impressed. 'How do you know that? Did you have to use that in your last posting? I was indoors all the time and didn't ever have to think of such things.' And to get home I just took buses, she thought. Good job I never had to tramp across a field.

'Not exactly,' said the stargazer, and then she abruptly shut up.

Clover drew her new uniform coat around her, glad of its warmth. There was nothing else to offer comfort. She was sitting on her kitbag, uncomfortably wedged between the rusty side of the truck and another volunteer. Everyone else must be equally uncomfortable, she realised, so no wonder conversation wasn't exactly flowing.

On the train down she'd been in a carriage with a different group of ATS women, who were all being posted to Southampton itself. Clover hadn't discovered until she alighted at the train platform that she was to continue her journey in this ancient jalopy, to the middle of nowhere.

She hadn't expected to miss Sylvia so much. They'd sworn to keep in touch but it wouldn't be like working together, day in, day out. She hoped some of the others on the truck would turn out to have a similar sense of humour, although hopefully not the same terrible taste in men. So far it was hard to tell.

Nothing to be done about it, she told herself firmly. They were cold, tired and hungry, just as she was, and probably with sore bottoms as well. The kitbag was a very poor cushion. She'd have bruises tomorrow. Not exactly how she'd hoped to start her big adventure.

'Ow!' she cried out involuntarily as they hit a rut in the road and she was thrown against the unyielding side of the truck.

Some of the others had also exclaimed in discomfort or shock and they looked around and made eye contact with one another. Some smiled. The one from the Midlands pulled a face and grinned. But the stargazer merely pressed her lips together and stared straight ahead, uncompromising.

Clover resettled herself on the rock-hard kitbag and hoped to high heaven she didn't have to share a hut with that one.

*   *   *

Of course, the first person she saw when she was allocated her hut was the stargazer.

The hut had six beds, arranged three along each side, under an arched roof, not unlike the one on the shelter at home. There was a stove burning at one end but the place was still freezing cold. The bed she was shown to was furthest from the stove. The woman from the Midlands and others from the truck had the good luck of the warmer end. Clover sighed out a long breath and the vapour from it showed white in the air in front of her face. If it was like this in summer, heaven knew what it would be like in winter.

She took in the corner of the room that was likely to be her home for the foreseeable future. The bed had a utilitarian blanket tucked in tightly, and there was a practical bedside cabinet for her personal items. There were some hooks on the wall and a coatstand was placed somewhat crookedly in the corner. Nobody had been here long enough to add anything to make it feel more homely, by the looks of things.

She tried not to let her dismay show. To think that she'd fought with Daisy for all those years because they'd had to share a room, but it had been warm, and brightly lit, and had a colourful rag rug on the floor and pretty curtains with matching cushion covers. There was none of that here.

'Better get that bag unpacked,' said the woman opposite, who was busy sorting out her own possessions. Clover glanced up and registered who it was. She frowned but knew that it was good advice.

'Yes, thanks, I will.' She began to loosen the fastenings, which was tricky as the bag was all lumpy from having been sat on.

The woman came across the hut and held out her hand. 'I'm Marigold,' she said, 'Marigold Pewsey.'

Clover set down the bag and shook the offered hand. 'Clover. Clover Harrison.' Then she smiled. 'You've got a flower name too. All my sisters have the same. Our ma always loved gardening, so we're Rose, Clover and Daisy.'

'Really.' The woman smiled tightly.

'Oh yes.' Clover was relieved now the ice had seemed to break. 'And our cousins are named after the virtues: Faith and Hope and Joy. Hope's all right but Joy's always miserable, and as for Faith . . . no, I shouldn't say. Our mums are Patience and Vera, so everyone thought we'd be Charity or something like that but like I say our ma loved gardening . . .'

The woman nodded. 'I see. Well, good to meet you. I must finish unpacking.'

Well, that's me told, Clover reflected grimly. Clearly the ice was not broken at all. Still, Marigold seemed to know what she was about, and Clover secretly watched how she arranged things and began to copy her. She might as well benefit from the other woman's experience in how to fit the maximum number of items into a small space. It wasn't so very different from when the storeroom had a fresh delivery, or the greengrocer's, come to that.

Ten minutes later, she sat back on her heels and stretched, yawning loudly, unable to stop herself.

Everything was stowed away, and she'd found the thick socks that Patty had knitted for her, so that her feet would not be like little glaciers overnight. Their cheerful pattern made her think of home.

'All done,' she said to nobody in particular.

'You'll be able to get a cup of tea or hot chocolate over in the NAAFI.' Marigold had come up behind her without Clover noticing.

'Oh, right.' Clover didn't want to give away that she'd been taken by surprise. 'Er, what's that? I wasn't taking much notice when we arrived.'

Marigold stepped over the empty kitbag. 'You must know, it's the Navy, Army and Air Force Institute – where we can get food and drink and whatever we need. Better get that bag put away as well as they're bound to do an inspection first thing. They'll want us ready before seven, you know.'

Clover's expression grew alarmed.

'A good night's sleep will set you right and everything will feel better after that,' Marigold said in her voice of experience. 'Come along, I'll show you where the NAAFI is, if you like. It's perishing in here, we'd benefit from a hot drink.'

Clover was surprised all over again; she'd thought this woman was standoffish at best, or downright unfeeling.

'Come on if you're coming. They've kept it open late because of us new arrivals but they won't stay open all night.' There was that note of impatience again. Obviously the kindness didn't last for long.

'Right, yes, I think I will.' Clover got to her feet, a

little unsteadily as her ankles had gone to sleep and they were tingling with pins and needles. 'Thanks.'

'Think nothing of it,' said Marigold, and it was hard to tell if she was being efficient, or abrupt, or both.

At the NAAFI canteen, the staff were making it clear that they'd stayed late as a favour and could the new arrivals please get a move on? Clover sighed; it wasn't the welcome she'd hoped for, but couldn't blame them. They were probably as cold as she was.

Marigold swiftly fetched them each a mug of cocoa and they made for one of the long tables that ran along the walls of the chilly building, not unlike a church hall. Some of the others from the truck had had the same idea, all warming their hands on mugs of hot drinks. Wafts of Bovril mixed with tea rose in the air.

'Shove up, you lot. Room for two more,' said the woman from the Midlands. 'I'm Elsie, and this is . . . ?' She turned to one of the other new faces, a little embarrassed that she'd forgotten the name already.

'Milly. Pleased to meet you. Didn't realise it got so cold down south!'

'Marigold,' said Marigold, giving a stiff nod, 'and this is Clover.'

Clover nodded, trying to stop her teeth from chattering all over again. She raised her mug. 'Cheers,' she said, but by now she was so tired that she could scarcely take in the new names and voices. She took a gulp of the drink, not as sweet as she'd like it but not bad. Anything was welcome right now. The bench seats were hard, the table surface scratchy, and the walls of the place not exactly homey; there were posters of regulations and pictures of the king and Winston Churchill, and that was about it.

'Clover, are you all right?' Suddenly she was aware that Marigold was speaking. The other woman's question cut through her sleepy daydreaming.

'Sorry. Yes, just a bit tired.' She rose to her feet, moving automatically. 'I think I'll turn in. See you all in the morning.'

The others nodded and returned to their chatter, as Marigold quirked an eyebrow to ask, 'Are you sure you're all right? Will you find your way back?'

Clover gathered herself. 'Yes, not to worry, I'll remember.' She hoped that was true. 'Just need to get my head down then I'll be fine.'

She could hardly recall the walk to the Nissen hut, one foot somehow going in front of the other, nor her exhausted collapse into her new narrow bed. Physically, it had been one of the toughest days she had known, and yet her final thought before sleep claimed her was: this is it. It's the start of the adventure you wanted.

Clover was glad of Marigold's prediction the next morning, when the inspection happened just as she'd said. She stood beside her bed, in her khaki uniform and shiny black shoes, hoping she'd pulled the blanket tightly enough and folded the corners correctly.

The officer, Section Leader Bellingham, was grim-faced and soon showed herself to be extremely particular. One of the newcomers nearest the stove was reprimanded for leaving her kitbag sticking out from under her bed. Elsie was torn off a strip for failing to polish her shoes. Clover escaped relatively unscathed apart from a sharp comment about her untidy hair, which was only to be expected. If she'd tried to restrain it properly then she wouldn't have had time to do anything else at all.

Only Marigold passed muster, and the officer gave her a brief nod before turning on the rest of them. 'Have some respect for the fact you are now serving at the Sector Station for the entire area,' she barked. 'We are responsible for all the airfields around. Sloppiness will not do.' Then they were summoned to breakfast, prior to the first session of marching.

Clover thought back to her first day with Miss Linton, and how she and Sylvia had groaned about their superior's strictness. But Miss Linton was friendliness itself when compared to this new officer. Still, perhaps the woman had hidden depths and would thaw a little once everyone got used to the new quarters and routines. She could only hope.

Clover did not fare so well when it came to the marching. She had never had to do it before and it showed. Beforehand she had assumed it was easy – surely it was simply all walking to the same rhythm and swinging your arms a bit. She soon discovered just how wrong she had been. There was a knack to it and she didn't have it.

Worse, everybody else seemed to be able to keep time and adjust their steps, moving neatly together. The harder Clover tried, the trickier it was, and before long she was stumbling and tripping, earning disapproving looks from the women next to her and, inevitably, getting singled out by the superior officer.

She stood silently while her failings were shouted at her for all to hear, knowing that she'd have to put up with it and that to protest would only heap more trouble upon her head. She had to miss her elevenses for extra practice. Her stomach rumbled but there was nothing to be done, only to try ever harder to get the steps right and keep her fingers crossed that she'd be more acceptable tomorrow.

This was to set the pattern for the next few days, as Clover struggled to keep up. Her lack of basic training showed and all she could do was to try harder. Still, on the other hand, she was quick to learn how to keep the hut in order, and to find her way around the big base.

At first it was strange to sleep in the same room with five strangers. That first night she had been too tired to care, but for several weeks after, she would lie awake listening to the various noises of five young women snuffling, sneezing which was made worse by Elsie's hay fever, and sometimes snoring.

The most disturbing thing was that Marigold talked in her sleep. The first time it happened Clover hadn't been sure what was going on, as she had almost dropped off to sleep and was jolted back to wakefulness by a low muttering. Now thoroughly alert, and far from happy about it, she strained her ears to catch the details of the words.

Yet that proved to be impossible as the sounds from the other beds drowned out the sense of the muttering,

247

and Clover had fallen asleep once more without working out what Marigold had been talking about.

It didn't happen every night, and gradually Clover stopped thinking about it. Sometimes she slept right through it, once she'd grown accustomed to it, and on other occasions she registered the sound but didn't try to understand the meaning. It was more important to get the best possible night's sleep herself, as her attempts at marching were even more miserable when she was overtired.

Then came a night when Marigold's voice was louder than usual and Clover gave up trying to ignore it. She punched her pillow to make it more comfortable and pulled her sheet and blanket up over her ears but it was to no avail. From the bed opposite came clipped exclamations and then a groan. These were followed by a short sentence repeated over and over.

The words made no sense though. Aid? Noose? Play? Try as she might, Clover could not figure out their meaning. Nobody else seemed to have woken up but Marigold tossed and turned, calling out the strange sentence again and again. Finally she cried out sharply, just once, and then fell silent.

Clover lay perfectly still, the moonlight edging around the blinds throwing a silvery gleam over her colleague. Marigold now seemed calm and soon there were soft noises of her deep breaths, followed by gentle snores.

Charming, fumed Clover. Now she was properly awake and Marigold was safely in the land of Nod. It struck her as deeply unfair, especially as the more experienced young woman never had any problem in marching to the required standard and her efforts at cleaning and tidying the hut were always immaculate. Whereas Clover was facing another morning of humiliation on the parade ground.

As she lay there, her thoughts became more charitable. It was hardly Marigold's fault. In fact, the woman would probably be mortified if she realised what had happened. She seemed so self-contained, joining in conversations just enough not to offend or appear rude, but giving away very little in the way of personal details. Clover was still none the wiser where her colleague came from, what her family was like, and where she had been stationed up till now.

Marigold was a telephonist and so their paths did not cross much during most of the day. Clover was thrilled to have been selected for anti-aircraft training, sure that this was exactly the kind of role that Miss Linton had had in mind for her. It was early days yet but it was a world away from the confines of the storeroom. If everything went well she would be angling the big searchlights above the base, tracking the skies to identify enemy aircraft. She could hardly wait. Adding to the excitement was the idea that, if she could help stop the enemy aircraft here, there was less chance of them making it through to the capital. Just because she'd left her family in London, it didn't mean she wasn't doing her bit to save them.

Meanwhile, Marigold's demeanour during the day was at odds with her disturbed sleep and especially those sounds of alarm that came from her at night.

Clover would even call them distressed. Something serious must have gone on to cause such a reaction.

Clover had no wish to pry but she couldn't help wondering if it would benefit Marigold to talk about it, to bring to light whatever was troubling her. She turned the idea over in her brain, not certain if she was the right person for the task. If only Rose were here. It was exactly the kind of thing she was good at.

Then again, Clover knew that she couldn't rely on Rose now, and that it was high time she stepped up in such situations herself. Rather, she should be considering what her big sister would do in the circumstances. Slowly a plan began to form.

Rose would recognise that something was wrong, for a start. This kind of crying out was a clear signal that all was not well in Marigold's world, no matter how calm and competent she seemed in the hours of daylight. Rose would be sympathetic but direct. She would pick a quiet moment and then take Marigold to one side, stressing that she was not interfering but telling her what she'd witnessed and reassuring her that she was only raising the subject out of a desire to help. She would be kind but firm. Whatever Marigold might say in response, she would not be horrified or shocked. She would hear the woman out and then offer advice, or a shoulder to cry on, or whatever felt necessary.

So, safe in the knowledge that this is what Rose would do, Clover resolved to do the same. In the absence of her eldest sister there was no choice: she would have to take on the job herself. There was no alternative. Having made this decision, she turned over and sighed into her pillow, then snuggled down into the hard mattress as best she could. The moonlit interior of the hut faded as her eyes grew heavy and at last she drifted off to sleep, satisfied that she would tackle her colleague the next day.

CHAPTER TWENTY-SIX

Rose had spent the evening celebrating the engagement of one of her colleagues. It was the second such gathering in as many weeks. Whether it was the shock of Dunkirk or the fear of imminent invasion, something was in the air, causing young couples to commit to their shared futures. There was tension everywhere, expecting the worst from over the Channel, confusion when it didn't happen. More planes were overhead, more barrage balloons, more activity from the ack-acks. No wonder people were doing whatever they could to find happiness.

First it had been Dora and her boyfriend in the navy, who had first met at school and had been going steady ever since. It was no surprise to anybody, and when Ian was home on his long-anticipated leave, they'd made their announcement and the other nurses had thrown a party. Dora had shown them all a pretty gold ring with a sapphire in the middle, which had belonged to Ian's grandmother. 'Make the most of it,' she'd grinned, 'because I won't be wearing it for work.

Imagine losing it down the side of one of the beds on the ward. No thank you.'

Much more startling was the news from Katherine, who had been single for as long as Rose had known her. She was already a sister when Rose had first started her training, and everyone had assumed that she was married to her career. Then she had dropped her bombshell: she had met an army doctor at Christmas, they'd begun to write to one another, and he'd been evacuated back to Britain from France. They'd decided not to wait, but to get engaged right away. 'Who knows what's going to happen?' Katherine had said, displaying another pretty ring, this time with an emerald at its centre. 'Richard could be shipped off to God knows where or he might be posted to somewhere near London. We have no way of telling. I can see you're all staring and thinking that we barely know one another, but I've never felt so certain about anything. So I hope you'll join us to celebrate on Wednesday.'

It would have been near-impossible to refuse and anyway, Rose had no intention of doing so. She had admired Katherine for years, for her medical expertise and her bedside manner, which brooked no nonsense but was deeply caring. What did it matter if the couple had met only six months ago and had barely seen each other in that time? It was a shock, though. Katherine must be nearly thirty.

Now Rose was back in her room once more, her ears ringing a little from the noisy party, down in the staff sisters' common room on the ground floor. Nurses had pitched in to make sandwiches and bring rare sweet treats, while the wireless had been turned up so that the evening concert could be heard above the chatter. They were all glad of an excuse to be happy, to show their delight that sober, steady Katherine had found such a suitable partner. 'They'll sit around the fire of an evening discussing advances in treating broken bones, I expect,' Dora had giggled to Rose as they'd stood in one corner. 'My Ian has absolutely no interest in the details of what I do. He just hopes he'll never end up in a hospital and have to find out. I feel the same about those pieces of radio equipment he spends all his time twiddling. But Katherine, she'll want somebody to talk about the finer points of preventing blood poisoning, I dare say.'

Rose had laughed. 'You're probably right. Do you want one of these sandwiches?' She passed along a platter that was doing the rounds, although the fillings were on the meagre side. There was not much cheese to go around and the butter had been spread very thin.

'God, I hate that two-faced Mr Prendergast,' Dora went on, nodding across the room to where the unpopular surgeon had stationed himself, typically by the edge of a big table so that the nurses would have to squeeze past him. 'Do you know what I heard him say?'

'Go on.' Rose was sure it wouldn't be anything pleasant.

'He was telling one of the trainees that Katherine should be grateful that she wasn't being left on the shelf at her age. Look at him! He's at least ten years older than she is! His hair is beginning to go thin, he can't see without glasses and he's getting a paunch

254

– though how he's managed that with rationing I don't know.'

'Best not to ask.' Rose took a bite of the not-very-cheesy sandwich.

'All right for him, though, he's a man and he's a doctor.' Dora took a vicious bite of her own sandwich. 'Nobody will ever say such things about him. Ugh, horrible man.' The two nurses had laughed, breaking the tension, sharing their distaste for the surgeon.

Now as she got ready for bed Rose couldn't help considering what she would prefer in a partner – someone who shared her interests, her profession even, or one who had a totally different career and hobbies.

She shook her head. She wasn't usually given to such idle speculation. There was nobody on the horizon, and therefore it was pointless to wonder. She had quite enough to think about, with work taking up nearly all of her time and energy. The hospital relied on nurses such as her, hard-working, well-trained, ready to cope with whatever emergencies were thrown at them.

Rose brushed her chestnut hair, which spent so long crammed under her white cap. All the same she liked to keep it clean and shiny, her crowning glory. Maybe one day she would meet somebody who would appreciate it, and she'd dress it up or wear it down, have some fun trying new styles. There was no call for any of that at the moment though.

She slipped into her serviceable cotton nightdress, which smelled of the soap powder used in the downstairs laundry. So did her bed linen; it was all fresh and usually she loved its clean scent. How different it would be to smell of expensive perfume . . . but that was an indulgence she could not afford.

Rose sighed again, realising this had been brought on by Katherine's unexpected announcement. Had she secretly been wondering if she was headed for a life on the shelf too? Did she feel that her youth was slipping away from her, her chances of future happiness made less likely by the war? She didn't usually allow herself to think like that, and if anybody had asked her outright she would have replied that it was ridiculous. Out of the question.

All the same, there was a sneaking sense of longing inside her that she rarely admitted to, a vague idea that things could be different. How good it must be to have someone to turn to, to share the best and worst moments, or even the most mundane – when you were tired and out of sorts, when the horrible surgeon had meddled with your cases or stood that little bit too close to you, when your bike broke down and you were late. All the silly little things that could build up over the course of a week, a month, a year.

Suddenly she felt as if she could cry. It was the uncertainty of the war, she knew, making her feel vulnerable and frightened. It would help to have someone to hold on to, who would hold her in turn. They could face the danger together. Rather than this overwhelming sense of being like a child again, alone in the dark.

Who that someone might be, she had no idea. Certainly not Martin, despite what everyone had once thought and he had obviously hoped for, at least for a while. She knew that plenty of her old classmates would have said that any boyfriend was better than none, but Rose had never agreed with that. She would far rather be on her own than stuck with a man for the sake of it. No, better to keep to the single life – unless the miracle of a soulmate should happen to come along.

The chances of that, she thought as she rolled over, were very small indeed.

Clover missed the chance to talk to Marigold at breakfast, as several of the telephonists had been commandeered to work early. Clover felt vaguely uneasy that this might mean something big was about to happen, a slow ramping up of the dread that was ever-present. But for the moment she was far more nervous about tackling Marigold. What if she refused to explain, or didn't believe that she'd been muttering in her sleep?

Clover got through the marching without any major mishap for once and then went straight to her anti-aircraft training. She'd felt intimidated at first by the size of the searchlights, wondering how anyone of her stature could ever hope to move them about, let alone with the degree of accuracy required. Yet as time went on she had lost her nervousness and could now handle the huge objects as well as the rest of the trainees. Of course it was one thing to manoeuvre the lights on a warm summer's day in bright sunshine. Now they were moving on to practising at night, which was colder, and with only as much torchlight as they strictly needed. That would be when she could spot the expected enemy planes headed for the East End. So she had every reason to be absolutely perfect.

This meant she had some of the afternoon free, and it turned out that Marigold did too, as she'd worked the unexpected early shift.

'Fancy a walk?' Clover asked brightly, coming back to the hut to find that Marigold was already there, changing her shoes. 'It's lovely out there – a bit of a breeze and only a few clouds in the sky.'

Marigold gave a small smile. 'There speaks somebody who's been outside for hours. I've been in that gloomy communications building and barely had a moment to think about the weather. Yes, now you come to mention it, I'd love a walk.' She picked up her big handbag. 'This isn't just for my gas mask, I've got some apples in here as well, so we won't go hungry.'

'Good.' Clover had always had a healthy appetite but there was something about working outdoors that made her ravenous. 'I'll change out of my uniform and then I'll be ready.' Hastily she shrugged out of the heavy khaki skirt and pulled on one of her old cotton ones, that she'd last worn in the greengrocer's.

Marigold had waited outside the hut, and slung the strap of her bag across her back as she saw Clover emerge. 'That's a pretty skirt,' she remarked.

'This old thing!' Clover laughed. 'I made it years ago, with Ma's help. She's very good at sewing and used to make all of our clothes when we were younger. I picked up some of her tips.'

Marigold inclined her head. 'Then perhaps you could teach me. My mother was never very interested in

258

sewing,' she said, and Clover thought that this was the first time she'd ever mentioned anything about her family. Perhaps it was a good omen.

'Well, there are five of us, as well as my parents,' she explained. 'We couldn't have managed if we didn't make our own clothes. We live near one of the big street markets so there's often bargain material to be had – well, at least there was before the war. Anyway, I quite like it, choosing the fabric, working out a pattern. I'll show you how to do it – it's not difficult.'

'I'd like that.' Marigold smiled again, and Clover thought how different her face was when she let down her guard.

There had not been much time to explore the area around the base so far, and now the two women headed out along a lane which ran between wide expanses of grassy downs, with no big towns nearby, just smatterings of cottages or farms. Clover gazed around, squinting in the sunlight. It was the exact opposite of what she was used to, the constant activity of a big city, where the noise never stopped and there were always crowds of people milling about. 'It's so quiet,' she breathed. 'You can even hear the birds.'

Marigold turned on the spot, looking at the remote horizon. 'You can see for miles,' she said. 'All those fields and farms and the downs themselves. No offices, no rows of houses, no train lines or tram tracks.'

Clover nodded. 'It is nothing like Dalston, where I'm from. That's in the East End of London,' she added, in case the other woman was not familiar with the name.

Marigold nodded. 'I've heard of it.'

'I was surprised at first when we got here, that it's so far away from all the cities,' Clover confessed. 'I thought I'd sound daft to say it, but I imagined we were being sent to defend the big ones along the south coast – but then we drove all that way from Southampton. We're not even near the big towns like Winchester.'

Marigold smiled. 'Well, they aren't going to put the major bases in the middle of a city, are they?' She gave a quizzical look. 'For a start there isn't the room. They need to land planes, don't forget. And then if you've got all this big bulky equipment, not to mention the likes of us experts in communication, you want to keep it all well away from any obvious centres, do you see? Although I'm more used to city life as well,' she added, which was news to Clover.

'Oh? Where are you from, then?'

'Liverpool,' said Marigold. 'Can't you tell, by my voice?'

Clover frowned. 'I'm not sure I know anyone from there, so I wouldn't have anything to compare it to. I didn't think you sounded that different to be honest.'

Marigold shrugged. 'Maybe not. I've travelled around quite a lot since joining the ATS, and besides my parents weren't from there so I didn't pick up the accent at home. But I've mostly been in cities . . . before.'

Clover swallowed hard. This was it – the obvious moment to broach the subject she'd been determined but also anxious to raise.

'Before?' she echoed quietly. Then, when Marigold did not respond, she repeated the word again. Don't let the chance fade away, she reminded herself. Think what Rose would do. She wouldn't give up right away.

Marigold still hesitated, and the only sound for a few moments was that of the birds. Some were swooping overhead, others cheeping or calling from nearby hedges. Clover wondered how she'd ever managed to miss the noise – when taken all together it was actually pretty loud, far more than the distant hum from the farms or the base.

'It was Paris,' Marigold said suddenly, and Clover looked at her in surprise.

'Paris? What, you were in Paris? You mean, you were stationed there?'

Marigold nodded. 'It's a long story.'

Clover began to walk slowly along the lane. 'Well, we've got all afternoon.'

'Yes. Yes, you're right, we have.' Marigold followed her, dragging her feet a little. 'All right, I'll try to explain. Like I said, I joined the ATS ages ago – back in 1938 in fact, before they had uniforms or anything. We just used to dress as if we were working in an office. After a while I was chosen to be trained as a telephonist. I liked it, I was good at it.' She paused, staring ahead straight at an old farm building but Clover could tell she wasn't really looking at it.

'Go on,' she said.

'Then as the war began, of course the army started moving into France.'

'The British Expeditionary Force,' Clover said. 'My brother was with them. We got his letters home from near the Belgian border.'

Marigold seemed to soften a little at that. 'Then you'll know a bit about what it was like. At first we travelled around. They called our platoon the soldier-ettes and it was like a big adventure.'

Clover drew in a breath, knowing how often she'd dreamed of her own big adventure.

'Yes, everyone was pleased to see us and we were treated like special guests. All the lovely food, the wine even.' Marigold's expression grew wistful and Clover remembered the jokes that Peter had made about their meals. Obviously Marigold had very different tastes.

'Then in, let's see, it must have been March, a couple of dozen of us were attached to the Royal Signals. So there we were in Paris, on switchboard duty at the telephone exchange there.'

'Blimey, however did you manage?' Clover couldn't begin to imagine.

Marigold came to a stop once more and gave a little shrug. 'It was easy. You see, my mother is French. I've always spoken it. They brought me up to be fluent in both languages. We used to go over to see her side of the family, and my grandmother's sister lived in Paris for a while when I was little. So for me it was like coming home, at least for a few months.'

Clover's eyes grew wide. Then understanding struck. 'Oh, but then—'

For a moment a look of pain passed across Marigold's face, but she soon had her expression under control. 'Well, yes, exactly. It all began to unravel as soon as the Germans invaded. We heard everything that was going on – that's what you do as a telephonist, you pick up all the messages and then you imagine what it's like, out there at the front. And then when the BEF retreated to the beaches . . .'

'Yes, I know. We . . . we knew some lads from home. We heard it all first-hand when one made it back.' Clover couldn't meet Marigold's eyes now, as the memory of Chalky's testimony flooded over her again.

'We stayed in Paris operating the switchboard for as long as we could, even when the troops were being evacuated.' Marigold had to clear her throat. 'We didn't know what would happen to us but our commander assured us they'd get us out somehow. So we had to carry on and trust that she was right. It wasn't until the enemy was on the outskirts of Paris that they decided we should go. It wouldn't have been safe to stay any longer. So we packed up as fast as we could, and all the French staff got out as well. They got us onto trucks just as the Nazis broke through into Paris but it was touch and go.' She shuddered despite the heat of the day. Clover, who had been feeling the warmth of the sun through her thin blouse, now shivered too.

'So we're all crammed onto trucks, the telephonists and our French liaison officer as well – we had to dress her up in one of our spare uniforms so she could come with us.' Marigold cleared her throat once more. 'The trucks are going as fast as they can but really it's not very fast, they aren't racing cars, and they're all laden down. We're sitting ducks, to be honest. So we get shot at, we think it must be machine guns by the sound of it, not once, not twice but three times on our way to the coast. We duck down but we've nowhere to hide, and we just have to hope for the best.'

263

'Shot at? What, out on the open road?' Clover couldn't contain her anguish.

'Yes, with nothing but the sides of the old trucks to protect us. Give them their due, it worked for most of the time and we almost made it. Then the roads were so crowded they couldn't get through. So our commander told us to walk for the final part of the journey. By then we were so exhausted we could hardly put one foot in front of the other but it's surprising what you can do when there's no choice. Somehow we got out of the trucks and walked along with all the crowds to the port. St Malo, it was. That's a long way from Paris,' she added ruefully.

Clover had no idea where that might be, but simply stared at her colleague.

'It's in Brittany. We used to go there when I was a girl, the beaches around there are lovely – well, they were then. Not so much now.' She pulled a face. 'But it was the most wonderful sight! There was a big vessel waiting for us – it was a hospital ship, and someone said it had been an old Channel steamer. It wasn't exactly the height of luxury but we didn't care. It was there, and we got on, and it brought us home.' She gave a short laugh. 'I can hardly remember that bit – we were so relieved, we slept for much of it. Then it was up and off again, to our new postings. And here I am.'

Clover turned her face up to the sun, seeking its warmth. Every inch of her body was chilled by the story. To think she had imagined a posting to France would be exciting. If she'd taken up Miss Linton's first offer this might have been her, left behind to find a way home after the main troops had gone.

Marigold stared up at the sky too, as if the retelling of the recent events had used up all of her energy. But as they slowly warmed up, Clover's resolution resurfaced.

'I don't know if you realised,' she began carefully, 'but sometimes you talk in your sleep. No, don't worry,' she added hastily, as Marigold looked alarmed, 'I'm the only one who hears, as I'm down the same end of the hut. Just this week you've been crying out and I'm not sure what it means, but perhaps it's something to do with your escape.'

'What did I say?' Marigold's voice was strained.

'It doesn't make sense to me. Something like, "aid, noose, play". Does that ring a bell?'

Marigold thought briefly and then nodded. 'I expect it was in French. I would have been calling out for help. *Aidez-nous s'il vous plait.* That's what we all did, after we were shot at – it's French for, help us please. It was not knowing the others were all right that was hardest. The shooting was so fast and so sudden we didn't have time to worry – but afterwards . . .'

'I know.' Clover gulped. 'When we knew that the troops had been forced onto the beaches but not who got off – well, we weren't sure what had happened to our brother. He was all right but we didn't know for what felt like ages.'

'So you understand a little of what it's like.'

The two of them gazed over the sunlit downs, cows in the fields, a few villages with their church spires pointing to the blue heavens above. It was such a picture-perfect scene. And yet a matter of miles away, young men had died in the seawater waiting to be rescued, and a few trucks full of brave young women had fled to another beach in the fervent hope of escape.

After a while, Marigold fished in her bag. 'Here. Have an apple.' She handed one to Clover.

'Thanks. Ooh, it's a nice one, and I should know.' She grinned at her colleague's questioning face. 'I worked in a greengrocer's for years. I'm an expert on such things.' She took a juicy bite and wiped the back of her hand across her lips. 'Yep, that's top quality, that is.' She took another bite. 'What happens now, do you think?'

Marigold finished her own mouthful of fruit. 'I have to say, we were in the thick of it in Paris, hearing all the latest news. It's not quite the same here – or at least not yet.'

'But?'

'The day after we got back from the hospital ship, there was a big speech – do you remember? The prime minister spoke in parliament and all the newspapers reported it.'

Clover made an apologetic face. 'That's more the sort of thing that my father would know about. Or my eldest sister.'

Marigold blinked hard as if it would help her recall the words. 'It went, "the Battle of France is over. The battle of Britain is about to begin." And then, "the whole fury and might of the enemy must very soon be turned on us." I don't suppose Mr Churchill would say that if it wasn't true.'

Clover shivered again, all that warmth disappearing like one of the small puffy clouds over Hampshire. 'So you think— Hang on, is that why you had to work an early shift this morning?'

Marigold finished her apple and tossed the core into the nearest field, wiping her hands on her handkerchief. 'You know I can't say. All the same, it makes sense, doesn't it?' Her tone of voice left little room for doubt. 'And here you are, Clover, newly trained to use a searchlight to protect a big army base. I'd say you're going to be right in the middle of it.'

CHAPTER TWENTY-SEVEN

Clover hoped that Marigold was mistaken, even if she recognised in her heart of hearts that the young woman had been involved in so much of the war so far that she was in a good position to make such a guess. It did not take long for her to be proved correct, however. Soon the skies above the south coast were alive with aircraft, some from the Luftwaffe, others from the many airfields scattered nearby. Airmen not just from Britain but from the Commonwealth and neutral countries such as Ireland and the United States all joined in the fight. There were even some from countries that had already been overrun such as Czechoslovakia and Poland.

The level of tension rose and rose but there was also a buzz of excitement in the hut, as a couple of the other girls had come up with a way to leave the base in the evenings.

'They've had me helping to mend the bicycles, so I can get hold of the keys to the big garage where they keep them,' grinned Milly, the fresh-faced Yorkshirewoman who was in one of the beds closest to the stove. 'We can go into town and meet some pilots. How about that!'

'Town?' asked Clover dubiously. 'What, you mean Andover? That's ages away.'

Milly shook her head. 'Not Andover. That's too far, but perhaps the big village on the other side of the hill, the one with the pub with the thatched roof. We could manage that in an evening.'

Marigold looked disapproving. 'That's still a fair distance and you know what will happen if you're caught breaking curfew. It'll be punishment duties from here on in.' She gathered up her uniform jacket and bag, ready to leave for her next session on the switchboard. 'I wouldn't try it if I were you.'

As the door swung shut behind her, Milly pulled a face. 'Well, she isn't me. What a misery guts. Clover, what do you say? Shall we make a break for it and try to meet some pilots in the pub? They say the Polish uniform is tremendously dishy.' She widened her eyes and Clover couldn't help laughing.

'You go ahead,' she said. 'I'm not sure I'm keen enough to risk it. I've only just got the hang of night operations so I don't want them to take me off them.'

'What, are you seriously saying you'd rather stand around in your greatcoat in the freezing small hours of the morning, aiming that giant torch beam into the sky, rather than come out to meet some gorgeous handsome men?' Milly's jaw all but dropped.

Clover grinned again because the young woman from Yorkshire spoke the truth. She didn't just enjoy aiming the searchlights. She absolutely loved it, every bone-chilling minute of it.

* * *

Sam was full of nervous energy as he bounded into the office and tore off his gas-mask carrier.

Daisy glanced up, wondering what was the matter. Now she came to think of it, he'd been on edge for a few days but she hadn't enquired further, still not sure of where they stood after his return from Dunkirk. There had been no repeat invitations to come for a drink on a Friday, and she had been quietly relieved about that. Her last experience in a Friday-night pub had put her right off.

'So,' he began, and stopped. Mr Rathbone was watching quietly from the back of the room, the really shadowy area.

'So, Daisy, this is my last week here,' Sam announced, and Daisy dropped her blotter in surprise.

'What? What do you mean, your last week? Where are you off to, Sam?'

Sam brushed an imaginary piece of lint from his shirt sleeve. 'I put in for a transfer and I've been accepted.'

Daisy rocked back in her chair. 'Transfer? What sort of transfer?'

He beamed with pride. 'I'm going on the buses. I'm going to be a driver. How about that?'

Daisy stared in shock. Even though she hadn't wanted to go out with him for a drink she'd assumed that he would always be here, ready to help her out when she couldn't understand the office systems or to lighten the atmosphere with a joke. Every time a difficult passenger had become angry with her, he'd made her laugh and realise that it wasn't her fault. It was impossible to imagine that he'd work anywhere else.

'Wh-when?' she stuttered.

'Like I said, this is my last week. I start at the depot on Monday.'

'But you can't even drive a car,' she protested.

'Doesn't matter. They'll teach me. They didn't mind about that at all, said it's totally different anyway.' He subsided into his seat but was still brimming with energy. 'I put in for it after I got back. Tell you the truth, Daisy, nothing's been the same since I returned from the rescue. I been feeling all antsy, like I had to keep moving or I'd go crazy. And also being stuck here half-underground don't do much for it neither. At least now I'll be up in the daylight again, after years down here.'

Mr Rathbone cleared his throat. 'It's not that bad, is it?'

Sam made an apologetic face. 'I haven't minded up till now. But once I got the idea, I knew it was the best thing to do. I want to do more, and if I can't join up then I can help above ground. Flat feet don't stop me pressing the brake and accelerator pedals,' he said knowledgeably, and Daisy pursed her lips.

'Bet you've never even tried.'

But Sam was not to be flustered. 'I'll know soon enough, won't I,' he said, his eyes gleaming with anticipation.

'It's very public-spirited of you to apply,' Mr Rathbone said steadily. 'Who knows what the conditions will be like soon up at street level. Hitler's clearly gearing up for something, now he's bombing the south coast for all he's worth.'

271

'Yep, I heard Southampton's been copping it pretty bad,' said Sam, and Daisy gasped.

'What, what have I said?'

Daisy looked down at her desk. 'We think that's not far from where Clover is.'

Mr Rathbone hurried to reassure her. 'Now, now, didn't you say she said she was in the middle of nowhere? The south coast is a big area, you know. Just because Southampton got bombed it doesn't mean it will affect wherever she is – and I realise she can't tell you exactly. But think of all the times something has happened in the West End and people ask you if you're all right even though you live and work miles away. You mustn't worry about your sister unnecessarily.'

'I suppose so.' Daisy knew that her boss was making good sense, but she did worry, all the same. Then another gloomy thought struck her. 'Who's going to take Sam's place, Mr Rathbone? Will we have Mr Fraser back full time?' She crossed her fingers as she said this, dreading his response.

Mr Rathbone raised his eyebrows. 'No, my dear, we will not. He is required more than ever at Wood Green. We shall have to train up somebody new. You'll still have your colleagues down at platform level so you won't be too lonely, and you can help me with any training of fresh staff. Now don't look like that, you are more than capable of taking on that challenge.'

Daisy was far from sure but she nodded, knowing that this was a compliment. Even so, she was not convinced that this was the sort of challenge she wanted to undertake. If she was to step up in some way, wouldn't it be better to push herself further? She loved working here, but if Sam was to leave it wouldn't be the same. What she really loved most was the dealing with customers, passengers who needed help, or calming down, or had a question she hadn't come across before.

Perhaps she too should make a move, try for another part of the transport system.

She inclined her head to one side. 'What did you have to do when you applied to be a bus driver?' she asked, all innocence.

Sam was on to her like a shot. 'Oh no, you don't. Don't you be thinking about copying me, Daisy Harrison.'

'I didn't say anything about that!' she protested, but Mr Rathbone was smiling.

'There might be a technical difficulty or two,' he suggested.

Daisy scowled, but recognised she didn't have a leg to stand on if anyone double-checked her age. She'd been lucky once but could not rely on anyone else being as understanding as her current superior. Nevertheless, she couldn't see why age would make her a better driver. She knew as much about it as Sam did – precisely nothing.

'I bet I could do it just as well,' she began, but Sam cut her off.

'Doesn't matter, it's not a question of what you think,' he retorted. 'It's not about your age, Daisy, and before you look like that I know you've not exactly admitted how young you are. It's more about your height.'

'My height? What's that got to do with it?'

Sam sighed, but he was still teasing. 'You aren't exactly

273

tall though, are you, Daisy? Your little legs won't reach the floor. They've got a strict requirement. I can't remember exactly what it is, but you aren't it.'

Daisy folded her arms. 'And you're tall enough, are you?'

Sam looked smug. 'As it happens, I am. They said I was an ideal candidate. So put that in your pipe and smoke it.'

'Now then, now then.' Mr Rathbone thought it prudent to intervene before their mock row became more heated. 'The die is cast, Miss Harrison. Our esteemed colleague will finish work here at the end of this week and then he will commence his bus driver's training. You and I will soldier on where we are. Now let that be the last of it. Miss Harrison, I see somebody in the ticket hall is in need of assistance.'

By the time she returned to her seat she was in a much better mood.

Sam smiled, picking up on the change of atmosphere. 'Well then, Daisy, you've been stringing me along for long enough. You won't have to put up with me again after this week. So what say you come out for a drink after work on Friday?'

Daisy could tell it would be mean to say no, this one last time. 'All right, Sam, you're on,' she said.

CHAPTER TWENTY-EIGHT

Clover was more exhausted than she could ever remember being. Learning how to manoeuvre the searchlights had been exhilarating, realising she could take on such a demanding role and do it to the exacting standards that were needed. She'd completed her training with flying colours. But it was an entirely other matter to operate those searchlights for long hours overnight.

Sergeant Williams had laughed when one of her fellow newcomers had complained. 'This is the best chance you'll ever get to prove your worth!' he'd exclaimed. 'I didn't train you to scare seagulls, you know. You're meant to show us all what aircraft are flying overhead, and look how lucky you are! Biggest aerial fights known to man going on right above your heads! You got the dogfights in the daytime and the bombers at night. Oh, you'll thank me in years to come, I can tell you. Be telling your grandchildren about this, you will. How you saved the day by lighting up the skies over Hampshire for king and country. So don't give me that long face, young lady.'

Clover had stepped into the shadows at that point so that the enthusiastic sergeant couldn't see her expression. She felt as if she had bags under the bags under her eyes. Her eyeballs itched with squinting upwards, her hands were chilled with the overnight breeze and her feet had gone to sleep. Now the reality had begun to hit her: this was not a game. It was, quite literally, a matter of life and death. One of those deaths might be her own, but she tried not to let her thoughts go down that route. She'd never manage to concentrate if she gave in to that impulse.

When she'd had a chance to grab a few hours' sleep she had regained some composure. To be sure, no one could have predicted she'd finish her training at such a momentous point. It was more than anyone might have imagined. But hadn't she wanted to do more, to save lives, just as her big sister was doing, but in a completely different sphere? Now was her chance – Sergeant Williams was right. Even though every bone in her body ached, her heart swelled with pride. This was it. History was being made all around her and, as Marigold had said, she was in the middle of it. Now everyone was calling it the Battle of Britain.

She was glad of a chance to escape, though, when Marigold suggested they take a bike ride one fine afternoon. It was now the height of summer and both young women looked forward to enjoying the sun, before returning to their posts: one on the raised ground to one side of the base as dusk fell, the other in the windowless, airless switchboard room.

The bikes were old and clanky but Clover didn't

care. She and Marigold had now covered most of the immediate area within walking range and this would allow them to venture further into the countryside, maybe as far as a local village. They might even manage a cooling lemonade in a pub. At the very thought her mouth began to water.

The clunking noise of the pedals on the ancient machines almost drowned out the birdsong, but Clover lifted her face to the sun and breathed out for joy. She got to the top of a small incline and lifted her legs clear of the pedals as she freewheeled down the other side, shouting out as she did so. 'Loooook! I'm going so fast!'

'Hang on!' Marigold realised she couldn't catch up without doing the same thing, and came flying down the lane, pulling to an undignified stop as her back wheel swerved alarmingly close to the hedge. 'Crikey, Clover, I thought I was a goner then. We'd better see to these brakes once we get back. I don't think anyone's checked them this century.'

Clover knew that this was a sensible suggestion but she didn't want to think about it right away, not when the sun was warm on her skin and the sky was a cloudless stretch of pure blue. 'Later. We'll think about it later,' she murmured, crinkling her eyes against the glare of the golden light. 'Hear that, Marigold? What sort of bird is that?'

Marigold stood silent and still for a moment, resting one leg on the ground and keeping the other foot on a pedal. 'Maybe it's a skylark,' she replied, scanning the air above her for any traces of the little bird. 'They like open ground like this. I'm not sure though.'

'Well, you're more likely to know than me,' Clover grinned. 'I can recognise a sparrow or a pigeon and that's about it. Or a robin. We didn't get skylarks in Hackney.'

'No, I suppose you wouldn't. Well, you didn't find many in Liverpool either.' Marigold sounded thoughtful. 'I say, Clover, did you mind about what I said the other day?'

'When you said what?'

Marigold gave a wry smile. 'When Milly wanted to take a bike to go to the pub and meet pilots. I know she thought I was being an interfering old fusspot. I wondered if you'd wanted to go.'

Clover shook her head with a small laugh. 'Honestly, that's got about as much appeal as a bowl of cold tripe. I've nothing against going to pubs in the normal run of things and don't really care if the others go or not, but I'm not risking what I'm doing here.'

Marigold got back onto her bike and resumed pedalling, only much more gently now, and Clover cycled along beside her. 'Good,' Marigold said. 'I mean, I didn't want to cramp your style. Go and meet airmen if you want to, it's not up to me to stop you, it's just that it's an insane chance to take. Breaking curfew like that – it's madness to think they won't find out.'

'Exactly.' Clover giggled. 'If we're going to do it then keep it for a special occasion.'

'Such as?'

'Well, I turn twenty-one quite soon. We could celebrate me getting the key of the door.' She threw back her head and began to sing, 'Twenty-one today, twenty-one today, she's got the key of the door, never been twenty-one before . . .' and Marigold joined in, at first hesitantly but by the end of the old song she was singing heartily too, laughing as the pair of them sped up along the deserted lane.

'That'll scare the skylarks,' Clover chuckled, now a little out of breath from pedalling while singing at the top of her voice. She cocked an ear to listen for any more birdsong, but there was none to be heard.

'Poor things. What have they ever done to harm us?' Marigold replied, but then her expression grew quizzical. 'Wait a mo, that doesn't sound like a bird. Can you hear it, Clover? What is it?'

Clover wrinkled her nose. 'Hear what? That was a distant seagull . . .'

'No, not that. Let's stop a bit.' Marigold was serious now, halting with a squeal of brakes, and coming to rest. 'It's not a bird, it's more mechanical. Coming from south of here.'

Clover tried her best to pick out the sound but struggled to begin with. Then she realised what her friend was talking about. 'The one that started like a background hum but seems to be coming closer?'

'That's it.' Marigold was deadly solemn now. 'Clover, I've heard this before, or very similar. You know, before . . .'

Clover swung her head around to meet her friend's eyes. 'Over in France, you mean? It's not like when the planes fly overhead at night though.'

'No.' Marigold swung around, scanning for what might be making the increasingly obvious noise. 'It's an engine in trouble, that's what it is. Try to see if you can make it out, Clover, your eyesight is better than mine. I'd put good money on it being an aircraft struggling to maintain height. Let's keep focusing on just above the horizon.'

For a few moments the two young women concentrated on the empty skies, turning in every direction, shading their eyes with their hands. Then Clover pointed. 'Over there. Look. It's almost coming out of the sun, that's why we couldn't spot it before.'

The noise was everywhere now, rumbling and grating and vibrating the ground beneath their feet. The plane came closer. 'It's a Spitfire, it's one of ours,' Clover said, almost to herself, as its distinctive shape became clearer. 'What's it doing?'

'Trying to find an airfield,' said Marigold. 'Or failing that, somewhere flat to land. Perhaps it's aiming for our base.'

Clover glanced in the direction from which they had come, and was struck by the realisation that they'd travelled a fair distance, almost without noticing it. 'It's too far,' she said. 'They aren't going to make it.'

For a few moments they stood transfixed, gazing towards the aircraft, powerless to change its fate. It sped across the horizon and dipped lower and lower, the sound of its struggling engine becoming ever louder. For a brief second Clover believed it was going to maintain height for long enough to reach the base after all, but then it grew clear that the miracle was not going to happen. With a scream of metal it narrowly avoided the roof of a tall barn and then scraped its fuselage along a flattish field, only a little way along the lane from where they were.

Marigold was first to move. 'Come on!' She pushed her bike upright. 'We've got to help. There's nobody else around.'

Clover couldn't see how they would be much use but she accepted that Marigold was better placed to know. She got back into the saddle and pedalled as fast as she could after her friend, whizzing along the narrow lane with the summer flowers bright in the hedgerows.

When they got to the field they could see the wrecked Spitfire through the gate. Marigold leapt from her bike and dragged the gate open. 'We'll never get the bikes through this,' she said, indicating the stubbly remains of an early crop. 'Let's leave them here against the hedge.' Then they ran towards the plane, trying to make out if there were any signs of life.

'Careful, it might catch fire,' Marigold warned, but she and Clover continued to run anyway. They came to a stop only when they had come close enough to get a better idea of what was going on.

A figure was fighting to get out of the cockpit, pushing with all his might, but the metal was bent out of shape. For a minute it seemed as if he was trapped, but then he suddenly broke free.

'Over here!' shouted Marigold. 'We're here to help. This way, this way.'

The man rushed towards them, limping badly, and then fell, whereupon they could see one of his legs was bleeding. He was gasping, breathless, not yet able to speak.

'We've got to get away from the wreckage, it could go up at any moment,' Marigold said. 'Can you walk any further?' The pilot couldn't answer. 'Right, we're going to lift you. Clover, carry him by his armpits, and I'll take the legs. I'm sorry, this is going to hurt but we've got to move you, we can't stay here.'

Clover's face showed her anxiety but she didn't want to frighten the injured man. Biting her lip, she did as Marigold suggested, barely registering the pilot's weight as she took hold of him, his flying jacket slippery in her grip. He still wore his goggles and so she couldn't see his eyes but his mouth twisted in pain as they half-carried, half-dragged him across the sharp stubble and back towards the gate to the lane.

'All right, this'll do.' Marigold could hardly talk as the effort had drained her strength. 'We'll set you down here, at the edge of the field.' Here at least the ground was softer, covered in grasses and weeds. They put him down as gently as they could, and he cried out in agony as his injured leg touched the earth.

'We need to send for help,' Marigold said, her voice a little steadier. 'Clover, you go. Ride back to base as fast as you can and raise the alarm.'

'Won't you be quicker?' Clover asked anxiously.

'Doesn't matter, I've got more first aid experience than you and this fellow needs it,' Marigold replied, and Clover could see that this made sense. She was getting to her feet when the explosion happened, the plane's engine going up in flames just as her friend had predicted it might. They'd got away from the wreckage just in time. One minute's delay and they would have been engulfed.

For a moment she staggered backwards but she couldn't think about that now. She would never manage to cycle back if she allowed those images to plague her. As it was, she felt sick to her stomach. As she turned towards her bike, she could see Marigold undoing the strap which held the pilot's goggles in place and the buckle under his chin to release the helmet. As she hauled herself onto her bike she could see his face. He was so young, she thought, perhaps even younger than her. She had to raise the alarm, to save this hero who was hardly more than a boy.

Clover had never ridden so fast, pelting down the lane, hoping there would be no farm vehicles or animals to block her way. She ignored the birdsong, the sweeping landscapes, the scent of the hedgerow plants. All her concentration was on reaching the base and finding help. Marigold might know first aid but she only had what she'd carried on the bike, no bandages or disinfectants or painkillers.

Her leg muscles screamed in pain but she willed herself onwards, turning the pedals again and again and again. Now her lungs were in agony too but she carried on, knowing there was no alternative. Even if anyone else had noticed the plane in trouble they wouldn't have known exactly where it had crashed. The plume of smoke would only just be rising, and there was no time to lose.

Sweat dripped into her eyes and her face was hot with effort as she finally rounded the corner to the entrance gate to the base. Fate was smiling on her at last as the first person she saw was Sergeant Williams, who was making idle conversation with the guard on duty. 'Harrison! Whatever have you been doing?' he said cheerfully but his manner soon changed when he caught sight of her expression.

'We . . . we . . .'

'Steady,' he said, and his tone was serious now. 'What's happened?'

She took a breath to calm down, knowing she had to get this right and as quickly as possible. 'A pilot's injured, his plane crashed in a field over there. Down the lane,' and she turned to point. 'He got out before the fire took hold but I don't know how bad he's hurt. Marigold's with him, I mean Volunteer Pewsey, and she can do first aid – but we didn't have any equipment.'

Sergeant Williams nodded once and immediately asked the guard to radio for assistance. 'You sure it's that way?'

'Certain,' Clover responded with no doubt in her voice.

'Then it's the Addison farm. Tell them that,' he said to the guard. 'Well done, Harrison. And now, you get back to your quarters and clean yourself up,' he said firmly. 'That's an order. You won't do anyone any good hanging around, least of all yourself.'

'But I want to see . . .' Clover could scarcely form a coherent sentence now that the adrenaline was wearing off. 'And Marigold? Will they be all right?'

Sergeant Williams' mouth twisted in sympathy. 'You've done your duty, Harrison,' he said. 'The medics will take charge now. Your job is to clean up and rest. Because no matter what has happened this afternoon

I still need you at your post this evening, on the search-lights. Do you understand?'

Clover nodded, too overcome to protest. Again it hit her: this was not a game. It was life or death, and she was in the middle of it.

CHAPTER TWENTY-NINE

It was not only in the skies above Hampshire that the Battle of Britain was being fought. While the planes engaged in combat over the coastline, from the far western curve all the way east to Kent, the fortunate air crew returned to land and regrouped, or had their injuries seen to, or snatched brief bursts of leave. The less fortunate were shot down or crashed, most of them as young as the pilot Clover had seen so briefly.

Even though she'd obsessively read the newspapers and listened to all the bulletins on the wireless, Rose was still surprised to find there was a new occupant on the ward when she went on shift one morning in August.

'A word, Nurse Harrison.' The harassed night sister took her arm and led her back into the corridor. 'We've got a curious case here, right enough.'

Rose, who had the advantage of a good night's sleep and filling breakfast of porridge followed by toast, looked surprised. Curious cases weren't unusual. You might say that every patient raised their own questions and problems; what difference would one more make?

She wasn't going to argue with Sister, though. The older woman's eyes were red from where she'd rubbed them through tiredness, her brow furrowed with worry lines. All the signs of a difficult night shift, in fact.

'Yes, let me explain,' she said, quietly enough that her voice would not travel as far as the room of patients in their beds. 'Young man, brought in yesterday afternoon. At first they weren't sure what was up. He's a pilot, home on a couple of days' leave from Kent somewhere. He's stationed on a base there, they said.'

'Lucky he could get away for a short time,' Rose observed, rubbing her bare arms as the corridor was shady and chilly first thing in the morning, despite the sun shining outside. 'I bet most of them have to stay on their bases.'

'Yes. Well. That's as maybe.' Sister had no time to speculate. 'The thing is, he's been fighting in the air battles you've heard about on the news, came back to see his parents who live on one of those big places overlooking Victoria Park.'

'Very nice.' Rose had often strolled past the tall, elegant houses, so different from the terraces around Victory Walk.

'Absolutely fine the first day, or so he told them, no visible injuries. Then started feeling pain yesterday around lunchtime, headaches, unable to breathe, sharp pains in his chest.'

'Ah, not so good, then.' Rose's interest had been piqued now.

'Exactly. Then he pretty well collapses. Winds up in here, unconscious. It's not looking good, Rose.'

Rose could tell that Sister was genuinely worried if she was addressing her by her first name. 'Doctor suspects a bad concussion and also cracked ribs. He'd had a dodgy landing down in Kent a couple of days ago, walked away from it and thought no more of it, but probably sustained a sharp bang to the back of the head. Oh, and turns out his entire left side is covered in bruises and scratches, and we haven't been able to tell if there are any minor breaks there. Least of his problems, anyway.'

Rose's eyes darkened in sympathy. 'The poor fellow. What's his name?'

Sister wrinkled her nose, trying to remember. 'Begins with an S. South . . . ? No, Sutherland. That's it, Philip Sutherland. Right, now you're aware of the situation, I shall be off. I'll see you this evening.' Sister hurried away, no doubt desperate for a few hours of uninterrupted sleep.

Sutherland, thought Rose. That was the name of the family who owned the factory where her father was foreman. Bert mentioned them sometimes, but just in passing; only the father concerned himself with the day-to-day running of the firm. It could be a coincidence. It wasn't an unusual name – but what were the odds?

None of that mattered, anyway, as son of a local factory owner or not, this young man was in need of care. Rose approached the immaculately made bed with its crisp white sheet turned back in a precise line, and it took all of her professional control not to give a small gasp.

The young man was as still as a statue. His skin was ghostly pale, as if he had been carved of marble. She had to look very hard to see any signs of inhalation and exhalation, as there was scarcely any movement in his ribcage or abdomen, beneath the functional wool blanket.

His hair was thick and the colour of hazelnuts, and she could imagine his superior officers admonishing him to get it cut on a regular basis. She was overcome with a sudden urge to run her hand through the sweep of hair on his forehead, and it brought her up short. Whatever was she thinking of? She'd better banish any such ideas at once.

His arms lay outside the sheet and blanket, positioned rigidly at his sides. His hands were strong-looking, the nails trimmed short, and she thought she could see a trace of oil on one thumb. Someone who knew his way about a plane's engine, maybe? There were no creases or calluses though. Most likely he hadn't worked hard with his hands all his adult life. Not like her father or Peter. If he was one of those Sutherlands, he would have been expected to keep his hands clean, sitting behind a desk or even in a library. He could have been a student, one of the lucky few. He was perhaps her age. Too young to be lying so still in a hospital ward.

'Good morning, Nurse Harrison.' Rose almost jumped as the doctor approached on his morning rounds. Thank God it wasn't the horrible Mr Prendergast but one of the older ones, Dr Oswald, with his receding hairline and sharp beak of a nose. 'I see you've met our latest patient.'

'Yes, Sister just told me about him.' She cast a worried glance at his ominously unmoving ribcage. Dr Oswald noticed and pursed his lips.

'I see you are worried about his respiration. What you see here is misleading. As Sister will have mentioned, we strongly suspect cracked ribs, and therefore have strapped him heavily – not that you can tell from here. They'll mend of their own accord if we can keep them supported. No, our main concern is the concussion. He hasn't recovered consciousness since yesterday afternoon, or so I am led to believe.' He folded his arms, a clipboard in one hand.

Rose nodded. 'That's pretty well what Sister said to me too. Well, we shall just have to see that he gets as much rest as possible. Not easy on this busy ward,' she added, as two junior nurses sped by with a creaky trolley full of medicines.

'Indeed.' The doctor paused. 'We might see if any of the smaller rooms become available. However, he mustn't be too out of the way. He requires constant monitoring. There's a conundrum for you, Nurse Harrison, and I shall leave you to ponder on that. Good day to you.'

He turned on the heel of his smart black brogue and moved off to check his next ward full of patients.

Rose sighed. Not ten minutes into her shift and already she had an impossible predicament. That was on top of the rest of the men in this ward, some here with ailments of old age, others from accidents thanks to the blackout, and increasingly more with conditions arising from the war. Every one of them required her attention and expertise to ensure they recovered as quickly as possible, ready to go back and rejoin the effort to clinch victory.

There was something about this young man, though, that crept beneath her defences and touched her heart. It was partly his age: she could relate so closely to him because of that. But it was also what he must have achieved already, the skills he must have had to take to the air in the first place, let alone in the conditions of battle. Her breath caught as she imagined what it must have been like up in the cockpit, so far above the ground, the fields tiny patches beneath him.

How brutal to be injured so far from safety and comfort. How unfair to reach that level of skill and to lose it all in a matter of seconds. It was unbearable. Her blood ran cold at the unjust nature of fate.

Then she gave herself a mental shake. Standing here allowing her imagination to get the better of her would help nobody. She had to complete her rounds and then devise a plan to situate this young man where she could keep a careful eye on him but not shunt him away in a corner where he might be missed once she finished her shift.

It was only what she would do for any patient. Him being a Sutherland had no bearing on matters at all, of that she was clear. She would show him no favouritism. The doctor had not mentioned his specific background and her own father would not expect it of her. He was a stickler for fairness and all of his children had been brought up to believe the same: that everyone deserved the best possible chance, no matter where they were born and in what circumstances.

It was the very look of this young man that had done it. He was asking nothing of her but Rose felt it all the same. Now and again it happened: a patient's plight touched her to the core. A connection sprang into being, as if from out of nowhere.

Standing at the head of his hospital bed with his notes attached to the metal rail, Rose vowed that all his training and courage would not have been for nothing. Somehow she would come up with a way to help him to recover, find a place where he could mend at his own pace, where those damaged ribs could heal and the rest of his injuries be treated. Where his brain could get over the devastating knock it had so clearly received.

Nodding firmly, she tucked in her chin and swiftly made her way to the ward table, to assess the wider picture of how everyone else was faring, and what might have changed overnight. The sunshine poured through the big windows, making the freshly laundered sheets bright, illuminating the surfaces and emphasising how clean they were, devoid of dust or smears. Everything was as it should be. Rose sighed and looked back to the young man, so perfectly still in the furthermost bed. Somehow, she would mend him.

Her mind was still on him as she opened the door to her family's house, after finishing her shift. Even though her feet were aching with standing all day long, she'd had a strong urge to sit at her mother's table rather than brave the noisy dining room in the nurses' home. She'd had a word with the night shift, so that any of those nurses could move Philip Sutherland if an opportunity arose. Rose had quietly earmarked the ideal bed for him but it was presently occupied and she didn't have the authority to discharge that patient.

Robbie broke her reverie by leaping the last few steps of the staircase and landing at her feet. 'Scuse me,' he said cheerfully, pushing the front door open before it had even closed.

'Hang on a mo. I haven't seen you for days. Is that all you've got to say to me?' Rose blocked his way.

Robbie shrugged. 'It hasn't been very long really. I got to go, Ricky says he's got something to show me.'

Rose frowned, instantly suspecting that this meant trouble. 'It's not that perishing go-cart again, is it?'

Robbie laughed. 'Nah, we crashed that good and proper yesterday evening. Ricky says it's beyond repair. No, he says he's found a pet.'

Rose still looked dubious.

'No, honest, he has. He won't say what so I've got to go and see. Let me through, Rose. Please.' He looked so piteous that Rose didn't have the heart to stop him.

'Whatever it is, don't let it bite you,' she warned.

Stepping into the kitchen, she found Daisy was already back from work and helping their mother lay the table. 'Hope there's room for one more?' she said, and Patty beamed at her.

'You know there's always room for you, Rose. Or for any of you.'

Rose smiled in return, enjoying the fragrant aroma of the stew bubbling away on the stove.

'Don't expect miracles, though. It was tricky buying any meat this week,' Patty told her, putting down the last fork and turning back to give the pot a stir. 'I had to bulk this out with barley and potatoes. Never mind, there's plenty of vegetables. And look what I got from the garden today.' She pointed to the windowsill.

Rose looked across as she was bidden and noticed a row of plump red tomatoes, their skins shining in the early evening sun. Now she could detect the ripe smell of them too, and it made her mouth water. 'What beauties!' she exclaimed. 'You're so clever at growing them, Ma.'

Patty chuckled. 'Years of practice and I save all our scraps to make compost. We all do, don't we, Daisy?'

Daisy nodded, putting a pile of side plates in the middle of the big old table. 'Wouldn't dare do otherwise,' she grinned. 'Can't have those plants going hungry, can we?'

'And you reap the benefits, young lady,' Patty reminded her. 'Now go and find your father. He's out the back, mending that lock that keeps sticking.'

Daisy went through the back kitchen and stuck her head out of the door to the outside. 'Rose is here!' she called. 'And tea's nearly ready.'

A couple of minutes later Bert came inside and washed his hands at the back sink, always mindful of Patty's strict rules about cleanliness. Even before Rose had begun her training, there was never any excuse for dirty hands in this house. As he did so, Robbie slipped back in to the kitchen, wiping straw from one shirt sleeve.

Rose decided to ask her father outright about her patient. As Bert took his place on the biggest wooden chair, she told him about the young man. 'And his surname is Sutherland. Is he related to your boss, do you think?'

Bert reached for the salt and pepper as Patty placed a big plate of stew in front of him. 'Oh, that does smell good, love.' She smiled in pride as he looked up at her. Then he frowned at his eldest daughter's question. 'I can't say as I know the names of his children, but I know he's got a couple and they're around your age, Rose.' He shook the pepper pot over his food, thinking further. 'Now you come to mention it, I do seem to remember someone saying the son had gone into the air force.'

'Where does your boss live? Is it over by Victoria Park?' Rose spread a piece of bread with a smear of butter, careful not to take more than her fair share.

Bert nodded. 'Yes, he does. Though I heard that his wife moved away for a while when we all thought Jerry was going to gas us, last year. Why?'

'Oh, nothing really. Sister said that's where the young man's family lived, that's all. Sounds as if it definitely is him, then.' Rose took a bite of her bread and butter, and then some stew. 'Delicious. Ma, you've done it again.'

Patty paused in raising her own mouthful to her lips. 'Thank you, Rose. You know I never want any of you to go without.' She looked carefully at her eldest as everyone tucked in and the topic of conversation changed. She hoped they wouldn't start talking about the way the bombing raids were getting closer to the centre of London; she was trying to put that to the back of her mind, although one had landed near Harrow and another towards the south-west of the city. To fight the creeping dread, she considered how Rose seemed today. Ever since the girl had started at the hospital, she had come home with tales of patients, difficult or unusual cases, staff problems or whatever other matters were on her mind. Yet today Patty picked up another element in her daughter's voice. It was nothing obvious, not worth raising, certainly not at the tea table. Yet she would put good money on it that there was something about this patient that had touched her daughter's often buried emotions, and it had very little do with him being related to Bert's boss.

Daisy, meanwhile, tucked into her food but she was only vaguely following the discussion. Her mind was elsewhere, and she had minimal interest in whoever might be on Rose's ward. She was recalling the recent evening in the pub when Sam had finally enticed her out on a Friday. Putting her memories of her previous disastrous night out firmly to one side, she'd reminded herself that she would miss him in the ticket office and one drink wouldn't hurt.

Then she'd found she'd enjoyed herself after all. Sam must have accepted that they were only ever going to be friends and didn't try any funny business. Not that she'd thought he would but, after Ted, she'd rather lost faith in her ability to predict what a man might do.

For a start it was a different pub and it had a lively beer garden, altogether much more cheerful a place to sit on a fine summer's evening. He didn't try to tell her what to drink, and was happy when she chose lemonade. 'Enjoy it while you can, they'll start watering it down fast enough,' he'd quipped.

Before long Daisy was wondering why she'd put this off and why she hadn't agreed sooner. They were having such a good chat that she didn't notice two young women taking the table next to them, and only looked across when the one with the dark plaits said, 'It's Daisy, isn't it?'

That had caught her attention. 'Yes,' she said, for a moment searching her memory for who this was, though she was very familiar.

'I'm Sylvia, I worked with Clover until recently. And this is my sister,' the woman said, and Daisy brought her hand to her mouth in recognition.

'Oh, of course. Silly me. You know how it is when you see people where you don't expect them.' She tried to cover her embarrassment. 'Er, this is my colleague Sam. Soon to be ex-colleague,' she added.

Sylvia had smiled brightly. 'Pleased to meet you, Sam. Yes, we don't often come here but it's not too far from us. We live in Tottenham, you see.'

Daisy automatically thought what route they must have taken to get here. One of the buses that ran straight down the Seven Sisters Road . . .

Then she remembered she wasn't at work and made more effort to be friendly. She must make a note of how Sylvia seemed so that she could write and tell Clover. Sylvia was relaxed and cheerful, a smattering of freckles across her nose, her face with hardly any make-up and her dress a simple checked cotton with a matching belt. Altogether a far cry from the girl Daisy had seen all those months ago with Victor. Clover would be happy.

'Yes, and we went to see *Gone with the Wind* again, didn't we?' she was saying, and her sister chimed in with 'Third time!'

Sam was lapping it up. 'Not my kind of thing at all,' he protested. 'Three times is three too many in my book. Give me a bit of action any day.'

'But there's plenty! It's set in a war!' Sylvia threw back her head in laughter and Daisy could see that Sam was enjoying it all hugely.

'No planes, are there? Or cars.'

'Hardly. Seeing as they wasn't invented then.'

'That's what I'm saying. I like a modern film. None of these silly costumes or whatnot.'

'They aren't silly, they're gorgeous, and do you know they take ages to make, ages.'

Daisy sat back for once and watched the two of them spar. Who would have thought it. She'd rarely seen Sam so animated, even after all those months of working closely together. Before she knew it, he had thrown down a challenge to Sylvia: that she come to a film of his choice and see if she didn't enjoy it. As a concession he would allow her to pick one for him, as long as it wasn't 'Gone with the bloody wind'.

Sylvia had told him off for being cheeky and too forward, but she hadn't turned him down outright.

'Penny for 'em, Daisy,' Rose teased her now, bringing her back to the tea table, the stew all but finished.

'Oh, er, nothing. Well, that's to say, I was just thinking of what I'm going to write to Clover later,' she improvised, which was, when you came to think of it, true. Clover would be in for a very pleasant surprise.

CHAPTER THIRTY

'Whatever is it? Your jaw just about hit the floor.'
Marigold was folding her hated army-issue underwear
and stowing it in her bedside cupboard. She and Clover
had the hut to themselves for once, the others having
lingered in the NAAFI. Now that they had been here
for a couple of months the place looked far more
homely; cushions had been added, some sent from
home and others made from any scraps that could be
found. Milly had crocheted a blanket and proudly
displayed it next to the stove, although it was now
so warm that neither were needed. Still, it added a
welcome burst of bright colour, with its vivid turquoise
and lemon pattern.

Clover rolled over on her bed, where she'd stretched
out to read the letter from home. The date on it showed
it had been delayed – again – but a letter was a letter,
when all was said and done.

'It's from my little sister,' she said. 'Well, not so little
any more. She bumped into my old colleague, you
know, the one who I write to sometimes, and who

writes back, except she's kept this bit of news quiet.' She giggled at the thought of Sylvia harbouring a secret.

'Why? What sort of news?'

'Good news for once, or at least I think it is.' Clover wondered how much to reveal of Sylvia's past, but decided it wasn't her story to tell. 'Let's just say my old friend hasn't had the best of luck with men, and was pretty low when I left for here. Now it seems as if my sister's friend has taken a shine to her. I suppose we'll just have to wait and see how it goes – but good for her.'

Marigold nodded, even though she had no idea who Clover was talking about. 'Can't begrudge anyone a bit of fun with all that's going on at present,' she said, shoving the final item away. 'Ugh, I hate those things. They make me itch.'

'They make everyone itch.' Clover turned over again and threw her arms behind her head, crossing her legs. 'You know what, Marigold? We've been here, what, over two months now, and I wonder if I could get a spot of leave. I don't usually miss my family too badly, they're all so regular at writing letters, but when something like this happens . . . I don't know, maybe I'm being silly, but I just want to sit for five minutes in our kitchen and see them all. Oh, whatever is wrong with me?' For a moment she was overcome with a longing, such as she hadn't felt in all the time she'd been away. How ridiculous that it was one small piece of information that had set it off – but she couldn't deny it. She was suddenly homesick beyond belief. All the news about the raids getting closer and closer to East London had been burrowing away and now it all felt as if it was too much. 'Sorry, Marigold, that came out of nowhere.' She couldn't meet her friend's gaze.

Marigold came over and sat at the bottom of Clover's narrow bed. She took a moment to frame what she would say.

'I understand,' she told her. 'Most of the time we're too busy to think about these things. It's only when we have a spare moment that it happens, as if our feelings ambush us. It happened to me in France some-times, and it was even sillier as there was no question of me getting leave. Also, to be honest, I'm not sure I would have got a warm reception even if I'd managed it. My mother believes in getting on with things, and my father wouldn't dream of admitting any kind of weakness. He doesn't like to see it in me either.' She pulled a wry face.

'My family isn't like that,' said Clover in an unsteady voice, and buried her face in her scratchy pillow.

Marigold sighed. 'You're lucky. From what you've said you might not come from a background as well-off as mine but they all sound so warm and friendly. Whatever you did, they'd help you if you needed it.'

'They would,' said Clover, muffled.

Marigold nodded even though the other girl couldn't see her, and turned to look out of the window. There was not much to see; rows of huts similar to this one. She knew it would be her view for the foreseeable future.

'Then why not put in for a spot of leave?' she suggested. 'To be realistic, though, you aren't likely to get it right away. You can tell as well as I can that the fighting is growing worse around us. All those planes we see, every night and day, up in the clouds, the dogfights and the bombers overhead. They'll want to keep you here on duty and you can't blame them. Still, if you make it known you would like leave, and you're fortunate enough to live close enough to get back relatively easily, you could get the chance when things calm down.'

Clover rolled over again, dashing her hand across her eyes. The wave of longing had passed and she spoke more clearly. 'Thanks. I will. Even knowing that I might see them soon makes me feel better. And I know we're in for another busy night. Ever since that first crash, it's been non-stop, becoming heavier and heavier.' They both fell silent at the thought. The pilot they had rescued had been taken to hospital with a badly injured leg but had survived. Since then there had been other incidents, although they had not been first at the scene for any of them. Pilots and ground crew had died – and the worst thing was, they were getting used to it.

'Buck up,' said Marigold suddenly, as voices drifted across the path between the huts. 'That sounds like Milly. Look, run to the bathroom and take your flannel. You don't want them to see you with red eyes.'

Clover hurried to take her advice, as the sounds of Milly's gales of laughter rose in the warm air.

Rose was not strictly on duty when she heard two of the other nurses talking in the corridor on their way to the dining room. Mr Roberts, who had had pneumonia, was being discharged, and his case would be managed at home by the local team of district nurses. Rose approved; the district nurses who lived at the other end of Victory Walk were all well-trained, and now and again their paths crossed. Their superintendent had a fearsome reputation and anyone in her charge could expect the very best of treatment.

That would mean a vacant bed in the men's general ward. The next bed along was occupied by Mr Cecil, who had been with them for some time, as his ulcers refused to heal. He had lived in Dalston for all of his life, as had his parents and grandparents before him, and he knew everybody. He would always joke about her father and what he'd been like as a boy, which Rose found very amusing. Bert's very few boyhood pictures showed a tidy, smiling schoolboy. Evidently there was a whole different side to him, which was possibly where Robbie got his mischief from.

Mr Cecil had let it be known that he particularly missed his old friend and colleague of many years, Ezra Soper. Mr Soper had also been admitted to Hackney Hospital, with what they thought was a stroke. He currently occupied the very bed that Rose had kept an eye on, it being in a corner, with light from windows on two sides, and thanks to the angle of the building, was slightly set back from the other beds, meaning it was quieter. Yet it was within easy observation from the ward table, the central nurses' station. She knew it would be the ideal spot for Philip Sutherland.

Rose told herself that she was making the most sensible decision for all the patients concerned. Mr

Soper could move to the newly vacant bed. He would benefit from being next to his old friend; a familiar voice often got through to a stroke victim. Mr Cecil would be delighted to see his companion, and was the sort of character who would love to know he was helping with his recovery. Philip would stand a much better chance in the window bed. He needed rest above all else; nothing else they could offer would bring him out of the coma from which he had shown no signs of stirring.

Rose set aside any thought of eating in the dining room. If she could find Dr Oswald and convince him of her plan, it would be better for everyone. She would hurry to do so right away.

CHAPTER THIRTY-ONE

Robbie hung back, hating what was to come. His idea of a good Saturday did not include going shopping with his mother. She would always bump into women that she knew and they would all say the same things to him, asking if he was enjoying school, even though it was the summer holidays, and remarking that he'd grown, which was stating the obvious. Although, he thought glumly, if he'd stayed the same size then he wouldn't have to be dragged round the shops for new school uniform.

Patty gave him a firm look, knowing full well that he was reluctant to go on the necessary expedition. It didn't matter; there was no choice. He would damage his feet if he continued to wear shoes that were too small. Already he'd trodden down the backs of his plimsolls and wore them like slippers. That state of affairs could not continue. Besides, she liked him to appear smart, and do credit to her and her family.

'Hurry up,' she said. 'The sooner we start the quicker it'll be over.'

'S'pose so,' Robbie muttered, sulkily following his mother around the corner of the side road leading onto Mare Street, the big thoroughfare through the centre of Hackney. It was bustling with eager shoppers, despite more and more goods being rationed. He knew that Patty had saved her clothing coupons to kit him out and that he should feel grateful, but he somehow couldn't. This then made him guilty, and even less willing to go through the yearly charade.

'Shoes first,' Patty told him. 'I can make your shirts, and you can still just about get into last year's trousers if I let down the hem, but you cannot go one more day without footwear that fits. Don't make that face, young man. You're going to get them whether you want to or not, so you'd better get used to the idea.'

Robbie hung his head but dutifully trailed after her, knowing he was being unreasonable. All the same he wished he was out playing football with Ricky and his brothers. Then he decided he was being daft. They could play this afternoon, as long as he got this over with as fast as possible.

'Tell you what, if you're good and agree to a nice sensible pair, then I'll buy you a lovely currant bun,' Patty said, neatly weaving between a group of older women who were pointing at talcum powder in the chemist's window. 'You'd like that.'

Robbie was struck with inspiration. 'Could I have something else instead?' he asked. 'I do love buns, but I was wondering if I could have something different. Something that would last,' he added, guessing that this would appeal to his mother's practical side.

'Oh, really?' Patty asked, sounding intrigued. 'It's not like you to turn down a visit to the bakery, Robbie. What were you thinking about?'

'A rabbit,' said Robbie.

Patty halted in her tracks. 'A rabbit.'

'Yes, a rabbit.'

Patty blew out her breath. 'And where exactly are you going to get a rabbit?'

'Ricky's got one and it's had babies.' He glanced hopefully at his mother's face.

Patty shook her head. 'Don't even think it. Where would it go? Then we'd have to feed it, clean it out, find bedding for it. It would be nothing but a nuisance. I'm surprised Mrs Glanville let Ricky have one.'

Robbie had known it was a long shot but he couldn't give up now. Ever since Ricky had shown him the creature he was hiding in a crate in the back yard, he'd wanted one as well. He'd fallen in love at first sight, with its silky fur and floppy ears. 'She didn't know at first,' he admitted, remembering the row that had erupted when his friend's mother had gone out to hang her washing and found the pet stowed in the corner where she kept the big pole that propped up the line. 'She likes it now though.'

Patty pursed her lips. 'Put that idea out of your head right now,' she told him. 'It's bad enough with food being rationed, and I wish they'd waited until the new term began before putting clothes on the ration too. We'd have to build a hutch—'

'I could do it!' Robbie offered eagerly. 'I helped Ricky, it's not so hard . . .'

'. . . and then find somewhere that sold straw, and food—'

'We could give it scraps,' Robbie protested but his mother's face hardened.

'You know we make good use of our scraps. We keep them to make compost for my plants. And who benefits? We all do – you included. What are you having for lunch, may I ask? Tomato sandwiches. Tomatoes from our pots, fed with scraps. No, Robbie, you are not having a rabbit. Don't glare like that. Now here's the shoe shop, and you can look cheerful while we're in there.'

It was when they emerged from the dark shop which smelt of leather and polish that the interesting thing happened. Robbie carried the box with his new good shoes inside, knowing that his mother had chosen ones of quality, and a size bigger than they needed to be so they would last longer, and realised that meant other members of the family would go without for a while. It didn't make him feel any better.

'Ooh, what have you got there?' He glanced up and his heart sank. It was his Aunt Vera, her hair held solid with spray, and clutching the arm of his cousin Faith as if she was going to make a run for it if she let go.

'New school shoes,' he muttered, staring at his feet.

'My, you've grown and it's only been a few weeks since I last saw you,' she went on. Robbie cringed. 'Hasn't he, Faith? You haven't seen him since Christmas, have you?'

Faith tossed her beautifully cut hair. 'That's right,' she said flatly. 'It would have been Christmas. Hello, Robbie. Hello, Aunt Patty.'

Even Robbie could tell she was not her usual self. He was not fond of her – she always talked down to him, even though she pretended not to. He preferred his cousin Hope but she was nowhere to be seen. He knew Faith had got some highfaluting job in town and he was quite happy that she spent most of her time there these days.

'We've been buying Faith some new clothes, haven't we?' Vera went on and Faith nodded.

'Well, that's nice,' said Patty. 'I thought you mostly went shopping in the West End, Faith?'

Faith gave herself a shake and perked up. 'That's right, but I thought I'd bring my custom somewhere closer to home. It doesn't hurt, does it.' She bit her lip and Robbie thought she was behaving very oddly.

'Very good of you,' Patty replied, earning a sharp glare from Vera.

'Yes, if I want something classic that will last me for years, then of course I choose the West End, maybe somewhere like John Lewis, but – but that won't be necessary at the moment.' Faith seemed to run out of steam.

Robbie knew that his mother dreamed of buying clothes from John Lewis but had to make do with Ridley Road market. Trust his cousin to rub her nose in it. He stood up straighter, now annoyed on his mother's behalf.

'Really?' Patty cocked her head and met her sister's eyes.

'Yes,' said Vera shortly, not elaborating further.

'I see,' said Patty, and her gaze moved to Faith, first her face and then the rest of her. 'Oh, I see.'

Now that Robbie followed where his mother was looking, he could see that Faith had put on weight. Not all over though. Just in front. That was a bit odd, he thought. It was just where Ricky's ma got fat before she had his little sister . . .

'Right, well, lovely to bump into you, but we really must be going,' Vera announced, steering Faith along the pavement. 'I'll pop in to have a chat later this week, Patty. I've some news for you but it can wait. Goodbye for now.'

'TTFN!' Robbie called after their departing backs. He'd heard his favourite wireless characters say that, when ITMA was on, and he liked the sound of the shortened version of 'ta-ta for now'. He turned his face up to his mother, his mouth spreading into a broad grin.

Patty breathed out heavily, for a moment not moving from the spot. Then she shook her head again, this time with a completely different look on her face. 'Oh dear,' she sighed. Then she turned as her son cleared his throat.

'Ma, Faith's gone all big in her front.'

'That's not very polite,' Patty said quickly. 'Don't talk like that about your cousin.'

'But it was how Mrs Glanville was like. You know, before Maggie arrived. Ricky said that's where babies come from.'

'Don't you say anything, Robbie!' Patty groaned inwardly. Trust Ricky to pass on that little gem before

311

she was ready to tell Robbie anything of the sort. 'You are not to breathe a word of this, not when we get home or out among your friends. Promise me.'

Robbie nodded. 'I promise. But,' and he saw this was the best chance he was ever going to get, 'may I have that rabbit now?'

CHAPTER THIRTY-TWO

The last of the daylight was fading and Rose should have finished her shift some time ago, but she had not left the men's general ward. Instead she had brought a chair to the far corner, where Philip Sutherland was now safely installed. Dr Oswald had agreed with her plan and put it into action, for which Rose was immensely grateful.

She scanned the young man's face for any sign of a change. He still had not stirred since lapsing into his coma, and she could only hope that beneath the surface he was able to recover and his damaged brain might heal itself. Now he was in this more secluded spot he would find it easier to rest, she was sure. There was no avoiding the constant background noise of the ward, which was busy day and night, but it was less evident here.

In the growing dimness it was becoming more difficult to see clearly but Rose wondered if there was a slight improvement in the colour of his skin. It might be wishful thinking but perhaps it was not so pale and waxy. Cautiously she put her palm on his forehead. It had been clammy and cold, but now it seemed closer to normal. Or was that her imagination, convincing her of what she badly wanted to believe? She took his temperature, just to be sure. Normal.

She sat back down on the hard chair, careful not to scrape the wooden legs along the floor. 'There, you're going to be well soon,' she said softly. 'You don't know me but I've been checking on you ever since you came in. I'm Rose, one of the nurses.' She paused and looked up towards the main ward, knowing that some of her colleagues thought she was crazy to spend so much time with one patient.

'You'll like this bed much better than the old one,' she went on, certain that the sound of a comforting voice would do no harm and could make him feel safer, deep down. 'It's got a view of the outside world for a start. You could see all the comings and goings, the nurses and doctors and cleaners. It's a big hospital and there are a lot of us. You're in good hands here, no doubt about it.'

Lights were coming on around the ward, but Rose got up and pulled the cubicle curtain a little way across to shield Philip's face from any bright glare. She turned and drew down the blackout blinds across the external windows, earning a wave of thanks from the harassed-looking night sister who had just come on shift.

'There, now we won't give away our position to any enemy planes.' She sat down again and impulsively took his hand. 'Maybe you'd like to know what's been happening since you arrived here. Well, those planes keep on coming but we're fighting back. They're calling it the

Battle of Britain but I expect you heard that already. You were part of it, after all. The RAF is winning the day – those Spitfires are nippy as can be, and then there are the Hurricanes too. I reckon Hitler thought he'd win this one easily but he's miscalculated.' She sighed and rubbed his hand a little to try to warm it. 'What nobody knows is what he will do next. If he was using the air to pave the way for invasion, like we've all been fearing, and it doesn't go his way, what else has he got up his sleeve?'

She paused again, uncertain that she wanted to voice her thoughts. Then again, it might help her to say them and face the dread that sometimes felt overwhelming. 'He'll have to step it up, won't he? He's gone after the air bases and hasn't managed to destroy them. So next it will be supply and manufacturing routes he'll target, and the cities to try to scare us into submission. Sorry, I didn't mean to worry you, it's just that I can't talk about this to anyone else because I don't want to bother the sisters and doctors, or frighten the newer nurses, and my family are scared enough as it is and insist on talking about other things, like growing tomatoes or how big my brother is getting to take their minds off it. So, I'm pouring it all out to you, thinking that you probably can't hear.' She looked at his face, at his fine features, the hair swept back from his forehead a little longer now. 'Because either way, it's us. The docks, the factories, all the people crowded in to these streets – it's the East End that's for it.'

From outside she could hear a bird calling in the last moments of daylight. Perhaps it was a blackbird, up on the roof of the nurses' home. Gazing at Philip's face she

315

felt something stir within her. She didn't want to give in to the fear. She wanted to live. Despite the bleak picture she had painted, there was a hope for a new life. She gave his hand a gentle squeeze. 'Well, so be it. We've been up against it before around here, haven't we? We always come through somehow. So you've got to get better and help see this through. We're going to stick together, that's what we're good at.' Realising that a nurse or doctor could come by at any moment she changed her hand position so that her fingers were resting with gentle pressure against his cool wrist. Taking a patient's pulse was something she could do as automatically as breathing but tonight it somehow meant so much more. Carefully she paid attention to what her fingers were telling her. The pulse was light but very definitely there. She would swear that it was more regular than when he was first admitted. And his face – no, she was not imagining it; he was improving.

'Come on, Philip, you're winning your battle too,' she breathed, knowing that she really should not stay any longer. 'Please, keep going. You can do it.' Rising to her feet, she set his hand back at his side and cast a final glance at his shadowed face. 'I'll see you tomorrow. Sleep well.' If this had been a fairy tale, he would have stirred and murmured her name; but it was not, and he remained as motionless as ever. Nevertheless, Rose thought as she moved down the central aisle between the long rows of beds, there was cause for hope. She had to hold on to that, against the dark waves of fear.

* * *

Patty tutted as she wrestled a big bag of potatoes from one side of the storeroom to the other. The new delivery boy had no idea of where to leave things. He'd said he was only temporary as he was waiting for his call-up papers, and she could only keep her fingers crossed that this was true. Not that he looked old enough to go into the forces, but perhaps he'd been less than honest about his age. People did that all the time. Look at Daisy, for a start.

Wiping the sweat from her brow, she stood up and stretched her aching back. It was still warm, the final days of August muggy and airless. She wiped her hands on her apron and went through to the shop. It had been a quiet morning so far. Which was more than could be said of the night before, with the ack-acks going more than ever, drumming through the walls of the house to interrupt her sleep and stoke her anxiety.

Meanwhile Clover had written to say that she'd requested leave but it hadn't been granted yet. Patty was even more worried for her middle daughter, out on the plains behind the south coast, braving the enemy attacks and using the massive searchlights to protect the bases and civilians. While she admired her courage, she had to admit she would love to see her back at the kitchen table, where she could protect her and feed her up a bit. Those army rations could be any old tasteless gruel, although Clover never complained.

The doorbell clanged and in came Vera, looking anxiously around. Patty had wondered when her sister would turn up, after their encounter on Mare Street at the weekend. Her expression was very different to her standard one of smug superiority; it was almost furtive.

'Morning, Patty. Am I your only customer?'

Patty had to grin, as there were very few places anyone could hide between the shelves. 'As you can see,' she said, trying to sound welcoming.

Vera nodded, and pulled at her collar. 'Dreadfully warm, isn't it.'

'Would you like a glass of water?' Patty offered. 'Or I've got some cordial somewhere?'

'No, no.' Vera sniffed. 'I don't want to put you to any trouble.' She checked behind her once again.

Patty frowned. 'If you're so worried about anyone coming in, perhaps we should talk somewhere else later? Come over for a cup of tea at the end of the afternoon. Or I'll come to yours.'

Vera sighed a very long breath out. 'No offence, Patty, but your place is always busy, what with Robbie, and Daisy, and then Rose dropping in, and Bert in and out. As for mine – well, Faith's moved back in, for the time being.'

Patty nodded, knowing full well that this was what all the fuss was about. She pointed to a wooden stepstool that she used to reach the highest shelves on the back wall. 'I'll just dust that down – here we go – and you can take a seat.' She pulled up the rickety tall chair she kept behind the counter for quiet moments. 'Right, now, you'd better tell me what all this is about.'

Vera hesitated, now the moment was upon her. Then she looked her sister in the eye. 'Don't tell me you haven't guessed. I saw your face on Saturday, so I shouldn't wonder it'll be no surprise to you to learn that Faith is in the family way.'

Patty stood. 'I think we might need those glasses of cordial after all.'

Ten minutes later, the whole sorry story had come out. In many ways Vera was right; it was no surprise. Faith had fallen for her married boss and his grand promises, of career advancement or the prospect of becoming his second wife, as of course he'd vowed to leave his first one. When it came to the crunch, though, he refused point-blank, and accused Faith of leading him on. So now Faith had no glamorous job, and no luxurious flat in the West End, and was left with the reality of becoming a mother before Christmas.

'Poor Faith,' Patty said sincerely. While her niece could be deeply annoying and insensitive, she'd been taken in by the oldest trick in the book. And she was only young; she wouldn't have known any better. More than that, when it came to it, she was still family. 'How can we help?'

Vera stiffened and the step-stool creaked. 'Thank you, Patty, but we have a solution in mind.'

This was a surprise. Patty's eyes widened. 'Is Arthur going round to convince the boss to do the right thing?'

'Don't be daft!' Vera snapped, all her tension causing her to lash out. 'Although Arthur will have his part to play, in the fullness of time,' she conceded. She swallowed hard and then sat up straight again. 'No, Martin has a spot of leave due very soon and he and Faith will be married when he comes home.'

Patty thought she must have misheard.

'Martin?'

'Yes, Martin.' Vera was piqued. 'You know very well who I'm talking about. Martin from the bank, who's now in the air force. The one you hoped Rose would take up with. Except he prefers my Faith, and just as well.'

'Blimey.' Patty didn't know what else to say for a moment. 'Er, does he know? About the baby, I mean?'

'Does he know? Of course he knows! How can he not know?'

Patty shook her head. 'Then why would he—'

'Because he's always been very fond of Faith,' Vera said, her voice determined, a hardness in her eyes. 'And Arthur will make it worth his while. When all this fighting's over, he will use his contacts to ensure Martin gets the best possible start in business. He won't be left waiting for some old codger to die in the bank so that he can be assistant deputy manager when he eventually reaches fifty.' Vera was almost spitting now, so desperate was she to convince her sister that the plan would work.

Patty nodded slowly; maybe it would. 'Then you'll let it be known—'

'That Martin and Faith, couldn't wait for the official ceremony last time he had leave. Which actually was back in the spring, though you might not have seen him. So really we are only making formal what was already agreed. Everyone who's ever seen them together knows that they are a young couple deeply in love.' Vera's tone brooked no argument.

'I see.' Patty leant back, aware that from now on there would be two stories: the real one and the official one, to which everyone must hold to avoid Faith being cast into disgrace. 'Well, if Faith and Martin are happy . . .'

'They are very happy,' Vera said grimly. Then she relented, a quiver in her voice hinting at her real feelings. 'I can tell you aren't, though. All right, we'll have to smile and say it's all worked out for the best. And maybe it will. All I ask is that you stick to the story, and nobody needs to know what really happened.' She glanced around again, as if to triple-check that the scandalous secret was safe.

'Well, she won't be the first.' Patty folded her arms, thinking that if only Faith hadn't been encouraged to believe she was so special and above everybody else, she would not have had so far to fall. Who knows, she and Martin might have been engaged by now in any case. 'I'll have to tell Bert of course. I don't keep anything from him.'

Vera pursed her lips and her lipstick ran into the fine lines that had begun to form around her mouth. 'I suppose so. It wouldn't be right of me to ask that of you. I know he isn't one for gossip.'

'He certainly isn't,' Patty responded hotly. Then she considered. 'And my girls will work it out, and so I'd best be straight with them too. I'll impress upon them that they aren't to spread it about.'

Vera's head went up. 'Really? Is that necessary? Won't Daisy go gabbing all around the place? Sorry, Patty, but she's very young when all's said and done.'

Patty's look grew steely. 'She's eighteen now, and with a very responsible job. She's not one to go gabbing, as you so delicately put it. Besides, with Rose being a nurse, she'll definitely realise what's really happened, and there's no point in feeding her a lie. Which I wouldn't anyway,' she finished with emphasis.

Vera pushed herself to her feet, her shoulders sagging with the weight of all that was to come. 'All right,' she agreed reluctantly. She tugged at the once-rigid lapels of her summer jacket, now wilting in the warmth of the shop. 'But nobody else, absolutely nobody.'

Patty nodded. 'Of course. Now, chin up, Vera. You've got to go out of here and face the world seeming like the happy mother of the bride-to-be.'

Vera shut her eyes for a brief moment and then briskly tossed her head, assuming something like her old air of confident respectability. 'You're right, Patty. And . . . and thanks.' She made her way to the door and ushered in a welcome light breeze.

'Leave it open,' Patty called as her sister went out to take on the world once more.

The one person Vera hadn't asked about was Robbie, no doubt presuming that he was too young to understand anything about Faith's predicament, but Patty knew full well that her youngest child had seen too much to be fooled. There was nothing for it; she'd have to start building a hutch, and the Harrison family would have a new member: a rabbit.

CHAPTER THIRTY-THREE

'So that's what we're going to do.' Patty set down her teacup and regarded Bert, Daisy and Rose, who had come over after finishing her afternoon shift. Robbie had already been sent up to bed. The blackout blind was down but the kitchen window was open behind it, allowing a current of air in the heat of the evening.

'You've got to be joking.' Daisy stared at her mother across the big table. 'We've got to pretend that stuck-up Faith hasn't conned Martin into marrying her?'

'Don't talk about your cousin like that,' Patty said automatically. 'We shouldn't wish misfortune on anybody.'

'It'll be Martin's misfortune to be lumbered with her,' Daisy fired back. 'Remember how hoity-toity she was at Christmas! My boss this, my boss that! What a load of old—'

'Daisy, enough.' Bert rarely intervened in the family spats but when he did, he meant it. 'What's done is done. Your mother is right. The die has been cast and it's up to us to help, not hinder.'

Daisy hung her head, admonished by her father. 'I know.' She couldn't help thinking of Sylvia and what she'd been through earlier in the year. There were no promises of a business career for any young man who stepped in. It wasn't fair. 'And what about you, Rose? What do you think?'

Rose had been taken aback by the news but her instant main reaction had been sympathy for Martin. She tried not to feel guilty, remembering his face as she'd turned him down. The last thing she'd wanted was for him to be stuck in an unhappy marriage. Then again, he had always had a firm eye on how he wanted his career to advance. He was taking a calculated risk. He was compromising, but who was to say it wouldn't work out for them?

'I think good luck to them,' she said. 'People get together for all sorts of reasons, plenty of them worse than this.'

'Well, serve him right, now he's going to be hitched to Faith for life,' Daisy huffed. 'We'd better hope the baby looks like her.'

'Daisy,' Bert said warningly.

'That's it. You, young lady, can help me carry the last of the tea things through to the back kitchen,' Patty said firmly, getting up and stacking the saucers and side plates. The crumbs of her flapjacks were all that remained; she'd sweetened them with the first blackberries from down on the canal path, stewed with a tiny amount of sugar.

Daisy pulled a face but did as she was asked.

Bert looked carefully at his eldest once they were alone at the table. 'Sure you're all right?'

'Yes. Of course.'

'Then we'll say no more about it.' He regarded her steadily in the light of the gas lamp. 'Well, no doubt we'll soon have bigger things to concern us anyway. You've heard the news about the increased aerial activity?'

Rose nodded. 'Right over Clover, isn't it.'

Bert nodded back. 'She'll be kept busy, no doubt about it. Raids over Southampton are getting worse, day and night. Have you had any increase in casualties? Any more like the Sutherland lad?'

Rose bit her lip. 'Not really, not yet. They aren't moving them. It was only because he was back on leave and taken ill then.'

'How is he?'

Rose glanced at her father, to see if there was anything other than a polite enquiry behind his question. She couldn't see any signs of it. 'Still hasn't come out of his coma,' she said. 'But that's not unusual. His brain might have taken some bruising and will need time and peace and quiet to recover. It has probably swollen and only time will give it the chance to go back to normal.' She was pleased with the calm, professional way she talked about the case, not revealing that she had been drawn in to the young man's fight for survival.

Bert inclined his head in acknowledgement. 'I'm sure he's in the best place,' he said warmly. 'I know his mother considered moving him to a private hospital but my boss convinced her otherwise. Said the least disturbance the better, and he wouldn't receive any better care elsewhere.'

'Exactly.' Rose approved. 'Disturbance is the last thing he needs. Or any similar cases,' she added, to keep things impersonal.

Bert sat back and clasped his hands. 'And what do you reckon about our new family member? Robbie's rabbit?'

Rose shook her head. 'I expect it's going to make a whole lot of extra work, and so he'd better do his fair share of it.'

'He swears blind that he will.' Bert pushed back his shirt sleeves and grinned.

'We'd better see that he does. Still, I suppose it saves the poor thing from winding up in the stewpot.' Rose raised her eyebrows. 'When is it arriving?'

'As soon as we can come up with somewhere to put it,' her father replied. 'It's the ideal time to begin to teach Robbie the basics of woodwork. We'll put together a few odds and ends, offcuts and the like, and see if we can assemble some sort of hutch. Otherwise it will run off and that will be that.'

'Is he old enough?' Rose wondered. 'And won't he just bash his fingers with the hammer?'

'Rose,' Bert said solemnly, 'he has to start some-where. And if your sisters can help me build an air-raid shelter then I'm sure your little brother can help out with a hutch.'

Rose stood up. 'Maybe . . .' She reached for her jacket and shaded torch. 'I'd best be getting back before it gets too late. I'll just say goodbye to Ma and Daisy. There's a special patient I need to check up on before the end of the evening.'

'Don't work too hard,' her father said, his voice full of affection.

Rose set off on foot, following the familiar pavements from Victory Walk to the hospital, guided by the dim beam of the torch, her mind far from her cousin's predicament. Part of her knew she could not achieve anything by checking that all was well with Philip at the end of the day; but another part hoped that the sound of a familiar, sympathetic voice would somehow help. Besides, she acknowledged, she wouldn't be able to sleep herself unless she'd sat by his bedside, even if it was for only a few minutes.

One of the many things Daisy liked about her job was that she had different days off every week, and was therefore not forced to cram into the shops or market aisles with all the other weekend shoppers. It was true that she rarely bought much, especially now that clothes rationing was biting, but that wasn't the point. It was the searching, the hunting for the perfect item, that was half the fun.

Of course many of the family's precious coupons had had to go on Robbie's clothes, as for some reason many schools had not relaxed their strict uniform rules. Robbie's wasn't too bad, but this was his last year of primary school and they'd all have to tighten their belts even further next year when he moved up to whatever secondary school was still open locally. Nobody could predict how many children would still be living at home, and there had been another big evacuation earlier in the summer. Daisy stopped her thoughts from going down that route. Nobody knew what would happen next week, let alone next year.

She wandered down the high road, heading south, and reached the big entrance to Ridley Road, the most bustling street market around. She was sorely tempted to browse the stalls, even without the chance of actually buying anything. She fancied treating herself, just for the enjoyment of it. Perhaps a little trinket of jewellery? She gave most of her wages to her parents, but kept a little back for moments like this. Everyone was muttering about the big attack which was bound to come so she should seize the day and pamper herself, before it was too late.

'Daisy!' a voice called out. It was a croaky sort of greeting but she half-recognised it, and turned around, away from the busy market. A young man stood a little distance behind her, his shoulders slouched, his face white even after the long summer.

'Chalky!' she exclaimed, taking in how he seemed to have aged since the last time she'd seen him a few months ago. 'Are you home on leave again?'

Chalky shrugged, and she could see how sunken his cheeks were. 'Sort of,' he said. 'How you been keeping, then?' He was making a big effort to sound perky, she realised.

'Oh, lots to do, you know how it is.' She launched into a description of life in the ticket hall, the changes there, what they might have to do if the platforms were opened up as shelters.

Chalky nodded, but drew away a little as if the blast of her enthusiasm was too much for him. 'I bet you do a grand job,' he croaked. 'You always was a live wire, Daisy. You'll do well there, I bet.'

'Thanks, Chalky.' Daisy couldn't remember him ever saying anything like that when they'd been at the factory together; in fact he was one of the gang who'd tried to make her life a misery, but that had mostly been down to Terry and it was mean to think ill of the dead. 'You out shopping, are you? Getting something for your ma, maybe?'

Chalky shrugged again. 'Nah, she never likes what I bring back, says I get it wrong every time.' He grinned sheepishly. 'I'm meeting an old mate for a cuppa in that tea place over the road. Fancy joining me? I'm a bit early,' he added, and Daisy couldn't decide if he was being polite or actually wanted her to come along.

Then she realised he was simply desperate to sit down.

'Oh, all right then. Yes, why not.'

'Not keeping you from buying your high fashion, am I?' He was making an effort, she could tell.

She laughed at the idea. 'What, from Ridley Road? Not likely. Anyway we put all our coupons towards my little brother's new shoes. It's very mean of him but he keeps growing, and he won't stop!' She prattled on as they dodged a couple of buses heading towards Liverpool Street and crossed the wide road, before turning into the little café's entrance. Daisy had often passed it but never been in.

It was a cheerful place, its small tables covered in bright gingham cloths, pictures of sunflowers on the walls, and the buzz of chatter from customers and

329

staff behind the counter alike. The woman who was obviously in charge came over, her wide face red-cheeked with the heat of the kitchen. Wiping her hands on her spotless white apron, she asked, 'Table for two is it?'

'Three,' said Chalky. He coughed a little and added, 'Me mate's coming along in a minute.'

'Come this way, then.' The woman expertly wove between the tables and chairs, some of which had bags and baskets of shopping at their feet. 'Table for three, in the corner there. Be with you in a mo.'

Chalky sank with evident relief into the chair against the wall. Daisy sat opposite him, and couldn't put off the question any longer. 'So, Chalky, how you been doing yourself? You seem a bit . . . er . . . tired.' In truth he looked terrible.

He gazed out through the big pane of glass, as people wandered by, visible either side of the lines of brown tape. He shuffled his hands on the table in front of him. 'Oh you know. Mustn't grumble.'

Daisy sighed. If she had a penny for every time somebody said that to her! 'Grumble away, Chalky,' she said. 'Up to you, of course, but I shan't tell anyone. Get it off your chest.'

'Humph, me chest.' He coughed again. 'That's part of the problem. Can't seem to get right, not after all what happened before. You know.'

'Dunkirk?'

'That's it.' He flinched a little, as if he could hardly bear to hear the word. 'I tried, I really did, I went back to my unit and everything. I couldn't keep up, though.

Couldn't march, couldn't do any other training, running or climbing or whatnot. Couldn't seem to think straight.' He was staring out at the passers-by.

'No wonder,' Daisy said. 'That was horrible, what you saw, and then being in that cold water. It's bound to take a while.'

Chalky would not look at her. 'That's what they said. But I don't understand, some blokes what had it worse than me are now fit as fiddles, volunteering for missions left right and centre. Me, I can hardly get out of bed in the morning, and they don't like that, oh no. So the doctor said I was to go back home for a couple of weeks for more rest. That's what I done. I'm due back to camp tomorrow.'

'Everyone's different,' she said. 'Not everybody will come out of the same event in the same way. At—'

'Don't say at least I did come out,' Chalky interrupted her. 'That don't help, Daisy. I see their faces all the time, you know. Terry, and Victor, and the others. I think I'm going mad, and when I come home I can't talk to Ma about it cos she's still upset over Victor. So's me auntie.'

'Course they are,' breathed Daisy, knowing that this would be true no matter what she privately thought of Victor. The red-faced woman came across, her face full of concern and Daisy brightly said, 'Two teas please,' so that she would not try to speak to them.

Chalky sagged in his seat. 'I'd rather be busy, you know, not have time on me hands.'

'You could work in the camp office,' said Daisy, remembering all the administrative roles Clover had thought

331

she might be eligible for. 'I know they need heaps of people to keep all the supplies coming and going.'

'Maybe.' He didn't look thrilled at the idea. 'Thanks, Daisy, I know you're doing your best. Look, here are our cuppas.' The woman set down a big pot of tea, a small jug of milk, and two cups and saucers. 'There you are. Let me know if you want sugar,' she told them in a tone which clearly indicated that she'd rather they didn't.

'Ah, no, no, this is lovely,' said Daisy hurriedly.

She poured the milk and added the tea, glad of a brief breathing space.

'Anyway I'm glad I bumped in to you,' Chalky said after a while, wrapping his hands around the cup as if needing the heat, even though the September morning was warm. 'I can't really say much to the other blokes, they never knew Terry and Victor, not like you.'

She nodded, again uneasily aware that she knew more about Victor than she'd ever wished to. That wouldn't help Chalky.

'That's why when I saw me old mate from the factory, I thought it would be nice to see him for a chat, cos he knew them, too.' His hands were shaking as he raised his cup to his mouth.

'Oh?' asked Daisy politely, stirring the tea even though there was no sugar to dissolve. 'Anybody I would recognise?' It was by no means a given; it was a big factory, now producing uniforms for the services if rumours were to be believed.

Chalky looked up. 'See for yourself. He's just walked in.' His face brightened.

Daisy swivelled around in her chair towards the door, and froze. She recognised him all right. It was Freddy.

Her heart was in her mouth as he came across to them, through the crowded tea shop, avoiding the shopping bags. He gave a quick wave to Chalky, who he saw first. Then he came to a stop as he saw Daisy.

He gave a broad smile. 'Daisy Harrison! Well, this is a surprise. Chalky didn't say.'

'I never knew I'd see her,' Chalky explained, getting up a little so that Freddy could shuffle into the vacant chair. 'Bumped into her by Ridley Road, so asked her to come along. Hope you don't mind.'

'No, no,' Freddy assured him, and his eyes were bright as he turned to her. He was in his naval uniform, smart and somehow more mature than he'd been when at the factory.

Daisy remembered how they'd teased him, in what felt like another life, that he'd chosen the navy because he thought the uniform would suit him. They'd been right – it did. She drank in the sight of him, his dark hair now cut short, his smiling mouth, his strong hands. Then she realised she was staring.

'Ah, um, it's good to see you, Freddy,' she stuttered, willing herself not to blush, but suspecting that her face was going red no matter what.

The owner bustled over with another cup and for a few moments she was spared the agony of trying to make small talk as tea was poured, milk added, cups topped up and passed around.

'So, what are you doing these days?' His gaze was on her again.

Daisy cleared her throat, and explained about her job and what might happen at the station in the future, all the while aware that her chatter was sailing along on the surface while underneath her heart was pounding so hard she didn't know how she managed to sit still.

Chalky was nodding but looked relieved that he could take a back seat, as if the energy he'd expended in their earlier conversation had drained him.

'So we've got to be prepared for anything,' she finished, her throat now dry. She took a sip of her tea but hardly tasted it.

Freddy nodded and then politely asked after Rose, who he remembered from their meeting in the market when he'd been on leave. Daisy instantly recalled the woman he'd been with, the one she had not liked much. She was damned if she was going to ask about her. 'Oh, she's working all hours God sends over at the hospital,' she told him. 'And, er, what about you? Can you say where you've been and how it's been going?'

Freddy's face grew more serious, and he gripped the edge of the table. 'Actually this is my first home leave for ages,' he said. 'I've just come from the Channel, where we've been guarding the shipping routes. It's been a bit busy.' He ran one of his hands through his hair, and Daisy thought this must be a habit he'd retained from when it was longer.

'And will you go back to that?' she asked. 'That's if you can say, of course.'

He shook his head. 'I'm being moved to a base in the north-west. We're going to be keeping an eye on the Western Approaches.'

Daisy nodded, glad for once that her father and Rose spent so long discussing the war, so that she at least knew what he was talking about. 'In order that the supplies can still come into the docks, say around Liverpool,' she said, and Freddy nodded, looking impressed.

'Exactly.' He smiled again and she loved the way it transformed his face.

Chalky gave a cough and then another. He drank a little of his tea but the cough would not go away. 'Scuse me,' he said, sounding embarrassed. 'I better step out for a minute till this stops. Sorry about that. It keeps happening.'

Freddy half-stood so that his old friend could get past, and they both watched him struggle through the busy café to the glass door.

'Poor Chalky,' said Daisy, realising how mortified the man was. 'Has he told you what happened to him? To the others?'

Freddy turned away a little as he sat back down, his features clouding over. 'Yes. Yes, he did, when I ran in to him the other day. Of course you hear about what went on, but it's another thing altogether when it was people you knew.' He gave a long sigh and Daisy waited for him to go on, sensing there was more to come. 'It's much worse for him. I didn't really hang around with Terry and his friends for long, and to be honest I don't think I would have been close friends if we'd all stayed at the factory. But Chalky, well, they all grew up together. It's shaken him up completely.'

335

Daisy nodded. 'They were all so excited when they signed up and then when they came home on leave that time – well, you weren't there but they were all down the pub in their uniforms, having the time of their lives.' She hastened on, not wanting to think what came of that gathering. 'Then he was back directly after Dunkirk and we saw him then – he told us the whole story. It was awful, just awful.' She drew in a breath at the memory.

Freddy looked at her, understanding all the layers of sorrow and fear beneath her words. 'And you, Daisy? How have you been, really, I mean, aside from the job?'

Daisy met his gaze and her heart hammered even more loudly. His eyes were deep, dark pools, and she felt as if she could stay like this for a very long time. 'I'm all right. It's hard not knowing what's going to happen or when, but that goes for all of us.'

'That's true.' He moved a little and for a moment she thought he was going to take her hand. 'It can't be easy, knowing that the raids are getting closer every day. Have you got a shelter nearby?'

Daisy nodded. 'My father built one in the back yard. Clover, that's my other sister, and me, we helped out, fixing the roof on it.'

Freddy's eyes widened and he smiled again. 'You did! Really!'

'Don't look so surprised,' Daisy mock-scolded. 'We knew it had to be done and our big brother wasn't around to lend a hand as he'd joined up already, so we just got on with it.'

'Well, I'm impressed.' Freddy sat back and drank the last of his tea, and Daisy enjoyed the moment. Then he leant forward once more, a little hesitantly.

'You know,' he began, 'I'm glad to hear you'll be safe if the worst happens. I hate to think of you in danger.'

Daisy raised her eyebrows. What was he saying?

'Yes, he continued. 'Daisy, I've got to say . . . I hope you don't mind. I mean, I don't know your circumstances or anything.' He shifted in his seat. 'But I must admit that, well, I think of you often.'

'Of me? You think of me?' Daisy's voice was almost shaking, with surprise, and with something else.

'Yes. I always noticed you, even back at the factory. That was why I introduced myself that time. And then when I saw you at the market, well, the sight of you there, it rather took my breath away.' He took a breath and carried on. 'You are unforgettable, Daisy Harrison. I hope I'm not speaking out of turn.'

Daisy looked down at her hands, tightly clasped together. This was something she'd dreamt of him saying and in the dream she would respond that she'd thought of him all the time, that she missed him, that she'd even made the mistake of trusting someone who looked like him. But then she remembered who he'd been with that day in the market.

She didn't want to spoil the moment that she'd waited for since that day outside the factory but she could not let him go on.

'I – I . . .' At first she hesitated but then she jumped right in. 'I don't know why you're telling me this, Freddy. After all you already have a girlfriend. You seem to have forgotten that I saw you together in the market that time. You certainly looked very close. So I'm not sure what your intentions are, saying you've been thinking about me, but I'm telling you now you'd better stop. I'm not going to be made a fool of.' She stood up, the teaspoons clattering in their saucers as she knocked against the table. 'I'd best be going,' she said, and she turned and rushed across the café, brushing past the staring customers.

Freddy got up equally as fast, thrusting his hand into the pocket of his uniform jacket and throwing some coins on to the tabletop. 'Wait, Daisy!' he cried, but she was paying him no attention.

'Daisy, wait! Let me explain!'

All eyes were on him now, and a few elderly women were tutting to one another on the table nearest the counter.

Daisy ran out of the tea shop, turning instinctively for home, blind to Chalky who was standing just outside, gasping for breath.

She could not bear to think about what had just happened. Was Freddy seriously trying to string her along, to make her believe he cared for her when she'd seen him blatantly out and about with another woman, and not fifty yards from this very spot? If there was one thing she'd learnt from the whole sorry Ted affair it was that she did not like to be made a fool of. Once was more than enough, thank you very much. Never again.

Her heart ached. She had thought better of him, had believed he wasn't like the others, with their jeering talk of girls – in Victor's case, more than talk. She couldn't bear the idea that Freddy was just like them. She'd been stupid enough to put him on a pedestal when in all likelihood he was as bad if not worse than all those young men. He had feet of clay after all. She sobbed but swallowed it down. She wouldn't show him how upset she was.

'Daisy, wait!' he called again, now from the door of the café.

She wouldn't, she couldn't. She would not be tormented by him any longer.

'Daisy!' he shouted, and now she could hear footsteps behind her. He must be drawing closer. 'Daisy! Stop, let me explain!'

Now she felt the stitch in her side that had been building since she made her frantic dash. With a gasp she had to stop, cursing the betrayal of the pain in her ribs. She did not turn round, did not want to see him running towards her.

'Daisy.' He was gasping too, having sprinted along the pavement. He took a moment to catch his breath. 'Daisy, don't run away. I've said this all wrong. I didn't mean to hurt you. You see,' and he had to take another rasping breath before he could speak again, 'Daisy, she's my sister.'

CHAPTER THIRTY-FOUR

Rose always found that September made her think of the start of the new term. Even though it had been many years since she was in any kind of classroom other than for nurses' lectures, she still got that back to school feeling when the sunlight reached a certain angle and the leaves on the big trees on Hackney Downs began to change their colour. As she finished her breakfast in the big dining room and then made her way to the general ward, she couldn't shake that sensation.

She was brought up short when she scanned the room. Where was Philip? She hurried, while trying not to look as if she was hurrying, to the far corner with two windows. The bed was empty, the sheets pulled back.

Ice-cold waves washed through her. What could have happened? She'd seen him yesterday and he'd seemed better, not exactly conscious yet but with much improved colour. When she'd quietly taken his TPR the results had been closer to the normal range. Surely he could not have died overnight?

Her hands were shaking and she quickly folded her arms to hide it. She could not be seen to favour one patient over the rest, although she was sure at least one of the sisters had spotted her preference. Everyone was meant to receive the same level of care. However she could not deny that she had singled out this one, and could not even say why. Now he was gone.

Her heart felt heavy as stone as she went over to the nurses' station, to check the handover notes from the night shift. They would spell out exactly what had happened. Before she could pick up the file, though, one of the younger doctors called across to her from a bed near the door. 'Nurse Harrison! Could you lend a hand here?'

She stood up and straightened her shoulders. The patient was Ezra Soper, and she knew his stroke had made him tricky to work with as he could not move his left side properly. Quickly she moved to his side, murmuring quietly to the old man, and so as not to wake his friend in the next bed, still managing to sleep through the early-morning activity all around. 'Try it this way,' she said to the doctor, realising that she had more experience handling such patients than he did. Several of the other doctors would have objected to being told what to do by a nurse, but Dr Edwards was far too sensible to put on such airs. He agreed to the way she'd suggested, propping Mr Soper sideways on a pillow so that they could reach the rest of him.

'Thank you, Nurse,' Dr Edwards said as they finished. 'He's on the mend, I would say. His lower left leg had little to no muscle control last week and now he's managing to flex an ankle and rotate it – well, as much as his arthritis will allow.'

Rose nodded. It was sadly true that even if Mr Soper recovered from the damage after his stroke there would still be his arthritis to contend with.

She kept her voice casual as she asked, 'I don't suppose you know what happened to the patent in the far bed?' She inclined her head towards the corner by the windows.

Dr Edwards frowned. He was not much older than Rose herself, and she'd heard that he had wanted to join up but his eyesight had prevented him. 'No, can't say I do, sorry.' He placed his stethoscope back in his pocket. 'Must be going, I've got to do the rounds on the women's surgical ward as Dr Oswald isn't in until later.' He gave her an appreciative grin and headed off to the corridor.

Rose went across to the nurses' station and picked up the handover notes once more, knowing that she should read them in order but flicking through to find the word Sutherland. That was the trouble with large wards; there were always so many pieces of information to record, and here was list after list of dosages to be changed or medicines to swap. Rose could feel her eyes swimming with the detail of it all.

She glanced up as one of the cleaners came past, mop and bucket in hand. 'Spillage to see to,' the woman said, and Rose recognised her, not only because she had worked here for several months but because she was the mother of a boy who'd been in her class in junior school.

'It's Mrs Pickett, isn't it?' Reluctantly she put the notes down again.

'That's right. Oh my goodness. It's little Rosie Harrison! Well, who'd have thought it. Look at you in your qualified nurse's uniform. Course, you always was a clever little thing.' The woman pushed back a lock of greying hair that had escaped from her headscarf. 'Now I come to think of it, can't say I'm surprised. Always knew you'd make something of yourself.'

Rose smiled but was itching to get back to her notes. Still, it paid to be on the right side of the cleaners, and anyway the woman was being kind. 'And how's . . .' she struggled for a second '. . . Maurice? Is he still around here?'

The woman shook her head proudly. 'No, he went down the docks for a bit but when all this malarkey started he signed up for the merchant navy. Said he knew a lot about boats already, might as well make something of it.'

Rose agreed. 'Good idea. And we'll need all of those ships we can get, to guard the convoys coming across the Atlantic.'

Mrs Pickett grew noticeably taller. 'They'll do a grand job,' she predicted. 'Now I better get to that spillage. I been on since six this morning, can you believe.'

'Oh, you must be tired out already,' Rose replied with sympathy. Then she added, 'Don't suppose you know what happened to the patient in the far bed? Did you have to clean down that area?'

'Oh, him.' Mrs Pickett could not get the stray lock of hair to fit where she wanted it and fiddled with it some more. 'The factory boss's boy, isn't he? Surprised he's not down Harley Street or whatnot. Anyway, he woke up.'

Rose started in amazement. 'Did he?'

'Oh yes, one moment he's out sparko and the next he's up and asking for tea. Me friend who does nights said he drank three cups one after another. Then they said he had to move as he didn't need the urgent bed no more.' She bent to pick up her bucket. 'Nice to see you, Rosie – sorry, Nurse Harrison. Anyway he's out in the courtyard now. Said he wanted to feel the sun on his face.' With a clank she made her way down the aisle, leaving Rose with her mouth hanging open.

As she slowly read through the notes, more methodically now, Rose reflected that if you wanted to know what really went on, best to ask one of the cleaners.

Patty bustled around the breakfast table, waving the envelope. Bert, Daisy and Robbie were about to tuck in to the freshly made porridge but waited to see what the big news was.

'She's got her leave! Clover's coming back!' Patty exclaimed happily. 'She'll have three whole days with us! Won't that be something? It's been so long since we've seen her!'

Robbie pulled a face. 'Not that long. June, July, August, and it's only just September.'

'Longer than we've ever been without her,' Patty insisted firmly. 'Don't pretend you aren't excited, Robbie. You'll want to hear all her adventures. Reading her letters isn't quite the same.'

Robbie dug in to his breakfast, unable to wait any longer. 'She can meet Snuffles,' he said, as he spooned it up.

'Don't talk with your mouth full,' Patty said automatically, at the same time as Daisy said, 'I'm sure that'll be the first thing she'll want to do.'

Robbie swallowed quickly. 'She might. She may not have seen a pet rabbit before. Or not one as cuddly as Snuffles.' The rabbit had moved in to his fine hutch and Robbie spent every spare hour playing with him, feeding him vegetable peelings and even clearing out his straw.

'When's she arriving?' Daisy asked.

'Tomorrow. She says afternoon but I dare say it will be evening.' Patty scanned the page covered in Clover's big, slanting handwriting.

'Oh,' said Daisy, suddenly very interested in her own bowl.

Her father gave her a straight look. 'Something wrong, Daisy?'

'No, no.' Daisy hastily began to eat, her mind racing. Of course she wanted to see her sister. Now that they no longer had to share a room, she realised how much she'd relied on her and had missed her dreadfully over the summer – not that she was going to admit this.

However, she had a stronger priority. She had promised to meet Freddy, and she could scarcely contain her anticipation. Now that the mix-up over his sister had been cleared up, there was no reason why they could not go ahead and – no, she dared not frame the words, even privately. Something big was about to happen, she could just feel it. All her senses were heightened somehow, eager for whatever was to come. She could not put him off. He only had a limited leave as well, and it was bad enough that he had to spend today with his family, including that horrible sister. Not that she'd described her like that to Freddy.

'Somewhere you'd rather be?' her mother asked jokingly, and Daisy blushed. She knew she'd better say something now rather than try to spring it on them as a surprise. After all it wouldn't be the first time that she'd gone out with a friend or two after work.

'I did say I'd meet one of the old gang from the factory who's home on leave,' she said as casually as she could.

'Oh, well, that would be nice,' Patty said, knowing that Daisy was sometimes lacking company now so many of her age group were away. 'But surely they'll understand when you say it's your sister? She's more important than an old colleague, I should say.' She finished her porridge, as she had had less in her bowl to start with. It was better to keep the other members of her family fed; she could perhaps pick up a snack at the greengrocer's.

Robbie looked up and gave a mischievous laugh when he noticed Daisy's red face.

'Daisy's got a boyfriend, Daisy's got a boyfriend!' he chanted.

'I have not!' Daisy said furiously. 'It's someone I used to work with, that's all, and he hasn't been home for ages.'

'See, it's a he!' Robbie crowed. Patty shushed him.

'Robbie, don't be so rude. It's not polite to start rumours, we've all got to keep civil tongues in our heads.'

Bert nodded approvingly. 'Why don't you go and see your friend immediately after work and then come back here to eat? You could bring him,' Patty offered.

Daisy drew a sharp breath. Yes, she dearly wanted to see Freddy – but didn't want to subject him to the scrutiny of her family so soon, not when they'd had no time to work out exactly how they felt, what they might be to each other. All the same, she knew how thinly the food budget was stretched, and what a generous suggestion her mother had made.

'I expect his parents will want him to come back to their house,' she said carefully. This was the right thing to say; Bert and Patty nodded in understanding. 'But if you don't mind, I'll do like you suggest and see him first, and then come back here, by which time Clover's train might have got her in.'

Patty began piling the bowls in order to take them across to the sink in the back kitchen, as Bert rose to pull on his work jacket. 'Then that's what we'll do,' she said cheerfully. 'I can make a stew or something like that, so it won't matter what time everyone gets here. I must send a message to Rose too. Now, Robbie, go and say goodbye to that blasted rabbit and get ready for school. He can do without you for a few hours.' She shooed her youngest up the stairs.

Daisy obligingly picked up all the unused cutlery and put it back in its drawer, knowing her mother was, as ever, pressed for time. She grabbed a tea towel and began to dry the bowls as soon as Patty had rinsed them. The two of them had done this so often that they didn't need to speak.

Even so, Patty turned to her daughter when the last one was done. 'Thanks, Daisy. That's saved me a few minutes.' She caught the young woman's eye. 'So, just a friend? Are you sure?'

Daisy knew that her mother could tell when anything had changed, even the slightest ripple in the family routine. 'Just a friend,' she said steadily, figuring that for the moment this was the truth. They'd hardly been in a position to declare undying love on the busy pavement opposite the entrance to Ridley Road market.

Patty nodded as she took off her frayed apron with its faded apricot stripes. 'Then you go and enjoy yourself,' she said. 'And if you decide you want to bring him to meet us, remember you're very welcome to do so. Now I can see you think I'm interfering, so I'll say no more.'

Daisy watched her mother disappear up the stairs to fetch her bag before going to work, and marvelled at the strange telepathic powers she seemed to possess. 'Just a friend,' she muttered, picking up her own bag. What tomorrow would bring, she couldn't even begin to hope.

CHAPTER THIRTY-FIVE

Of course it turned into one of the busiest mornings on the men's ward that Rose could remember, with a seemingly endless list of urgent tasks to be performed over and above the usual duties. One man's medication had been changed and he didn't like the result. Another slipped and hit his head on his bedside cabinet, resulting in blood everywhere. Mr Soper couldn't understand why, if he could now move his left ankle, he wasn't suddenly completely better, and became upset.

Rose was run ragged with a score of extra jobs to do, leaving no time even to think about Philip, let alone go and find him. Today's ward sister was called over to a case where a routine appendectomy looked as if it had become peritonitis, leaving Rose effectively in charge, meaning that the more junior nurses came to her. It took all of Rose's control not to snap when one asked about the best way to fold a sling, when that should have been second nature to anyone who'd done basic first aid, not to say full nursing training. Still, it was easy to forget the essentials when under pressure.

By eleven o'clock the poor man with peritonitis had been rushed into theatre and the sister could return to supervise her staff. 'He's going to be in there for a while,' she predicted, huffing as she finally took a seat at the nurses' station. 'Thank you, Nurse Harrison. I could see you were keeping the show on the road, when I had a moment to glance across from my patient. What a morning.' She took a second to draw a breath. 'I dare say you could do with a cup of tea. Why don't you take ten minutes? I'll ask one of the others to find one for me,' she added swiftly, seeing that Rose was about to offer.

Rose smiled and thought how lucky she was that it was this particular sister in charge today. 'I might just do that,' she said gratefully. Her head was spinning with all the tasks she'd been juggling since starting her shift. A little fresh air would put her right – and if that happened to lead her into the courtyard, then who could complain?

She all but ran down the corridor, barely registering the familiar smell of detergent, until she reached the door to the outside courtyard. Pausing, she smoothed her hair, then told herself she was being silly. There was little she could do about her appearance. She looked exactly like what she was: a nurse who'd already done several hours of a heavy shift, with a creased uniform and hands red from constant washing between patients.

Besides, what did it matter? She had to be careful not to build on any of the stories she'd told herself in the long hours sitting beside Philip's bed. Now it came to it, he didn't know her from Adam. It was all one-sided, all on her part. She was cold with nerves as she stepped into the warm sunshine of the little courtyard.

She cast about for any sign of him. For a moment she was dazzled by the bright, direct light, as the sun was nearly overhead. Blinking, she turned fully to one side and there he was, propped up in a wheelchair by lots of pillows. He moved his head slowly, having heard the courtyard door open and close.

Hesitantly she stepped towards him. 'Hello,' she said, wondering what his reaction would be. 'You don't know me, Mr Sutherland, but I'm one of the nurses from your first ward. I'm Rose Harrison. It's good to see you awake and sitting up.'

Philip turned towards her. 'Rose,' he said, and for someone who had been in a coma, his voice was deep and steady. 'You say I don't know you but I know your voice. Am I imagining that? You sound very familiar, though I can't say why.'

Rose came across to him and sat on a wide window-sill to his side. 'I used to sit with you, talking even though you couldn't answer,' she told him. 'Some of the doctors think that unconscious patients can hear far more than we realise. If that is the case, we thought it might help if somebody talked to you regularly. So that's what I tried to do.'

'I see.' Now his face lit up with understanding and she had her first taste of his smile, which dispelled any remaining chill of nerves. 'Then I must thank you. I can't quite explain it and I wasn't sure if I was dreaming, or whatever you call it when you're out cold as I was. I just knew there was somebody there, and I could

351

sense that it wasn't a threat, that I was being cared for. I used to look forward to you speaking to me, I think.'

Rose laughed and had a horrible feeling that she was blushing. 'Well, I used to like to do it. I had to assume you could hear at least some of what I was saying and perhaps understood it. So I'd tell you what's been happening in the news, or just around the ward. Anything to make a connection really.'

'A lifeline, in fact.' He grinned at her and she could see the beginnings of fine laughter lines around his eyes, even though she now knew he was only a year older than she was.

'Maybe not quite that,' she smiled back.

He gave her an inquiring look. 'Was I imagining it or did you sometimes hold my hand?' he asked.

Rose hesitated, feeling caught out. But then, where was the harm in admitting it? 'Yes, I did. I had no idea if you could feel it, but I thought it might help.'

He nodded, squinting a little in the bright sunlight. 'I reckon it did. It made me feel safe, when I wasn't sure what was happening, or where I was. Then you'd speak to me and I didn't have to worry. At least, I think that was how it was. It's so hard to make sense of it all.'

Rose nodded. 'There's no hurry. Now you are awake you can take all the time you like. You had a bad blow to the head – it's bound to make you confused for a while.'

He nodded back. 'That's what the doctor said. Told me I'd been lucky not to be killed outright, and lucky again that my concussion was spotted and treated. It's a lot to take in.'

352

'It must be.' Rose met his gaze and that sensation she'd experienced on first seeing him raced back, that of a powerful connection that went beyond words. It made her shy but she could not back away. 'I'm glad it's worked and you're feeling better, Mr Sutherland.'

'I am. And please, call me Philip. As it turns out I *do* know you, it seems strange to be so formal.' He tipped his head back so that the sunshine could fall fully on his face. 'It's nice out here, isn't it?'

'It is.' They sat in companionable silence for a few moments, absorbing the warmth, the background sounds of the busy hospital merging with the cheeping of sparrows which hopped around in the far corner of the paving, searching for crumbs.

He shifted around on his pillows and Rose instantly got up to see if she could help. 'No, no, I can manage,' he said at once. 'I haven't lost any movement, I'm just a bit weaker than I'm used to being.'

Rose drew a breath, sitting down again. 'That's to be expected. You'll regain your muscle strength gradually, now that you are up and about.'

'Or almost.' He grinned again. 'Not quite moving around under my own steam yet.'

'Yes, but that'll come,' she said reassuringly, certain that she was speaking the truth. He seemed so wide awake and animated, it was hard to imagine he would regress now.

'Am I keeping you from your work?' he asked suddenly. 'I don't want to do that. I can tell how busy you all are.'

Rose surreptitiously checked her watch and saw that her ten minutes were almost up. 'No, no, it's all part

353

of my business, checking up on my patients – or former patients,' she assured him. She saw the spark of humorous understanding in his face, just as she had foreseen, when she'd dared to think about what he would be like when he recovered.

He shifted again, turning towards her as well as he could. 'Will you come to see me again? Would you mind?' he asked. 'Sorry, that probably sounds very forward. It's just that it's so good to put a face to your voice.'

Rose stood, smoothing down her uniform. 'Of course. I know where you are now, after all. It's all part of your ongoing treatment,' she added, smiling more broadly.

'Then I'll see you soon, Rose.'

As she walked away, she could tell that he was tired; even their short conversation had used up his depleted reserves of energy. Yet she knew, beyond a doubt, that she had not been imagining it: there was a true and fundamental connection there. It hadn't all been in her overtired mind. She didn't know what it was yet or where it would lead, but it was real.

Daisy had a big dilemma about what to wear for the evening. She didn't want to dress up to the nines, as they were only going to a local pub, and she didn't want to draw attention. Besides, she would have to get changed at work, and that would cause Mr Rathbone to raise an eyebrow.

She wanted to make an impression on Freddy, though. She knew that he'd first seen her in her factory clothes, which were about as unglamorous as you could get, but now things were different. She'd grown up, in so many ways. She wanted to show that she'd made an effort for him – that she thought enough of him to do that. Everyone said that women dressing up was good for overall morale. He'd be there as a serviceman home on leave; he deserved to be seen out with someone who looked smart.

She really, really wanted him to like what he saw when he looked at her.

On the other hand, she would have to go home to her family, including Clover, who would take one look at any special outfit and guess what was going on in a millisecond. So would her mother. She didn't want to face a barrage of questions; it was bad enough already. Everything with Freddy was still too new, too uncertain. She wanted to make her way slowly, to be sure of what they felt for one another, before making any kind of announcement.

She definitely did not want a repeat of Robbie chanting that she had a boyfriend.

So she was forced to tread a fine line. Also, she was made to rely on her own wardrobe as borrowing anything of Clover's was out of the question if her sister would be there to discover her wearing it. There were still a few items of Rose's that she'd left behind but now, with her more mature eyes, Daisy thought they were just a little dull.

She had combed through her options, and chosen a navy skirt, neutral enough not to draw comment, but which was cut on the bias and she knew swung around her legs in exactly the right way. She'd uncovered an old cream blouse that she'd secretly refreshed with new mother-of-pearl buttons, and which had a good collar on it, meaning she could open the neckline just a little further than normal. It had a background pattern of dark blue flowers and the two pieces could have been made to be worn together. She'd chosen the highest heels that she could comfortably walk in, not wanting to repeat the night out with Peter when her feet had been in silent agony.

A quick slick of subtle coral lipstick and a dab of Vaseline on her eyebrows and she was ready. She didn't want to be stuck sitting on her own by arriving too early, as despite her several visits to pubs she was still not happy to venture in alone. Yet she had to go straight from work. She dawdled along the pavements, stepping neatly over the painted kerbs, once white but now more like grey.

To her surprise, the first people she saw on entering the lounge bar were well known to her. There was Sylvia, her usual plaits now brushed out and her gorgeous near-black hair cascading down her shoulders in a smooth sheen. Opposite her sat Sam, a far smarter Sam than had ever been seen in the ticket hall. He'd scrubbed up well, Daisy acknowledged, taking in how he'd styled his hair with a razor-sharp parting. He was wearing a crisp white shirt but in deference to the warmth of the September day, he'd rolled back the sleeves a little and loosened his tie – a new one, she would be prepared to bet.

To an outsider, they might be sitting at a respectable distance from each other, but Daisy could spot the signs.

Sam was leaning towards Sylvia, his arm resting on the top of the bench seat, and she was angling herself towards him, her hand playing with her hair. An untouched glass of lemonade sat on the table in front of her. It was a far cry from that long-ago scene with Victor.

Daisy was tempted to move swiftly to the far corner of the room, but then she might miss Freddy. Besides, Sam had seen her now. He was waving.

'Daisy! Fancy seeing you here. Do you want to come and sit with us?'

It was a kind offer but she could tell he'd much rather she didn't accept. Besides, she didn't want to share Freddy with anyone. 'No, thanks, I'm meeting a friend,' she told him, 'but it's good to see you. You too, Sylvia.'

Sylvia smiled at her. 'Give my best to Clover – I hear she's coming back for a few days and I'm sorry I'll have to miss her. Nice blouse, Daisy. Wherever do you find them?'

Daisy grinned. 'Somewhere that Clover hasn't thought to look.' She spotted a table a little way off, far enough that she couldn't hear what they were saying and where they couldn't hear her either, but with a line of sight to the main door. 'Have a nice evening.'

Sam and Sylvia had turned back to gaze into one another's eyes before she had properly left them.

Now she was seated at the vacant table, Daisy wished she had brought something to occupy her hands, to stop them tapping with nerves on the wooden surface. Rose or her father would have brought a newspaper. She herself never paid much attention to anything other than the *Radio Times*, but there was no chance of taking that out of the house. Her mother would have been on to her like a shot. Besides, it was too late for that now.

Perhaps he wouldn't turn up. His horrible sister would have come up with an excuse to detain him at home, or his parents would have invited friends round to hear him tell his adventures. Or, worse, he could have changed his mind, had second thoughts. She was so horrified at that idea that she missed Freddy coming in and walking across to her.

One look at his face and she saw her fears were groundless.

Time flew by. Daisy turned down the offer of shandy, preferring to be like Sylvia and stick to lemonade. Freddy had chosen a pint of beer but they found they had so much to talk about he barely had time to drink it. She described her family, from the respect her father earned as foreman of the factory to the latest addition, Robbie's rabbit. Freddy told her about his, how his parents had not been happy about him working in the factory as they'd hoped he would take a job somewhere more prestigious. 'But I didn't want to,' he'd explained. 'I couldn't see myself behind a desk all day. I did my best when I was there, learning bookkeeping, but I like to be properly busy. Funny, it turns out being in the navy is exactly what I was after.'

'Do you think you'll stay in, after all this is over?' Daisy asked.

Freddy fell silent for the first time since he'd arrived. 'I don't think it'll be over very soon,' he said after a heavy pause. 'I don't expect I'll have to choose for a long time. Sorry to be so gloomy.'

Daisy nodded, realising that she'd wanted a different answer but respecting that he felt obliged to speak the truth. 'I know what you mean,' she sighed. 'If there wasn't a war, I'd never have been able to work in the tube station.'

'So we'll make a go of it,' said Freddy, and Daisy loved the way he was determined to make the best of what fate had dealt them. She smiled at him, recognising how his eyes were warm and inviting in return. She could look at them all day. A thrill went through her, that she was sitting with this man, the very one she'd been thinking of for so long, after waiting all that time. She could hardly believe it.

Then reality crept in and she knew she did not have all day, or even many more minutes, not if she was to avoid a major family scene. She was torn; she dearly wanted to stay here, bathing in Freddy's admiration, but she also wanted to see Clover. She sighed, and could avoid it no longer. 'I'd love to stay here talking to you,' she said, her voice full of regret, 'but you know I said about my middle sister? I've got to get back to see her. She's only got a few days' leave as well. They'll be waiting for me. I'm so sorry, I wish we had longer.'

Freddy nodded at once. 'Of course I understand.' For a moment she thought he was going to take her hand, they were so close. 'You must see her, it's only right. I wish we had longer too,' and something about the way he said it made Daisy tremble inside. He meant it, she was sure.

Freddy rose, and lifted up her light jacket from the back of her chair. 'I'll walk you home,' he said.

'Oh, there's no need.' She realised she wasn't sure exactly where he lived. He might be going out of his way.

He shook his head. 'It wasn't a question,' he grinned. Then as he helped her on with her jacket she felt the warmth of his hands through the light material, and she knew that she was not going to argue one bit.

CHAPTER THIRTY-SIX

Patty thought her heart would burst with pride when Clover came through the front door, in full ATS uniform. She was late, of course, but it was not yet fully dark. She swung her grip into the hall and then hugged her mother, before Robbie and Bert rushed into the hallway to check that it was really her, home at last.

'Come and sit down, come into the kitchen and let me see you properly,' Patty urged, thinking that Clover had put on muscle. One hug had shown her that. 'You'll be dying of thirst, I dare say. The kettle's on, I'll make a pot of tea at once.'

Clover took off her uniform jacket and shook out her hair. 'Oh, it's good to be back.' She gazed around the kitchen, where nothing had changed. 'Is that stew I can smell? Oh Ma, I have missed your cooking something awful.'

'Don't they give you much to eat?' Robbie asked curiously, giving his sister the once-over. 'You haven't shrunk or anything.'

Clover waved his comment away. 'Of course they do, but it's not like Ma makes. Not even close.' She gratefully accepted a cup of tea. 'They did have tea at the station from the WVS but the queue was so long, and by then I was so late, that I didn't bother.'

Patty nodded. 'Not to worry, you're here now.' She regarded her daughter carefully while they all sipped their tea. She'd changed in those months away. Quite in what way, she was yet to find out.

'Where are Rose and Daisy?' asked Clover, looking round.

Bert leant his elbows on the kitchen table. 'Rose was working this afternoon,' he explained. 'She hoped to get away but you remember how often her shifts overrun. She'll be here if she can, but she said not to wait for her.'

Clover dipped her head, knowing what Rose's work-load had been like before she left, and expecting that it would only have grown heavier. 'What about Daisy?' She hadn't wanted to admit it even to herself but she'd missed her younger sister, despite all their arguments and turf wars in the shared bedroom.

Patty wondered how much to say. It was not her place to divulge what she so strongly suspected about this friend her youngest girl was meeting up with. 'Oh, she went for a drink with someone who she used to work with at the factory,' she said neutrally. 'She said she'd be back in time to eat. She'll be here soon.'

She stood to take away the teapot and to stir the stew. Almost ready. She had saved some of her cheese ration and would grate it over the top, just before serving. Clover would not be disappointed, and tomorrow they could have a proper meal of meat and two veg. She would pull out all the stops to make her brave daughter's visit a very special one.

'How long before we eat?' asked Robbie, hopping from foot to foot. 'I'm starving.'

'Five minutes,' said Patty, while Clover laughed and said, 'You're always starving, Robbie. Some things never change.'

Robbie put out his tongue. 'I am not! But I've been smelling the stew all evening so no wonder I'm hungry. Tell you what, do you want to see my rabbit?'

Clover pulled a face back at him. 'Must I?'

'Yes, he's part of the family now,' Robbie said solemnly, bending to pull up his grey school socks. 'He's just outside the back door. I made his hutch. You'll love him, everybody does. Come on.'

Clover rose reluctantly, and moved to the back kitchen with her brother.

As they reached the door to the yard, the sirens sounded.

Daisy froze. It had been a while since they'd heard the air-raid alarm and she'd almost convinced herself that it would not go off again. A shiver of foreboding crept down her spine as she realised it was almost dark and prime time for a raid.

Freddy had had his hand through the crook of her elbow, a sensation that she did not want to end. While he'd been nothing but a gentleman, that pressure and warmth through her cotton sleeve had felt both reassuring and thrillingly exciting, a promise of more to come. Now he swung her around a little and caught hold of her other elbow as well. 'Daisy, are you all right?'

'Yes, yes, a bit shocked, that's all.'

'We need to find somewhere safe. How about the closest church hall?' He was thinking faster than she was.

'Of course.' Then her brain kicked into gear. 'We're only five minutes from my house. Less if we run. We'd be better off going there.'

Freddy looked down. 'Can you run in those shoes?' He seemed doubtful.

Daisy knew she hadn't wanted him to meet her family yet but now was not the time to quibble. 'Just watch me,' she said, and her eyes danced with excitement even with the sudden danger all around. 'It's along here.' She grabbed his hand and they set off, the very last of the daylight giving just enough illumination to guide their way – a way that Daisy knew like the back of her hand, as she sped down a back alley that served as a useful shortcut.

The siren continued to wail as she led them onto the side road that would end at the downs, off which was the turning to Victory Walk. 'Here's where we are,' she breathed, the silhouette of the terraced houses beckoning like a longed-for beacon. 'My father dug a shelter in the back yard, like I said. We'll be as safe in there as anywhere.' Freddy cast his glance around and Daisy wondered if he was assessing the situation as he would when on duty. 'Do you agree?'

She could just about make out his profile as he nodded, now lit by the anti-aircraft beams that rose over the rooftops into the skies above, strobing across the high clouds. 'Sounds like a good plan,' he said, a little short of breath. 'Which house?'

She held his hand as they came up to the front door. 'Here.' The door was still unlocked, and she brought him into the hallway. 'I expect they'll all be out the back already.'

It was dark inside, not only because the blackout blinds were all in place but because the lamps had been put out. Everyone knew you shouldn't leave the gas on in case of a direct hit. Daisy swallowed hard at that prospect but it would do no good to think about that now.

'Daisy? Is that you?' Bert's voice sounded from the kitchen. Daisy had never been so glad to hear him. Now she was safely back home she could acknowledge how frightened she had been out in the open like that, even if the adrenaline had powered her run to safety, adding to the excitement of being with Freddy.

Of course her father had waited for her, to check that she was home.

'I'm here – *we're* here.' Daisy pushed open the door into the kitchen, and there was Bert, holding a candle in a jar, the only light in the room. Its flame flickered and the shadows danced across the walls. 'Er, Pa, this is Freddy. Freddy, this is my father.'

Bert stretched out his free hand. 'Pleased to meet you.'

Freddy extended his, and they shook. 'Pleased to meet you too.'

Daisy felt as if she was in a very strange dream, introducing Freddy in this way. She didn't even know what she should call him. Was he her boyfriend? Her admirer? If she had ever dared to imagine him meeting her family, it had never been in circumstances like this.

'Through here,' Bert said, ushering them through to the back kitchen. 'Daisy, grab anything from here that you might need, but your mother's got the meal all ready to eat on trays on our knees, along with enough emergency supplies to keep us going for a month of Sundays.'

Daisy hoped that wouldn't be necessary, but thinking fast she picked up a cushion from one of the dining chairs and thrust it into Freddy's arms, before feeling carefully along the draining board and picking up an extra plate, fork and cup. She had her bag and gas-mask holder slung over her shoulder. That would have to do.

'Right, it's out here.' Once into the yard they were lit once more by the anti-aircraft beams, and it was only a few steps to the opening to the shelter. Daisy squeezed in, thinking that if she found the space tight at her height, then Freddy would be bent almost double. 'Mind your step,' added Bert, as Freddy swayed at the threshold, not realising there was a change in floor level where the ground had been dug out.

In they went and Bert swung the corrugated metal door shut behind them. 'Room for two more,' he said cheerfully, as Daisy gazed at her family crammed into the little shelter. They were lit by the flame from a Tilley lamp which swung from the ceiling.

Patty had set up her methylated spirits stove at one end, and had balanced the pot of stew on top of it, a pile of trays and plates beside it. She looked up and even in the wavering light Daisy could see the relief on her face. Before she could speak, Robbie jumped in.

'Good, you're back, we can eat now.' He pointed. 'Who's that?'

'Robbie!' Patty exclaimed, but Freddy laughed.

'I'm Freddy, and I used to work at the clothing factory with Daisy,' he said, lowering himself onto the bench seat, nearest the door, wedging his cushion behind him. 'We'd almost got to the high road when the siren sounded so she said I should come here. I hope you don't mind.'

Patty was momentarily flustered. 'No, no, not at all. I said to her that she should feel free to bring you round, I just didn't expect it to be like this.' She rallied and pointed to the big iron pot. 'Some stew?'

She began dishing up and passing trays and plates along, which meant that Daisy didn't have a chance to introduce everyone else. She caught Clover's eyes across the shelter and smiled in greeting, knowing that any heart-to-hearts would now have to wait. Then she felt something moving at her feet.

'What's that? Is it a rat?' she almost shrieked.

Robbie tutted. 'No, silly, it's Snuffles. I couldn't leave him out there.'

'Oh, for God's sake, I nearly spilled the stew,' Daisy groaned, reaching down and finding the creature. She tickled its ears with her spare hand, to make it keep still.

Freddy grinned in the twilight and turned to Robbie. 'I had a rabbit when I was your age. He kept me company for years,' he said, and Robbie smiled at him, any hostility vanishing in a trice. Daisy could tell Freddy had made a friend for life. She was also grateful that her little brother had something new to think about, to distract him from what was going on outside.

As they ate their stew, the noises grew louder, aircraft engines, ack-ack defences, and then the dreaded muffled thuds of explosions. Finally their fears had come to pass; there was an actual raid taking place over East London, and evidently not too far away. Daisy could feel a cold lump in her stomach, the knowledge that this could mean serious damage and injury, or worse.

'What about Rose?' she gasped, wondering why her big sister was not here with the rest of them, but Bert rushed to put her mind at ease.

'She'll have been working late. They're better off in the hospital – they've made arrangements for raids,' he said with authority in his voice. If he was worried, he showed no trace of it.

'They're bound to have,' said Freddy, and for some reason this comforted her even more deeply. It showed he cared how she was feeling, and how her family were too.

Clover, sitting at the far end, stacked the plates and trays on a shelf running along the back wall of the shelter. 'They'll have a plan, all the hospitals have,' she added. 'We just have to sit tight. They don't sound as if they're directly overhead.'

Daisy turned to look at her sister full in the face. 'This isn't your first raid, then?'

Clover shook her head, and her chestnut curls bounced in the uneven light. 'No, far from it, I'm sorry to say. At least I'm in a shelter this time, not out on the ack-ack defences.'

Robbie perked up. 'Do they let you fire a gun?'

'No, but I stand alongside those who do. I direct the beams, you know, those big white stripes of light you see in the sky.'

'Blimey.' Daisy was struck by the reality of just how hard that must have been for her sister. 'Aren't they huge? How do you do it?'

'There are several of us, you aren't up there on the hill on your own,' she teased, managing to lighten the mood even though the subject was so grim. 'Have you got enough room there, Daisy?'

Daisy nodded and moved a little closer to Freddy, for warmth and security. Snuffles had settled down, and they all grew quiet, listening to the activity all around them.

'We could be in for a long night,' Bert said. 'We'd better try to get some sleep. Everyone got some blankets? Right you are, then.'

Patty turned the Tilley lamp to its lowest setting, and they all shuffled to get comfortable, and wait for the oblivion of sleep.

Daisy woke several times in the long night, sometimes because of the noise of explosions, sometimes because of the discomfort of sleeping in the unfamiliar position.

She would wake confused and then very scared, cold where her rough blanket had slipped down, the smells of last evening's stew mingling with the damp earth all around the shelter. The final time she woke, she realised her head had fallen onto Freddy's shoulder, and he had his arm around her. Her face was pressing into the dark serge of his uniform jacket.

He didn't seem to mind. She could hear his steady breathing as he slept. Perhaps he was used to snatching forty winks whenever he could, on board his ship. Even though it was a night like no other, it felt familiar and safe to be leaning against him, absorbing his warmth. Even though part of her was terrified, having him here and so close made it bearable. She couldn't imagine how she would have coped if he hadn't been here. His presence made her feel complete, and it gave her a sensation like nothing else she could ever remember. She snuggled in more tightly and was soon asleep again herself.

At last a silvery dawn broke over Victory Walk, and with it came the sound of the all-clear. Everyone slowly roused themselves from sleep, stretching as much as the cramped space would allow. Bert was up and out first, needing to make sure that the house was undamaged and in a condition for them all to come in. Clover followed, being accustomed to disturbed nights and strange sleep patterns from her summer of frequent raids and nocturnal shifts. Patty stifled a groan, not wanting anyone to tell that she was not really cut out for a night sitting up, quietly easing her stiff joints.

Robbie was last to wake, having managed to sleep half on his mother's lap, scarcely sitting at all.

Freddy stirred quietly but his movement brought Daisy out of the last vestiges of her doze. She sat upright and rubbed her eyes. 'All right?' he said quietly.

'I think so, yes. You?'

'Absolutely.' His voice was steady. He moved carefully, keeping his head low as he stood, and stepped up and out of the small shelter. 'Everything all right?' he called across to Clover and Bert, emerging from the back door.

Bert's reply was tired but full of certainty. 'Yes, looks as if we have come through it unscathed. A few ornaments have fallen over, probably just from the strength of the shocks, but otherwise it's all in one piece.'

Clover cleared her throat. 'Not sure that everyone has been so lucky. There are plumes of smoke in the air – there are fires nearby, and you can smell the smoke once you get outside.'

Patty moved to the shelter door, stiff joints forgotten. 'In what direction? Not towards the hospital?'

Bert hastened to put her right. 'No, to the south, probably towards the docks. I hope your sister is all right,' he added, knowing that Vera's house was not far from one of the fires they'd spotted.

'I'll go down there later,' Patty said. 'After I've checked the shop. I do hope she's not hurt. Or any of the girls, of course.'

Daisy felt slightly guilty that she hadn't even considered what it must be like to be pregnant and stuck in an air raid. Her only thought had been for Rose. Then she realised she wasn't sure in which direction Freddy's home lay, and turned to look up anxiously at him. 'How about your family?' she asked quietly.

371

He took a deep breath. 'They've got a shelter too. My father saw out the first war; he'll know what to do. And they'll know I can take care of myself.' He smiled seriously down at her. 'And look, I got all the home comforts. You and your father did a good job there.'

Clover laughed. 'And me as well! That's how nothing fell through the roof, I'm telling you. In particular, that back corner.'

Patty was all action now. 'We could all do with a cup of tea,' she announced. 'And you, young man, get yourself washed and changed. You have to look respectable for school.'

Robbie's face fell. 'Do I have to go? Won't we all get a day off?'

'You will not,' said Patty firmly. 'Don't you think that's what Hitler wants, all you children to miss your schooling because of him? No, we carry on as normal. So don't you even think otherwise.'

Robbie made a face but did as he was told, disappearing inside.

'I'd love to stay for a cup of tea,' Freddy said sincerely, 'but I had better get back to my family. They're not far from here – I'm sure they'll put the kettle on first thing.' He smiled at Patty, appreciating all she had done to make her own family and the unexpected guest as comfortable as possible under the terrible circumstances.

'If you're sure . . .'

'I'd better,' he said firmly.

'I'll see you out,' Daisy offered, leading him into the dimness of the back kitchen, through the bigger room into the hall. By the front door, she paused. 'Thank

372

you for seeing me home,' she said, suddenly unsure what to say next. Everything was still so new between them, and yet after the night in the confines of the shelter she felt she knew him as if they had been together for years.

'It was my pleasure.' He smiled down at her and then very swiftly bent his head to kiss her softly on her lips. 'Forgive me, I've wanted to do that for too long. I'd best be going . . .'

'I wish you could stay,' said Daisy honestly, one hand flying to her mouth in delighted disbelief. 'When can we see each other again?'

He shook his head as he opened the front door and stepped onto the brightness of the pavement. 'I really don't know. I can make a good guess that I'll be called back from leave early, after all this. So I might be off this afternoon in fact. I'm so sorry, Daisy. I wish we could spend all week together but I don't think we'll be able to.'

She looked into his face, seeing it properly now in the early sunshine. 'I understand. I'll wait for you, Freddy.' Just yesterday she could not have imagined saying such a thing or at least not so soon. But now, it felt exactly right. His expression showed he felt the same.

'Perhaps I'll be home for Christmas,' he said, half-joking, but she could tell he would count the hours until they met again.

She nodded, and despite the destruction around, the disturbed and frightening night, the prospect of worse to come, her heart was singing. 'Yes, come home for

Christmas,' she breathed, as he took her hand, squeezed it, and then stepped away. 'I'll be here, Freddy. Waiting for you.'

Exhausted but thrilled, she watched as he strode off along Victory Walk, his back straight and for all the world as if he hadn't spent the night in a cramped bomb shelter.

'He seems nice,' said Patty, coming up behind her, and gently ushering her youngest girl back into the comfort of the kitchen.

'Thanks. He is,' said Daisy honestly, her heart full.

Her father smiled at her and then at all of them gathered around the table. 'We got through it,' he said. 'We didn't panic, and we managed. That's how we'll carry on.'

'Thanks to you for building the shelter,' his wife said, tired but proud.

'And to Clover and Daisy for helping to finish it. and to you for making it comfortable,' Bert added.

'We all did it,' said Daisy.

Bert nodded once more. 'We did. We've shown we can survive and that's thanks to all of us. As long as we're together, we'll be all right.'

Patty looked up at him and at her girls, lit by the bright beams of the early morning sun. 'That's what's important,' she breathed.

Why not dive into **more** of Annie Groves' engrossing stories?

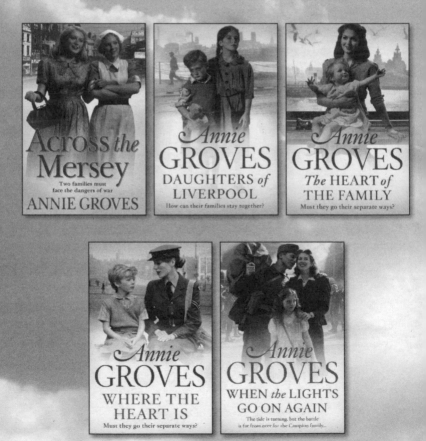

'**Heartwrenching** and **uplifting**
in equal measure'

Take a Break